A Touch of the Sun

David Evans

Prologue

The warder has a shiny bald head, pouches under his eyes and a potgut: a gone-to-seed front-row forward. On the wall behind him hangs a large picture of another fat man. Prime Minister Balthazzar John Vorster. The clock next to the picture says ten past eight. A young *boer* stands at my shoulder, intensifying my unease.

'You said I'd be released at eight,' I say. 'My sister will be waiting for me outside.'

The warder shifts his bulk in the swivel chair and sniffs as though I've farted. 'Not any more,' he growls. 'We told her to come back later.'

'How much later?' I fight down the bile which is beginning to seethe.

'You'll be informed. My instructions are to keep you in for just a *bietjie* longer.' He reaches for the smeared mug on the desk and slurps some coffee, then takes a bite of a half-eaten sandwich.

Does he really have instructions, I wonder, or is he just exercising his own bit of power? In eight years I've learnt that prisoners – especially my kind – can expect to run the gauntlet of acts of malice and casual cruelty. Or maybe someone in the Special Branch has let the old *boer* know who I am and that it's in order to give me a bad time.

'Can't I phone my sister, *meneer*? She'll be worrying.' I try to keep my voice even. No point in making a fuss yet.

'This is Victoria Prison, Brown, not the bladdy Victoria Hotel.' He gives me a glimpse of tobacco-stained dentures and half-chewed sandwich. The unfamiliar reek of the egg turns my stomach. *Bandiete* don't get eggs. 'Besides, you've got nothing to tell her.'

The young *boer* chuckles appreciatively.

'Then perhaps *you* could phone my sister, *meneer*?'

Mouth still stuffed with sandwich, Potguts shakes his head. 'I told you. No calls.'

'Why can't I go now? I've served my sentence.' I'm beginning to tremble. Stay calm, I tell myself. This is prison. Use the boopcraft the years inside taught you. You've signed for your cash and belongings. You've been fingerprinted. You're wearing your new clothes.

'You'll go when we decide you can go,' Potguts says. 'We're busy now.'

Grobelaar's remark during my interrogation comes back to me. *'We can keep you until infinity – and beyond.'*

'I can see you're busy, *meneer*,' I say, careful to filter all satire out of my voice. 'Can I see the commanding officer, please, and put my request to him?'

The heavy-jowled face reddens. 'He's not here yet.'

'His deputy is. I saw him at inspection.'

'He's not available.'

I take a deep breath, deciding to abandon caution. 'I want to lodge a complaint.'

The warder's neck seems to grow thicker. 'Take him back to the section, Frik.'

'*Kom.*' The younger warder touches my arm and jangles his bunch of heavy keys. Defeated, I turn to go with him.

'Brown!' Potguts rasps.

'*Meneer*?'

'I'll phone your sister, hey.'

Can I trust him? I doubt it. Nonetheless I say

8

fake respectfully, ' *Dankie, meneer.* Thank you.'

' *Loop!*'

A yard ahead of the young *boer* I walk down the narrow corridor. The walls are the same depressing green as the front office, the cement floor polished to a high shine by generations of *bandiete.* Occasionally the *boer* stops at the locked door of a cell to peep through the judas hole. At the first grilled gate he halts, jams a big key in the lock and turns it with a sharp twist of his wrist. We pass through. Another section, another gate. We go through it the same way and then through a third. A sickly sweet odour is creeping out of the lobby at the end of the *gang*: recently emptied sanitary pots.

Ten yards and we're at the door of the cell I'd left so hopefully an hour ago.

'Was that your sister with the legs and short hair?' the young *boer* says. ' *Sy's mooi.*'

I decide he's not being deliberately offensive, just conversational, even friendly.

'She's also married,' I say curtly. 'To a farmer. Very big and very jealous.'

He laughs, unlocks the grille, then the heavy metal door. I step inside and the door clumps shut. The key rattles in the lock.

Alone in the small space with the enamel sanitary pot, the rolled-up felt mat and blankets folded into a square to resemble an old-fashioned radio, I begin pacing up and down. My stomach clenches and the ugly question throbs in my head.

Further charges? Every political prisoner's dread. Euphoric first moments of freedom after a long spell inside, then, with exquisitely malign timing, the tap on the shoulder, the charge sheet thrust in your face. They've done it hundreds of times. New allegations. Anything to keep enemies of the State locked away. Dug up, made up. Not that they'd need to invent in my case.

'They won't do it to you, Blackie,' Sam Glass had tried to reassure me in the thick dark of our cell. 'You've pushed your time. That'll be enough for them.'

'Sure,' I'd said bravely. But later that night the old dream recurred: Robert Oldcastle's body, sodden, the face eaten half away by crabs, being winched out of the quarry on Long Mountain while Grobelaar stands beside a weeping Melanie, whispering in her ear and pointing at me.

The town hall clock strikes in the distance, too indistinctly for me to count the strokes. The prison authorities have returned the watch confiscated after my sentence, but it's stopped and won't rewind. I glance at the floor where the sun through the high barred window is painting strips of light. Long-termers calculate the time from such scraps of information. It's close to nine now. In Pretoria Prison six hundred miles away my fellow-politicals will be in the carpentry shop making cupboards for other prisons, repairing items of furniture for warders' homes or, tops for irony, bending sheet metal into cabin trunks for the police.

The town hall clock strikes again. This time, ears better attuned, I manage to count the chimes. Nine o'clock. The usual hour for release.

Or not.

Sounds in the corridor. Rattle of keys in the lock of the section gate, the click-click of metal toecaps on the cement floor, then a key scrapes in the lock of my cell door. It coughs open. 'Come,' says the grinning young warder. 'Unless you like it here so much you want to stay.'

The steel portcullis of the prison clangs shut. I'm

left with my suitcase on the pavement. No sign of Kathy.

Wide, treeless and empty of people, the street stretches towards the bridge which links it to the rest of the town. The sun, already blazing down from above Long Mountain, strikes a dull gleam from the corrugated iron roofs of the whitewashed houses opposite, squatting in neat gardens: warders' homes constructed while I was serving my time in Pretoria. Beyond them is a row of shops, low and still shuttered.

Nothing moves in gardens or street. No dogs or cats, not even a *mossie*. I can hear nothing either, though I'm straining for the sound of Kathy's car. Momentarily I'm seized by a lunatic urge to turn and hammer at the prison gate for readmittance. At least there's life in there.

When I was a kid, the street was only a dirt road leading up from the river to a dusty clearing among the thorn trees where the prison stood. A grey stone building with high crenellated walls, converted from a fort built during the settler wars with the amaXhosa: a place of mystery and terror.

'If you don't *pas op* you'll get locked up there and never come out,' Violet Lategan used to say to us kids.

Well I *was* locked up and her son Kepler played his part in it.

Now I'm out and as jumpy as a meerkat. Where the fuck is Kathy? Did Potguts not bother to phone her?

A grey Ford is dawdling up the street from the bridge. It's not Kathy: she'd told me at her last visit that she'd be driving a red Dodge. Grobelaar? For all I know the Special Branch drive Fords now. Is this what the delay has been all about: to give Grobelaar time to have his breakfast, kiss his wife goodbye and get to me, charge sheet in hand?

The car draws nearer. Through the windscreen I can make out a fair-haired woman behind the wheel and for a delirious moment I'm convinced it's Elizabeth Carter. Then the car is level with me and I see that the driver is a stranger, middle-aged and coarse-featured. It accelerates away and I let my uplifted hand drop limply to my side. How could I have imagined that Elizabeth would come to pick me up? Kathy would never allow it.

The sun is cooking my neck. The material of my new jacket is scratchy against my skin and sweat begins to leak down from my armpits.

A woman approaches, holding the hand of a toddler whose steps have the uncertainty of a drunk's. My eyes mist. After years of living only with men, and with children barred from visits, the boy seems miraculously small and defenceless.

The woman is young, about twenty-three, dark haired and sturdy. I take in the tight yellow blouse, the brief, hip-hugging blue skirt, the tanned thighs. I know her, though when I last saw her she was only a chatty teenager serving behind the counter of the Victoria Milk Bar with Carol Lategan, Violet's daughter. In the same instant I feel a welcome tickle of lust. For the past week, though I've fingered and rubbed and summoned every fantasy I can think of, I've been unable to get a hard-on.

She gives me a quick sharp glance, then, ignoring my mumbled hello, hurries past me, jerking the child after her.

I'm a lot thinner than I was and it's just possible that, with my prison haircut and jacket a size too large, my appearance has altered beyond recognition.

But no, there was no misreading that look.

The snub has shaken me though I hadn't, in long hours of brooding on my release, expected to be welcomed back with open arms by white Victoria. Grobelaar in his gloating way had spelled it out during my interrogation: *'If you side with the kaffers, jongetjie, you'll be treated like a kaffer.'*

I take off my jacket, remove my tobacco tin, matches and slatch, then drape the jacket over the suitcase. Fumbling the tin open I pick out one of the skinny cigarettes I rolled at dawn, feverish after a sleepless night. I light up, coughing as the prison-issue tobacco attacks my throat.

A figure in jeans has emerged from one of the houses opposite and is watching me while puffing at a cigarette. A teenage girl sneaking a smoke? Startled, I spot the beginnings of a beard. I'm looking at a boy with shoulder-length hair, my first sight of a fashion I've only heard about along the prison grapevine. It makes me uneasily conscious of my near-bald look.

The boy pitches his cigarette into the gutter and saunters off in the direction of the bridge. A man is raising the shutter of a shop window. Still no Kathy. Should I risk setting out with my suitcase on the hour's walk to Songololo Street? No, better not. I might easily miss Kathy on the way.

A Volkswagen Beetle putters up the street, the sun flashing off its windscreen. Definitely Special Branch.

The car stops. Grobelaar is on the pavement in front of me, tall, hollow cheeked and stooped in his familiar navy-blue suit: the walking cadaver, Sam Glass termed him. Kepler Lategan is a pace behind, lumpy shouldered under his sports jacket, a scowl on his heavy face and a briefcase swinging from one large hand. I suck frantically at my cigarette.

'*Goeiemore,*' Grobelaar says. ' *Jy lyk effentjies bleek, ou Simon.*'

I don't doubt it. I feel pale. My legs are boneless and I desperately need to shit.

'You aren't afraid of us, are you?' Grobelaar smiles, showing the spaced teeth which have always put me in mind of a hungry tyrannosaur.

'Should I be afraid?' I try, unsuccessfully, to match his smile.

'That depends on what you get up to.'

'As I told your colleague in Pretoria, I'll take it easy at home for a bit, then look for a job.'

'You can stay at home all right, but finding a job might be a problem.' He beckons to Kepler who comes forward, taking a thick typed document out of the briefcase and handing it to Grobelaar. 'You know what this is, Simon?'

'No.' My tongue feels enormous in a mouth of mud. My head is a dull echo chamber in which *Further Charges* reverberates.

'Have a look.' He holds out the document.

I take it, the pages fluttering though the morning is windless. The print is a blur, through which I can just make out the seal of the Republic, my name in black type and the capitalised names of the Minister of Justice.

Then, as my vision clears, relief comes, like a sudden cessation of breathlessness. What I'm holding is not a charge sheet. The winding bureaucratic sentences with their whereases and hereinafters and references to Acts and subsections of Acts are informing me that with effect from the time of my release I'm confined to the premises of sixty-nine Songololo Street except for the hour on Monday and

Friday when I'm to report to the Rhodes Street Police Station. I'm to have no contact with anyone beyond the members of the household, my doctor and other designated persons.

No further charges. Only house arrest. I want to drop to my knees and give thanks.

'What do you say, Simon?' Grobelaar is studying me, the smile still disfiguring his face.

There's no time to reply. A red Dodge pulls up behind the Volkswagen and Kathy bursts out of the driver's door. Red skirt, red top, bobbing breasts, short dark hair, a dash of bright lipstick.

Ignoring Grobelaar and Kepler she hurries to my side and grips my arm. 'They've just phoned to say they were releasing you at last,' she pants. 'Come, let's get out of here.'

'Just a moment, Kathy,' Grobelaar says smoothly. 'There's a few details to discuss.'

'You've had all the time you're getting today,' she snaps. 'I'm taking my brother home. And I'm Mrs Roberts to you.'

The smile vanishes. 'Careful, *meisietjie*, we can make things difficult for him and you. Remember what he did and *pas op*.'

'He's paid for that. He's entitled to a bit of peace.'

'Why are you so keen to get your *boetie* home?' Kepler sneers. 'Isn't that fat husband of yours man enough for you?'

The crudity of it stuns me and before I can speak or move, Kathy has released my arm and is advancing on Kepler. 'Everyone knows your problem,' she hisses. 'If street dogs could give evidence you'd be inside for rape. But you can't make it with a human being – not that you haven't tried.'

Blotches daub Kepler's face, as if he's contracted

a skin disease. He raises his hand, but Grobelaar steps swiftly between him and Kathy.

'*Genoeg*, Kepler,' he growls. 'Leave it, man.' He turns to Kathy. 'All right, Kathy – Mrs Roberts – the details can wait. You take your brother home.' The tyrannosaur smile returns. 'See he behaves himself and you'll have no problem with us. We might even get that house arrest order amended.' He points a long finger at me. 'You heard that, Simon.' He taps Kepler's arm and indicates the Volkswagen. '*Kom*, Kepler,' he says. 'Tomorrow is another day.'

'I'll be seeing you, Blackie.' Kepler looks past Kathy to me. It sounds more like a threat than a farewell.

Kathy, hands on the steering wheel of the Dodge, waits until the Volkswagen has disappeared round the corner before putting her arms around me and kissing me. The embrace, after the womanless world I've inhabited for so long, is strange, yet at the same time familiar, slipping me back through time. I stroke her neck and shoulders awkwardly, aware of the soft breasts against my chest, my first taste of lipstick in seven years, the sweet smell of soap and scent and skin mingling with the slight familiar tang of coffee and tobacco.

Kathy disengages. 'We should be getting home,' she says, her hand on the ignition. 'Just in case those bastards decide to return.'

I slump back, dizzied by a confluence of sensations. 'There's no great hurry,' I say. 'I'll be home a long time. They've given me a little homecoming present: a five-year house arrest order.'

Her head jerks round. 'Oh, *boetie*,' she says. 'Those vindictive pigs.'

'It could have been worse,' I say, wanting the sympathy, but wanting, too, to impress: the prison graduate, complete with correspondence course university degree, who has come through, cool and intact. 'I thought they were going to hit me with further charges.'

'What?' Her fingernails dig into my arm. 'What charges could there be?'

Her hazel eyes, flecked with green, scan my face in the way I've always found difficult to counter.

'That's anybody's guess,' I say as nonchalantly as I can. 'You know them. If they can't find anything, they're perfectly capable of making something up.' A picture of Kepler's sneering face flashes into my mind. 'That was quite an insinuation from our old pal and neighbour just now.'

She flushes. 'Kepler? He's always had a thing about us, remember? Mom, me, you. Liberalists and *kafferboeties*, the lot of us. While you were in detention he was around nearly every day, fishing for information, trying to get around Dad when I wasn't there, sliming up to Norman.'

'Yes, but *that* suggestion!'

'Jealousy. He tried to persuade me that if I slept with him he could get your sentence reduced. When I said no bloody chance, he started hinting about the things he'd seen through the hedge ages ago. All our non-white callers. Mom and me dancing on the *stoep* once with *swartgatte*, as he put it. Oh, yes, and he saw me coming out of the *rondavel* in my nightdress late one night. That really excited him.'

'I bet it did.' Unsettling memories are stirring.

'He's sick, evil.' She twists the key in the ignition and the Dodge's engine murmurs its response. 'Let's get on, hey? Straight home, or shall I take us the long way? Not that Victoria has changed much.'

I'm not quite ready to face home and what might await me there. 'How about a turn around the reservoir?' Grass verged and tree lined, it was a favourite spot for picnickers by day and lovers by night.

'Can't.' She accelerates past two overalled African cyclists. 'It's fenced in now – with a gate they keep locked between eight and eight, ever since two MK guys tried to blow up the filtering plant.'

I find myself laughing. 'Good for them.'

She frowns. 'We'll never agree about such things, little brother. Anyway, they failed and got fifteen years each on Robben Island.'

We've reached one of the two bridges which span the narrow, twisting Songololo river. I glimpse a grubby trickle between the cracked brown banks. 'I don't know what it's been like in the Transvaal,' Kathy says. 'But we seem to be having seven years of drought here. Norman talks of selling the farm and going to New Zealand. I say if he leaves the country he goes without me.'

I want to say, 'Good idea.' Instead I say, 'How are you two getting on?'

'So-so. My losing the baby set us back. And he hates the political situation – can't stand the government but doesn't want to see an African majority running things. A sort of fifty-fifty partnership is as far as he'd go.'

'Not nearly far enough.'

'He treats black people better than you did once.'

'You should never have married him.'

'Maybe not.' Her hands tighten on the steering wheel and her jaw juts. 'But I did and I'm staying married to him. Understand me well, *boetie*. You're my brother and I love you, but Norman is my husband for better or for worse. I know it's hard for you. It's been hard for him to accept what you did. For me, too. But that's all behind us now. You're alive. You're out. That's something to celebrate, isn't it?'

'Yes.' I look away from her, out of my open window and up towards the rock-topped crest of Long Mountain. She's right, as usual. Except about the past being behind us. It isn't for me. It's all around me, meshing with the present, moving into my future. The people I've been hoping to see. The people I'm afraid of seeing, their names scored into my conscience. The people I'll never now see: the banned, the exiled, the imprisoned, the dead.

One

Elizabeth Carter was my first love. I thought her the most beautiful girl I'd ever seen.

She strolled into my life on my first day at Victoria Prep as I stood at the playground gate in an embarrassed sweat. Indifferent to my moonstruck stare, she walked past me to join two dark-haired girls who, standing apart from the playground games, had been inspecting me with casual interest. One was short and very pale and the other taller with long tanned legs. Elizabeth was tall, too, taller, I guessed, than I was. Her long hair had the colour and sheen of mealie grains in the sun. She glanced disdainfully at me and I just had time to register high cheekbones and a nose which tilted slightly before she said something to the others, which caused them to turn away with her.

For weeks I tried to get her to notice me by shooting my hand up every time the teacher asked questions in class and by prowling about near the trio in the playground.

It was her cleanness which captured me. My mother made my sister Kathy and me bath nearly every night, and Florence Zondi, the maid, washed and ironed our clothes daily. But Elizabeth's cleanness shone out as though she was lit from inside. Her white shirt and green gymslip were always spotless. Her hair gleamed. There wasn't a spot or a freckle on her soft, lightly tanned skin: you felt afraid to get too close in case you soiled her by accidental touch.

Break was the time to make a play. Once outside the classroom boys and girls usually divided, with us boys roaming the playground, fooling with a ball, spinning tops, swapping marbles or wrestling and tripping each other up. A lot of the tripping and bumping took place in the corner of the playground, where the girls gathered to play quieter games like hopscotch or to sit and talk. When the boys became too boisterous some girls might plead and protest an threaten to tell Miss Ferreira, our large shaggy-haired class teacher, but they seldom did. Others, like Sarah Bentley, clearly didn't mind being jostled and did some robust shoving themselves. Elizabeth and her friends always withdrew at once to another part of the playground. The withdrawal had in it no enticement: no provocative remarks, no backward glances, no hints of flaunting. Led by Elizabeth, they simply left. If they minded taunts about being snobs or toptown stuckups they gave no sign.

Two weeks into the term Miss Ferreira introduced a new exercise into our PT session. She told the girls to kneel in a circle with arms outspread: they represented flowers, while us boys, representing bees, danced round them, flapping our arms to a lively tune from the piano. When Miss Ferreira stopped playing we crouched in front of the girls until the playing restarted and the pattern was repeated. Most of us thought it stupid, though Harry Lewis more knowingly called it 'the fucking game'. Stupid or not, it was quite popular because it allowed us to rush about in lesson time and gave any boy who fancied a particular girl a way of letting her know it.

Whenever the music stopped I dutifully crouched in front of whichever girl was nearest. It took Harry to point out to me that some boys were kneeling to the same girls over and over again. 'Watch Jacky Hughes, Blackie,' he whispered as we galloped to the music.

I watched. When the music stopped burly Jacky

thundered past two girls and knelt in front of a small kid with red hair and freckles. 'He gave her a ring from a lucky packet the other day,' Harry added. 'Sissy stuff.'

The next time the music stopped I headed for Elizabeth, who instead of spreading out her arms was kneeling with her shoulders gracefully slumped and her fingers touching the floor. I dropped down in front of her, lowering my head in the way Miss Ferreira had taught us, not looking at Elizabeth but aware of the sweet, fresh smell coming off her body.

There was a light tap on my shoulder, then another, harder. I didn't want to look up. The third tap was on my head and more like a slap. I raised my eyes. Elizabeth was mouthing something which I didn't at first catch. Then I got it. 'Go away.'

My face hot, I glanced quickly round. All the flowers had bees. 'There's nowhere,' I whispered miserably.

'Just go,' she gritted.

'Please!' I begged.

She gave me a sharp little push. 'Go away,' she said more loudly. 'I don't like you. Buzz off.'

I stumbled up. Moving a few paces, I dropped into a crouch in an empty space. Dust was rising from the floor, invading my nose and throat, choking me. Tears burned my eyes. I hated her. Worse, I loved her.

I tried to avoid her. But by some perverse trick in the order of things I saw more of her than ever. We came face to face constantly on the school verandah or in the lobbies. She kept appearing just ahead of me or just behind me in the line for assembly. Saturdays, shopping with my mother or Kathy in Victoria High Street, I would be bound to encounter her with her mother, an older, oddly tired-looking version of her daughter.

Elizabeth never gave any sign of recognition. It hurt. But I endured it as I endured the irritation of being called Blackie, a label stuck on me because of my curly hair and dark skin.

I was doing well at my lessons, coming first in reading and writing and second to Sarah Bentley overall. Elizabeth was third, while her friends won prizes, too, Jessica Leighton taking the art prize and Melanie Oldcastle winning a special award for music. My delighted mother told everybody in Songololo Street about my triumph. My dad bought me a three-bladed pocket knife and Kathy stood me to the bio out of her own pocket money. My father's sister, Aunt Betty Roy, sent me a card telling me to keep up the hard work.

The unexpected present came from the maid's gangling son, Sipho: a span of oxen made out of clay.

'Me, I'm going to school next year,' he said, as he handed them over, neatly packed in a shoebox. This surprised me even more than the gift. I'd taken it for granted that he would be hanging around until he was old enough to go and work in somebody's garden or as an errand boy for a local store.

On the morning of the rehearsal for the prize-giving the class was formed into a crocodile to march to the town hall. I was to lead off with Sarah.

But Sarah was at the dentist's.

Miss Ferreira looked down the line. 'Elizabeth,' she said, 'you come and lead off with Simon.' She smiled at us all. 'I have a few things to check with the principal so I want you to stand quietly on your own. If the school bell rings while I'm away, each of you must take the hand of the child beside you and, keeping your lines neat, walk briskly round the corner until you get to the principal's office where you'll fall in behind the classes already there. All right?'

'All right, Miss,' we chorused.

I felt a rush of exhilaration as Miss Ferreira walked away. Then I noticed Elizabeth's mutinous expression.

She looked at Melanie and said, 'Change places with me.'

'I can't, Liza,' Melanie said worriedly.

'Of course you can,' Elizabeth snapped. 'Come on.'

'I daren't,' Melanie replied. 'I'm sorry.'

'Jessica?' Elizabeth said.

Jessica hesitated, then said, 'Sorry.'

Elizabeth tried a smile on Jacky Hughes's little red-haired girlfriend who was standing beside Jessica. 'You'll change with me, won't you?'

Red hair shook her head regretfully. 'I'd like to, Elizabeth, but Miss Ferreira specially said we were to keep our places.'

'She changed *me*.'

'Yes. *She* changed you.'

'Well I'm not going to stand here,' Elizabeth scowled. 'I don't care what Miss Ferreira said.'

It struck me, cold with the humiliation of it, that I had never heard Elizabeth say so much.

The bell clanged. Unsure of what to do, I put out a hand to take Elizabeth's. When my fingers touched hers, she flinched. 'Don't,' she cried. 'I'm not walking with you.'

I reached out for her hand again. 'Miss Ferreira said you must.'

She twisted away from me. 'I won't. I don't like you. And you're dirty.'

The bell had stopped, as if silenced by her words. 'We must go,' Melanie said. 'They'll all be waiting for

25

us.'

'I don't care,' Elizabeth said. 'I'm not going with him.'

'Elizabeth!' Melanie chided.

I no longer felt cold. My body was hot, as if licked by flame. 'I'm not dirty,' I said. 'I'm as clean as you are.'

Elizabeth was looking at me scornfully. 'You're dirty,' she said. 'You smell of train smoke and that horrible street you live in. You should have stayed there.'

The blood was boiling in my head. I wanted to push my fist into that small contemptuous face, but she was a girl. Hardly knowing what I was doing, I stooped down and, scooping up a handful of sand, rubbed it over her forehead and down across the spotless white of her shirt.

She seemed to explode. Blows smacked my chest. Nails scorched across my cheek. Heels hacked at my ankles. Then Melanie and Jessica were pulling her away. Miss Ferreira appeared, grabbing my arm and marching me off past lines of children to the principal's office.

'You shouldn't have done that, Simon,' Miss Ferreira scolded, 'whatever she said to you.'

Miss Robinson, lean, silvery and with hair cut short like a boy's, said much the same thing half an hour later after she'd interviewed Elizabeth, Jessica, Melanie and the red-haired girl. 'At least you didn't strike her,' she added. 'But you must know that what you did was very wrong.' Standing by the window she looked gaunt and grim, something carved from bone.

'She was wrong, too,' I said, shakily.

'She says you're always bothering her.'

'That's not true, Miss. I just wanted to be her

friend.'

The beginnings of a smile, gone as quickly as it came, touched the severe lips. 'Sometimes the people with whom we want to be friendly don't want to be friendly with us. They have that right, you know, without being smeared with dirt.'

'She called me dirty. I wanted her to know what it felt like.'

Again I caught a faint smile. 'I decide the punishments here, Simon. Would you agree that three cuts with the cane was just punishment?'

'One cut would be fairer, Miss.'

An eyebrow went up. 'Oh. Why?'

'Because she provoked me, Miss.'

'Provoked you? You know what provoked means then, Simon?'

'It means doing things that make people so cross that they do things they didn't mean to.'

'That's near enough.' She was looking at me intently. I found myself wondering why she wore her hair so short. Was it because she was the principal and the principal had to look like a man or was it just because – like Kathy – she thought long hair got in the way?

She began to move towards the door. I supposed she was going to fetch one of the canes which were kept in a cupboard in the passage. But at the door she stopped. 'Your work has been good since you joined us, Simon. But school is about more than good marks. School is a place where you are taught to think – to use your mind – and where you should learn to live decently with other people. All kinds of people. Even people you don't like or who don't like you.'

She waited and when I didn't say anything asked, 'Do you like it at this school?'

I thought it wise to nod.

She went on in a softer tone. 'I do think Elizabeth provoked you, though I feel bound to say' – the blue eyes travelled across my shirt and shorts and socks – 'you could keep yourself a little tidier. And you should have shown more self-control. That is part of what you are here to learn. Remember that in future. You may go.'

She opened the door and I went.

The next day Melanie Oldcastle spoke to me for the first time.

I'd stayed for a few minutes after school to help Miss Ferreira tidy the classroom, and by the time I reached the lobby only Melanie remained. She was down on her knees trying to ram her raincoat into an already overflowing schoolbag. Her failure didn't surprise me. Magical at the piano, she was clumsy in craftwork classes and hopeless in the gym.

I took my cap, raincoat and tackies out of my locker and stood watching her. I wasn't going to help a friend of Elizabeth's, not ever.

She looked up. 'I can't get it in,' she said tearfully.

'Too bad.'

'Please!'

I hesitated. Then the desire to show off won over the desire to punish. 'You're folding it wrong.' I took the bag from her and knelt down beside her. She watched while I unpacked the bag, rearranged the books, the gym things and the lunch tin, then carefully folded the raincoat and pushed it in on top. The bag closed easily.

'I can never do things like that,' she said.

She was quite pretty in spite of being so pale and her brown eyes were very large and appealing. But I wasn't ready to forgive her. I pushed the straps of the bag through the buckles and pulled them tight. 'So you talk to people when you want help,' I said.

A slight flush coloured her face. 'I talk to anyone who talks to me,' she said.

'You don't,' I retorted.

'Yes I do.'

'Your friend Elizabeth doesn't and you do what she does.'

'I don't.'

'I bet you wouldn't talk to me if she was here.'

The flush had stayed. Now it deepened. 'That isn't true. Anyway, she isn't here.' Awkwardly, she got her arms through the straps of her bag and wiggled it into place on her back. 'I've got to go to my piano lesson with Mrs Katz.'

'Is that why you didn't go off with the others in one of those smart cars of yours?' The Carters had a white Chrysler, Mrs Leighton a blue Cadillac and Melanie's father a green Buick.

'Yes. Mrs Katz is just round the corner.'

'I know.' I didn't add that I had delivered dresses there which my mother had altered. I slung on my own schoolbag, nodded at her and said, 'Bye then.'

She didn't move. 'I think that was an awful thing Elizabeth said to you yesterday. It isn't your fault that you're dark.'

'She didn't say I was dark. She said I was dirty and I smelled.'

'She didn't really mean it. It began with a silly joke of Jessica's about your skin being dark because of you living behind the railway line and getting all that smoke in your house.'

'It doesn't blow in and I bath every day. I've got a dark skin because some of my great great great

29

grandparents were from dark people in Europe, that's all.'

'It's a nice skin. Like a Spanish pirate's. Or Mario Lanza's. Jessica said that, too. Actually, Elizabeth's sorry.'

'She hasn't said sorry to me.'

'It isn't her way. You mustn't mind.'

'I don't care what Elizabeth says or does,' I lied. 'I don't care what any of you think. You can all hate me if you want to.'

'No one hates you. But when you came you seemed – well, what my dad calls a hard case. A bit rough.'

'That's good,' I said, fingering the long cut left on my cheek by Elizabeth. 'That girl scratches my face and kicks my shins and then you say *I'm* rough!'

'Really, we don't hate you, Simon. I don't anyway.'

'Show it then,' I challenged.

She looked uncertain. 'How?'

I cast around for inspiration. Useless to ask her to make Elizabeth apologise. So what? An idea came. 'You could give me a kiss.'

Her pallor had returned. 'Oh, I couldn't.'

'See!' I jeered, turning away, hurt but determined she shouldn't see it. I'd invited the rebuff after all.

'Wait!' She caught up with me. 'I could walk with you if you like.'

'Why should I like?'

She flinched at the brutality of it and I felt a twinge of regret. Nonetheless, I said, 'Aren't you afraid someone might see you and tell your friends?'

She shook her head. 'No.' She took a step towards me, then another. Before I realised what she was doing she encircled my neck with one arm and kissed me on the cheek before breaking away. She smiled. 'Will you walk with me now?'

'All right,' I said.

The next day I reached the school front gate at the same time as the three friends. Melanie said hello and Jessica ducked her head. Elizabeth walked on as if she hadn't seen me.

Two

Songololo Street was hot and still and waiting for a cleansing storm.

Cars and motorbikes would soon be grinding and farting along it. But at this moment, just before the five o'clock rush, the street was veiled in the haze which came off the corrugated-iron roofs of the single-storey houses and the shimmering tar of the broad potholed road with its chipped kerbs and clogged gutters. The houses, their rough-cast, whitewashed walls grimed by the soot from the trains which passed along the tracks behind them, seemed to be waiting, too, for the noise and activity of the absent school children and their working parents.

The houses and front gardens were similar: squares of lawn, rose bushes, lines of flower beds and painted statues of characters from Disney films. Every second house had a concrete bird bath and ferns crowded most verandahs: Songololo Street residents cared about the look of things, unlike the inhabitants in Pretorius Street, two blocks away, among them riff-raff like the Viljoen family: too lazy, drunken or defeated to bother whether their front spaces were tidy or not.

The back gardens in Songololo Street were another story. Some were wasteland, others maintained like orchards. Ours fitted somewhere in between. What made it different was that it had a *rondavel* built by the previous owners. For a while it had been a playroom where Kathy and I could romp and row without disturbing our mother or Florence the maid at their work, or my dad when he slept late after night shifts or was off ill with one of his recurrent asthma attacks. This year it had become my bedroom.

Kathy, as the older, had wanted it, but my mother had insisted on her sleeping nearby in case she was needed to help nurse my father. Kathy had yielded reluctantly, extracting a promise that she could play records and entertain friends in the *rondavel* when I wasn't there. I didn't mind that or the occasional hint of tobacco. Since I'd gone up from the Prep to Victoria Boys' Junior School I'd risked a sneaky puff or two myself.

I rode slowly down the street, skirting the potholes. Some black kids, including Florence's skinny, runny-nosed daughter, were playing five-stones on the grass verge outside our house. Swerving up onto the pavement, I bore down on them shouting and pretending to fire a six-gun: they scattered, laughing, and regrouped as I passed. Mrs Greyling from Number sixty-five was leaning over the fence and talking to Mr Lategan as he worked on his old Ford V8: he must be having time off from his duties at the local jail.

They returned my wave, though neither of them liked me much. Mrs Greyling, who rightly suspected me of raiding her fig trees, had been overheard calling me a *skellem* and a sly little dago, and Mr Lategan didn't like anybody as far as I could tell. But Songololo Street prided itself on being neighbourly and Mr Lategan had been noticeably pleasanter since he'd decided to take his son Kepler out of Frontier Lane School and get him into Victoria Boys' Junior because he believed it would improve his English.

I rode through the front gate and round to the back garden. I parked my bike against the *rondavel*, growled a greeting at Florence, who was throwing mash to a half-dozen squawking Rhode Island Reds, then headed towards the kitchen.

And stopped dead.

A lean brown man in a chauffeur's uniform was coming down the back verandah steps. I didn't like Joshua March or the way my mother tolerated him. It didn't make any difference that he'd worked with her in the binding department of the *Victoria Daily News* or was said to be one of the owner's Coloured bastards, or had been decorated in the war. As far as I was concerned he was an arrogant old *Hot'not* who didn't know his place.

'Hello, Simon. How's it going at the Junior School?' He'd stopped on the steps, a smile adding to the creases of the leathery face, one stringy hand cupping a lighted cigarette. One of my mother's Commando Round, I'd bet.

'All right,' I muttered.

'You're winning lots of prizes, I hear. That's good.' The yellow-irised eyes took in my bulging satchel.

'Only for English.' I edged past him and went through the open kitchen door.

'You're late, son.' My mother, a tube of icing in one hand and a smouldering cigarette in the other, was standing back from the kitchen table, examining an almost completed wedding cake.

'I had to stay behind to help out with the library books,' I said. It was true, which wasn't always the case. Mostly I came straight home, but occasionally I cycled into Mountside to the huge white double-storey in Gladstone Drive where Melanie lived with her widower father.

'No trouble – no fights?' My mother pushed a dank strand of hair back from her forehead.

'No trouble and no fights, Ma.' It was one of her illusions that I enjoyed fighting. The truth was I fought only when I felt I had to, either to try and forestall what threatened to be prolonged persecution or because I couldn't escape. I wasn't brave and I didn't like pain. Kathy had taught me that spirited resistance, even if it failed, made most bullies think twice about picking on one again. So I fought when I would rather have run, and tried to keep my funk a secret.

Now I tried to shift my mother's focus: 'Kathy not back yet?'

'Yes.' She smacked my hand lightly to stop me scraping a bit of icing from the table with my finger. 'She's taking a dress to Mrs Landau, then she's going to see Mrs Adams who owes me for a birthday cake.'

'Me and Kathy were supposed to be going to ju-jitsu.'

'Damn! I forgot.' She stubbed out her cigarette in an overflowing saucer and rubbed a hand across her cheek, leaving a streak of flour. 'You'll have to go another time. And you say Kathy and I not Me and Kathy.' She nodded towards a bunch of flowers lying in the sink. 'Joshua gave me those. Sweet of him, wasn't it?'

I'd have liked to ask her why Joshua always called round when my dad was at work, but didn't dare. Nor would I say anything to my dad, though I'd heard him grumble that she was far too easy-going with non-whites. What was worse, Kathy had started imitating her.

When I didn't respond my mother fixed me with a hard look, then dug in her apron pocket and pulled out a list. 'I want you to go to Rangisamy's and get me some curry powder and brown rice on tick. I'll pay next week.'

This was worse than Joshua's call. 'I'll go to Jessup's, Ma.'

'What for? He's at the other end of Victoria High

Street and I haven't got no credit with him. He shortchanges, too.'

I shuffled my feet. 'Can't Florence go? She could do with a bit of exercise. Get some of the fat off that big black bum of hers.'

My mother lit another cigarette. 'Florence can't go. She's got other work to do. And I don't want none of that kind of talk about her. She's a good girl.'

'Good and fat,' I said. 'And it's *any* not *none*, Ma.'

Stepping forward quickly, she gripped the lapel of my school blazer and pulled me towards her. 'Listen, son,' she rasped, 'I didn't have many chances to get on, but I took the ones I had and I'm seeing you get yours. There's more to life than smart talk, more by a long way, so don't get too big for your *broeks* or I might just take the strap to you, old as you are. I want you to get on in the world, but you won't do it by giving me lip or by running down Florence or pulling faces when you're asked to do a small job.'

'All right, Ma,' I said, shaken by her untypical anger. 'I'm sorry, but I don't like that shop.'

'And why is that?'

She knew what I wanted to say and what anyone else in the street would have said but no one in our house was allowed to say straight out – that Rangisamy's shop stank.

I shuffled my feet. 'You know, Ma.'

'No. Tell me.'

'It smells.'

'Go on.'

'And it's always full of...' – I stumbled out the words she and Kathy had taken to using lately – 'Africans and Indians.'

'They're his customers and they pay just like

36

anyone else,' she said. 'His shop may smell different but it isn't dirty. Nobody talks about the smell when they want tick. Nobody talked about the smell when I was a kid during the Depression and Rangisamy's father kept my father and half this street alive. He was a good man and so is his son and no bugger from this house is going to treat him without respect.'

She released me and resumed her puffing. 'I don't like the way people have got lately – since this crowd of Nationalists took over. You wonder what the war was fought for sometimes when you hear the talk about Jews and Indians and blacks. You've never had no talk of that kind in this house.'

'But Dad...'

She silenced me by holding up her hand. 'No, Simon, I don't want to hear it. Just remember we're all God's creatures.'

I was tempted to repeat Harry Lewis's remark that God must have been pretty malicious to invent some of His creatures, but thought better of it. My mother seldom went to church, but she believed passionately in a benevolent creator.

'What are you two arguing about?' Kathy was in the kitchen, dumping her jersey on top of my satchel and heading for the biscuit tin on the dresser.

'Nothing.' I was pleased to see her, but I knew she'd only side with my mother.

'Let's see.' Kathy took a Tennis Biscuit out of the tin and, breaking it across, lobbed half to me. 'Fighting? Stealing Mrs Greyling's fruit? Telling dirty jokes with Harry Lewis and Norman Roberts? Annoying Kepler? Or chasing posh little toptown girls?'

'Annoying me,' my mother put in. 'And you're back very quickly, miss.'

'I met Mrs Adams in town outside the bookshop. She'll post you a cheque.'

'A cheque! Bugger!' My mother drilled smoke through her nostrils. 'I wanted cash in hand. Never mind. Off with you, Simon. No, wait, get me some cigs as well.' She walked to the dresser and took an old raffia purse from a drawer. 'You can get yourself an ice cream at the Victoria Milk Bar, and Kathy, too. You'll have time to get to ju-jitsu after.'

'I'll come with you,' Kathy said. Her eyes fell on the flowers. 'What nice dahlias, Ma.'

'Aren't they? Joshua brought them.'

'I'm off.' I didn't want any more news of Joshua.

'I'll give you a lift, little brother.' Kathy moved with me towards the door.

'No, you won't. I'll ride my own bike.' It galled me that Kathy was still stronger and taller than I was and I didn't fancy any of my friends seeing me as her passenger.

In Pretorius Street we met Carol Lategan, Kepler's younger sister, trailing home from school, her Frontier Lane blazer slung over her arm and her satchel dragging along the pavement. I'd have ridden on, but Kathy stopped.

'Long time no see, Blackie,' Carol said, wrinkling her snub nose at me. 'Where are you going?'

'Just to the shops,' I evaded, not wanting to name the Indian store.

'Rangisamy's,' Kathy said.

'Oh, the *koelie* shop,' Carol said. She closed her fingers round the handlebar of my cycle. 'Will you lift me? I'd like some sweets.'

I hesitated. The last time I'd tried to ride with Kathy on the crossbar we'd almost crashed and Carol, though shorter than me, was chunky. But I was remembering how willing she'd always been to trade furtive peeps and kisses and exploratory fondling.

'Ride with me if you like,' Kathy said.

Pride decided it. I patted the crossbar. 'Climb on.'

Rangisamy's was on the corner of Jameson and Albert Streets on the way into Vilakazi, the black location. Boxes of fruit and vegetables crammed the small front window, and above them, clipped to a clothes line, hung curling magazines and comics. Inside, it was hot and stuffy with revolving stands filled with jars of curries and spices and tinned foods. An icebox with bottles of Coca-Cola and lemonade occupied one corner and, behind the long counter, shelves buckled under more tins and trays of sweets.

The place was always crowded. White women with their hair in curlers half hidden by scarves. Black nannies carrying white children or a baby of their own strapped to their backs. Xhosa men in dirt-stained overalls. Old Coloured women with pleated faces and missing front teeth. Lounging young men with hair slicked,down to suppress the curls which suggested their black origins. Everyone milled about, fingering the wares and jostling each other, their body smells mingling with the odour of the spices and vegetables and ripening fruit.

Rangisamy was standing behind the counter, a small, sharp-faced girl in dungarees at his side. Unlike most of his customers, Rangisamy gleamed, his smooth brown face contrasting with the white linen of his shirt. Gold links fastened his cuffs. When he smiled, as he did for us three, he showed teeth which were bright and even. Touching the shoulder of the girl, he nodded in the direction of a wizened black woman, who was slowly loosening the knot of the grimy handkerchief which held her few coins. Then he moved along the counter towards us.

'Well, Mister and Miss Brown,' – he was always lightly formal with Kathy and me – 'What can I do for you, please?'

I reeled off the order as quickly as I could.

'That is very easy,' Rangisamy smiled. 'How about some fresh garam masala, just in from India, and some very fine brown rice. Your mother would like that, yes?'

My skin was heating up. I didn't know what garam masala was, but I didn't want to admit it to Rangisamy.

'That's fine, Mr Rangisamy,' Kathy said, 'if it doesn't cost more than curry powder.'

'Same price to you,' the shopkeeper said. 'What else?'

'Twenty Commando Round and two packets of peppermints – XXX, please.'

'And my mother says she'll pay you next week,' I put in quickly.

'Of course, of course. Mrs Brown is a very old customer.'

'A bar of milk chocolate for me.' Carol proffered a coin.

'No credit for you, eh?' Rangisamy said. The sharp-faced girl had taken money from the old woman and handed her a small bag of tobacco. Rangisamy spoke softly in a language I didn't know and she slipped away. 'My niece, Shantih,' he said to us. 'She is staying for a while.'

'She's very pretty,' Kathy said.

'Yes, very pretty and very clever.' He began to move towards the spice shelves. 'I get the rest of your order and give you some chapati and samosa, too, eh?

On me.'

'Thank you, Mr Rangisamy,' Kathy said. 'You're an angel.'

'Only a man. No angels in dialectical materialism, not even for a Hindu.'

'I don't get that,' Kathy said.

'Never mind. I explain one day.'

The niece returned and handed over the sweets with a smile.

'Hello, Shantih,' Kathy said. 'I'm Kathy Brown.'

'Hello Kathy, how goes it?' said a voice behind us. It belonged to a young Coloured of about eighteen with a knife-scar on one cheek and a baseball cap slanted down over his eyes.

'Ben March!' Kathy exclaimed and for one terrifying moment I thought she was going to hug him. 'When did you get back?'

'Yesterday. No work in Cape Town for labourers these days – not if they're brown.' He looked at me with narrow yellow eyes which reminded me of his father's. 'You've forgotten me, eh, Simon?'

'No,' I gruffed, not believing he thought so for a moment. He'd remember my sulkiness a year ago, just as I remembered him and his father sitting in our kitchen like white people and drinking beer from the bottle while my mother fussed around them.

'My old man says you're playing rugby now – up at the boys' school.'

I didn't reply and was glad when Kathy started asking him questions about his doings in Cape Town. Rangisamy came back with three large packets and a smaller one and I hurried out into the street to where our bicycles were propped against a lamp-post.

Kathy and Carol came out a few minutes later. Kathy wagged a finger at me. 'Rude boy, snubbing Ben

March like that. I'll tell Mom on you.'

'Tell her,' I said, knowing she wouldn't. 'Anyway, he's a *skollie*, you can see it from his face.'

'I thought he was quite good-looking for a *Tottie*,' Carol said. 'I *smaaked* that scar – like a pirate.'

She and Kathy were grinning at each other in a knowing, girls-together way that I hated. A pirate, she'd said. That was how Melanie had described me years ago. I'd been pleased then. Now it didn't seem so flattering.

'Kathy will lift you, Carol,' I said. 'I'm off.'

'Where?' Kathy demanded. 'I thought we had ju-jitsu?'

'We did. But I've changed my mind. I'm going to see Melanie Oldcastle.'

Kathy's eyes flared. Carol pouted. I grabbed my bicycle, did a cowboy leap onto the saddle and pedalled away.

Three

My visits to Melanie followed a pattern. I'd cycle up the long drive between the palm trees, prop my bicycle against one of the two pillars which supported the cement canopy over the front door and ring the bell. Even though she knew who I was, Dorcas the maid would make me wait in the hall while she went upstairs to see if I was welcome. With a face which showed as much expression as a brown eggshell, she'd return to send me up to the airy pink attic, with its piano, its pastels on the walls and its view of a large back garden and white-tiled swimming pool.

I got to the attic to find Melanie talking to Jessica Leighton about Table Rock Hill, the highest of the mountains which surrounded Victoria and the only one regularly capped by snow in Winter. It was the furthest from the town and the least accessible by road: to reach the foot took about two hours through dull scrubland and unfriendly cacti, which yielded to slopes made inhospitable by lumpy rocks and *wag-'n-bietjie* bushes with fishing-hook thorns. Too steep to attract casual ramblers and not steep enough to challenge the serious climber, it nonetheless rewarded those who scaled it with a view of Victoria and the lesser mountains which encircled it. And it had its own legend.

Kathy and I had meant to make the climb for years, but had never got round to it.

'Let's do it next weekend,' Melanie said.

'You'll find it tough going,' I said, astonished by her enthusiasm.

Her pale face reddened. 'I'll be all right if I take it in stages and others didn't mind slowing down a bit. I so long to see it. Dorcas told me its story ages ago.'

I knew the story. Two black lovers from feuding clans had met there secretly until they were betrayed and forced at spear point to jump to their deaths.

'It's so beautiful and sad,' Melanie said.

' *Ag,*' I said, 'who cares about what happened to a couple of Natives?'

'Oh, I do.' She looked sorrowful for a moment, then brightened up. 'We could make up a party and have a picnic at the top.'

'I'll come,' Jessica said, green eyes glinting. 'I've got to see that view.'

She left shortly afterwards and I was about to go, too, when there was a heavy footfall outside the door and Melanie's father came into the room. I stood up at once. Mr Oldcastle was a figure in Victoria, a builder who had been the town's mayor. A tall fleshy man with a ruddy face and very black hair, he had a searching stare and a bullying manner. Not a man to annoy, according to Harry Lewis, who had been forbidden to visit Melanie 'for no reason at all'.

'Hello, Angel,' he said, kissing Melanie heartily and motioning me to sit down. 'What have you done with yourself today?'

Melanie went through a summary which included what had happened at school, her lunchtime music lesson with Mrs Katz, and Jessica's visit, but didn't mention the proposed expedition.

'He worries about my health,' she said when we were alone, 'because I had a heart murmur when I was born. There's nothing at all the matter with me now, but it'll be better if I tell him about Table Rock nearer the time – or even after I've done it.'

Would you do that?' I asked, remembering what an honest soul she had been at the Prep, admitting that she'd been whispering or hadn't been paying attention.

'Yes.' She smiled a wincing smile. 'I'm not the little goody-goody you think I am. I'm very wicked sometimes.'

Wicked? I mulled that over as I rode home. Not a word you could use to describe Melanie.

Four

'Not far now.' My cousin Rex halted and pointed at a rocky ridge ahead. 'If I remember correctly, the summit comes only a little way after that *rand*.'

I didn't reply. Rex had climbed Table Rock Hill before and I knew I should be grateful: we'd made steady progress up the mountainside, following the rough, sometimes almost undetectable path, not hurrying and, on his advice, taking regular brief drink breaks to counter the growing heat of the cloudless summer day.

Instead I was unreasonably resentful that what I'd secretly hoped would be a party of four – five if Melanie could persuade Elizabeth to join us – led by Kathy and me had become eight... without Elizabeth. Learning of the expedition, Rex and Kepler had invited themselves. Then to make matters worse my mother had insisted at the last minute that we take Sipho and Thandi along. She and Florence were doing a serious house clean, she said, and didn't want any kids underfoot. I fumed and foamed and muttered that there were enough monkeys on the mountain already, and Thandi at nine was too young for the climb, but my ravings were futile.

It didn't sweeten my mood that no one else but Kepler had objected – though only to me – and that Thandi's skinny legs seemed to scissor her effortlessly up the mountain. I tried to compensate by imagining that I was a white hunter – Stewart Granger or Clark Gable – and the black siblings were biddable porters, there to carry the crammed rucksacks of drinks and sandwiches prepared by Florence and my mother. Unfortunately, abetted by Kathy, they sabotaged this fantasy by only taking an occasional turn hefting the provisions, and by chatting unabashedly to Rex who, like most farm-raised children, spoke fluent Xhosa. Besides, being blond and hulking, he fitted the white hunter image more exactly.

As Rex had predicted, after clambering over the rocky ridge and circling a copse of thorn bushes, we came out under the summit. Above us, Table Rock jutted, a great slab of grey stone which nudged the sky.

A few yards ahead of us all, Kathy stopped. 'Someone's there already,' she said.

We listened and heard the murmur of voices.

'Shit.' I dragged a hand across my sopping face. 'All this climbing and we aren't going to have the place to ourselves.'

Rex, his broad face glowing with the effort of the steep haul, treated me to the grin of the non-smoker. 'They might say the same, cuz.'

'At least we're here.' Melanie, dry faced and pale in contrast to the flushed faces around her, lowered her bottom gingerly onto a jagged rock. 'There were times when I didn't think I'd get this far.'

'Nor me.' Jessica slipped her rucksack off her shoulders. 'I'm fagged out.' A kindly lie, I thought.

'Perhaps we should picnic here,' Melanie said. 'It could be that we're hearing the voices of those Natives in the legend and it would be bad luck to disturb them.'

'Those aren't *kaffer* voices.' Kepler was listening intently. 'I can't quite make them out, but no *kaffer* talks like that.'

'Say Native, Kepler, or, even better, African,' Kathy said. 'Not kaffir.'

'I say *kaffer*,' Kepler retorted gruffly. 'You *kafferboeties* can say African if you like – and one

47

day you'll end up calling them *baas*.'

'Kepler's right,' Rex put in. 'Those people aren't Natives.' He turned to Sipho and Thandi who were standing a few yards downpath: 'amaXhosa *na*?'

'Not Xhosa,' Sipho said, while Thandi shook her head in agreement.

Kathy was seething. 'I'm no *kafferboetie*, Kepler Lategan, just because I don't talk like a member of the Ossewa Brandwag .'

'Why don't we go and find out who they are?' Jessica said quickly, smiling at Melanie. 'If you're ready, Dame Myra Hess?'

'I'm ready.' Melanie smiled back at her.

'Let's go then.' Kathy started off and soon her crimson shorts were fifteen yards above us on the twisting route to the top.

I hung back. I no longer cared who was first. Besides, bringing up the rear meant I could be ready with a steadying hand if any of the girls stumbled. Disappointingly, no one did, but I was able to enjoy the flex and flow of their bodies as they climbed above me. My interest in Jessica was growing. Never mind that she'd hardly said a word to me since we'd set out from Melanie's house. Her hello had been warm and once or twice I'd fancied that the green eyes were studying me. She wore her dark hair in a jaunty ponytail, her mouth was attractively red and I'd discerned the beginnings of tits. Discounting Thandi's *kiewetjie bene*, she had the longest legs of the party and the most fluent movements. Watching her scramble over a rock I found myself wondering if she had fluff in her crutch now, like Kathy, unknowingly spied on in our newly installed shower. The thought set off a pleasant tingling between my legs. I began to enjoy myself.

Not for long. As we straggled over the rise onto the flat top of the mountain the speakers came into view: an Indian girl and two Coloured lads sat on a rug laid out on the expanse of stone which gave the hill its name. At their ease, chewing samosas and sipping orange juice, they looked up, surprised but untroubled.

I recognised them at once. The bird-like Indian girl, dressed in a smart blue cotton tracksuit, was Rangisamy's niece, and there was no mistaking the piratical face of Ben March or the more delicate features of his younger brother Seth.

I wanted to spit with disappointment. It was bad enough meeting others on the mountain top, but to find these non-whites here was maddening. Out of the corner of my eye I could see Kepler scowling. He'd jibbed at the news that Thandi and Sipho were to accompany us. But at least they were 'household'. These were usurpers.

Kathy was already moving forward. 'Hello, you two,' she said to the brothers, then shot out a hand to the Indian girl. 'We meet again.'

'Yes!' Smiling, the girl got up and took Kathy's hand.

Ben March lounged to his feet, compact, stocky and vaguely menacing in his baseball cap, white T-shirt and tight brown corduroys. An expensive-looking pair of binoculars hung from his neck. Stolen, I'd have bet. Though he returned Kathy's hello, his narrow-eyed inspection of our party suggested that he was as little pleased to be sharing the hilltop as I was. Seth had risen, too, rumpled in khaki shirt and longs, sockless and wearing old black tackies. He had a sketchpad in his hand: I could see charcoal lines and some writing. 'Greetings, Kathy,' he said and nodded at me. 'Hello, Simon.'

I didn't reply.

'Isn't it wonderful?' the girl crooned, her arm sweeping in an arc to encompass the high ridges of Basutoland, a blue frieze in the distance. 'If you go to the edge you can see Victoria as clear as anything – Kokville and Vilakazi townships, too.'

Her proprietary air irritated me. 'Strangely enough,' I said, 'we're here because we'd worked that out for ourselves.'

She was undeterred. 'Mr Seer – you know him? – said he'd spotted a booted eagle on one of his walks. They are very rare around here.'

I knew plump old Seer with his womanly trot and habit of chatting to anyone he met about everything under the sun. I'd often found him interesting but now I wanted to show these dark interlopers my antipathy. 'Never an eagle,' I scoffed. 'Indian mynahs – he must have seen mynahs. You people brought them out to Natal. Now they're everywhere.'

'Not true,' she said. 'There are some in the Transvaal now. But you won't find any in these parts.'

'They're sneaking in all the time,' I said. 'I hear their chirping and chattering whenever I'm around Jameson Street. I heard one on this mountain just now – I've even seen one.'

I was aware of Kathy shaking her head and Melanie looking anxious. Beside me, Kepler was breathing hard.

'Then aren't you lucky?' The Indian girl smiled up at me. The large black eyes were a little too brilliant. But her verbal ping-pong was better than mine and it goaded me.

'Funny, but I don't feel lucky.' I retorted. 'Who

wants dirty, noisy *koelievoëls* making the place untidy?'

'Simon!' Kathy exclaimed.

She might have said more but Ben March had stepped forward. 'I'd watch what I was saying if I was you, *boytjie*,' he said evenly.

The smart-arse reply leapt out before I could check it. 'You aren't me, so why should I?'

The narrow yellow-irised eyes examined the old rugby jersey and black shorts I'd pulled on for the climb, then lifted to my face. 'You know why. In the first place we got here before you and if anyone is making this place untidy it's you. In the second place you know better than to insult this girl because of her race.'

I could see Kathy's face, bleak with anger and embarrassment. Time to wriggle off my own hook or there would be reprisals from her later. 'Who says I was insulting her race?' I said. 'I was only talking about mynah birds.'

'Bullshit,' he said. 'You were insulting her. You as good as called her a dirty *koelie*.'

'I did not. And I was talking to her not you. It's none of your business.'

'She's my friend. That makes it my business.'

'Leave it, Ben.' The girl touched his arm. 'It's all right.'

'It's not all right, Shantih. I know this *ou* and it's time we had something out.' He turned to face me again. 'What's it with you, Simon Brown, that you think you're so superior to the rest of us and can walk around as if we're a stink under your nose? Your ma doesn't act that way and neither does Kathy here. Why you?'

His insolent right-to-know air disconcerted me. No non-white had ever asked me to explain my attitude, and I didn't want to start now. But, equally, I didn't want him to think I couldn't. 'Kathy and my mom must speak for themselves,' I said. 'As far as I'm concerned I'm white and proud of coming from pure European stock and from Western European civilization, the most advanced the world has known. So I believe in white leadership in this country and separation of the races.'

I was echoing my father. But here on the mountain top, with Ben March's tawny gaze on me and a hot dry wind plucking my words away, the argument didn't sound so impressive. Nonetheless, I plugged on: 'I've got nothing against Indians or blacks or even you Coloured people as long as you keep to yourselves and stay out of my way. And I don't go around holding my nose – except when people really do stink.'

'White Western civilisation?' The wide mouth dripped the words out scornfully. 'Don't you know that Indians and Africans and Arabs and Chinese were civilised while Europeans were still running around naked and painted blue – savages?'

'*Pas op jou.*' Kepler was quivering at my elbow. 'That's no way for a mongrel *Hot'not* to talk to a white *baas*. Us whites are in charge of this country now and you'd better not forget it.'

We were edging into deep trouble and Kepler butting in was the last thing I wanted.

'You're in charge now but not forever – and I'll talk to you any way I like.' Ben's glance was dismissive. 'Being white doesn't make you special or my *baas*. You may think you're part of a master race, but in my eyes you're just rubbish – poor white rubbish.'

I could see Seth March's almost girlish face over Shantih's shoulder. It was serious, watchful. 'Ben,' he said. 'Easy brother.'

The others had gone very quiet.

Ben grinned – a grin that was more like a snarl. 'This is commonage. It's still the people's land. And we got here first – just like our Xhosa ancestors. So if you don't like us being here, you can just bugger off.'

'Are you going to *moer* this bladdy *boesman*, Blackie, or must I?' Kepler gritted.

It was a common belief among my schoolmates that any white could flatten any non-white, because all non-whites were cowards, and it was true that I'd won a few fights against cheeky *kwedini* down by the Songololo River. I'd grown fast since leaving Victoria Prep and at five foot seven was taller than my adversary. But he was eighteen or thereabouts to my fourteen and his muscles had definition and an adult hardness. Everything about him, from the taut posture of his body to the scar on the rough-skinned face, proclaimed toughness. The myth of superiority looked increasingly flimsy.

I could tell that Kepler, a year older and much bigger than me, itched to have a go, but the street code required me to stand up for myself. It was some consolation that he – and maybe Rex, too – would pitch in if I started taking a really bad hammering. Seth March didn't look the fighting type so Ben would be on his own. All the same I didn't want to be the first to take him on. But with the others watching, I couldn't back off.

There was no point in waiting. 'No *skollyboy* tells me to bugger off,' I said. Grabbing the binocular straps with my left hand I jerked downwards and swung at his face with my right. It connected with his cheek, but only glancingly. In return I felt a hard thump on my shoulder. A fist dug painfully into my ribs. I heard the Indian girl cry out, 'No, Ben, please.'

Then Kathy was between us. Her palm met my ear in a stinging slap.

'That's enough!' Her eyes were flaring her fury. 'Stop this. Now!'

I stared at her dumbly, the blood thundering in my ears. She'd always fought on my side before, always.

'Do you hear me?' she snapped. 'This is stupid. There's room up here for all of us.'

Angry with her, feeling betrayed, I battled a stupid urge to cry. 'He was cheeking us – called us names.'

'You started it.' She turned to Ben whose upraised arm was clasped restrainingly by Shantih. 'I'm sorry, Ben,' she said. 'I don't know what gets into him sometimes.'

He dropped his arm and shrugged. The snarl faded, mutating into a grin of amusement. 'The women want peace between the tribes. We'll have to settle with each other another day.' He shot out a hand. 'All right?'

Everyone was waiting for my reaction. Kepler was boiling, but I sussed the others wanted an end to the embarrassing confrontation. Melanie was paler than I could remember. Jessica was turning over a pebble with a shoe. I felt foolish and at the same time defiant, and also aware of a sneaky sense of relief.

I took the tendered hand. It felt like any other hand.

'Brilliant,' said Shantih. 'Now we can all be friends.'

'*Ag, nee wat.*' Kepler turned away in disgust.

Most of the others were clustering round. I heard Jessica introduce herself and Melanie say that her father had seen eagles up in these same mountains.

Rex was translating some of the discussion into Xhosa for Thandi. It chafed me that they could all bring themselves to be so friendly. After a moment I followed Kepler to where he was standing at the rock edge.

Shantih hadn't exaggerated the view. Below me Victoria was spread out across the valley. I could easily make out the richer suburbs, Mountside and Albertville with their double storeys and blue-glinting swimming pools, edging up to Long Mountain, and the breast-like shape of Mapassa's Hill beside the reservoir. Further on the poorer suburbs stretched south of the railway line. Then across the twisting Songololo River lay Kokville, the Coloured township, and, beyond it, Vilakazi location sprawling flat and drab across the plain until it faded into the dongas and thornbush.

I'd thought of Victoria as small. Harry Lewis called it a *dorp* compared to Johannesburg and Cape Town and even East London, and my Aunt Betty Roy, who often boasted about her two visits to Europe, dismissed it as lilliputian. But I was thinking the opposite: from up here, Victoria, if you included the non-white areas, was far larger than I'd ever imagined.

Kepler's mind was elsewhere. 'You should have carried on fighting, man,' he grumbled.

'No,' I defended. 'Not in front of the girls.'

'*Ag*,' Kepler said. 'You let that sister of yours boss you too much, Blackie.'

'It's not that,' I said. 'She'll tell my mom and then there'll be hell.'

'Your house is run by women,' Kepler said. It had the sound of a pronouncement repeated; something heard from his dad perhaps.

'Never.' I was beginning to go hot.

Ben March had sauntered up to us. 'Fancy a cig?'

He produced a packet of ten Gold Leaf.

'Don't smoke,' Kepler grunted and moved away.

Ben was still holding out the packet towards me.

He might be a Coloured, but he was doing the decent thing. I glanced over my shoulder. Kathy and the other girls, helped by Seth March and Rex, were unpacking the rucksack. 'Thanks,' I said. 'But not here.'

He laughed, moving down the slope and beckoning me to follow. 'A smoker on the sly, eh?' When we were out of sight of the others he stopped and handed me a cigarette.

Sipho emerged from behind a rock adjusting his fly.

' *Molo*,' Ben said.

'*Ewe*,' came the reply.

' *Unjani*?'

' *Ndiphilile. Wena*?'

'*Ndiphilile nam.*' He proffered the packet to Sipho. ' *Ufuna isigarethi wena*?'

Sipho took one. ' Thank you. I speak English.'

Ben chuckled. 'Better than my Xhosa, eh?' He held out the binoculars to me. 'Have a look through these. They're very strong. My father took them off a German soldier in the desert war. He was decorated, you know.'

I didn't want to hear about Joshua's bravery. I took the binoculars and aimed them at the view.

The side of the mountain leapt into sharp focus. A winding road which had seemed like a thread of brown cotton was now clearly discernible: I could even make out a familiar-looking green Buick moving slowly up from the bottom.

I handed the binoculars back and Ben passed them to Sipho, who juggled them in surprise, then, recovering, swivelled to train them on Long Mountain.

Ben drew on his cigarette and eyed me quizzically. 'Did you really think you could take me just now?'

Pointless to lie. 'Not really. We had you outnumbered, though.'

'Think so? Seth's not as soft as he looks. Besides...' His hand darted to his back pocket. Metal glinted in the sunlight and I found myself staring shakily at an open flick knife. 'This helps equalise things.' He snapped the knife closed and returned it to his pocket. 'We *skollyboys* go around prepared. We have to.' For a moment the menacing grimace was back. Then it vanished.

'We could be friends, you know?' he said. 'My dad and your ma have got on ever since they worked together on the *Daily News*. She's a real *mens*, your ma, and your sister's like her. Seth's a clevvy, like you. You'll change your mind about this colour thing. It's *kak*, man. We all come from the same ancestor and she was African. And us Marches got whiteys' blood on one side of the family, did you know that? White and African mixed. We're the future, *ouboet*.'

'That's what you think,' I retorted, as unsettled by his apparent friendliness as by the earlier hostility. 'It's not what I think. And I'm not your *ouboet*.'

'Don't be too sure,' he countered. 'Anyway we're all here now – and all South Africans, whatever the *Boerenasie* says.' He broke off at an exclamation from Sipho. '*Yintoni*?'

Sipho, talking excitedly in Xhosa, was pushing the binoculars at him and pointing.

'What is it?' I looked in the direction he was indicating. The car on the mountain opposite had stopped, a stationary green blob. I could just make out two specks beside it.

Ben had the binoculars to his eyes. 'He says he

saw the man open the boot and a girl get out. That's right. There is a girl.'

He handed me the binoculars.

A blur, then I had the focus. The car was parked in a clearing, close to a clump of tall trees. A heavily built white man was closing the boot. A black girl stood by holding a blanket.

'Caught you – sneaking a smoke, eh?' sang a voice. Kathy, followed more slowly by the others, was charging down on us. She fetched up at my shoulder. Before I could stop her she had flicked the cigarette out of my mouth and snatched the binoculars. 'What are you looking at?'

She swung up the binoculars. 'Great,' she breathed. 'They really are good. I can see...' She went silent and very still, the binoculars pressed to her eyes.

'What?' Jessica demanded. 'What can you see?'

'Nothing,' Kathy said quickly. 'Just a green car.'

'Can I look?' Melanie was staring out across the valley, her face wrinkling with concentration. Following her gaze, I thought I could see the specks moving away from the green blob.

'No. Yes. Just a tick.' Kathy was fiddling with the binoculars again. 'I've messed up the focus.' She thrust the binoculars at me. 'You fix it, *boetie*.'

I took the binoculars. Kathy had blurred the focus all right, but I could still make out the car and the clearing. The man and the black girl had gone.

'I'll do it.' Melanie reached for the binoculars. But Ben was before her, gripping the binoculars and lifting them out of my hands.

'Let me,' he said. He was some time, his fingers toying with the focus wheels. At last he handed the binoculars to Melanie. 'All clear now,' he said. His eyes met mine, then slid away.

'Oh!' Melanie cried. 'It's our car.'

'Is it really?' Kathy spoke carelessly, but I knew she'd recognised it. Everyone knew Oldcastle's car.

Melanie lowered the binoculars and clasped them to her chest. She looked searchingly at Kathy, then at Ben and finally at me. 'You didn't see anyone?'

Kathy shook her head. 'No.'

'Only a man,' I said, not quite certain why I was lying but sure I had to. 'I don't know if it was your dad.'

'That's right,' Ben said. 'There was just a guy going into the bushes.' His eyes strayed to Sipho who was doing his blank act, then to me, to Kathy, to Shantih, to Seth, and finally back to Melanie. 'Call of nature, perhaps.'

'What would your pa be doing up the mountain?' This, heavily, from Kepler.

'I don't know,' Melanie said uncomfortably. 'He goes to look at things, I suppose.'

Ben's hand closed round the strap of the binoculars, forestalling any movement to use them. 'Time to move on. I think we'd better *waai*. We'll go and leave you to your picnic.'

'Won't you stay?' Kathy pleaded. 'I thought you were going to stay.'

'No, Ben is right. We must go.' Shantih was smiling, but I sensed that she would have preferred to linger. 'It was nice meeting you.' She touched Kathy's arm. 'Come and see me at my Uncle's.'

Melanie surrendered the binoculars reluctantly to Ben. 'I thought there was someone else there before.' She looked past us to where Sipho stood, separate and impassive. 'Did you see anyone else?'

He didn't answer immediately. I was aware of my heart ticking. Then he shook his head. ' *Hayi*. No.'

'Easy to make a mistake even with the binoculars,' Shantih said. 'Our eyes sometimes see something not there.'

'Yes,' Melanie said. But her face was full of misery.

Five

After the meeting on the mountain Kathy and Shantih Patel began to live in each other's pockets.

Though I didn't like it, I didn't have a lot to say, knowing that my mutterings would have no effect. I was glad that they usually met at Rangisamy's, away from the policing stares of the neighbours, my mother's hospitable fussing and my dad's frigid politeness. I did protest at their habit of lounging about in the *rondavel* when I wasn't there, but Kathy got round my mother by reminding her I'd agreed to share.

'It's no use pulling faces, little brother,' Kathy said. 'Shantih's more interesting than the other girls. You'd like her, if you let yourself. She's clever and she knows all about Islam and Hinduism and Buddhism. Christianity, too, though she says her parents don't believe in any god and Rangisamy doesn't either. Anyway, I'm going to be her friend. You can like it or lump it.'

Shantih treated my sullenness as a joke, choosing to pretend that I was shy around girls. Laughter, I soon realised, was her defence whenever I tried to be rude, as if my gibes and grimaces were merely in fun. She kept up the tactic even when we were alone together. 'You like me really, Simon Legree,' she'd say, with an irritating simper. 'But you're afraid I'll trifle with your affections if you admit it.' She was also crafty enough never to criticise me to Kathy, which made my attempts at undermining her look cheap.

So I played along, trading barbs and trying to look as if I didn't mind being called Simon Legree.

Another unwanted consequence was that Seth March called round a few days after the visit to Table

Rock. I would have brushed him off but Kathy had already tongue-lashed me for my behaviour on the mountain. I was unsettled by his bringing a gift: an old dog-eared book called *Mhudi*, by Sol Plaatje. I didn't want to read any epics of Native life, especially one written by a black and set in the past. But faced by the frail, copper-skinned boy, no taller than I was, though about two years older, I felt unable to refuse his gift or rebuff his shy goodwill.

He didn't stay long that time but appeared at the kitchen door a couple of weeks later with a sheaf of poems which he diffidently handed to Kathy and suggested we might read them sometime. 'He obviously fancies you,' I said sourly to Kathy after he'd left.

She merely laughed. 'You aren't very observant for a writer, *boetie*. He's sweet with me and Ma, but you're the one.'

'That's all I need. A *Tottie* who's also a queer.'

'He's not after your body, stupid. It's your mind. He probably hasn't told you that he's won bags of prizes for English at school and has had his poetry published in magazines, including one in America. *He* didn't tell me that. Joshua did. And he's getting a bursary to go on to teacher-training college soon.'

I had to admit to myself that the poems seemed clever, particularly a long poem about Mapassa, the Xhosa chief who ruled the area alongside the Songololo River and rose against the Europeans when they seized some of his land in the eighteen-fifties. But friendship with a Coloured was a gauntlet I wasn't keen to run. I was in a fine sweat over what would happen if Kepler dropped in and found Seth ensconced in the kitchen or my *rondavel* – and glad of the tall quince hedge between our property and the Lategans's.

Kepler had been cold for a while after the Table Rock episode, avoiding me and hanging about with Harry Lewis and Jacky Hughes. But proximity and his need for help with his English homework brought a thaw.

I was pleased. His powerful shoulders and muscular arms made him someone to cultivate rather than cross and his friendship was an insurance against trouble with the three Viljoen brothers.

The year moved on. Holidays came and went and soon it was past Christmas and we were back at school, adjusting to a higher class with more homework, coping with stricter teachers and getting to know a new pupil or two.

One of these was Sam Glass, who came to Victoria from Johannesburg with his family when his father opened up a furniture and carpeting store.

He was tall with a dark thin face topped by strong black hair. He was clever and quietly confident, speaking up in class and even challenging the English teacher's interpretation of our set text, *Hard Times*. He was sporty, too, nearly as fast on the track as Harry, skilful with a rugby ball and an uncomfortably fast bowler.

Sport was a bond not only with Harry, Jacky and me, but also with Kepler once the rugby season began, cricket not being a game *ware Afrikaners* could take seriously. Sam didn't hurry to be friendly, but he wasn't aloof either and, after a while, began coming down to Songololo Street fairly regularly. Kepler didn't take to him at first, but changed his mind after seeing him kick three penalties and a drop for Victoria Colts.

'He's not a bad *kêrel* for a Jewboy,' he said. 'You watch: he'll be first team full-back in a couple of years' time.'

If Kepler had any ambition greater than becoming a policeman it was to play for the Springboks.

He wasn't the only fanatic. The entire school was obsessed with sport from the headmaster, a former Springbok cricketer, down to the smallest standard three pupil. Boys who didn't or wouldn't participate enthusiastically were regarded as wets or sissies and, on top of that, disloyal to their school, their town, their province and ultimately their country.

But in my class something even stronger was moving than the urge to excel at sport. Sex.

Suddenly there was a lot of talk about girls and what you did with them. It was *the* topic in the playground, in the school lavatories, on the way home and down at the river – everywhere in fact. Words like cunt, bubs, *poes* and *broekslang*, and phrases like stinky finger, *kaal* tit, tossing off, number twelve and all-the-way, became common currency. Blurred and grubby pictures began to circulate of foreign-looking men and women in acrobatic and improbably complicated positions. Harry produced a card on which cartoon figures were ingeniously linked to create numbers and letters of the alphabet. Another showed a naked couple, heads nuzzling between each other's thighs. 'It's called sixty-nine, Blackie,' Harry chuckled. 'Like your house number.'

There was also a lot of fidgeting and fooling around at break-time with comparisons of penis sizes in the lavatories and some jokey-aggressive ripping open of flies. I learnt this way that Jacky Hughes had a cock shaped like a syringe. Harry's cock was a pale sausage. Norman's pink and chunky. Kepler's was long, brown and thick – a 'veritable python', said Harry in admiration. Sam's, rarely seen, looked rather like a long-stemmed mushroom, the impressive head, Harry explained, a result of circumcision. My cock he described as a little black mamba, whether jokingly or insultingly, I couldn't decide.

Those of us with sisters, as supposed experts, were expected by our schoolfellows to supply a lot of anatomical detail and information about female body functions, from the location of the hymen to the mysteries of conception and menstruation. Kepler and I were evasive. I didn't know his reasons: he'd never seemed particularly fond or protective of Carol. I knew mine: nothing would compel me to tell them how in earlier days Kathy and I had bathed together and my prick used to grow whenever, in soaping each other, our hands encountered private parts. I feared her fury if she learnt that I'd been discussing her, but also felt a reluctance to share any part of our intimacy. Nor did I want to talk about my clumsy fumbling with Carol in the *rondavel* and the Lategans's garage. Loyalty came into that somehow, too, though I was no longer on really friendly terms with Carol since she had started working at the Victoria Milk Bar and taken to lipstick and high heels and going out with much older boys.

Harry, though sisterless, seemed to know more about girls' bodies than any of us. He knew words like labia and vagina and vulva and talked impressively about ways of avoiding babies and of the diseases you could catch from prostitutes. He didn't say so directly, but let us infer that he had been initiated by a friend of his mother's one sultry afternoon in a beach cottage at Kofi Bay.

Norman, never very talkative, had a farmyard view. His tales were of the mating of cats and dogs, of rams tupping ewes, pedigree bulls serving selected cows and a stable boy coaxing a reluctant stallion to eagerness by diligently massaging its long member.

Kepler, like Harry, claimed to have been all the way with an older woman, knowing it to be a sin in the eyes of his God and his church, but unable to help himself. He wouldn't say who had led him 'into shame'. Harry muttered, safely out of Kepler's hearing, that it must have been Tilly Peters, the cross-eyed young woman who worked alongside Carol at the Milk Bar and who allegedly let anyone fuck her: for money – or even for nothing if she liked him.

Sam refused to be drawn on the subject and, oddly, no one insisted.

While 'going all the way' was a widely shared ambition, one area of experience was fiercely taboo: sex with non-whites. Only Harry, as we strolled along the Songololo one Saturday, dared float the idea. According to my dad,' he said, 'unless we can get more white people to come to this country we'll have to mate with non-Europeans or we'll all become inbred and produce idiots.'

'Would you actually fuck a Native?' queried Norman.

'No,' Harry said. Then he grinned. 'Mind you, I might just once, to see what it was like. You know what they say? Once you've shagged a black woman you'll never want a white one.'

' *Sies jong*, Harry,' Kepler said, 'that's filthy talk.' Harry held up his hands. 'Okay, Kep. Only joking – no poking.'

'Whites have been mating with non-whites ever since Van Riebeek landed,' Sam put in, to my surprise. 'That's why we have a Coloured population.'

'It's wrong,' Kepler said heavily. 'It's a sin and

it's against the law.'

'It may be against the law here,' Sam said quietly. 'But there aren't that many pure races in the world. History will sweep so-called race purity away.'

Kepler glared and shook his head, but didn't reply.

Inevitably, there was talk of masturbation and discussion of its pleasures and imagined hazards. Most believed it was wrong and probably harmful, while rather shamefacedly admitting to risking blindness. Only Harry was unrepentant and Norman, with the practicality of a farm boy, was certain that it couldn't do more damage than coupling even if it was impure. Sam, as before, shrugged his refusal to say anything. 'I'll bet he's stinky fingered some Jewess,' Jacky whispered. 'They say it's seven years good luck if you doodle one of them.'

While the others talked of 'coming' and 'shooting' a secretive urge kept me from admitting to the others that I'd begun handling myself but was unable to carry on beyond the almost unbearably thrilling sensation which preceded ejaculation. I didn't know why I held back: only that I'd a confused conviction that I should wait until some future time.

That was the counsel of my mind. My body was mutinying against any restraint. Unsought, unwanted, erections came. From the lightest brush of a female body. From the mere glimpse of a thigh. From the hint of my sister's nipples against her T-shirt. The cleft between Carol's breasts as she served me with ice cream on Saturday mornings. Filmy underwear on a washing line. Any description of a sexual act. Scents from women and girls which brought on thoughts I hadn't known were in my head. Anything, it seemed, could bring my cock to uncomfortable, often embarrassing, stiffness.

And I was bedevilled by perverse and vivid, if fragmentary, dreams involving people known and unknown, in which the objects of my lust usually dissolved or altered as I engaged with them. In one dream I was a baby and Kathy was helping my mother wash my knob in a way that was rousing and frightening at the same time. My mother's head came down and I felt the soft exquisite movement of her lips. Then it wasn't my mother's mouth sucking me, but Kathy's. I woke bewildered and guilty, squirming in my own sperm.

I couldn't bring myself to mention these and other images which plagued me. Nor could I talk about my compulsive need to spy on Kathy when she showered, because my hideous secret would be out: a boy criminal, evil and beyond salvation.

Six

Hacksaw Markham, our coach, had flu, and after-school rugby practice had been cancelled. There was no rush to get home and I pedalled slowly towards the High Street. I wanted time to think about Norman Roberts's revelation that he was 'keen on' Kathy and his awkward request that I 'put in a word'. I'd agreed, though I didn't want to. I liked Norman well enough and he might edge out Shantih, though Kathy hadn't shown any more interest in him than in any other boy, which was nil lately: the days were past when she'd demanded to be included in every game going. But his amiable face and big body seemed intrusive and threatening, invested with a dangerous new power and appeal. Could Kathy possibly fancy him? I didn't want to believe it. I wanted the old tomboy Kathy who liked her *boetie* best.

In the High Street I passed the *Daily News* building with its front window full of black and white photographs of events and notable personalities and registered idly a board on the pavement carrying the announcement: *Non-white Alliance Announces Plans to Defy Race Laws.*

I skirted the Sunken Gardens with its well-watered lawns, weeping willows and artificial lakes. Would Kathy and Norman come here for a *vry*? My dad had once volunteered that he'd courted my mother in the gardens. But I didn't want to think of courting or lovers. Only two days ago Elizabeth Carter had snubbed me again. I'd come out of the Athena Café and she was with a boy in a St Michael's School blazer. My heart bouncing against my chest wall, I'd choked out some kind of hello. The boy gave a half-smile. Elizabeth stalked past with a stare of non-recognition.

Altogether I was in a bad way. The randiness which had come like a virus had developed into a fever. A rash of pimples had appeared on my face as if to betray my ugly inner state. Unable to have the girls I wanted, I was unwilling to approach others, though this didn't stop my lusting after them. To add to my misery, most of my schoolmates appeared to be doing better. Harry had been to the bioscope with Jessica Leighton and claimed she'd let him fondle her through her clothes afterwards. Sam was friendly with Sarah Bentley. Norman had his hopes of Kathy. Even Jacky was calling on some girl in Albertsville. Kepler, like me, had nobody. But, Harry claimed, he compensated by regular tossing off.

That might have been my answer, too. But I remained reluctant to complete the act, choosing instead the daily agony of frustration and the unpredictable scenarios of frequent wet dreams.

I'd reached the bridge which spanned the Songololo – only a thin brown trickle. The grass on the banks was pale and lifeless. A black girl was pedalling towards me from the direction of Songololo Street. As she drew nearer I saw it was Thandi on the battered old bike Sipho had hauled out of the garden shed, repaired and taught her to ride. In spite of the winter chill she was wearing only a cardigan over her blouse and a cotton skirt which fluttered up above the long thighs.

She greeted me cheerfully in English as we passed. I said *Molo* sourly, annoyed by her use of my name without the respectful prefix of Master or *Baas*. I didn't agree with everything my father said, but I thought he was right about blacks getting cheekier. That went for Thandi's brother, too, really full of himself now that he was a student – calling to see

Florence in his flannels and blazer and ostentatiously carrying a book. He didn't go out of his way to talk to me. I didn't want him to, but it niggled nevertheless, particularly as he talked freely to Kathy and my mother.

I crossed Songololo Street and cycled into the lane behind. A minute later I was at our open back gate. I rode through, dismounted, and made my way up the path between the vegetable beds and the grapevine and round the chicken *hok*. Florence's *khaya* door was closed and so was our kitchen door. She would probably be out with my mother delivering orders.

I passed under the fig tree. A gleaming new red Humber cycle was propped against the side of the *rondavel*. Shantih's. Believing that I was at rugby practice, she and Kathy would be inside the *rondavel*. The curtains of the *rondavel* window were closed and so was the door. Unusually, no music was playing.

Lowering my bike onto the grass under the fig tree, I walked up to the door of the *rondavel* and grasped the handle but didn't turn it immediately. I could hear movement and murmuring on the other side. Then there was silence, followed by what could have been crooning, but somehow wasn't. I twisted the handle and stepped through the doorway.

My first impression in the gloom was of a blur of red and green on the floor beside the bunk and, on the bunk, a gently shimmering mass of red, white, green and brown. Then my eyes, adjusting fast, identified the blur on the floor as a pair of red panties and a green jersey.

The tangle on the bunk clarified into two people. Kathy, in the white shirt and green serge skirt of the convent, was on her side, her back to me. She was pressing up against Shantih, who lay with her dark head flung back on my pillow. Shantih's bright red dress was rucked up above her waist and Kathy's hand was a pale smudge between the brown thighs.

Standing there, it was as if I was registering the scene on the bunk with every sense: the heavy-scented air, the suddenly vibrating colours of the room around me, the lurch in my belly, the unbidden hardening of my cock.

As I hovered, sick with a confused medley of feelings, Shantih's thin hands went to Kathy's shoulders and gripped. In that fraction of a moment her gaze met mine and locked as if welded. Then her hands fell away from Kathy's shoulders and she was sitting upright, tugging her skirt down. Kathy twisted round and saw me, stupid and trembling in the doorway.

'Simon!' Her face was a knot of fury. 'What are you doing here?'

'What are *you* doing?'

'Never mind,' she spat. 'Get out.'

I was about to obey, but the enormity of it was like a match to benzine. 'Why should I?'

I jabbed a trembling finger in the direction of Shantih, who, having slid off the bed, was hastily wriggling her bare feet into the red pumps which lay on the floor. ' *She* should get out.'

'I said *you* get out, Simon!' Kathy came off the bunk, her fists clenched. Her shirt was unbuttoned. I glimpsed the pale curve of a breast, dark aureole, jutting pink nipple. 'Go on, get!'

'No! Kathy.' Shantih was shaking her head agitatedly. 'I'll go. It's his room.' She rolled up the jersey and turned to me. 'I'm sorry, Simon.'

She put a hand on my arm, but I shook it off.

'Simon,' Kathy grated, 'if you don't get...'

She didn't complete the threat because Shantih stepped forward and hugged her. 'No, Kathy. Not now. I must go.' She looked at me, distressed. 'I'm truly sorry. Truly.'

Then she was out of the door. It coughed shut behind her, leaving Kathy and me staring at its blankness.

'Well, *boetie*?' Kathy said, refastening her bra. Her tone was unapologetic, even defiant. Her hair wild, her eyes blazing out from behind slitted lids, she reminded me of a feral cat.

'I never thought you would do a filthy thing like that with a *koelie* girl.' My eyes were itching with tears. I was still clutching the schoolbag containing my rugby kit. I let it drop to the floor.

'Don't call her a *koelie*,' she said. 'She's my friend and we were only cuddling.'

'That's a lie,' I cried. 'You were stinky fingering her.' At the revived image of the tableau on the bed I felt a treacherous reprise of the arousal I'd experienced then.

'Don't use those words,' she retorted. 'Don't talk about down there as if it was a dirty place. It's where you came from.'

'Not me – not from any Indian twat.' I wanted to hurt her, to spoil beyond recovery any pleasure she'd got. 'Just wait till I tell Mom and Dad what you've been doing.'

She winced. 'You'd never tell. And anyway what we were doing wasn't wrong. It's what girls do, that's all.'

'Tell that to Dad,' I countered. She'd shrunk a little. With an odd, ugly thrill I realised what was blending with her anger. Under the belligerence, she

73

was frightened. The knowledge was like a tonic.

'I could tell things about you,' she said. 'Looking at girls and thinking dirty. Spying on me in the shower. Tossing off with your friends.' That was Kathy. Not one to accept defeat readily.

'Not me,' I said. 'That was Kepler and Harry and Jacky having a competition to see who could shoot furthest. Norman told you, didn't he? Sucking up to you because he wants you to be his girlfriend.'

'He can want. I don't want to be his girlfriend – or any boy's.' Her tone changed, became earnest. 'Listen, *boetie*, I've got a thing for Shantih and she's got it for me and I'm not giving her up.'

She was rallying. It was time to use my advantage.

'You'll have to give her up if I tell. Dad will see to that.' I turned and walked to the door. 'He'll see the mynah bird flies away.'

'Simon,' she said – a rare use of my name. 'Don't tell, *boetie*. Please don't tell.' She moved towards me. 'Please.'

I halted, my hand halfway to the doorknob. My heart was drumming so hard I wondered if she could hear it. 'All right, I won't. If...'

'If what?'

Her expression changed. I thought I read anger and disdain, but I was simmering with need and had gone too far to stop. I could barely get the words out. 'You know,' I croaked, gesturing at my crutch.

Her gaze went to my fly and the bulge there. She stepped closer and my stomach flipped in anticipation. Then her hand shot out, gripping me, the nails digging painfully into my cock through the fabric of my trousers and underpants. 'Listen, to me, Simon,' she said in a voice gone quiet and cold. 'If you think you can use what you saw here to get what you want, you'd better think again. And while you're about it you'd better think about what Dad will do if I tell him that you're a randy little rat who tried to blackmail me – your own sister – into jerking you off.'

Her breath was hot against my ear as her fingers tightened. 'Take my advice, *boetie*,' she went on. 'Get a girlfriend – and quick. Then you and me will be all right with each other.'

With a final squinch which made me yelp, she left me to my shame and hurt.

Seven

I knew Kathy's advice was sound. But, Elizabeth Carter apart, there was no girl around that I strongly fancied. Though I liked Melanie Oldcastle and visited her quite often I was too inhibited to ask her out. It had to do with a conviction that she was delicate and should be protected. We hung round the pool when the weather was warm enough and played records or talked in the pale pink attic. She taught me chess and tried unsuccessfully to teach me to play the piano; and I taught her Battleships. Sometimes Clive White turned up and he and Melanie played duets while I croaked out the words of some of the songs I knew.

I liked Clive. Slightly built, fair and with a drooping moustache and languid manner, he was my idea of a sensitive artist and intellectual. He was friendliness itself, offering me cigarettes from his box of De Reskes and chatting to me about books and films and music as if I was his age and knew as much. He was witty about his work in Landau's bookshop, which he enjoyed but regarded as a dead end, and amusing, too, about the customers and old Abel Landau.

'I don't know how we make a profit. He's always donating books to this or that non-white school or selling them to Natives at half price. I could understand him being polite to the principal of the Native school in Vilakazi, but to call him Mr and take him into the back for tea is going rather too far, though I must admit Caleb Mdonga is well read for a Native.'

'Better read than Clive White, I'll bet,' was Kathy's comment when I repeated his remark. She didn't like Clive and was much more interested in Melanie. 'She's nice, but she is strange. The house, too. It gives me the shivers: so big and empty. And only that sour maid to look after her.' She shot me a glance. 'Do you think she knows about her dad?'

'She's never said anything to me. Jacky Hughes says the police brought a court case against him after they caught him with a black girl in the car, but he got off by saying he was just giving her a lift. It didn't get into the papers because he was a friend of old R.B. Alexander.'

Kathy frowned. 'That sounds like one of Jacky's tall stories.'

'Jacky's dad says old Alexander was always in Vilakazi when he was a young man. That's where Joshua March comes from.'

'You'd better watch what you say in front of Mom about the old man and Joshua.'

'Mom's too soft. People should stick to their own kind.'

She blinked angrily. 'You mean their own colour, don't you?'

'Same thing.'

'It isn't the same thing. Seth March is more your kind than that *domkop* Kepler or slimy little Jacky Hughes. You'd soon find that out if you weren't such a bigot.'

'Bigot?'

'Prejudiced, what Mom calls biased. Like the Lategans and even Dad sometimes. Like the people who call the Landaus and the Katzes Yids. Like people who call us names because we live this side of town. Like the people who call Mr Seer a queer.'

'Queer. That's you and your friend Shantih, too, isn't it? Lezzies.'

She grinned at me. 'Not so queer, little brother.' She picked up my cricket bat, oiled in readiness for the new season, and played a passable imitation of a cover drive. 'Your friend Norman has asked me to go to the farm with him.'

'He never.' I stared at her, my feelings in turmoil.

'He did and I'm going. I've always wanted to see the Robertses' farm.'

I swallowed hard. 'How does Miss Paw Paw like that?'

Her grin looked more like the snarl of a feral cat than a human smile.

'About as much as you do, *boetie*,' she said.

Eight

The Victoria public library was the last place I would have expected to find trouble. But I hadn't taken into account Kathy, Shantih and the Viljoens.

It was a hot February afternoon. Daydreaming about the coming Saturday's cricket match while cycling along Kitchener Drive, I only vaguely registered the white facade of the library with its blank oblong windows and soaring palm tree. But as I drew nearer, I could see that three boys and a dark girl in a red dress were jostling about under the tree in what looked like a clumsy dance.

Then I recognised them. The boys were the Viljoen twins, Conrad and Sarel, and their younger brother, Gert. The girl was Shantih. On the ground beside the bench, and clearly knocked over in the scuffling, lay Kathy's Raleigh bicycle.

Instinct told me to leave Shantih to the brothers. I didn't fancy the odds at all and, as far as I was concerned, the Indian Mynah had a hiding coming.

But a three-pronged goad pricked me on. First, Kathy would never forgive me if I abandoned her friend. Second, if I pedalled off like a coward, my name would be worse than shit in the neighbourhood. The third was that Shantih had spotted me and, true to the nickname I'd given her, was screeching my name. Cursing her, Kathy, the Viljoens and my luck, and with the chill of fear already in my belly, I swerved into the kerb, flung my bike down and rushed towards the mêlée.

She was fighting gutsily, biting, kicking and scratching. Conrad Viljoen had a cut running down his face and Sarel was flinching from her skittering feet. But numbers were telling. Conrad had her by the hair and right arm and Gert, from behind her, had one arm across her throat and was twisting her left arm up her back with the other. Her skirt was torn. There was a bruise above one eye and her face was flecked with spittle.

Sarel was nearest so I went for him from the back, catching him by the shoulders and ramming my foot hard into the hinge behind his knee. He went down. I jumped at Conrad, who twisted round to confront me, loosening his grip on Shantih. I drove a fist at his face, but missed and he closed with me. A knee found my groin. Our heads clashed and we lurched apart gushing blood. Out of one streaming eye I could see that Shantih had got free of Gert.

'Get Kathy,' I rasped. Then a fist smashed into my temple and Sarel scythed my legs from under me.

The pavement hit me hard. Dazed, I dimly made out Gert and a bloody-faced Conrad looming above me. Sarel's blunt face was also in the muzzy frame. I was for it: a rib-bruising kicking, just for a start.

But not at once. Viljoen pride demanded a gloat and Conrad was the mouthiest one. 'What did you have to butt in for, hey Blackie?' he demanded, his foot dangling over my stomach. 'I never thought you were a *koelie*-lover like your mad sister.' He gestured towards the bench under the tree with its *Europeans Only – Slegs vir Blankes* sign. 'That little *gamat* actually had the cheek to put her black *gat* on a white person's seat. You could get syph that way.'

They were playing with me. If I defied them I was going to be tagged up and down Victoria as a traitor to my skin. If I grovelled I was betraying my sister. Whatever I did they weren't going to let me go without injury. And the longer I stayed down the worse the damage was going to be.

'So, Blackie,' Gert jeered. ' *Wat sê jy*?'

His over-confidence was my only chance.

'I say you're fucking cowards, packing one girl, even if she is a *koelie*.' With the speed of terror, I grabbed Conrad's menacing foot and jerked furiously. Unprepared, he staggered off balance. Gert's toecap thudded into my back as I rolled onto my side and, as I got to my knees, another kick scorched my ribs so that I howled.

And all this for the sake of that bloody little mynah bird, I thought.

There was a clatter of feet: Kathy, her hair flying and her crammed bookbag swinging. 'Pigs!' she yelled. 'Shits!' Her bag crunched into Gert's face, once, then a second time, causing him to cringe away, his hands held up protectively as she steadied herself to swing again. Shantih ran straight at Sarel, arms and legs pumping. He squawked and ran.

Groggy, I faced Conrad. He was breathing hard and looking fierce, but he didn't come any nearer.

'Okay, Kathy, okay! Let's call it quits, hey?' It was Gert who spoke, his hands spread in a gesture of truce. 'The *koelie* was taking liberties. We didn't know she was with you.'

'That's a lie,' Shantih said. 'You saw us arriving and the moment Kathy went inside you started on at me about who did I think I was going around with a white girl.' She pointed at Sarel, who, safe across the street, had stopped running. 'And that little thing tried to take the bicycle. When I grabbed it back, Mister Bloody Nose there spat on me.'

'Only because she fought and scratched like an animal,' Conrad said.

'An animal,' Kathy said, 'and what kind of creature are you – a *rinkhals*? – to spit at her?' Still clutching her schoolbag in her right hand, she stepped forward quickly and spat in his face. 'That's for Shantih,' she said, 'and' – spitting a second time – 'that's for me. Now why don't you and your scummy *boeties* bugger off?'

His face swelled, his fists knotted and for a moment I thought he was going to try his luck. So did Kathy: she lifted her bag warningly. At the same time there was a shout from the library entrance. Two women had appeared. Miss Wilson, the angular, grey-haired librarian. Miss Robinson, my former principal. They paused on the steps then hurried down towards us.

'We'll get you and your *koelie* pal,' Conrad said. 'Just wait.' But he was already moving off, followed by Gert.

'Bring your big brother, Hendrik, next time,' Kathy jeered. 'Your mom and dad, too, if you like.'

'Well Simon Brown – in the thick of things as usual, I see!' Miss Robinson was examining me, a frown pleating her forehead. Though I was now inches taller than the grey-suited principal, I felt like the five year-old who had stood apprehensively before her a decade ago.

She looked enquiringly at Shantih. 'And who are you?'

'Shantih Patel,' Kathy said. 'Our friend.'

'You should have come into the library with Kathy, child,' Miss Robinson said.

'I'm not allowed,' Shantih said. 'And there was Kathy's bicycle.'

'I would have let you in,' Miss Wilson said, 'and there's a shed at the back for bicycles.' She looked at Kathy. 'I'd report those boys to the police, if I were you.'

'We know them,' Kathy said. 'And it's no use reporting them. They live by crime and they'd just call us narks and break every window in our house.'

'You and Shantih have cuts,' Miss Robinson said to me. 'I'm sure Miss Wilson will let you use the bathroom to wash and patch up a little.'

'It's nothing,' Shantih said, touching her eyebrow. 'The spitting was worse.'

'They can wash at our home,' Kathy said. 'Mom's expecting me. I just popped in to return a book.'

'*The Well of Loneliness*,' Miss Robinson said. 'I noticed it on the counter. An interesting choice.'

'You've read it, Miss?'

'A very long time ago. What did you make of it?'

'I thought it was fantastic. Shantih did, too.'

'But too sad,' Shantih said. 'Stephen is too unhappy. I'll never be unhappy like that.'

I felt myself going hot. Miss Wilson was staring at Shantih as if she had just parachuted into our company from a passing spaceship. Miss Robinson was looking thoughtful. *She knows*, I told myself. *She knows and she doesn't mind.* My head spun with the complexity of it.

'You girls must come for tea sometime,' Miss Robinson said. 'You, too, Simon, if you like.' She touched Kathy's arm. 'I'll telephone your home.'

She's one, I thought, *she's one of them.* The idea was shattering.

After she had gone Kathy fussed over Shantih for a bit, then turned to examine me. 'Are you all right, Simon?' she queried. 'You look a bit green.'

'I'm fine,' I said. It wasn't entirely true. I felt dizzy and my body was aching. 'Let's get on home before Miss Paw Paw gets us into another fight.'

Shantih laughed. 'You're my hero. You should

have seen him, Kathy, riding to the rescue like a Pathan warrior on his horse.'

In spite of her mocking tone, I felt a surge of pride. But I wasn't going to show it. 'Well, you're not my heroine,' I retorted. 'You're too much trouble.'

I began to walk towards my abandoned cycle.

Instantly they were on either side of me, their arms enclosing me.

'Don't desert us, Simon Legree,' Shantih cooed. 'We think you're wonderful, we really do. So did those old women. They were eating you up with their eyes.'

'You're disgusting,' I said. 'They were old enough to be my mother.'

'All the better,' Shantih said. 'Boys like being mothered.'

They were clipping me tight. I could feel the softness of their breasts against my chest, their cheeks warm against mine. It was soothing and comfortable and I would have liked to submit to it. Instead, I wriggled free and strode over to my bicycle, shaking my head at their laughing challenges to remain and be cuddled.

As I pedalled away they called and waved, arms around each other's waists. Unrepentant. Happy. Infuriating.

Nine

My dad was shouting.

This was astonishing because he never shouted. He hardly ever spoke. He was the quietest man I knew. Shifts, a willingness to work overtime and to relieve holidaying colleagues out in the district, meant he was often absent. But even when he was in the house he was so silent that it was easy to forget he lived with us. Paradoxically, forgetting him was less likely when he was confined to his room during his bouts of illness, because my mother, Kathy and Florence bustled backwards and forwards tending to him.

He wasn't unfriendly in the normal run of things. He answered if spoken to. Occasionally, he volunteered a thought on some topic under discussion at mealtimes or an item in the news. He said enough for me to know that he was pro-British and had been a Smuts man, but considered the present government to be on the right lines concerning non-whites. But generally he preferred to withdraw to our seldom-used dining room or the bedroom and read his paper or some travel book. He'd got a taste for foreign parts in the war before he was invalided out. It was a grievance that he hadn't been able to see the world.

He'd started shouting when my mother told him after supper that she was joining a Black Sash women's vigil. But the real reason for his rage, it turned out, was that he'd heard about the fight outside the library. Worse, he'd heard about it from a workmate who was friendly with the Viljoens. The story had developed in the telling. In the revised account, the *koeliemeid*, Kathy and I had been trying to steal Conrad Viljoen's bicycle and had started a scrap when caught.

'It's your fault, Phyllie,' he stormed. 'You've

never been firm enough with the kids. They're out of control, fighting in the street like that.'

'They'd no choice, Eric.' Pale with anger in her turn, she clicked her recently acquired lighter furiously at the tip of her cigarette, then exhaled a jet of smoke. 'Shantih was attacked by those guttersnipes and the kids charged in to defend her.'

'Why is Kathleen running around with the Rangisamy girl? Can't she make white friends?'

'It's Patel, Dad, and I've got white friends. But I like her best.' In contrast to my mother, Kathy was a violent red.

'Well, you'd better stop liking her. I don't want to see her around here, whatever her name is.' He swung back to my mother. 'This comes from you being so familiar with every Tom, Dick and Harry. I know you once worked with Joshua March and everyone thinks the sun shines out of his brown backside because of what he did in the war. But he's a Coloured and that's bad news. What do you suppose the neighbours think, seeing him round here every other day and those sons of his being treated like family?'

'It's not every other day – it's once every couple of months. Joshua and his boys *are* like family and I don't give a bugger what the neighbours think.'

'They don't look like family and I do give a bugger about the neighbours.'

'Eric,' my mother said, expelling more smoke, 'you've never objected to the Marches before and you've been quite happy to go to Rangisamy's yourself. You're only making a fuss because of those Nats you work with.'

'I am a state employee, Phyllie,' he said more calmly. 'It's not like the old United Party days. It's got very political and you have to watch your step.'

'Not me.' My mother doused her cigarette stub in her coffee mug. 'And I'm not going to turn the kids into little yes-men, not never.'

They faced each other across the kitchen table. Mom in her apron as usual, a bit greasy faced, her hair sticking to her forehead, looking more solid than I'd ever seen her, as if rooted in the kitchen floor. Dad in his black suit and tie, SAR badge on his lapel, his face muscles jumping. This was the first open row I could remember. I'd heard him grumble and I'd heard her shout at him as she shouted at us, more because it was her style than through any deep anger. Now I waited for him to reply, fascinated but uneasy. I wanted him to stand up for himself. He was the man, why couldn't he act like it?

He moved first, picking up his copy of the *News* and half-turning towards the door. 'I'm not asking for yes-men, Phyllie.' His tone had changed: there was a faint whine in it. 'I'm asking them to remember who they are and behave themselves like white people should, not get mixed up with non-white kids and rubbish like the Viljoens. And I can't stop you joining those posh women from Mountside in their games, but I wish you wouldn't. Mrs Landau and old Mrs Alexander and all their bridge friends can afford to stick their fingers up to the government. But we can't and you shouldn't let them drag you in.'

My mother reached for her box of Commando Round. 'They aren't games,' she said over the clicking of the lighter, 'and I'm not letting anyone drag me in. I'm going because I agree with what they're doing, not because of who they are. Now listen, Eric. I've tried to bring the kids up right. They're not perfect, but they're not bad neither. They don't steal, they're doing well at school and they help me when I ask them. If you took more interest you'd notice that they're growing up with minds of their own. I try to let them choose their own friends, even if I'm not too keen on their choice. I like Shantih and I don't like Jacky Hughes or Harry Lewis, but I don't interfere because the boy chose them for himself. And I'll say this, too. Good on the boy that he stepped in to help his sister's friend.'

My father waved the paper vaguely as if to brush away midges. 'You're going to ruin those kids. But you've always done what you liked. Always got your way with everything.'

He walked out of the room. I took a hesitant step after him, stirred by a half-impulse to show I was on his side, my father's son. But I got no further, halted by the sight of my mother's brimming eyes.

'Never everything, not nearly everything,' she said as if to herself.

Ten

Florence Zondi was a plump, smiling woman who often sang as she bustled about her work. So it was a shock to find her between my mother and Kathy at the kitchen table, her apron up over her face, keening. Joshua, his chauffeur's cap on the back of his head, sat opposite, holding a coffee mug. Thandi, stork legged and wooden-faced except for an intermittent chewing of her lip, stood at the sink watching.

'It's Elias,' my mother said. 'He's been arrested.'

'Why?' Elias was Florence's husband, a jovial, bearded petrol pump attendant at Illingworth Motors.

'For going into the European section of the Post Office in High Street,' Kathy said. 'Joshua saw it and came to tell us.'

'The Post Office?' I'd passed it two hours earlier that afternoon and noticed nothing unusual, beyond a small knot of blacks dressed as if for church on the steps. One, a large woman in a dark green dress and black beret, had been handing out leaflets and I'd taken her and the others for members of one of the many black religious sects.

'Elias and Maisie Matomela were chosen to lead volunteers into action at the Post Office,' Joshua said. 'Another group went into the Europeans Only waiting room at the railway station today after phoning the police. And Mr Seer got himself arrested for walking into Vilakazi township without a permit.'

'What's the use of trying to get arrested?'

'Haven't you heard of the Defiance Campaign?' Joshua demanded. 'People all over South Africa are showing the *Boere* they would rather go to jail than obey their colour bar laws.'

'He's not very interested in politics, Joshua,' my

mother said quickly. 'Eric doesn't like politics neither. Kathy's more the one.'

'He should be interested,' Joshua said. 'This is a struggle of all the people against the *Boerenasie*.'

'Then why aren't you in jail with the others?' I said. 'And what's Florence so upset about if it's the right thing to do?' Kathy was frowning warningly, but Joshua's remarks had riled me. Besides, he was sitting in the chair my dad usually occupied.

'Elias didn't tell her,' my mother said. 'That's men for you.'

'He was only called on to lead this morning,' Joshua said, 'because Thabo Modisi was taken by the Special Branch last night.' He laughed contemptuously. 'The Specials said it was to stop him trying to get himself and others arrested today.'

Florence pulled the apron down from her face to reveal wet, swollen eyelids and puffy cheeks. 'I knew Elias was volunteering, madam. We talk about it weeks ago, because I am ANC also. Women's League.' She dabbed at her eyes with the edge of the apron. 'But today is too soon, too soon.'

'ANC?' My mother reached for her box of cigarettes. 'That's communist, isn't it?'

'Not communist, madam,' Florence said. 'Is the organisation of the African people.'

'You never told me that you belonged to it, bad girl.' For a moment my mother looked put out. 'Don't you go telling the master. He wouldn't like it.' She lit a cigarette and took a few puffs, her forehead wrinkled in concentration. 'I can't get over it, Elias chucking up his job to go to jail and leaving you to look after the kids. And what good will it do? The government won't change their mind about the laws. I know these Nats. They'll never give in, never, not to your ANC. I think this thing Elias is doing is mad, Florrie, mad and stupid.'

'Yes madam.' Florence's face closed up.

'My father is not mad,' Thandi cried out from beside the sink. 'Not stupid. He is brave.'

We all stared at her. She was standing erect, large tears rolling slowly down her cheeks.

'Mom!' Kathy was up and at Thandi's side, wrapping her arms around her. 'Of course he's brave, Thandi. Very brave.'

'Oh my child,' my mother said, getting up and going to them. 'I'm so sorry.'

Thandi was crying in earnest now, great sobs shaking her body. I turned my head away, not wanting to see a skinny kaffir girl blubbing.

Joshua was examining me coldly. 'You asked me why I wasn't in Elias's group. There's a rota. My turn is coming.'

As I glared at him, searching for a cutting retort, I heard footfalls in the passageway. Swinging round I saw my father, in his dark railway clerk's suit, framed in the doorway.

His face pale, he surveyed the room. 'What's going on? What the hell is this all about?'

Joshua put down his coffee cup, but didn't rise. 'Florence's husband has gone to jail for leading a group into the white section of the Post Office.'

'It's the Defiance Campaign, Dad,' Kathy said, her arm still around Thandi.

'That!' my father almost spat. 'We've had Natives swarming all over the station today. Going into the Europeans' waiting room. Sitting on Europeans Only benches. One cheeky bitch even tried to go into the women's lavatory. Bloody chaos. If I'd had a gun I'd have shot them.'

'You'd have been making a very big mistake, Mr Brown,' Joshua said quietly. 'The people don't want violence. But things can change.'

'So you know all about it, do you?' My father's face was twitching. 'Well, I'm buggered if I'm having a communist demonstration in my own house. So you can push off.'

'Hang on a tick, Eric,' my mother said agitatedly, coming forward. 'We're all a bit upset over Elias. Let's cool down and talk sensible.' She motioned vigorously at me. 'Off you go, Simon. Take Thandi to the *rondavel* with you. Play her some records or something. You too, Kath.'

'I want to stay, Ma.' Kathy's eyes were huge as she stared at my father.

I stared, too. He hadn't moved from the doorway, but seemed to swell to fill it. His face twitched and his hands closed into fists. He was even angrier than after our scrap with the Viljoens.

Joshua had straightened in his chair, his eyes on my father. Would they fight? At the prospect, a lump of ice formed in my gut. Yet I was aware of half-wanting it to happen. Mixed in with the fear that Joshua would win was a lust to see the insolent Coloured man bested.

'I said off you go, you kids,' my mother rasped. 'No arguments now. Us grown-ups need to talk.'

It was a voice which reached into childhood discipline. We went.

We listened to records for a while. Then when *Blue Moon* dropped onto the turntable Kathy got up and held out her hands to Thandi. The girl looked surprised but took them and let herself be pulled into the space between the bunk and the door. Soon they were moving together to the music. I filched a cigarette from Kathy's illicit pack and went to the door, puffing the smoke out into the dusk and trying to imagine what was being said in the kitchen.

The music stopped. The *Tennessee Waltz* came on. Kathy tapped me on the shoulder. 'Your turn with our guest, little brother.'

My chest had gone tight. Me dance with a black girl? It was bad enough for Kathy to do it, but she was a girl, which made it different. What was the contemptuous word Kepler used of any white man who went with black girls? *Kaffermeidnaaier*!

My mouth was already shaping my refusal when Florence emerged from the kitchen with Joshua behind her.

'*Siyahamba kuVilakazi*,' Florence said, holding out her hand, which the girl took.

'What happened, Joshua?' Kathy was tense. 'Where's Mom and Dad?'

'Having a little talk. It's all right, girlie. Understand that it's hard for your dad. He was a Smuts man. But now that Smuts is dead and the *Boere* are running things they don't even bother with *kakpraat* about justice for non-whites. Their talk about the *swart gevaar* and the red menace worries a lot of folks. Not your ma, because she just sees people and that's what they're talking about now.'

'Was talking about it.' My mother had come out to us. 'You'd better go, Joshua. Eric's none too happy, but never to worry. He's got his views, but he's a kind man.'

Joshua gave his yellow grin. 'Okay, then. Stay well, you kids. You, too, Phyllis. I'll walk with Florence and Thandi.'

My mother was sniffing. 'Have you young

93

buggers been smoking?'

I left it to Kathy to reply. Joshua had called my mother Phyllis. For all his insolent familiarity I'd never heard him use her first name before.

Eleven

Elias served a week in jail. Shortly after his release he was sentenced to three more for walking down Victoria High Street after curfew. This was followed by a two-month sentence for entering a train compartment reserved for Europeans.

Mr Seer, who'd been given a suspended sentence for entering the location, was also arrested again: he'd gone into the non-European section of the Post Office and tried to send a telegram to the prime minister protesting against the Pass Laws. He was sentenced to three weeks' imprisonment.

Joshua went to prison for two weeks, then again for a month, both sentences for ostentatiously sitting on a bench in the Sunken Gardens reserved for whites. Seth March, who was with his father on the second occasion, was jailed for a month.

Even more unexpected was the news, brought round by a highly excited Shantih, that Mrs Rangisamy was one of a group of campaigners arrested in nearby Cathcart. They had entered a Whites Only railway restaurant, sat down at a table and coolly requested tea and cakes. They got a month in Victoria Prison instead.

The second time Elias was arrested Florence cried briefly on my mother's shoulder. The third time she didn't cry at all, but her face seemed to have gone thinner and she no longer sang while working. My mother said this was because Thandi had begun cheeking her teachers, truanting and mixing with dubious township characters.

As the campaign continued through July and August into September, we became a house divided.

Kathy followed it in every way she could:

through the scanty reports in the daily newspapers, the more detailed accounts in papers like *The African People's Voice, Advance* and *Indian Opinion*, and anyone she knew who was involved. Her enthusiastic chatter about the power of passive resistance led to a series of mealtime spats with our father. He'd become uncharacteristically voluble, as if resentment stung his tongue to eloquence: he derided the campaign as something inspired by communists and supported by misguided white philanthropists who didn't really understand the colour problem.

He didn't try to hide his satisfaction when Joshua was sentenced. 'That one thinks he can act like a white man just because he's got a vote,' he said, his gaze switching from Kathy to my mother. 'But he can't, not with this government. And they'll soon be taking that vote away.'

He became finger-jabbingly angry when Kathy accused him of siding with Afrikaner Nationalists to protect his job on the railways.

'My job pays for the food you're eating and the clothes you're wearing,' he snapped. 'Your trouble is that you're letting some people fill your head with a lot of rubbish. A pity the Rangisamy woman couldn't take that chatterbox of a niece off to jail with her. The more troublemakers locked up the better as far as I'm concerned.'

'Shantih would have joined the campaign if she hadn't been too young. And I would have, too.'

'More fool you,' he said. 'No good will come of this law-breaking.'

'Bad laws deserve to be broken. Doesn't it make you think, Dad, when good people like Elias and Joshua and Mrs Rangisamy – even old Mr Seer – are prepared to go to jail?'

'I don't see good people. I see a communistic black man, R.B. Alexander's arrogant half-caste bastard, a silly Hindu woman and an old homo. Queer old Seer will be in his element locked up with a bunch of men.'

'Mr Seer has never done no one any harm, Eric,' my mother put in. 'And a lot of other white people are quite sympathetic.'

'*Ag!*' he said disgustedly. 'Softheaded liberals. The laws have got to be obeyed even when we disagree with them. Otherwise there's chaos. And that's what the communists want: chaos and violence.'

The wrangling at table became so heated that my mother threatened to eat alone unless there was a ban on discussing the campaign at meals.

I kept my nose out of the dispute. Though I agreed with my father and would have liked his approval I didn't want to take sides against my mother and Kathy.

Kathy was concerned about Mom. We'd always thought of her as the strongest of us. But she seemed to have been knocked by the arrests and was going around looking drawn.

'It's Joshua,' Kathy said. 'She's worried about them all, but about Joshua most. He's so proud. She thinks he'll get into trouble in prison.'

Florence got word from Julian Richards, the reporter on the *News*, that both Joshua and Elias were coping with prison . Lanky and ungainly, his sallow face scarred with acne, Julian was clever, energetic and often to be found chatting to Clive White in Landau's bookshop. He was also unapologetically for the protesters and critical of his paper's timid coverage of the campaign.

'Oh, Julian, you're so romantic about our non-white brethren,' Clive grimaced. 'Surely agitators are behind this dreary lawbreaking? Left to themselves Natives always seem to me rather cheerful and contented with their lot.'

'Several thousand have chosen to go to jail in protest so far,' Julian retorted. 'I don't think that reflects contentment or could be put down purely to agitation.'

He was exasperated by my lack of interest in politics, but unexpectedly opened up a chance for me to earn some money. 'You're sporty and don't write too badly,' he said of a piece on the annual cross-country race I'd written for the school magazine. 'How about writing a para or two about some of your school matches? I'm killing myself trying to get round to everything and I hate sports reporting anyway. I'll speak to the editor about it, if you're game.'

I was game. The payments, though small, came in handy and I found the writing easy. My mother and Kathy were pleased, while Joshua, undeflated by his spells in jail, was annoyingly paternal. 'You've got a foot in the door now,' he said as I passed him on the stairs of the *News*. 'When you leave school you'll take over from Richards. He's all right, but you'll be better.'

It was typical of his insolence that he never prefixed any white man's name with the courtesy Mister. 'I wouldn't count on my replacing *Mister* Richards, Joshua,' I said. 'I'll probably go onto the railways, like my dad.'

The yellow eyes flared, but he merely shook his head. 'Never mind the railways. You come onto the paper.'

I was too busy swotting for the end of year exams,

battling to keep my place as an all-rounder in the Colts XI, and writing up weekend matches to pay much attention to the news of riots in Port Elizabeth and Kimberley, though I couldn't help overhearing Kepler and Sam having a set-to over clashes between stone-throwing township dwellers and armed police.

Everyone else, it seemed, was getting worked up, including Kathy and my mom, because Elias and Joshua were preparing to lead a group of non-whites into the white section of Barclays Bank, and Florence had raised the possibility of taking part herself, which meant telling my father. Thandi was floating about, too, stork legged and sulky faced, thickening the atmosphere of crisis.

As it turned out no one went to jail. Just as the number of defiers climbed to over two thousand a month, further rioting in an East London township resulted in the death of a white nun known for her humane work. Scores of blacks died, too, gunned down in clashes with the police. But it was the prominence given by the newspapers to the shocking image of the nun in a flaming car which effectively destroyed the passive resistance campaign.

My father blamed communist agitators. Joshua blamed the government and police. Kathy and my mother mourned the dead.

Twelve

When the final bell of our final school day rang, some of my classmates began cheering and thumping each other on the back. Harry Lewis lit a cigarette inside the classroom and Jacky Hughes went into a Caliban imitation, yelling 'Freedom, high day! High day, freedom!' until Kepler told him to shut up unless he wanted a *klap*.

Sam Glass smiled at me as he emptied his desk and said, 'Now our real education begins.'

My feelings were mixed. I relished the idea of earning real money, the right to smoke and drink openly and the possibility of opportunities with unsupervised girls. There was, as Harry said, quoting Coriolanus, a world out there. But though I knew I'd done well in the state exams, it galled me that I had to choose between jobs on the railways, bank clerking or joining the *Victoria Daily News* as a cub reporter while dimmer boys were going on to university because their parents could afford the fees, which mine couldn't. And, all in all, I'd had a good last year at the school. I'd won the English prize and come second overall behind Sam. I was probably proudest, though, of my part in the first rugby fifteen's historic victory over St Michael's, a tackle on Jim Farraday, their captain and star centre, inches from our try-line: it was all the more satisfying because Farraday was Elizabeth Carter's boyfriend, and she'd been watching from the packed stand. Instinct told me few such triumphs lay ahead.

Above all, I felt a certain regret that alliances forged in the classroom and on the playing fields would be broken.

Already a distancing was evident. Kepler was spending a lot of time at the Police Station or knocking about with his policeman cousin. Not that I'd anything against the police beyond suspecting, like most people in our area, that there was no such thing as an off-dutycop and they were best given a wide berth.

Jacky was going to the University of Cape Town if he got his 'matric' which was by no means certain. The official goal was an arts degree. His real goal, Harry said, was to try to get into the Ikies' first fifteen. Whatever the aim, he was taking on the irritatingly knowing air of the student and ostentatiously carrying around with him books like Yeats's *Collected Poems* and F.R. Leavis's *The Common Pursuit*. 'You should be coming to varsity, too, Blackie,' he said.

'I've got a job here,' I said. 'University is a waste of time.' But I was aware of the clench of envy.

Harry was staying on in Victoria to work in Lewis Tanneries, the hide and skins firm he would one day inherit. He'd arrived at school this morning in the MG his father had given him to mark his seventeenth birthday.

'We'll see a lot of each other, you and me and old Norm now that he's courting your sister,' he said. 'Get a girlfriend and we'll make up a sextet sometime, with the emphasis on the sex.'

'Sure,' I said, not thrilled to be reminded of Kathy's inexplicable but manifest liking for Norman. 'But what do I do for a partner?'

'Try Jessica Leighton,' he said. 'She's free and willing.' While I gaped, he jumped into the MG and roared off.

I was still thinking about Harry's remark when I reached the footbridge which arched over the railway line. As a kid I'd often paused there to watch the activity on Victoria Station, the locomotives gasping and clanking, the loading and offloading of livestock and freight, the comings and goings of passengers, including the tribal blacks recruited to work in the mines of the Witwatersrand.

The tribesmen's strangeness hooked me. Most had bright bandanas about their heads, carried *knobkieries*, and wore trousers clipped below their knees with circlets of string or wire. Some were draped in multicoloured blankets and had brass bangles on their muscular arms. Others wore cotton-reels in the lobes of their ears. Gaudy, tinkly, cheerfully shouting at each other, they moved about the platform, vivid presences against the drab grey of the station buildings. They didn't rouse the antagonism I felt towards town blacks, seeming to be men from another world, not imitation whites.

Lately, and it was somehow connected with my final days at Victoria Boys' High, I'd resumed my old habit of pausing there and waiting for the arrivals and departures to stir up the scene, or to hail my dad on one of his frequent scuttles along the platform. Sometimes this led to a descent for a quick cup of coffee and chat with the friendlier of his colleagues.

The noon sun was slapping against my neck and bringing the sweat out under my arms. I dropped my old schoolbag at my feet, took off my jacket and draped it across the parapet. It would be ten minutes before the Cape train arrived on its journey to Johannesburg.

I fished in my jacket pockets and found a packet of ten Gold Leaf and a box of matches. The cigarette, no longer forbidden, nonetheless tasted illicit.

My tie was throttling me. I jerked it from my neck and on impulse flung it over the parapet so that it snaked down to the greasy furrow which ran parallel to the lines of rail. I'd have liked to send the blazer after it, but couldn't face explaining such wilful waste to my mother. Instead, I opened my overflowing schoolbag and removed the two ballpoint pens, a Penguin copy of *Sons and Lovers* and a dog-eared notebook in which I jotted ideas for a story I'd started to write. These I stuffed into my jacket pocket. The rest I emptied over the furrow. The thick history of South Africa, the atlas, the bowdlerised Shakespeare, the fat copy of *Adam Bede* and the general science textbook fell fastest. The English and Afrikaans grammars dropped nearly as swiftly and my exercise books fluttered satisfyingly down to join the ragged circle of litter. I threw the schoolbag after them and stood there breathing hard, shocked by what I'd done. A good thing there had been no one on the platform to see me. Black cleaners would clear the furrow pretty soon and perhaps find a use for some of the books and even the tie. Birch, the headmaster, had been insistent that we shouldn't pass on items of our school uniforms to non-Europeans. 'We want no honorary Victorians strutting around the locations,' he was always saying. 'Fuck you, Birch,' I said, flicking the cigarette after the rest.

'Blackie Brown!' said a voice. A girl, almost my height and wearing the black stockings and navy blue gymslip of Victoria Girls' High, had come up unnoticed from the town side and stopped to stare. She was dangling a string-tied parcel.

I recognised the dark hair and quizzical brows. Jessica Leighton.

'Why did you do that?' she asked.

'I give you three guesses.'

She thought for a moment, then nodded slowly. 'A bit extreme, isn't it?'

'Perhaps. But I felt like it.' Down by a side

platform a locomotive was creeping up to some trucks loaded with cattle for the Witwatersrand. It struck, jangled, linked. On the main platform the signalman was ambling towards his box.

'Do you always do whatever you feel like doing?' An eyebrow twitched.

'Whenever I can.' I searched for a quip which might impress and decided to hijack a quotation which Julian Richards said came from the hedonist's creed. 'If it pleases me and does others no harm, then it must be good.'

She considered this, not noticeably impressed, yet apparently in no hurry to move on.

'Have you seen Harry lately?' she asked.

'An hour ago. We broke up today.'

'Our school did, too – early enough for me to get to town to buy these shoes.' She patted the parcel then added, 'Talking of breaking up, did you know Harry and I had?'

'He sort of mentioned it.' I took a quick decision not to repeat Harry's parting suggestion.

'Did he tell you why?'

'No.'

She hesitated. 'He wanted me to go all the way with him and I wouldn't.'

Doubly bewildered, it was my turn to stare. First, because of Harry's stories about her. Second, because she was confiding in me.

'He's taking out Celia White now. Perhaps she'll give him what he wants.'

I couldn't think of any response other than a shake of the head. That seemed enough for her. 'So that's it,' she said. 'I liked him a lot but he turned out to be untrue and untruthful. Well, it's water under the bridge.'

'Or a runaway locomotive, maybe?' The wires beside the Cape line were vibrating, a noise like Christmas beetles.

'Maybe.' She smiled, a touch bitterly.

'Listen,' I said. 'It's magic.'

In the distance a train wailed twice. Small groups were forming on the platform. A woman in a hot-looking red coat carrying a baby. A man in a wide-brimmed hat. A few steps behind them a nanny, wheeling an empty pram, her head bound in a blue *doek*. Further down the platform stood a cluster of well-dressed blacks: they would travel in the third class compartments. A black porter was pushing a trolley and calling, '*Lumkha, lumkha*! Look out! *Pas op!*' Two other men, bare to the waist, their milk-chocolate skins glistening, were carrying a crate of cackling fowls. The approaching train hooted again, the wail eerily amplified by the mountain cuttings.

'I wouldn't quite say magic,' she said, coming closer. 'It's just noise and smoke to me. But it makes a difference being from railway people, I suppose.'

'You suppose right. The railways have opened up countries – the United States, India, Britain. They helped turn South Africa into a rich country after gold and diamonds were discovered. Look! Recruits for the mines.'

As if to illustrate my point, a colourful crowd of tribesmen was assembling on the platform. The hooter sounded again and now the train was visible, racing down the track towards the bridge on which we stood, smoke pluming out of its funnel. Jessica began to walk away, but I blocked her path and wrapped my arms around her.

'Wait!' I said. 'This is the good bit.'

'No!' she cried, struggling. 'Let me go.' A hand

thrust against my chest, but I held on, tightening my grip.

'Remember saying I was dark because of the train smoke,' I said. 'Let's see if it works on you.'

'It was a stupid thing to say,' she panted.

She'd stopped struggling. The impulse to subdue her went as quickly as it had come and I let my arms go slack. She didn't move, but simply stood there, leaning against me. The train roared under the bridge. For a long moment we were enveloped in a damp cloud, warm and stifling. Then the train was past. The smoke cleared.

Still she stood, not moving, a smudge on one flushed cheek. I had the feeling that if I tried to kiss her she'd let me. I raised my hands to her shoulders, but too late; she stepped back.

'We were awful to you,' she said. 'But we were just kids and you *were* rather different.'

'You mean dirty!'

'No. Different. My mother calls it class difference. People with different ideas and different habits.'

'You being posh, and people like us being trash – poor white trash?'

'No. But you were rather rough – rough and wild. Like just now. I think we were rather scared of you. Except Melanie. Melanie always stood up for you.' She paused. 'She says you two are just good friends.'

'It's true.'

She patted her lips, frowning, and seemed about to walk on, then turned back. 'Would you be interested in going to *The Moon is Blue* with me? It's supposed to be very good. Very funny. Rather risqué. I was going with Celia, but I'm not very pleased with Celia at present. Of course, you might have better plans...'

'No.' I surprised myself by my eagerness. 'No

plans. I'd like to go with you.'

'Super. It's on tomorrow night. Could you pick me up about seven-thirty?'

'I'm afraid I don't have a car.' I hadn't thought of that complication. No bus ran to Mountside and clearly girls like Jessica expected to be driven.

'Oh?' She frowned. 'That is a problem. You do drive?'

'Yes.' It wasn't the time to confess to not having a licence.

'I don't yet. Could you borrow?'

My embarrassment deepened. Kepler, once a possible lender, wouldn't want to aid and abet an illegal driver now that he was obsessed with law and order. Norman and his truck would be on the farm. Harry would be more likely to go without shoes than without his MG on a Saturday night.

'Probably,' I said, not wanting to admit failure so soon. 'I'll have to ask around.' My mind was flipping through possibilities and discarding them. Sam didn't drive and his father was out of the question. Clive? I didn't know him well enough. Jacky? He got his father's car quite often, but why should old man Hughes agree to me having it? It was all hopeless unless I risked 'borrowing' from Victoria Motors forecourt or outside someone's house. No, that was madness, especially in summer when the danger of being seen was high.

She was watching me. 'What about a taxi?' I said.

She grimaced. 'Not Victoria Taxis. They're foul.'

My mood was changing. Jessica was posing problems. She was clearly used to being ferried about. No courtship by cycle for her. Then she would be going away to university soon. I'd probably be just a filler while she waited for someone more her type: she'd shown no sign of wanting to be friendly until now. Besides, I didn't much like the idea of taking on one of Harry's rejects. On the other hand, she was pretty, intelligent and part of the toptown set.

She seemed to sense my conflict and put on a bright smile. 'Never mind. We'll think of something. She glanced at her watch. 'I'm late. I have to rush. I'll ring you or you ring me – tonight. All right?'

She began to walk away, turned and stepped back towards me. 'Just one thing you might think about, if you're taking me out. I'm for keeping things strictly platonic.'

'So am I.' I produced my best smile. 'Definitely.'

She looked at me, trying to assess the extent of my seriousness, then laughed. 'We're on then?'

'We're on.'

I said it firmly. But where the hell was I going to find a car.

Thirteen

I was passing the oak-guarded Public Gardens when I heard footsteps and a slender brown hand was inserted between my arm and my side.

'Dreaming of me, Simon Legree?' Shantih cooed, matching her step to mine and clipping my arm so that I couldn't withdraw it.

'Get away, Shantih,' I said. 'You'll get us into trouble.'

'Aren't I worth a little trouble?' she demanded cheerfully. 'Aren't we practically family?'

'You're mad, Mynah Bird. They'll lock us up.'

'And not together,' she smiled, releasing my arm. 'I'd be all right among the women criminals, but you're not very drawn to men, are you?'

Scanning the street ahead, I didn't reply. The touch of her hand, the brush of her hip against mine triggered an arousal which was escalating my anxiety.

'Why have you and Kathy been so scarce lately?' she said reproachfully. 'Your mother has been into the shop quite a few times, but no sight of you two.'

'I've had exams and Kathy has been hell of a busy standing in for Dr Kramer's receptionist.'

'I believe you,' she said drily. 'Not a single moment in the past three weeks.'

We had reached the library and she pointed to the Europeans Only bench under the palm tree. 'Let's sit here a moment and have one of your cigs.'

'Let's not,' I said.

'Are you just a bit of a chicken these days, Simon Legree? You fought a battle for me here once.' She plumped down on the seat and held out a hand for a cigarette. 'You can stand if it makes you feel safer.'

She was looking up at me with her bird-sharp

smile. There was no one in the street. I sat down, careful to leave space between us.

She waited till I'd lit her cigarette, then said, 'Kathy's seeing a lot of your friend Norman, isn't she?'

'Not so much.'

'You don't have to pretend. I know she is and I know why.'

I couldn't resist. 'Because it's natural.'

The chestnut eyes flashed. 'No. Because it's easier for her. She hasn't gone off me. I know that. She just finds it hard to face up to being' – she drew on the cigarette – 'different. You would say queer.'

'Perhaps it was just a phase?'

'No! Never! I know that, too.'

'You can't be sure.'

'I can.' She turned the sharp face towards me. 'Anyway the problem will be solved quite soon. I'm being sent back to Durban.'

'Why?' I was conscious of a jumble of emotions. One was relief at the removal of a complication. Another was the obscure regret that a contest between her and me was being stopped before its time.

'Many reasons,' she said. 'Going backwards and forwards between here and Durban is too expensive. Ranjith, my brother, is there most of the year. I could follow his footsteps and enrol at the University of Natal.'

'As what?' I knew my mouth had fallen open. This Indian girl was for university now while I, a white boy, had to go to work.

'Medical student. The family would like that. But I think the main reason for sending me away is that someone has said something to my uncle and aunt about Kathy and me.'

She smiled wanly at my 'Hey?' and jerk of

110

surprise. 'Nothing has been said directly. It's not their way. They like Kathy. But they've hinted that perhaps we're too much together, and as progressive Indians they think I should be serious about a career.' She gave a small sniff. 'Progressive. My family is very politically progressive – only not about this.'

'But who'd have told them?'

She dropped her cigarette stub and extinguished it with a swivel of her sandalled foot. 'I don't know.' She tilted her head so that she was looking at me obliquely. 'It wasn't you, was it?'

'It bloody-well wasn't.' Indignation turned my voice into a yelp. 'I'm no snide.'

The thin brown hand was on my sleeve. 'I didn't think so. But I had to ask.'

'Ask someone else. Ask your uncle and aunt.'

She shook her head. 'Not yet. Things are too – too delicate. But I can guess.'

'Go on?' Her hand was still on my arm and the distance between us had narrowed to almost nothing. It was a good thing the street was still empty.

'When I'm sure I'll tell you.'

'Give us a clue.'

'No. But tell me you'll miss me, Simon Legree.'

Her trousered thigh was against mine now, warm and disturbing. I could make out the outlines of her breasts under the thin smock-like top. Her face was only inches away. Was she unconscious of what she was doing and its effect? It would serve her right if my hand brushed her breast accidentally on purpose. I gulped down some smoke, squinched my cigarette and stood up, trembling.

'I've got to get going.'

'Say you're sorry, Simon.' Her eyes were misty with appeal. Or was it mischief?

'I'm not sorry. No mynah birds west of Natal.'

'Not just a bit sorry?'

The big eyes were liquid now in the narrow face. 'Maybe just a bit,' I grunted.

'Good.' Her smile was like the flash of a kingfisher wing in the sun. 'Because I'll be back some weekends.' She got up. 'I'll walk with you to the High Street.'

A car hooted behind us. I turned. Harry Lewis swept past in his MG, waving. I raised two fingers in reply and swore.

'Why did you call him a shithouse?' Shantih asked. 'I thought he was your friend.'

'A real friend would have stopped.'

'Perhaps he was being tactful.'

'Not him. He was showing off.'

'Good riddance then.'

'Good riddance. Only I wanted a favour.'

'What was the favour?'

'He was driving it.'

'His nice car? That *is* asking a favour.'

'I've got a date who expects a car.'

She chuckled. 'Upper class, eh?'

'Sort of.'

We'd crossed Prince Edward Street and were entering Cobbler's Lane, which led to Victoria High Street. There were people about now, making their way in and out of the dry-cleaner's shop or the florists or cutting through to the main street. A couple of shabby Coloured women were joking with a young black man in a smart lightweight jacket. Sipho. The women looked at us incuriously as we passed on the other side. Sipho waved and Shantih waved back. I nodded. Shantih slowed as if to stop, but I marched on and she followed.

'I'll tell you what,' she said after we had walked a little further, 'you could borrow my Volkswagen.'

'What?' Incredulous, I stopped. 'Your car?'

'Well, actually it's my brother's as well – left to us by a relative.'

'I couldn't.' But my mind was alight with the bright chance of it.

'Why not?' Her lip curled in amusement that held a trace of derision. 'Because of whose car it is? She needn't know.'

'No,' I said, too vehemently, knowing I deserved the taunt. 'Not that.'

'What then?'

The red was staining my cheeks. 'I haven't got a licence.'

She laughed easily. 'I know. I'll risk it. But there are two conditions.'

There would be, I thought. She was an Indian after all.

'Go on.'

'Nothing much. I want you and Kathy to come to a little private do. A kind of farewell. Some young people you know, some you don't.

'Like who?'

'Wait and see. Bring your new lady friend. There'll be curries and bhajis and poppadoms and so on... a few lagers for you drunkards. Nice talk. A little politics.'

'Politics?' I groaned. 'You know I'm not interested in that stuff.'

'You should be. Your friend Sam Glass is. He'll be there. And Julian Richards, too. Also Elizabeth Carter.'

'Elizabeth!' I could only stare at her.

'Yes. The Carters are liberal people.' Ignoring the

fact that we'd left Cobbler's Lane for the much thicker flow of Victoria High Street, she closed her fingers round my elbow. 'You'll enjoy yourself. Now when do you want my car?'

'Tomorrow evening. We're going to the bio.'

She grimaced. 'Lucky for some. *The Moon is Blue*, isn't it? Us third class citizens won't see it for years. If ever.'

I stared at her. I'd never thought of her life as lacking pleasures I took for granted. 'That's tough.'

'Never mind. I'll see it one day when I go to England – and all the other ones that are banned here even to you lucky whites.'

'What's the other condition?'

'You let Kathy and me have the rondavel while you're at the bioscope.'

'*Simon! Si-mon!*' A voice like that of a *hadedah*, familiar and unwelcome, cut through the street noise. Jerking my head in a panicky reflex I saw, across the street, my Aunt Betty Roy, large, ginger and imperious. Then a lorry and trailer rumbled between us, followed by a crawl of cars, nose to tail.

Shantih had heard, too. Her face, inches below mine, was crinkling with inquiry.

'Trouble,' I said. 'My aunt. The biggest gossip for miles around.'

'I'll be off then. See you tomorrow.' The teeth flashed, the chestnut eyes glowed. Tightening her grip on my elbow she lifted her head and kissed me lightly on the cheek. Then with a flutter of her fingers she was gone.

Fourteen

Victoria High Street was taking the shock of the end of term discharge.

It oozed traffic and the parking bays were clogged with large American cars. There were dusty farm lorries, loaded with black farmhands who squatted patiently in the sun among stacked bales, rolls of netting wire, shiny new farm implements and pens of bleating sheep. The pavements were quick and noisy with people. Large men in wide hats, pumping each other by the hand or shouting greetings across the street. Brisk farm wives, fresh and metallic from the hairdresser, their smart clothes and gloves marking them off from the dowdier townswomen. The children they had come to fetch: neat in their striped blazers, cheese-cutters, ironed gymslips, panama hats. All of them flowing in a thick, shifting tide along the pavement, ebbing into shops and cafés and hotels, surging back into the main stream again, gathering in eddying groups before draining away to their farms.

Waiting reluctantly for Aunt Betty to cross the street, I'd time to consider the farmers' regular occupations of the town. On days like this they took over the shops, sending sweating shop assistants racing up ladders or into back rooms to find what they wanted. They took over the hotels and cafés, carelessly pulling together tables and chairs so that they might gossip more comfortably about the weather, wool prices, the government's subsidies, shopping, sports and the eternal unsatisfactoriness of their kaffirs. They asked no one's permission ever.

They didn't need to. They held Victoria in fief. On show days their animals might foul up the lower end of Victoria High Street. They themselves might leave shops in disarray after dragging the merchandise about. They might strew wrappers, shells and peels over the public gardens and showgrounds. Their older sons might sing and squabble and scrap in the popular hotels on Saturday nights and harass off-duty nurses in the small hours of Sunday morning. But they were licensed by their money. The town thrived because of them: it rode on the backs of sheep as surely as Johannesburg balanced on deposits of gold.

I knew many of the farmers and their wives because they had sons or daughters at the main local schools, had followed the fortunes of the school rugby team, and because my father's sister Betty had married Wilf Roy.

She puffed up to me now in a cloud of face powder and strong perfume. I took a deep breath and kissed the plump cheek.

'Well, bad lad,' she said. 'I'm glad I spotted you. I haven't had time to visit your mother, sad to say.'

That didn't surprise me.

'She'll be really sorry, Aunt.'

She eyed me disbelievingly. 'Come and have a meal with your uncle and me in the Athena Café. I want to hear what you've been doing – and Kathy, too. We never see either of you nowadays.'

'Sorry, Aunt, I can't. I've got bags to do and I'm expected home.' I began edging away, but she caught hold of my wrist.

'Not so fast, young man. I've not finished talking to you yet. When are you coming out to the farm?'

I'd been hoping to escape that question. 'One of these days, soon,' I said.

'I think you're dodging us.'

'No. I love the farm.'

That had been true, once. When small I'd found

it an entry into a strange, privileged world, where my Uncle Wilf had been a god over fields and animals and the labourers who came out of smoky huts in the halfdark to do his bidding. I'd loved perching on the seat of the puttering two-stroke tractor as it hauled the disc plough through the dusty lands. Or riding two-up as my uncle guided Pegasus, his huge grey horse, through an early morning bulky with the dim shapes of animals. I'd followed my uncle and cousin Rex everywhere, rushing into the pens as they did to catch sheep for the dipping tank, straining to count the stock in the evenings, proudly carrying my uncle's rifle over the stubbly hills while he searched for the meerkats and other creatures which attacked the crops. I'd longed to grow up like Uncle Wilf, tall, slouching, fair with a lean, lined face – or even to be like Rex, ruddy and tall and his father's shadow. I'd ignored Aunt Betty's teasing about my soft townie ways and shown that I could trudge the lands without complaining and wrestle for hours in the sun with the stiff handles of the seed drill. As the years passed I learnt to ride and shoot and drive a tractor, not as well as Rex, but well enough to earn my uncle's praise.

Kathy, too, had spent time on the farm. But she'd chafed at being expected to stay around the farmhouse. 'Such a tomboy,' Aunt Betty said huffily, watching Kathy smashing the ball about in our informal games of cricket or defeating Rex's attempts to throw her in wrestling contests on the wide front lawn. Uncle Wilf's kindly interventions sometimes led to Kathy joining us in the lands, but Aunt Betty's desire to have her close usually prevailed.

Back in Songololo Street, Kathy raged to my mother that Aunt Betty was boring and wanted to play at being a great lady, treating her, Kathy, as just another maid, unpaid at that. My mother argued at first, but after several stormy sessions agreed to talk to Aunt Betty. The conversation took place while we were at school and she'd never told us what was said. But Kathy's visits to the farm stopped.

Over the years my own attitude changed. I didn't lose my feeling of enchantment, but I came to see that the farm's power lay in its otherness, its separateness from what was going to be my environment. I could admire the life, its ruggedness, its usefulness, its practicality. But as my sense of its virtues grew so did my awareness that it was precisely those virtues which ruled it out for me. I might think about it, I might write about it, but I couldn't live it. I wanted streets, cars, shops, cinemas, girls in flimsy dresses.

'If you love the farm, you've got a funny way of showing it,' my aunt said. 'You've become a regular townie again.'

'I'm afraid so, Aunt.'

'What about coming to see us just after Christmas?' she demanded. 'You could really do with a bit of fresh air and farm food. You look quite yellow.'

'Can't, Aunt,' I said, glad of a legitimate excuse. 'I'm beginning my job at the *News* and I'll be pretty busy.'

'You could fit us in,' she said, adding beadily, 'I suppose you go to the Robertses' farm now that Kathy is courting with young Norman?'

'Kathy goes. I've only been once.'

'I hear they plan to marry. She should give that a bit of thought.' Her mouth looked as though she had just sucked a lemon and I remembered that she'd always disparaged the Robertses as too rich for their own good and too soft with their labourers. The Roys were not rich and not soft employers. I'd seen good-natured Uncle Wilf lash out with his whip at *kwedeni* he judged to be idling.

'I don't think anything's decided, Aunt, but I'll pass on your advice.'

'Do. We act in haste and repent at leisure.' She brought her face a little closer. 'Who was that girl you were talking to just now?'

'Just a girl I know.'

'She was dark. Very dark.'

'That's her name,' I said. 'Dark. Vera Dark.'

'Don't be silly, Simon.' She glowered at me. 'She's Indian, isn't she?'

'Yes.' Had she seen Shantih's quick peck on my cheek?

'Hmm.' She regarded me balefully.

'How's Rex?' I enquired. 'How does he think he did in the final exams?' This was a nasty spinner. Competent and at ease on the farm, Rex was out of his element in the classroom, and in the words of one teacher as dim as a Toc H lamp. When he'd failed the mid-year mock exams, Betty withdrew him from Victoria Boys' High and enrolled him at a private school in East London.

She sighed. 'He's sure he's failed Afrikaans again, and he needs it if he's going to get into the agricultural college.'

'You never know with exams,' I said with fake solicitude, 'and he could always resit if the worst came to the worst.'

'The problem is to get him to do any work now that term is over,' she moaned. 'Catch him looking at any book at the best of times. He isn't like you. Besides, he's courting. When he isn't in the lands, he's on the phone to some little Afrikaans madam he met in East London.'

'If they stick to talking in her *taal* it might get him through his supp,' I offered.

She glared at me. 'I can't stand those upstarts and their bird-language. Do you know that a slip of a thing at the Magistrate's Court tried to insist on speaking to me in Afrikaans? I felt like answering her in Xhosa.'

'A good thing you didn't, Aunt. She might have sent you round to the non-European counter.'

She didn't smile. 'I think I prefer the Nigs,' she said. 'At least they respect the Monarchy.' She pinched my arm. 'Come and have an ice cream, at least. Your Uncle Wilf needs cheering up. Things haven't been going too well on the farm lately. First the drought and then a very bad Native who tried to stir up the others. You know how angry your uncle can get when he thinks a black is trying it on. The other day he just turned on our old boss boy, Dodo, for no reason at all as far as I can tell.'

She stopped. The pale blue eyes had registered my restlessness. 'All right, Simon, I can see that you want to be off. Go on then, but don't forget to give my love to your mother and Kathy. I'll drop in one of these days. Meanwhile you find time to come for a visit.'

'Sure, Aunt,' I said.

Fifteen

My uncertainty about just how far Jessica went, and what moves to make, was giving me gut cramp as I sat beside her in the dark auditorium of The Odeon. Songololo Street savvy had it that you didn't make any kind of grab at 'good' girls on a first date and probably should hold back until the third. But what if the girl was fast? She might think you too slow and not give you a second date, let alone a third. With Carol I'd have risked an exploratory touch or two. But I'd no idea how a girl like Jessica would react. Her talk hinted that she'd be outraged and I didn't fancy an account of my shame travelling around her circle or reaching Mrs Leighton.

But Harry had said Jessica was hot. If so I was missing a glorious chance to score at last.

Nonetheless, I decided to keep my hands in my simmering lap and concentrate on Maggie McNamara's efforts to retain her virginity.

I was glad I had. In the Athena Café after the film, Jessica was emphatic about the heroine being right to hang onto her virtue.

'Boys are allowed to sow wild oats,' she said. 'If a girl does anything she's called ugly names. Anyway, I want to keep myself for the man I marry. Not even William Holden or Clark Gable could tempt me, though Anthony Perkins or Montgomery Clift might. Harry Lewis certainly didn't.'

She politely turned down my hesitant suggestion that we drive to the reservoir.

'I've had a lovely time, Simon,' she said warmly, 'and I'm so glad you asked me, but we're off to Cape Town early tomorrow and I should be getting to bed.'

Outside her house, a large white-walled single-storey behind a high privet hedge, she waited in the passenger seat while I got out from behind the wheel and went round to open the door on her side. I walked with her to the gate.

She didn't go through immediately. 'We should do that again. I'll ring you when I get back. There's a dance coming up at the Hotel Victoria and Melanie is making her debut with Clive White's *Semiquavers*.'

'I'm game,' I said. Melanie had told me that Clive had formed a small band and that she might join it as part of her plan to become more outgoing.

'Super.'

She kissed me quickly on the cheek and sped off down the path.

Kathy and Shantih were sitting in the *rondavel* drinking coffee. The air was heavy with smoke and an odour of chips and vinegar explained by the plates on the floor near the door. They looked heavy eyed and the bunk was suspiciously tidy.

'We didn't expect you back so early,' Kathy said. 'How did it go?'

'Fine,' I said, handing Shantih the Volkswagen keys. 'And thanks for lending me your birdcage on wheels.'

'We were expecting you'd take Miss Jessica for a spin around the reservoir,' Shantih said.

'Well I didn't.' I tried not to sound sour.

'I've never been to the reservoir at night,' she went on. 'It's out of bounds to us.' She giggled. 'Next time there's a Defiance Campaign we'll have to throw a party there and all get arrested.'

'Good idea.'

'What was the movie like?' Kathy lit a cigarette. 'Very funny. Quite daring. Jokes about mistresses and seduction and losing virginity.'

'Did Maggie McNamara lose hers?' Shantih took the cigarette from Kathy's fingers and puffed it, then held it out to me.

'No.' I puffed gingerly.

'Perhaps that's why your girlfriend wouldn't go to the reservoir,' Shantih said. 'Or perhaps my little car wasn't quite smart enough for her to want to sesh in?'

'Did she know whose it was?' Kathy had repossessed the cigarette.

'That didn't come up.'

'I think cars are taken for granted in her suburb,' Shantih smiled. 'There are bigger and better ones than my Beetle.'

'That girl's using you, *boetie*,' Kathy said. 'She's showing Harry Lewis that if he can slum it, so can she.'

'It wasn't like that,' I said. 'Anyway, everyone uses everyone else.'

'That's not true, though sometimes it seems like that.' Shantih stood up. 'Time for me to go.'

'Bedtime for me too.' Kathy stubbed out her cigarette.

Passing, Shantih touched my hand. 'Don't be sad, Simon Legree. It was only a first date. Anyway, *we* love you.'

'Sure. Thanks again for letting me use your car.'

'Thank you for letting us use your nest.' She delivered the second kiss to my cheek that evening.

Sixteen

I'd expected Elizabeth Carter to ignore me. But after the lank-haired sitar player had completed his eerie repertoire and Mrs Rangisamy and Shantih had wheeled in trays of aromatic eats, she walked over to where I stood nibbling at a bhaji. In a pale blue shirt and skirt, her shining hair shaped to frame her fine-boned face, she looked as beautiful – and untouchable – as ever. Ben March, leaning against the wall under a framed photograph of Nehru and smoking a roll-up, eyed her appreciatively as she passed.

'Jessica tells me you've been taken on at the *News*,' she said.

Incense, curries, cigarette smoke, and the dozen or so people milling about in the small room, were combining to make the atmosphere stifling, in spite of the recently opened window. But that wasn't why I felt feverish. It was, as far as I could recall, the first time she'd spoken to me since our playground clash.

I tried for poise. 'It's a start.'

'Would you rather have gone to university?'

'No. I want to be a writer one day – short stories and novels.'

'Journalism is a good way in, they say. I'm thinking of it for myself after university.'

So that, not me, was her interest.

Before I could follow this up, she added, 'Jessica said you invited her to come along tonight, but she felt it wasn't her sort of thing and she's not keen on Indian food.'

Should I play the game? Was being willing to mingle in a room with a few non-whites the way to make an impression on liberal people like Elizabeth? Did they believe it was achieving anything, this genteel socialising? The smoke and smells of Kokville and Vilakazi didn't blow over their neighbourhood at night. The residents of Victoria's richest suburb didn't get the black riff-raff and beggars drifting through the lanes behind their houses, often after curfew. What would they say, I wondered, about having somebody like Joshua habitually dropping in uninvited? Or about having black servants whose problems became yours because your mother was too soft to keep them in their place? How would they feel about an Indian girl who thought it was quite all right to crawl all over your sister? Or about being in debt half the year to her uncle? But they didn't get into those predicaments. They were the superior people who could do what they liked.

It irked me. 'It isn't my kind of thing either,' I said. 'More my sister's.'

'But you're here.'

'I like the food.'

The grey eyes assessed me: as coldly as ever, I thought.

'I think there must be more to it than that,' she said.

She was right, of course. Shantih had insinuated herself into my life, coming between me and Kathy, bringing change, complication and embarrassment. But she'd also brought a certain style and gaiety. And in her way, perhaps because she knew about the bitterness of thwarted desire, she'd tried to be my friend.

'Not really,' I said.

A hand closed on my elbow. Shantih's. It would be Shantih. Sam Glass was behind her, and behind Sam, Kathy. 'A favour, Simon Legree,' Shantih said. 'Sipho and Thandi have to get back to Vilakazi and

Sam has volunteered to drive them in my Beetle. But he'd like a bit of company on the way back and we voted for you.'

I looked down at her smiling face. She knew it was after curfew and the risk involved in going into Vilakazi. Mischievous to the end, she was testing my nerve and her power.

From across the room, Thandi was looking our way. Every time I saw her she'd grown taller, her legs longer, her skirt shorter. She said something to Sipho and the pair started to move towards us.

'I want to come,' Kathy said. 'I've never been in the township. It's time.'

'No!' Shantih said. 'You'll stay here with me, till the men get back. Then I can drive you and Simon home.'

'Five is quite a tight fit, Kathy,' Sam said.

'All the same, I want to go.' Her lower lip thrust out in a way I recognised as trouble.

'And I want you to stay here with me,' Shantih said.

'I want to go,' Kathy repeated.

The static between them was almost audible. Then Shantih smiled. 'Why don't we all go? The VW will take six at a pinch.'

'Let's do it then.' Kathy smiled back at her.

'It's mad,' I said. 'Two blacks, three whites and and an Indian stuffed into a small car in the township after curfew and without a permit among us! It's asking for trouble.'

'Not necessarily,' Sam said. 'According to Sipho the cops will be busy raiding the shebeens or getting drunk themselves and there are no informers around sober at this time.' He turned to me. 'There's only a little risk, but it is a risk.'

'I say we go,' Kathy said.

'What do you say, Legree?' Shantih was obviously relishing my dilemma.

The space around us had filled up. Thandi and Sipho had arrived, followed by Ben and Sarah Bentley. Thandi's eyes were on my face. I read challenge there. Elizabeth Carter's expression was inscrutable. Yet I sensed she was waiting to hear my reply.

That decided it. 'Why not?' I said.

Seventeen

Sipho climbed into the front of the car with Sam to navigate us into Vilakazi and Kathy and I got into the back. Shantih was quick to perch on Kathy's knee, leaving me no choice but to let Thandi settle on top of me. I tried not to speculate on what would happen if the police stopped us.

Sam drove past an unlighted row of rangy trading stores and towards the raised boom at the end of the tarmac road. This border of Victoria with Vilakazi township was a point I'd never been beyond, though it was less than a quarter mile from Songololo Street. On the other side were more shops, smaller and shabbier with crooked verandah pillars holding up sagging roofs of corrugated iron. Further on, starkly caught in the car headlights and flanking a dirt-surfaced road, were the single-storey breezeblock houses of the township.

Vilakazi, Sipho was telling us, got its name as a result of the unlikely collaboration of old Caleb Mdonga, the principal of a township school, Major Illingworth, Elias's boss, and a group of Afrikaner Nationalists. English-speaking town councillors had wanted to name it Smutsville. 'The *Boere* didn't want Smuts because they saw him as a traitor to the *volk*. Our people didn't want to honour the man who had put down uprisings by giving orders to bomb and machine-gun blacks. Then Mdonga and Major Illingworth came up with the idea of an African name. Some residents wanted Mapassa, but the whites blocked that. Eventually they compromised on Vilakazi, after the Xhosa poet, B.W. Vilakazi.'

We'd reached the boom. Sipho pointed at an empty kiosk to the left. 'We're in luck tonight. Vuka, the *polisa*, is probably in a shebeen. So straight on, then left at that house where the gate is broken. But *hamba kahle*, the road is not good.'

'I've never been to a shebeen,' Kathy said.

'That house with the nice garden over there belongs to the mother of Sibongile Sibande,' Sipho said. 'She runs a shebeen in the back. A bad woman who finds young girls for white men. She tried to get Thandi for that business one time.'

At the mention of her name Thandi squirmed and ducked her head – whether out of embarrassment or some other emotion, I couldn't tell.

'What kind of white men?' Kathy asked.

'All kinds. Lorry drivers. Gangers. Business men.' I waited for him to mention names, but he didn't.

The car had hit dirt road and Sam slowed to negotiate a pothole. 'You're right about the condition of the street,' he said. 'No doubt it'll get better when there's more trouble and the government wants to send in armoured cars.'

'Roman Catholic church.' Sipho pointed at a large building with a steeple set back from the road. In front of it was a wooden Christ with outstretched arms and golden hair.

'The little children say he's asking us to kiss him,' Thandi said. 'But we cannot because he is white and we would go to jail.'

'*Tula*, Thandi,' Sipho said indulgently, 'that's a *tsotsi* joke.' To Sam he said, 'Go left now.'

The street we entered was wider than the one we'd left and deeply rutted where recent storm rains had broken out of the kerbless gutters and gouged the sandy surface. The houses were older: square structures of chipped brick with crumpled downpipes and weather-worn roofs. Many had broken windows blocked with cardboard and sacking. The gardens, cruelly caught in the light of the full moon, consisted mainly of scanty flowers and grass struggling bravely in patches of soil behind slack fences. The cut down drums which served as dustbins were overflowing with rubbish. Litter lay everywhere. Through the open car windows the night smelled acrid.

'These houses are better than the newer ones,' Sipho said, 'and the next will be worst of all. All over the country contractors are making illegal profits by building with poor materials and the government is doing nothing about it.'

'I hope you're taking note of this, Simon Legree,' Shantih said. 'You'll have to write about it all when you're a reporter.'

I didn't answer. I was concentrating on trying to control the upsurge of randiness caused by the soft chafe of Thandi's bottom in my lap as the car jolted across the rutted road surface. At moments it felt as if the cloth between us was dissolving in the warmth generated by the contact and that flesh was about to meet flesh. Was she aware of my growing erection? I began to sweat at the thought.

'Simon!' Kathy said, giving my arm a pinch. 'You're not paying attention.'

'Shantih's a bit early with the advice,' I said testily. 'I'm being told how to do my job before I've even started it.'

The Zondis' house was much like the others from the outside, though there were lace curtains in the windows and a good show of rose bushes supervised by a cement gnome in the small front garden. The moment the car stopped Thandi was off my lap and speeding down the short path to rap on the door. Had she registered my hard-on? Was she going to report it? I looked up at the moon and wished for deliverance.

'Please to come in,' Sipho said. Kathy and Shantih were already following Thandi. I climbed out reluctantly and joined the others at the gate.

A small girl opened the door and Thandi ushered us into a dimly lit front room which led off the narrow passage. After indicating that we should seat ourselves on the large faded sofa and wooden chairs she disappeared. She had hardly left the room when Florence appeared in a dressing gown spattered with tropical-looking flowers, her head bare of the usual *doek*. She had clearly been asleep, but she greeted us warmly, taking our hands in hers in turn and submitting, laughing, to a hug and a kiss on each cheek from Shantih. Then, standing in the doorway, she questioned us in English about the meeting while breaking off to shout instructions in Xhosa to Thandi and the little girl deeper in the house. She brushed aside protests that we had already eaten.

'Never mind,' she said firmly. 'You are in my house now and I am giving you only sandwiches.' Her eyes twinkled at me. 'They are getting you into the politics, too, young master .'

'He's coming along slowly,' Shantih said. 'But what's all this young master talk from a member of the ANC Women's League?'

'*Ag!*' Florence chuckled. 'I am too old to change my ways now.'

A man of about thirty appeared, dressed in a tracksuit. Tall and thin, he had a triangular face and a wide mouth. 'My nephew, Thabo,' Florence said.

'Thabo Modisi.' He shook hands elaborately, looking at each of us as if recording our faces for later use. 'I've heard you are going to be a reporter on the newspaper,' he said when he got to me. 'That's good.'

I was beginning to wonder.

Kathy and Shantih were asking Florence about the framed pictures on the heavily polished cabinet which stood against one wall. Several were wedding scenes: a young man in a suit who could only be Elias, standing beside a young Florence on the steps of the church we had passed on the way to the house. A picture of the pair dancing. Another of them holding up a silver cup. The pair with bridesmaids in swathes of white. Florence holding a baby. Florence, flanked by Sipho, holding another baby with Elias looking on. Individual shots of Sipho and Thandi in school uniform. Florence with the little girl who had opened the door.

There was another photograph, mounted on cardboard. It showed Elias, uniformed and wearing a forage cap, shaking hands with a grizzled black man.

'I know who that is,' Kathy said. 'Chief Luthuli, president of the ANC.'

'Yes,' Florence said. 'It was when Elias was in the Youth League.' She walked over to a small sideboard and took out a newspaper cutting showing Elias in a group which included a leather-jacketed black man with a boxer's build and a small fair-haired man in a neat suit. 'Our heroes,' she said.

'I don't know them,' Kathy said. 'Except for Elias.'

'You will know them one day,' Modisi said. 'Mandela will be the top man in the ANC when Luthuli gets too old and Bram Fischer is one of the lawyers who have been defending the treason trialists.'

Thandi came into the room carrying a tray with teapot, milk, sugar and cups and saucers. She was followed by the small girl who, on the verge of giggling, was balancing a large tray of sandwiches on her head.

'Moya! *Hayi*!' Florence said sharply.

The girl reached up and adroitly brought the tray down in front of her. 'Moya is my niece,' Florence added. 'Her mother, my sister, died a year ago and her father has to work in the mines. So we spoil her and she is a bit cheeky sometimes.'

The child dutifully handed round the sandwiches, which were made of thin white bread and rather greasy ham. The ceremony was disconcertingly like that in any Songololo Street front room where house pride usually took the form of offers of food to visitors. *Aping their betters; pretending they're whites*, my Aunt Betty would have said. But tonight scornful judgment wasn't so easy. Florence in her own home was a different woman both from the cheerful servant I'd taken for granted for years and the wife weeping at the arrest of her husband. Listening to Shantih's chatter, she kept a watchful eye on Thandi and Moya as they poured the tea and offered around more sandwiches. At the same time she exuded a good-natured power which reminded me of my mother.

On the way back to Victoria Shantih insisted that I sit in the front alongside Sam while she and Kathy got into the back of the car. 'What makes you think the Congress Alliance you were all talking about in there will be good for whites and Indians?' I asked her.

'It will be good because we'll have played our part in making it good,' she said. 'We'll have shown we are with Africans in their struggle. Also we should do what is right, even if it isn't good for us.'

We drove along streets glistening and slithery in the drizzle which had begun while we were indoors. Groups of people were trudging through the wet, most of them headed towards Victoria. Some were in oilskins, others in raincoats, but many were in improvised coverings of sacking or cardboard.

'Early morning shiftworkers,' Shantih said, 'or domestics setting out to walk the ten miles or more to the other side of town.'

A cycle shot past our left mudguard, the rider hunched over the handlebars, straw hanging damply out of the tattered tyres. A skeletal mongrel abandoned a scuffle with a larger dog over a piece of offal and flung itself at the cyclist's pumping legs: he wobbled and swayed but kept going and the dog returned to its scavenging.

'This is why there is often trouble,' Shantih went on. 'People shouldn't have to live this way while others are so rich. Even liberal white employers like Illingworth, Tewson and Lewis underpay their non-white staff. And your future boss is as bad as anyone. Big profits, low wages. Ask Julian Richards.'

'What about your uncle, Mynah Bird?' I asked, irritated by her know-all air. Kathy stirred and her knee pressed warningly into the back of my seat.

'Fair,' she replied. 'He doesn't employ many people. He pays the pound a day the Congress asks and a bit more, and he's good about time off. He also gives to the cause.' She laughed. 'He exploits *us* – me and my aunt. I tell him I'm going to start a union for wives and nieces.'

'He's a good man,' Kathy said. 'Simon shouldn't provoke.'

'I don't mind,' she said. 'There are too many fat cats in the movement, talking like Karl Marx and acting like Harry Oppenheimer. My uncle isn't one of them. A decent petit bourgeois.'

'All this talk,' I said. 'I won the English prize two

years running and I heard words tonight I don't understand.'

'That's because you've been kept ignorant,' Sam chipped in. 'I must lend you some good books.'

'He won't read them,' Kathy said maliciously. 'Sex, sport and snobby novels, that's what Simon likes.'

'Don't let them tease you, Simon Legree,' Shantih said. 'You were very good tonight, except for letting that Elizabeth Carter mesmerise you and then looking a bit too hard at Thandi's legs.'

'I wasn't staring at Thandi's legs,' I protested.

We'd reached the exit from the township. The barrier was still raised and the kiosk still empty.

'You were, Simon Legree. And you were getting quite warm in the car earlier. Watch out. Thandi is growing up.'

A green Buick, going fast, drew abreast of us. The driver shot a glance our way and for an absurd instant I started to raise a hand in greeting. Then the Buick was past, sweeping Mr Oldcastle on towards Mountside.

Sam appeared not to have noticed him. I turned towards Kathy and Shantih in the back, wondering if they had. But they were oblivious, wrapped in a hungry embrace.

Eighteen

'Come and have a drink at the Vic,' Julian Richards said. 'You look as if you need an alcohol transfusion.'

I did. I'd been shadowing him for three weeks and my respect for him had grown as my self-esteem had shrunk. There was a lot for one reporter to cover, beginning with the daily round of visits to the police station, the courts, the town clerk's office and other regular sources of news. I trailed after him to meetings of the Town Council, the Chamber of Commerce, the School Board, the Hospital Board, the Women's Institute and a score of organisations connected with the running of the town. I also went along on interviews with individuals who had stories to tell and phoned around the district for items of interest to farmers.

Weekends meant attending a chosen sporting event, then cycling around gathering in reports about matches not covered by the *News's* underpaid stringers.

Julian managed it all in his seemingly languid way. At meetings he took copious notes in a mixture of Pitman's and his own shorthand and asked crisp questions at interviews. Back in the office he typed his reports quickly on an old Remington then telephoned contacts, selected items for following up from the minutes of municipal committees or, in slack periods, culled fillers from the larger dailies.

As part of my training I was expected to take notes and to construct a report which the editor could compare with Julian's. After that I would be given Julian's 'blacks' to make my own comparisons.

I couldn't remember a time when I'd felt more stupid and inept. My laborious longhand notes proved disastrously inadequate. I got facts wrong, left out important information and included trivia, missed the point of what I'd heard or presented it poorly. My typing was slow and disfigured by corrections. I managed to make interesting news dull and dull news dreary.

Ian Grantley-Pearson, the editor, pointed all this out with savage satisfaction. Pipe in mouth, he studied me with unconcealed distaste each time I came trailing into his office to stand in front of his desk. He made no secret of the fact that he had thought R.B. Alexander's choice of me to understudy Julian mistaken.

'This is journalism, not school composition, Brown,' he said on my third day, holding my messy copy between finger and thumb. 'For this paper you don't meander up to a neat little climax: you begin with the climax or the outcome. In other words you start with the most striking fact – usually the judgment in a court case, the result in a sporting event, the decision in a meeting, the price of a deal or the death toll in an accident. I'd have thought that was obvious from a study of the paper – or Richards's blacks – but you don't appear to be absorbing the lesson.'

The next day he was on about my vagueness. 'It is no use writing about Mrs Smith,' he growled through teeth clenched on his pipe. 'There are thousands of Mrs Smiths, just as there are thousands of Mr Browns. We need initials, address, age and occupation. Nor is it enough to say that the government is going to order large-scale cattle culling among the Natives in the Glen Grey district. Richards reported a figure. You should have had one too. Journalism is about fact. Lots of fact. Correct fact. I notice in your version of the interview with the town treasurer you write about a rent rise. The treasurer was talking about a rate rise. The location superintendent is Mr J.S. Hughes, not J.F. Errors can lead to misidentification, complaints and libel actions.'

He had mild praise for my sports reporting. My general reporting was 'skimpy and pedestrian,' my sentence construction 'flatulent.'

He also objected to my leaning on his desk in my anxiety to follow his criticisms.

'It's *my* desk, Brown,' he said acidly. His irritable gaze moved to my chest. 'Who chooses your ties for you?'

'I don't know, sir,' I stammered. 'I mean, some are presents, some my mother or sister bought, some...'

'Try for something more subdued. Just one or two or at most three colours.'

'I will, sir.' I thought of R.B. Alexander's vividly dotted bow ties but said no more, focusing instead on the picture on the wall behind Grantley-Pearson. It was a calming technique perfected in dozens of appearances before Dr Birch, my school principal, usually while waiting to be caned. There it had been a print of *Vita Lampada*. Here it was of Montgomery of Alamein.

'Remember you represent this paper wherever you go, Brown,' Grantley-Pearson went on in tones which reminded me of Birch. 'You're not just taking notes at this function or that. You're the *News*.'

'Yes, sir.' Montgomery was shaking hands with a row of young men in battledress. Was Grantley-Pearson one of them, I wondered. He had, Julian said, distinguished himself in the war. I didn't like him any better for it, nor find it any easier to call him the expected sir. But he scored higher than Maitland, the business manager, who expected the same respect and disliked me as much.

'Grantley-Pearson thinks I'll never learn the job,' I moaned to Julian once we were settled in the public lounge of the Hotel Victoria.

'You don't know that and anyway it takes time to learn the drill, as he would say.' Julian sipped a brandy and coke. 'He likes to be stern with cub reporters. He was the same with me when I started or, to be fair, a little more lenient, because he plays golf with my dad.'

'He despises me.'

'He doesn't despise you. He thinks you're a bit unpolished.'

'He despises me,' I repeated. 'I come from the wrong side of town.'

'There's something in that. He's English and they see social differences where we don't. He'd probably be more at ease with a black lecturer from Fort Hare than a white mechanic from Illingworth's garage – not that he'd want much to do with either. He's uncomfortable with his own father-in-law, because old R.B. is a self-made man with little time for public schoolboys. I suspect he thinks R.B. chose you just to annoy him.'

'I'm going to have to resign,' I said. 'I could get a job in a bank or a shop while I looked around – I might even try my luck in Jo'burg or Cape Town.'

'Don't resign,' Julian said earnestly. 'You'll get the hang of things if you work at it. I'll try to be more helpful and peep at your stuff before it goes in to Grantley-Pearson. I've neglected you. But if Elizabeth Carter comes onto the staff as a sort of Girl Friday that'll give us more time together.'

'Elizabeth Carter?' I mumbled. 'But she's going

to Rhodes University.'

'Apparently she isn't too happy about academe. She might take a few months overseas and then join us and see how she likes it. You know her, of course.'

'Yes.' I took a big swallow of my beer. Elizabeth in the office watching me struggle to learn a job I might have no talent for promised exquisite pain.

Nineteen

The shower was playing up, but I'd sluiced off most of the oil and grime acquired during two hours under Kepler's old Ford when Kathy walked into the bathroom.

'Your lady love is here,' she said.

'Jessica? She said she was going shopping with her ma.'

'Well, she hasn't. You'd better hurry. Mom's next door and I haven't time to entertain the Madam from Mountside. Norman is picking me up in half an hour and I'm not nearly ready.' Kathy whisked a towel off the back of the old oak chair and held it out.

'I'll be five minutes.' I put a hand out for the towel, but, grinning, she tweaked it away.'

'I'll tell her. Wash that soap out of your hair first.'

She waited until I had rinsed my hair then handed me the towel. 'Are you serious about her, little brother?'

'Dunno. She's off to university.'

'Have you slept with her yet?'

I didn't answer, concentrating on towelling myself. She came closer, almost touching me. 'Have you, *boetie*?'

Her proximity was having an effect. 'None of your business,' I said, 'but no.'

'Good.' She twitched the towel again, grinned meanly at my budding erection, then made for the door. 'She's pretty, I'll say that. But trouble. All nerves.'

When I got to the kitchen Jessica was at the table drinking a coffee and paging through *Outspan*. She was wearing a bright green T-shirt and black shorts; her bare legs were nicely tanned. 'I should have phoned,' she said rather jerkily, 'but I thought I'd surprise you.'

'You have,' I said, aware of the pile of dirty dishes in the sink, the clutter of jars and bowls on the table and the hole in the linoleum under her sandalled foot. 'Saturday is Florence's day off. My mom's with a neighbour and Kathy's been a bit idle because she's going to the Robertses' farm.'

'Don't apologise. As long as I'm not in the way.'

'Never,' I said, too heartily. 'I'm glad you've come.'

'Kathy told me you've been fixing a car. And this morning you were working for the paper. You keep busy, don't you?'

'Quite busy.' I was trying to think. Parked outside her house in Shantih's VW the previous night we'd gone in for some wild kissing. But when I'd touched her breast, she'd called a halt, protesting that she felt ill, and got out of the car. Then at her door she'd let me pull her to me, not drawing away when my cock hardened, and responding to my cautious rubbing against her before breaking away. Was she here to carry on from where we'd left off or was curiosity the spur?

The gauze door to the *stoep* squeaked and my mother stepped into the kitchen carrying a large basket of peaches and a packet of Commando Round.

'From Violet Lategan's garden,' she said, placing the basket on the table and sitting down heavily on a stool next to Jessica. 'Part payment for that alteration I did to her dress. We've got enough peaches, but what can you say? Her hubby has been keeping her a bit short lately – he's a tight bugger.' She smiled at Jessica. 'You're the young lady who got Simon brushing his teeth, combing his hair a dozen times a day and getting books on art out of the library. I'm glad somebody gave you a cup of coffee.'

'Kathy did,' Jessica smiled, not missing, I was painfully certain, the rollers in my mother's damp hair.

'Cig?' My mother held out her pack of Commando Round.

'No thank you. I don't smoke much.'

'You're wise. Coffin nails. I've been on them since I was fourteen.' She produced a lighter from her apron pocket and lit up. 'How is your mother? She won't remember, but we met once or twice when I was catering for one of those wartime fund-raising do's.' She blew a smoke ring and grinned.

Uncomfortable with the conversation, I itched to get Jessica away to the *rondavel* but couldn't think up an excuse.

'Are you going to study to be an artist at the university, dear?' my mother asked. 'Simon says you're a very good drawer.'

'No,' Jessica said. 'I'll be reading English literature. I'm not good enough to be a painter, not even a commercial one.'

'I was quite artistic as a girl,' my mother said. 'I loved drawing and painting and making things, but I left school early and that was that. I suppose some of it has stayed and goes into what I do.'

'I'm sure it has, Mrs Brown.' Jessica said. 'Everyone talks about your cakes and how wonderfully you decorate them.'

'Have you seen any?' my mother asked eagerly. She got up quickly, stubbing out her cigarette. 'If you've got a mo I'll show you some photos.'

'Ma,' I said desperately, 'Jessica doesn't want to look at them.' But she was past me and out of the room.

'It's fine,' Jessica said softly. 'I'd like to see them.'

I shook my head helplessly. My mother's cakes

were always in demand in our part of town, but she got few commissions from Mountside. I wanted to say something in her defence. But no phrases came before she was back with the folder that she used to tout for business and was spreading photographs out on the table with a mixture of shyness and pride.

I knew them well. A castle with drawbridge. A ship based on the *Queen Mary*. A Spitfire which had graced a squadron banquet during the war. And the one which had started it all: the rendering of Beaumaris Castle, which the young Phyllis Joubert had seen in a picture and decided upon for her own wedding.

'They're wonderful.' Jessica managed to sound sincere. She pointed to the wedding picture. 'You and your husband look brilliant, too.'

'I think wedding dresses are flattering. I was never no beauty.' My mother's vanity was confined to her baking and icing. 'Eric was always thought quite a catch.'

'Kathy looks a lot like you and Simon takes after your husband.' Jessica glanced at me mischievously. 'Not nearly as handsome, of course.'

'Simon has never looked very much like any of us. He's a throwback to some Spanish or Portuguese great-grandad.' Kathy, in the brown slacks and bushjacket she usually wore to the farm, was in the doorway, suitcase in hand.

'I don't know, Kath,' my mother said. 'Our families were never no good on ancestors.'

'There's French in our family, on my mother's side,' Jessica said. 'German, too, though she hates that mentioned.'

The talk about families continued, never lively but not quite stalling either. For all her effusiveness I

144

suspected that my mother wasn't at ease. Eventually she collected up her photographs and disappeared into the pantry 'to get on with things' after urging Jessica to drop in whenever she felt like it.

Kathy, one buttock hitched onto the kitchen table, surveyed Jessica in a way that sent a warning tingle down my neck. 'So how are you finding it down here among the peasants?' she said at last.

Jessica flushed. 'Fine. Only I don't think of you as peasants.'

'How do you think of us? Isn't this slumming it for you? Not the kind of area where you usually show your face.'

'I haven't been here before, it's true,' Jessica said steadily, 'because I haven't been invited.'

'Most people we see don't get invited,' Kathy said, 'because they're from here.'

'It's my misfortune that I'm not.'

'What's that supposed to mean?' Kathy flashed.

'Lay off, Kathy,' I said.

'I don't like being patronised even if you and Mom do.'

'I'm sorry you think I'm patronising.' Jessica had gone pink. 'I like Simon and I think your mother is sweet.'

'No one round here is sweet. Hard-working. Poor. Decent. But not sweet.'

A car horn sounded outside. Kathy unhitched herself from the table. 'That'll be Norman.' She looked across at Jessica with a half smile. 'What I think of you doesn't matter. What Simon thinks does. But he's my little brother and I watch out for him.'

'I'm sure you do,' Jessica said, 'and I get the message.'

She waited until Kathy had left the kitchen, then

burst out: 'She doesn't like me, not one little bit.'

'She'll change her mind.'

'I hope so. She's very intimidating.'

'You should see her at full moon. Now would you like to see my hovel?'

She sat cross-legged on my bunk, smoking the cigarette I'd given her while her eyes roved.

Following her gaze, my taste seemed crass, adolescent. The photographs I'd taped to the walls, mainly magazine pictures of sportsmen – though there was one of John Steinbeck and a shot, torn from *Esquire*, of Arthur Miller. Framed pictures of school teams. A cardboard-mounted snap of Kathy at fifteen on the Orient Beach at East London. A snap of Kathy, my parents and my cousin Rex tacked to the back of the door. Toppling piles of records, paperbacks and magazines on the tables and the floor. Clothes scattered about.

Standing awkwardly at the end of the bunk, I waited for the judgment. Instead, she appeared nervous; her fingers plucked at the coverlet. Clearly she felt unsure of herself in my territory, perhaps even on probation.

'No painters,' she smiled. 'But no smutty pictures either. And lots of good books.' She touched the pile beside the bunk. 'I'd expect Somerset Maugham and Hemingway and Steinbeck, but not Oscar Wilde and Camus *and* Rosamond Lehmann. I'm impressed.'

'I read anything I can get – including a lot of trash.' I didn't mention Clive's role in my choices, or the westerns, pulp detective stories and yellowing copies of *Men Only* under the bunk. 'You'll have to help me pick some pictures.'

'Surely.' She moved her legs and I was treated

to a glimpse of tanned inner thigh and white panty under the shorts. 'I remember how well you read aloud at the Prep, never stumbling over the big words.'

'And I remember how you and Elizabeth sneered at the way I spoke and imitated the way I said my vowels – *teeown, and greeownd* and *meeooon* – behind my back.'

'Don't remind me.'

I sat down next to her. 'I suppose I sounded like a *plaasjapie*. My mother is half Afrikaans.'

'You're a real South African then, not outlanders and – what do the Afrikaners say? – *rooinekke* like us.'

'Joshua, the boss's chauffeur, says the blacks are the real South Africans and the Coloureds the new South Africans.'

'It must be strange being Coloured – neither black nor white, but in between.' She shivered a little. 'I'd hate it.'

'Me, too.' I took the cigarette from her, stubbed it out in the ashtray and, putting my arms around her, kissed her.

After a minute she put a hand against my chest and nodded towards the door. 'I'm not sure about this, Simon.'

'No one will bother us. My mother never barges in – just shouts.'

'Even so.' But she came back into my embrace and after a while let me press her back against the pillows. Soon we were on our sides at full stretch, kissing ardently and straining together. Her hand crept under my shirt and up my back.

'You've a very smooth skin,' she said.

'So have you.' I eased her T-shirt free of her shorts. My fingers went up her back and met the catch of her brassiere but, remembering her reaction last time I'd tried to touch her breasts, I made no move to unhook it yet. Instead I inserted one leg between hers. Her mouth became looser, wetter. She snuggled closer, scissoring my leg. Now I fumbled with the catch of her bra. It sprang loose.

Immediately she pulled away. 'What are you doing, Simon?'

'What comes naturally,' I said hopefully.

'To boys, and some girls, I'm sure, but not to me.'

'It's only petting,' I said, 'not going all the way.'

'I don't like anyone grabbing at my breasts. I'm sorry but I just don't.'

'Perhaps you just don't like me,' I said, sulkily.

She touched my cheek. 'Don't be silly. You know I do.'

'Prove it.'

She didn't answer immediately, but looked at me soberly. 'Right,' she said at last. 'But you're not to try to take over.' Grasping me by the shoulders she pushed me onto my back and, straddling me, began to undo the buttons of my shirt. 'No, I want to,' she said when I raised my hands to help. My chest bared, she quickly reached down to the hem of her T-shirt and lifted it, sweeping up the loosened brassiere as well. I saw the pale mounds of her breasts and the dark pink of her nipples, then their softness was against my chest.

'Promise to keep still – no grabbing,' she said.

'I promise,' I said.

Her lips fastened on mine. Her tongue slid inside my mouth. After a while, she began to move on me. I kept still, not daring to move. There could be no doubt that she was feeling the stiffness of my cock through the thin material of our shorts, or – judging by her quicker breathing – that she was affected by it. I was, too. How long could I stay still before this exquisite friction made me come and soak us both?

'See, I do like you,' she whispered.

Then she was sitting up, pulling down her T-shirt and twisting her arms up behind her to refasten her bra. I reached out to pull her back, but she twisted away. 'No, Simon. This is where we stop.'

'Why?' I thought wistfully of the slim tin of French letters bought with shuffling embarrassment from the High Street chemist and now lying unopened in my jacket pocket.

'Because it's as far as I go. Farther than I've been with anyone. Also because I'm going to be at varsity for years and only around here in the vacs. You'll surely want to go out with someone else.'

'No.' At that moment, still feeling the imprint of her body, it was utterly true.

'Be realistic, Simon. We hardly know each other. We're too young to be serious.'

' *They tried to tell us we're too young*
too young to really be in love...' I sang creakily.

She shook her head, smiling. 'Good try, but the fact remains that we're going to be apart and shouldn't try to tie each other down.' She bent down and kissed me quickly, then slipped off me and swung her feet to the floor. 'Let's see what happens this term. Will you write me?'

'If you write me first.'

She looked at me sharply, then nodded. 'Fair enough.'

Twenty

'Would you mind blowing your smoke in some other direction?' Elizabeth asked. After two months sharing a table, it was a familiar request made with familiar disdain.

'So sorry.' I looked at her disapproving face across a surface littered with newspapers in various states of disembowelment, galley proofs, magazines, overflowing steel trays of cuttings and the blacks of news stories. Taking two quick puffs of the cigarette, I stubbed it out in the ashtray at my elbow and resumed my assault on the old Remington I'd acquired from Julian when he left.

'Thank you,' she said ironically. 'We might both live just a little bit longer.'

'And we might get run over tomorrow by a learner driver.'

It was a childish jab. She was taking driving lessons and they weren't going well, as a crumpled mudguard on the Vauxhall Velox bought her by her father testified.

She gave no sign of having heard, but continued her scissorwork on the Johannesburg *Star*. She'd been making an obvious effort to be pleasant since she'd joined the paper, and for my part I wanted to please her, but seemed fated to annoy.

Her presence was a daily reminder of my miserable childhood infatuation. Worse, I was stirred more strongly than ever. A turn of the neck, a movement of a bare arm, the lines of her body under the simple, elegant clothes made me stupid with desire. I fantasised about overwhelming her in the office one night when she had to work late and alone. It didn't happen. I imagined scenarios in which we went on assignments together and she was as impressed by my skill as I'd been by Julian's in my early months on the paper. No joint assignment came our way.

Instead Elizabeth moved about the office with the infuriating air of an inheritor. Secure in her position as the fiancée of Jim Farraday who, I'd discovered, was R.B. Alexander's grandson, she drifted in about mid-morning and left immediately after helping to proofread the galleys in the afternoon. In between she spent long periods talking to her friends on the telephone she shared with me. Grantley-Pearson treated her with the geniality older men usually exhibit towards pretty young women and old R.B. was gallant and flirtatious. I hated them while envying their ease.

'You're a masochist,' Kathy said when I confessed my longings. 'You've got that silly Leighton girl keen on you, and Carol, too, if you bothered, but you've got to get all horny over Miss Stuck Up. Like a *jags* stray dog. Get focussed, *boetie*.'

'You played around with Shantih and Norman,' I countered.

'That was different,' was the reply. 'Anyway Shantih has gone to Durban.'

'And Jessica is in Cape Town.'

'She'll be back. Meanwhile you get letters.'

She would and I did. I also had the memory of our last night before she'd left. In the dark of the Leighton's garden she'd not only let me touch her nipples but had let me slip my hand briefly inside her shorts while for a moment her fingers had squeezed the fierce bulge in my trousers.

It wasn't enough.

Twenty-one

Grantley-Pearson leant back, puffing at his briar. 'I want you to take Elizabeth to the courts. Time she got acquainted with the routines.'

'Yes, sir,' I said happily. 'Only...'

He peered past me into the reporters' room. 'Not here yet? No matter, she can follow you down. Take her on police calls as well.'

'Certainly, sir,'

But if Grantley-Pearson was no longer quite as hostile as he'd been he couldn't quite conceal his dislike.

'Off you go then,' he said, 'and for God's sake knot that tie properly.'

I left him blocking in a press telegram. Julian had confided that the editor supplemented the far from handsome salary R.B. Alexander paid him by sending versions of our more interesting local stories to other newspapers.

The low sprawling building which housed the Victoria Magistrate's Court was of the same grey stone as Victoria Boys' High but had in addition a green corrugated iron roof and a drooping South African flag. The court where most of the criminal cases were heard was at the back. In the gravelled yard behind the courthouse blacks of various ages were standing or sitting, and a *kwela-kwela* was parked near the yard gate. This police pick-up van, which looked like a cage on wheels, was crammed with black men. Most of them would be pass offenders who could expect a two-minute appearance and a summary sentence to hard labour, probably on a white-owned farm. Possibly on my Uncle Wilf's.

Six whites were standing on the highly polished

stoep. I recognised two of them. Detective Sergeant Grobelaar, tall and hollow cheeked, rather like a down-market undertaker in his navy suit, had given evidence in several cases since I'd begun court reporting. He had a reputation for cleverness and was expected to go far. Beside him in a crisply ironed, tight-fitting uniform was Kepler Lategan. Grobelaar greeted me as I passed. Kepler nodded stiffly.

The long courtroom had plain wooden seats like church pews, a dock which looked like a cattle pen and a high bench for the magistrate. It smelled of pungent polish and stale sweat.

'*Molo nkosi*,' said Silas Mkize, the grizzled black interpreter, who was standing at the prosecutor's table.

'*Molo*, Silas.' I offered him a cigarette, a tactic learnt from Julian. 'What's on the roll?'

He took the cigarette and put it into the top pocket of his cotton jacket. 'Lots of *dompas* cases. Two accused to be remanded for HB and T – you saw the complainants outside with Sergeant Grobelaar.'

'White accused or Natives?' I asked. 'And how much stolen?'

'Africans,' he said, 'and they are charged with taking a few hundreds' worth.'

'Anything else?'

'An Immorality Act case. These two.' Silas jerked a thumb towards the dock into which a uniformed policeman had ushered a white man and a Coloured woman. The man was about thirty, small and thin with sunken cheeks and a slack mouth. He wore a shabby grey suit, which hung loosely from his narrow shoulders. His white shirt was fraying at the collar. Aware of my inspection, he smiled at me nervously.

The woman was also shabby with a faded yellow face and puckered mouth, which made her look older than the man. She had a drab purple scarf over her unruly black hair and wore a faded blue dress with pink flowers on it. On her feet were down-at-heel tackies blancoed white.

Van Rensburg, the prosecutor, a man with the build of a wrestler, entered the court, briefcase in hand. 'Has Silas told you about our two lovebirds?'

I nodded. 'I'm surprised they found each other worth it.'

He laughed. 'Your colleague Richards would have felt sorry for them. I will say it must be love. It can't be beauty.' He snapped open his case and looked at me, his large head tilted. 'I suppose your rag will want to cover this case.'

'My rag will,' I said. In the few months I'd been attending the courts I'd learnt Van Rensburg disliked and distrusted the *News*.

'Will your rag also want to cover a case of receiving stolen property?'

'Naturally,' I said.

'The police are still investigating, but you'll find it's big, friend, very big. Thousands of pounds.' He flipped over a page of the document he had taken from his case. 'One of the town's leading citizens is involved. Still interested?'

'Of course.' He was beginning to irritate me. 'Who?'

Van Rensburg's smile was almost a sneer. 'Wait and see.'

'Can't you give me a hint?'

'No.' He was staring past me now, a leer on the blunt face. I turned. Elizabeth had come into the courtroom. Clutching a small bag and notebook she looked about her curiously, then walked forward to join us at the prosecutor's table.

'Elizabeth Carter,' I said. 'She works on the paper with me.'

'Van Rensburg.' The prosecutor stuck out his hand. 'Pleased to meet you.' His eyes travelled appreciatively from her face down the neat maroon jacket to the short matching skirt and slender legs. 'If I'd known you were coming I'd have arranged a nice murder trial or at least a culpable homicide.'

'I'm glad you didn't,' she said quietly. 'I'm not too keen on blood and gore.'

'Me neither,' he said, 'but that's what sells papers, isn't it?' He turned to Silas. 'Put another chair at the reporters' table.'

The courtroom was filling up. The public benches were divided by a rail down the middle to keep the races apart. Blacks filed slowly into the left side while the few whites sat on the right. I led Elizabeth over to the press table.

'What an appalling man,' she said, sliding onto the chair Silas had provided.

'Good prosecutor, though.'

'Oh, I'm sure he is.'

'*Staan op*,' a court orderly shouted. 'Stand up. *Stilte in die hof.* Silence in court.' The magistrate, plump in a blue suit, entered through a door to the side of the bench and bowed before sitting down. Van Rensburg handed up a sheaf of documents for signing: admissions of guilt for petty offences.

Next, ushered in by a policeman, a dozen black men entered the dock one by one to plead guilty to a variety of misdemeanours, a dreary list which included being without a pass, or having an out-of-date pass, not having permission to seek work in the Victoria area, or being in one of the white parts of the town after curfew.

'Those people aren't criminals,' Elizabeth murmured. 'Just work-seekers.'

I hadn't thought of it that way. 'Van Rensburg would say that they're all chancers. They know they have to get permission to enter town, but they don't do it.'

'Imagine having to get permission to enter a town to look for work. We don't.'

'There's too many of them. Hughes, the location superintendent, is always telling the council that Vilakazi is overcrowded. They breed too fast.'

'That sounds rather fascistic to me.'

'You should try living right next to the problem. I do.'

She shot me a glance, but said no more.

When the court adjourned I waited until the magistrate and Van Rensburg had gone, then went over to Silas who was watching the Immorality Act pair being directed into the dock by an old sergeant.

'What have you heard about the receiving case, Silas? Who is the accused?'

He looked towards the empty bench, raising his finger to his lips. 'Tewson,' he said, 'Mr John Patrick Tewson.'

I lit a cigarette. John Patrick Tewson *was* big. The eldest son of J.L. Tewson, owner of Victoria's largest departmental store, he usually ran the Albert Street branch, which served the townships. He was a member of the town council and the Victoria Club and a vice-president of the golf club. At present his father was away and J.P. was in overall charge of the firm.

'He bribed Africans to steal from other firms for him,' Silas said. 'A bad thing.'

'Sir. Sir!' The white man in the dock was miming the smoking of a cigarette. 'Can you spare a fag, sir?'

'Sure.' I walked over.

He took the cigarette from me with hands which shook. I noticed that the frayed shirt was very clean. The woman didn't look at us, but stared in front of her.

'You from the paper?' The man had a weak, plaintive voice.

'Yes.'

The man glanced quickly at the sergeant. 'You going to report this case?'

'Yes.'

He drew shakily on his cigarette. 'Do you got to?'

'That's what I'm paid to do.'

The man's face quivered. 'My old ma lives in Molteno. She's Dutch Reformed Church. If you put the case in your paper she'll read it and it'll break her heart.'

'They tell me this is your second offence,' I said coldly. I was regretting the moment of softness which had led to me giving him the cigarette.

'Last time was in East London,' the man said. 'The papers didn't get to know about it.'

'This time they did. I'm sorry, but that's it.'

'Can't you help us out – just this once,' the man begged.

'I can't make exceptions. You broke the law. That's news.'

'The law's no good,' the man said agitatedly.

'I didn't make the law,' I said. 'I just report the news. You took a risk and you got caught. That's tough, but I can't help it.' I turned away, annoyed at his distress.

Van Rensburg had come back into the courtroom with Detective Sergeant Grobelaar. '*Knyp daardie sigaret, Krige*,' Grobelaar said. '*Dis 'n hof, nie*

157

'n hoerhuis nie.'

'What's he want from you?' Van Rensburg asked.

'He doesn't want me to report his case.'

'But you will, won't you?' Van Rensburg sneered. 'He's got an Afrikaans name.'

'We'd report it whatever his name was,' I retorted. 'Anyway, it's an Afrikaner law.'

The magistrate returned to the bench. The public benches which had emptied during the recess filled up again. Elizabeth, who had also slipped away during the interval, resumed her seat beside me. Her scent was subtle and disturbing.

Kepler stepped into the witness box and took the oath. His cap had left a red mark on his forehead. He said he had been on duty in the Coloured district, Kokville, on the evening of March fourth. As a result of a report he had gone to number twenty-six Smuts Street and entered a small room at the back of the dwelling. Krige and his fellow accused, Hannah Meintjies, were in bed together. He'd pulled back the blankets. Both were naked. He'd concluded that sexual intercourse had taken place not long before.

'On what evidence?' Van Rensburg asked.

'I detected what appeared to be semen on the private parts of both accused and on the bedclothes also,' Kepler replied.

'Any questions?' the magistrate asked the couple in the dock.

'Please, sir.' Krige's hands were gripping the dock, the knuckles showing white. 'When you came into the room we was sleeping,' he said to Kepler.

Kepler looked at the magistrate. 'That is not so, Your Worship. The accused were both awake.'

'We woke up when you shone your torch in our faces.' The man's lips were trembling. Next to me

Elizabeth gave a faint hiss.

'They were both awake, Your Worship,' Kepler said. 'The accused, Krige, cried out, *Jesus, dis die Polisie.*'

'You woke us up,' the man said. He'd gone very pale. 'You took out your revolver and said I must *naai* Hannah, or you would shoot us. So we did it while you watched and used the hand on yourself.'

Kepler turned towards the magistrate. 'That is not true, your worship. Krige suggested that I should have intercourse with Meintjies and forget about charging them. I refused.'

'Before God, you are telling a lie,' shouted the woman from the dock. 'Before God in heaven. You made me touch it and suck it.'

'Silence!' the magistrate snapped. 'You are not to interrupt. You will have your turn to ask questions.' He said to Kepler. 'Constable, why didn't you refer to the suggestion from the male accused in your evidence-in-chief?'

Kepler's neck went a deep red. 'I knew the accused was making such a suggestion to avoid being charged. I paid no attention to it.'

'But surely it was an attempt to bribe you, constable?'

'I didn't understand it that way, your worship. He didn't offer me money.'

'It was a bribe nonetheless,' the magistrate said, 'and you should have reported it.' He looked towards the dock. 'Any further questions? Accused number two, Meintjies? No? You may stand down, constable.'

The acting district surgeon was next in the witness box, sleeking back thick fair hair. He had examined both accused and found evidence of recent sexual intimacy.

'Did you discover anything else, doctor?' Van Rensburg asked.

'Yes,' the young doctor said. 'The female accused is pregnant. I'd say about three months pregnant.'

'Was there any evidence she had masturbated or fellated anyone?'

'She made no report to me so I confined my examination to her vagina.'

A figure stirred at the back of the non-European section of the court. I recognised the dark, piratical face. Ben March.

Detective Sergeant Grobelaar testified next to the effect that Krige was a European, carrying a European identity card. Meintjies had no identity card – or claimed she hadn't. But she was classified as a Coloured born in East London and at present living in Kokville. All her associations, except for Krige, were with Coloured people.

The magistrate wrote for a minute then said to the couple. 'You may make a statement from the dock, or you may make a statement on oath, in which case you may be cross-examined by the prosecutor.'

Krige's throat rippled. 'From the dock, please, sir,' he said.

The magistrate waved a hand.

'I never had no trouble with the law, sir,' Krige said, 'except about this. I do my work for the municipality road gang. I do it honest and I earn my money. I was married to a white woman but she was no good. She drank and went with other men. No woman really cared for me, not properly, not even my ma, till I met this woman. She's a good woman, sir. She cooks and sews for me and she washes my clothes regular. I been in jail before, for living with Hannah in East London. We got three months that time. So I

160

came here with her, hoping we'd be left alone, but somebody snided us. I can't help this thing, sir. I know what the law says, but I love this woman. That's all, sir.'

The woman looked around the courtroom. For a moment she seemed taller, younger. Speaking very clearly she said, 'In the Bible it tells us that what God has joined let no man put asunder. In God's eyes I am Koos's wife and I am proud to be his wife.'

There was silence, except for the scratching of the magistrate's pen. The man gripped the rail, his face gaunt. The woman stood upright, hands at her sides. But as the magistrate looked up, she put her hand over the man's.

'You have pleaded guilty,' the magistrate said heavily, 'and I find you guilty. You have a previous conviction for a similar offence and I am obliged to take that into account. You have said in mitigation that you love one another. That is of no concern in this case. The law forbids carnal intercourse between European and non-European, as you well knew, yet you have both twice disobeyed the law. You made allegations about the behaviour of Constable Lategan in an attempt to discredit his evidence and I will say here that I disbelieve your story. Accordingly, I sentence you both to one year's imprisonment in the hope that it will deter others and give you time to reflect on the error of your ways.'

The pair were led out from the dock and out of the courtroom. Krige looked over his shoulder and towards the press table, but the woman walked straight, staring ahead of her.

'How sad, especially for her,' Elizabeth murmured.

I didn't answer. I'd noticed Ben March rising and

stalking out of the court. Van Rensburg was standing up, smiling and suggesting an adjournment for lunch.

'You're very quiet,' Elizabeth said as we made our way out of the courthouse into the street. 'Not a word about what a good story you've got.'

'It *is* a good story. A very good story.' I lit a cigarette.

'You don't seem very happy about it, Simon.'

The smoke from my cigarette was drifting into my eyes. I avoided looking at her.

Grobelaar had caught up with us, Kepler in step. 'You'll report this case, eh, Brown?' he said.

'Yes.'

'Including the remarks about Constable Lategan?'

'It'll be a full report.'

'Those people are rubbish,' he said. 'Drunkards and wasters with no morals who will say anything to get sympathy.'

'They got mine,' Elizabeth said crisply.

'*Ag*, you liberalists burst into tears every time you see a little kaffir baby,' he laughed. 'But you don't like them so much when they grow up. That old boss of yours can be glad there wasn't an Immorality Act when he was sneaking in and out of Kokville and Vilakazi township. Kokville! They should have called it Alexanderville.'

Some weeks after the Krige case I was late getting home, delayed by an interview with the local MP. As I turned into our back lane I came face to face with Joshua in his chauffeur's uniform and wheeling an old Humber cycle. He stopped, removed the cigarette from his mouth and grinned at me.

'Hello, young man. How goes it?'

'Okay.' I didn't grin back. He'd have been visiting my mother and Kathy.

His grin didn't waver. 'My hens been laying good this month and I thought your ma would like some eggs so I left half a dozen on the back step. See she gets them and maybe you'll get omelette for breakfast.'

'We've got hens of our own,' I said. 'And I'd watch out how you go round here if I was you. Kepler Lategan next door is a policeman. He might just arrest you for trespass or even take a pot shot at you.'

He shook his head. 'I'm not scared of any *Boer* policeman .' He drew on his crumpled cigarette. 'Remember that Immorality case?'

'What about it?'

'Well, last night the constable that told all those lies about Krige and Meintjies was beaten up in Kokville. Badly beaten up. Coming out of Ma Horner's, that's a red light house, where he was dipping his wick. So I don't think Constable Lategan will be messing with us *Hotnots* for a bit.'

Chuckling, he wheeled his bicycle past me.

Limping along Songololo Street Kepler Lategan looked like the victim of a vicious rugby maul. Elastoplast clamped his nose, his forehead was furrowed with grazes, his eye-sockets were a blend of black, green and gold and his left arm was in a sling.

He wiggled a finger at me. 'Your rag reported it wrong the other day. I was going into that *hoerhuis* from the alley – investigating, you understand – not coming out. A bladdy *skollie* jumped me from behind, man,' he gritted. 'Twisted my arm up behind my back and slammed my head against the wall so fucking hard that I went lights out. Stamped when I was down, too. I got two broken ribs under this shirt.'

'But why, Kep?' My expression was all concern.

He shrugged, grimacing. 'Robbery. The cowardly bastard took my wallet, my watch, my small change, my identity card – even my cigarettes and my Ronson lighter. Who told you all that stuff, anyway?'

'I don't know,' I lied. 'Someone reported you'd been assaulted. Any idea who did it?'

'Not yet but there's plenty of informers in Kokville. I'll get that bliksemse *Hotnot*. He'll try to put off that stuff he thieved sooner or later.'

'Good luck with it, Kep.' I resisted an impulse to mention the Krige case or Ben March's presence in the courtroom.

Twenty-two

Rain was sweeping in heavy gusts against the half-open office window and sprinkling water over the table. I jumped up and slammed the window closed.

'So the drought has broken at last,' Elizabeth said. 'The farmers will be pleased.'

'They'll find something else to moan about. Washaways or soil erosion or trouble with their workers. But we'd better ring around for a few quotes. I'll try those I know and you can chat to some of your smart country friends.'

'In a while. I'm looking through this at the moment.' She held up a copy of *The African People's Voice*. 'The ANC are talking of a nationwide consumer boycott. I thought it might be worth a paragraph.'

'You're wasting your time. Grantley-Pearson won't run it unless it actually happens. He's afraid of the paper being charged with incitement.'

'Would you run it if you were editor?'

'I'd run anything that sold papers. That won't.'

'I suspect you're a lot softer than you let on – and for the underdog.'

'Underdog not kaffir-dog.'

Her mouth turned down. 'That remark is typical of your pathetic attempts to sound cynical. It only succeeds in making you sound very small town.'

'I *am* small town and your remark is typical of you toptown people who think you can tell the rest of us what to think just because you've got pots of money.'

'I give up.' She went back to reading the paper.

Immediately, I felt regret. We'd been getting on quite well in recent months. 'Look, I'm sorry. That wasn't a good joke.'

'It wasn't, but I've no right to tell you what to

think. My parents have always been liberal, but they never do anything about it. Your family has actually made friends with people of another race.'

'Not me. Kathy and my mother.'

'I couldn't help noticing at the Rangisamys' that people treated *you* like a friend.'

'Well, they're not my friends.'

The phone rang. She picked it up, listened, then held it out to me.

'Mr Brown?'

Though I couldn't place the voice it seemed familiar. 'Yes, Brown here.'

'This is Thabo Modisi. We met at the Zondis' one time. I would very much like to show you the council's wonderful new housing scheme. Could you meet me at the entrance to Vilakazi?'

'I'm busy,' I growled. The man had a nerve assuming I'd be readily available.

'Some houses have a foot of water inside them. If you come now you can see for yourself.'

'I haven't got the time,' I said. 'Sorry.'

'It would not take long,' Modisi persisted. 'This is a very bad thing.'

'Some other time. I'm really very busy.' I hung up, annoyed but also disquieted by the call.

'What was all that?' Elizabeth laid aside *The People's Voice.*

'A guy called Modisi trying to insist that I come and look at what the rain is doing to a new housing scheme in Vilakazi.'

'Shouldn't you go?'

'I can't be rushing off into the township just because some black trouble maker thinks I should.'

'I thought you said that papers should print whatever sells copies.'

166

'Who cares what happens in Vilakazi?'

'Perhaps more people than you think.'

'That's all you know.'

I said it curtly, because I knew she had a point.

It was drizzling when I left work at five. I hadn't heard from Jessica for a while and I'd decided to call on Melanie. But I was barely five steps beyond the *News* door when two blacks stepped in front of me. I was about to butt past them when I recognised Sipho and the triangular face of Modisi.

'You really must come and look at those houses, Mr Brown,' Modisi said quietly.

'Simon, when you see how people must live there you will want to write about it,' Sipho put in.

'Listen, I'll come look tomorrow,' I said irritably. 'I've had a hard week and I'm not very interested in doing over time, especially as I don't get paid for it. Also I'm on my way to meet someone.'

'Tomorrow it may be dry,' Modisi said. 'Now is the time. If you write about this the council will have to do something.'

'There isn't a car. Joshua has just set off with the chief. And my bike's at home.'

'We can walk there in half an hour,' Modisi said.

'In this?' I stabbed a finger heavenwards.

'We walked here in this,' Modisi smiled. 'It's nothing to men.'

I thought of Melanie and her comfortable attic. Then I thought of Elizabeth's expression at my response to Modisi's call. I thought, too, that I might be turning my back on a good story. 'All right,' I said, grudgingly. 'It had just better be worth it.'

The route Modisi chose took us past the far end of Songololo Street and on into Joubert Street, a white area which fringed Kokville and the no man's land next to the black township. I hadn't been that way for some time and was startled by the littered pavements and untended gardens. Modisi nodded at a house with a broken gate and smashed front windows. 'Government policies are hitting some white workers, too.'

'Don't blame the government,' I said. 'They've always been lazy in Joubert Street.'

'They are uncertain about their future,' Sipho said. 'There are rumours that the government doesn't want white and black living so close and the people don't know whether this area will be declared black or whether the township will be moved.'

'They will learn that they must join our struggle if they want to be secure,' Modisi said.

I tried to picture the Viljoens siding with people like Sipho and Modisi. 'Don't you believe it,' I scoffed. 'No whites are going to join you. Not this bunch, anyway. They'd shoot you first.'

'You'll see one day,' Sipho said.

We crossed a footbridge over the Songololo and were soon in a broad dirt street, flanked by stores which had once been gaudily painted but were now faded. People were trudging along in twos and threes, the kids splashing in the puddles; some of the adults were carrying umbrellas and picking their way, others were simply walking with their shoulders hunched against the drizzle, their feet ploughing indifferently through water and mud.

Glad of my light mac, I thought of the last time I'd been in Vilakazi. It had rained then, too.

'Not far now,' Modisi said. He and Sipho were without raincoats and had turned up their jacket collars. Moisture hung like sequins from their curly hair. It struck me that they might pass as handsome if they were white.

Beyond the trading stores lay the ragged shanty town we'd passed on the night of Shantih's farewell. It had sprung up, Modisi explained, because people who were starving in the countryside had crept into the urban area to look for work. 'They'll bring in bulldozers soon,' he said. 'They are better at knocking down the people's houses than building them.'

'They're slums,' I said. 'You can't let slums develop.'

'They are slums to you,' Modisi retorted calmly, 'but they are homes to the people who live in them.' He indicated the row of breezeblock buildings on a rise behind the shanties. 'The new scheme. It will end up a slum, too. New slums for old.'

A big white Vauxhall heading for Victoria bumped by us, sending a spray of water over our feet. Modisi swore. 'Hughes, the location superintendent. I'd hoped we'd avoid him this way.'

The car stopped, turned, then, hooter blaring, splashed past us again. A dozen yards on, it slewed to a halt. Hughes got out and stood waiting for us, frowning, his legs slightly apart. A short, strutting man with a harsh voice, he'd regularly watched Jacky play in school rugby matches.

'What are you doing here, Brown?' he grated. I recalled that the last time he'd spoken to me he'd slapped me on the back and called me Blackie boy.

'I want to take a look at the new housing scheme, Mr Hughes,' I said carefully.

'Any particular reason?'

He'd know the reason and, I suspected, wouldn't like it.

'There was a reference to it in the council minutes and I decided I'd like to see it for myself.'

'You can see it later this year when it's officially opened by our MP.'

'I'd like to see it now.' I could feel my pulse beginning to hurry.

He frowned. 'You know you aren't allowed into the location without a permit.'

'I came in earlier this week without one. For the blanket distribution. Nobody minded then.'

'That was by invitation.' His frown had deepened to a scowl.

'So is this – residents' invitation,' I said, and heard a soft chuckle beside me.

Hughes didn't like the joke. His hard gaze shifted to Modisi then Sipho then back to me. 'Only the department can invite you.'

Beyond Hughes I could see his black driver listening intently. I took a deep breath. 'Mr Hughes,' I said as propitiatingly as I could, 'I only want to take a very quick look at the scheme.' I could feel the small camera I carried around with me in my hip pocket, but decided not to mention pictures. 'I will, of course, ring you tomorrow if I'm going to write anything. Surely that's fair enough?'

'No,' Hughes said. 'I'm not going to let you in without a permit from our office or from the town clerk's office. They're both closed now.'

'Surely you can authorise my going in?'

'Not unless you go through the proper application procedures.'

'You don't want him to see what's there,' Modisi said.

'I'm not talking to you,' barked Hughes. 'So shut up.'

'I would very much like to go in, Mr Hughes,' I said as winningly as I could. 'The scheme was very highly praised when it was proposed and our readers have a right to know how it's working now.'

'Apply tomorrow.'

'I'm here now.'

'I can't allow it.'

'Why not?' I felt anger boiling up, but tried to keep my voice even.

'I don't have to give you reasons. We'll discuss it tomorrow.' He dashed drizzle from his hair. 'Come on, Brown. We don't want to stand arguing in this. I'll give you a lift back to town.'

I turned to Modisi. 'It looks as though a visit's off for the moment.'

Before Modisi could reply, Hughes's voice cut in: 'I know you, Modisi.'

'I know you, too, Mr Hughes,' Modisi said calmly.

'So you run to the newspaper with complaints?'

Modisi smiled. 'No, I go to your office first. Then I go to the newspaper.'

'Watch out for this man,' Hughes said to me. 'He likes to make trouble.' He swung open the back door of the Vauxhall. 'Do you want that lift or not?'

'Is that offer for all three of us?' The words were out before I could think.

'No!' Hughes's eyes were bulging. 'Just you.'

Modisi and Sipho were watching me. I was conscious, too, of the surprised stare of Hughes's driver. I knew what the sensible course was. But Hughes's attitude made me reckless. 'I'll stay with them, thanks.'

'Suit yourself,' Hughes said curtly. 'Just get out of my location quick. You're trespassing.' He slammed the back door shut, opened the front door and got in. The driver started the engine, but didn't engage the gear.

'What will you do now, Mr Brown?' Modisi was smiling again.

'Go back to the office and write this up.' Turning my back on the car I began to walk away. Modisi and Sipho fell into step with me.

'You could come in later tonight,' Modisi said.

The man was relentless. His idea, though risky, had merit and I was tempted. But a cold inner voice was telling me I wouldn't get away with it. I shook my head. 'No. I'd better not get caught breaking the law. But once we're out of sight of Mr Hughes I'll slip you my camera and you can take some pictures or get someone else to if you don't know how.'

'I know how.' Sipho chuckled. 'I was so pleased when you said no to Hughes. I am glad you are with us.'

'I'm not with you,' I said. 'I'm not with anyone. I'm doing my job, that's all.'

'That's enough,' Modisi said. 'For now.'

Twenty-three

Grantley-Pearson took a few pulls at his pipe. 'I've been meaning to tell you how well you're doing, Brown,' he said. 'The chief is pleased, too, and I think you can expect a salary increase soon.'

'I could do with it,' I said. My eyes were on the typescript of my Vilakazi story on his blotter.

'I'm sure you could.' He tapped the copy with a fingernail. 'Personally, I was for running this. I fought for it with Maitland, the business manager, and I fought for it with the chief, but they wouldn't budge. Policy.'

'What policy?' I was too angry to include the usual sir. 'My Vilakazi story is being killed. I suppose that's because of the big printing contract from the municipality.'

He frowned. 'I could tell you that your Vilakazi story was spiked because it's likely to irritate race relations in a time of stress. This isn't stable old England and we can't publish and be damned like Cudlipp's *Daily Mirror*.' He leant forward. 'You'll know there is talk of nationwide boycotts on top of the unrest among the Pondos across the Kei River. There's industrial trouble in Port Elizabeth and East London – probably the work of the same agitators. The Vilakazi housing scheme is a very sensitive issue and might become inflammatory.' His tone became almost benign. 'But you're right, of course, about the municipal printing contract. Advertising and printing contracts make this paper pay and provide your salary and mine. A paper is more than an editorial department, it's a business. Being young you want a crusade. Hurt pride comes into it too, I suspect.'

His pipe had gone out. He relit it. 'Look, Brown,

we've compromised but we haven't just bowed the knee. The chief is insisting that the municipality looks into the complaints from Modisi and Zondi – types to avoid, by the way – and put right what needs putting right. As for the contretemps with Hughes, well, that's best quietly forgotten.'

'But should it be forgotten?' Heat was rising through my body. 'Surely that's a matter of press freedom?'

'Hughes was being officious, but he was within his rights.'

'Perhaps he was, legally. But he was also blocking an investigation. Those pictures Modisi took do show water right inside the houses.'

'That's how you see it,' the editor said. 'Hughes is claiming that you swaggered into the location without a permit, accompanied by a well-known agitator, and that you were provocative and insolent.'

'I wasn't swaggering,' I said. 'Swimming would be more accurate. Modisi was with me to guide me. I'd no time to apply for a permit and I swear I was polite to Mr Hughes. I used to be friends with his son.'

'Hughes says you were even a bit of a red at school.'

'Me a red?' I exclaimed. 'I'm not even a liberal. I believe in white rule. All I was after was a story.'

He smiled, a first in my experience. 'That's what I told the chief. I'll be honest with you. I didn't want you on the paper. I was wrong. You were very raw to begin with, but you've learnt fast and you've worked hard. A fact which has been noticed even by Maitland who has – just between us – the soul of a cash register.'

Careful, I thought . *He's trying to soften you up.*

'Yes, you could go far,' he went on, 'but by the time you've got to the editor's chair you'll have had to make a few compromises. Profits aren't a matter of ethics. It's a sad fact, but I live with it. You'll have to, too.'

Elizabeth was reading a bound January nineteen thirty copy of the *News* when I stalked out of the editor's office.

'They carried advertising and not news on the front page in the old days,' she said.

'That was honest at least,' I said, halting beside her. 'It was all about selling then and it still is. The news is just a bit of jam to make readers swallow the commercials.'

Her grey eyes lifted to my face. 'Ian didn't like your story?'

'He *liked* it. But he's spiked it.'

'I'm sorry, Simon. That's too bad.' She put her hand on my arm and even in my angry state her touch sent rills of warmth through me. I had to check a powerful impulse to drop my head onto her shoulder. Instead I hoisted my best Bogart smile.

'The editor thinks I could go far if I suck up to the right people.'

She didn't smile back. 'Could I see your story?'

'Be my readership. There's a copy and some pics on my desk.'

Outside it was darkening fast. Another storm was boiling up and Modisi and his friends would have more to complain about. Should I give a shit if a lot of blacks got wet? Strangely, I found I did.

Twenty-four

I'd arrived at my desk early. Grantley-Pearson stalked out of his office, his pipe puffing smoke like a steamroller's chimney, and thrust the tabloid at me. 'Did you have anything to do with this, Brown?' he demanded.

The African People's Voice, the masthead announced in heavy red type. A box in eigtheen point bold offered a clue to Grantley-Pearson's anger: *A Story The White Man's Papers Won't Print: See Pages 4,5 Inside.*

Pages four and five consisted of three items about Vilakazi. There was a picture of Thabo Modisi and an interview in which he accused the municipality of negligence and the *Victoria Daily News* of suppression; a report, backed by pictures, on the inadequacies of the new houses; and the story, printed in bold type, of our confrontation with Hughes under the ironic headline *Expelled From Eden.*

'I know nothing about this,' I protested.

'That's very lucky for you,' Grantley-Pearson said gruffly. 'The question is who does? The old man is livid. Luckily this kind of paper has no circulation worth mentioning outside a small group of half-educated blacks and white communists. Can you think of anyone who might have written it?'

'No, sir.' I couldn't.' But I believed I could. Modisi's hand was in it somehow and probably Sipho's as well. But the style seemed too punchy to come exclusively from that serious pair.

Elizabeth drifted in at ten-thirty, just after I'd returned from the courts. When I held out the paper she took it, her eyebrows climbing slightly as she scanned the middle pages. 'You didn't write this?'

'I'd never write for a commie rag. But no one's ever going to believe me.'

'I believe you,' she said.

'You should. You wrote it.'

She smiled. 'With a bit of help from Joshua and Seth March who interviewed Thabo Modisi.'

'You're mad,' I said. It was close to a yelp. 'There's going to be a hell of a fuss – and if it gets out you did it...' I couldn't finish the sentence.

'It needn't get out, need it? And if it does' – her smile seemed to have doubled its wattage – 'I'll own up. As you've pointed out to one or two people, I'm privileged by being almost family.'

'I still don't get it.'

'I'll explain, then. I don't want to be a proofreader and women's page hack all my life. So I'm learning journalistic skills whatever way I can. Ian is a little slow to appreciate women's efforts and *The Voice* isn't. Also, I believed some principles were involved. You've a low opinion of us liberals, Simon, but perhaps we aren't quite as weedy as you think.'

Twenty-five

On my return to the office after a boring meeting of the school board, I wasn't pleased to find Thabo Modisi lounging in my chair and talking to Elizabeth while Joshua hovered within earshot.

Elbows on the table, her pile of cuttings pushed to one side, Elizabeth looked up with a smile which carried a hint of embarrassment. 'Mr Modisi has come in to tell us that he'll be leading a contingent of PAC anti-pass campaigners from Vilakazi in March.'

'That is so.' Black suited, elegant, quiet voiced, he exuded confidence. 'We will go to the Rhodes Street Police Station and invite arrest. No bail, no defence, no fine. It will be an uncompromising challenge to the Government countrywide.'

I knew something of the proposed campaign. There had been perfunctory coverage of the preparations in some of the big dailies, and a recent edition of the *Evening Post* had carried a sympathetic profile of the Pan African Congress leader and university lecturer, Robert Mangaliso Sobukwe, stressing his anti-communism and commitment to non-violence. Elizabeth had shown me a copy of *The Voice*, which described the proposed action as 'pure adventurism', a 'poor imitation' of the Defiance Campaign of nineteen fifty-three and a hasty and irresponsible attempt to pre-empt an ANC campaign, planned for the end of March.

'I thought you were ANC like the Zondis,' I said, grumpily dragging a nearby chair to the table.

'I was, and I've argued this thing out with Elias, Florence and Sipho also, but they are too confused to see it. They are of my family but principles must come first. I once believed that the African National

Congress would never be run by communists but I was wrong. Since then I've seen how white communists have disregarded the African majority and slowed down the struggle on instructions from Moscow. They are always talking about the need to create revolutionary cells and cadres but they are really afraid of the black masses who are non-communist and Africanist.'

'*The African People's Voice* says the PAC is an unrepresentative organisation of opportunists and outright black racists backed by the CIA,' Elizabeth said softly.

The smooth, triangular face tightened. 'That is communist propaganda. We argue that there is only one race, the human race. The PAC will accept anyone whose loyalty is to Africa, pan-Africanism and the African people.'

'Could I join your organisation?' Elizabeth said, more softly yet.

Momentarily, Modisi looked nonplussed. Then flawless teeth flashed white in the serious face. 'If you threw away your white identity card and lived among us as an African.'

Maitland, *en route* to the chief's office, cast a hostile look at the three of us. Elizabeth didn't notice. She was smiling back at Modisi. An element, absent before, was thickening the air.

'I'll consider it,' she said lightly.

'Well,' Elizabeth said after Joshua had escorted Modisi downstairs, 'which of us is going to write up the interview?'

I couldn't bottle my bitterness. 'You'd better do it,' I said. 'You're the one who is ready to go and live with him and his lot in Vilakazi.'

'I didn't say that,' she protested, flushing. 'I said I'd consider living as an African. You're reading far too much into a joking remark.'

'You mean flirting don't you?' I was slipping a cog, but I couldn't stop. 'You really have come on. I was too dark and dirty for you to even hold my hand, but now you can laugh and joke with a kaffir from the townships.'

The blood ebbed from her face, leaving it ashy. 'I was hateful and horrible, but that was long ago. Can't you accept that I've changed and see things quite differently? Why must you harp on about it? Do you dislike me so much?'

'I don't dislike you.' It came out a low snarl. 'Can't you see it's quite the bloody opposite.'

The colour flooded back to her cheeks as if I'd slapped her. 'Oh, Simon,' she murmured. 'It never occurred... I'm sorry, really sorry.'

Angry tears were stinging my eyes. 'Don't be sorry. You don't know what really being sorry is. You're sorry for those blacks in Vilakazi. And you're sorry for me. But it's not personal. You don't know what it's like to be us. You've got everything you want. Money. Looks. Bloody Jim Farraday. Wait till you want what you can't have. Then you'll know.'

Maitland, emerging from the chief's office, stopped to stare at us. I lurched up, grabbed my notebook and headed blindly for the stairs. Going down I met Joshua coming up. 'Modisi is a brave man,' he said, 'and some young men are so *gatvol* with the pass laws they will follow anyone. But the campaign will fail because the ANC is the true organisation of the masses.'

'I don't want to hear any more about kaffir politics,' I said and shouldered my way past him.

It was my day for unpleasant surprises. When I got home from work a letter from Jessica was waiting for me. She was, she wrote, looking forward to her return to Victoria. Her term was going well, but she'd missed me *terribly*. Then came the pinprick:

Your cousin Rex pitched up at Res. He's enrolled at an agricultural college outside Cape Town and decided to pay a call. Very formal and proper and rather awkward, but quite sweet in a Gabriel Oak sort of way. He's offered to give me driving lessons in his car, an Austin A40. He's also asked me to partner him to an end of term hop and I've said yes. I knew you wouldn't mind.

I did mind. I didn't want my large, fresh-cheeked cousin taking Jessica dancing or giving her driving lessons: activities too intimate not to be disturbing.

On the way to the Hotel Victoria for a restorative drink I met Kepler, strutting along High Street in his uniform. 'No, man, I'm doing well,' he said in reply to my query. 'There's talk of my going into the CID one of these days. Maybe the Special Branch in time.' He laughed. 'Keep an eye on you, eh?'

'Sure, Kep.' I wondered what he'd heard. I was about to move on when he said, 'Seen Harry lately?'

'Here and there. Why?'

'Just something an *ou* from Vice Squad said to me. Harry was quite keen on dirty magazines and pictures, *né*?'

Was he sending a friendly but indirect warning, or on the probe? 'Weren't we all – when we could get them?'

'Not me.' The heavy face wrinkled. 'They were disgusting.'

'I don't think Harry's into that kind of stuff any

more,' I said. I wasn't sure it was true. But it seemed the thing to say.

Harry was scornful when I phoned him. 'I remember bloody Kepler getting a hard on when I showed him some pictures of a negress and a white guy doing mouth jobs on each other. Now he's snooping around looking for promotion. Put a man in uniform and he becomes a hypocrite. Well, I'll watch out. And so should you.'

Twenty-six

'No, Simon. *No*!' Jessica's hand grasped mine, halting its exploration inside her panties. 'We've gone far enough – too far.' She sat up abruptly on the bunk where we'd been lying entangled, and, pushing me to one side, adjusted her skirt and pulled her T-shirt and bra down over her breasts. 'I should really be getting home.'

'If you have to.' I burned to continue and sensed that under her fear a similar desire was smouldering. This was the third time we'd reached this point since she'd returned from Cape Town for a brief visit and tonight, as we'd kissed and touched and strained against each other, I'd believed we'd go the full distance.

She rehooked the catch of her bra, swung her feet to the floor and stood up. I got to my feet, too, a little inhibited by her downward glance at the stiffness in my groin. Only minutes ago her hand had been there, squeezing and rubbing and – blissful moment – fiddling with my fly. Then she'd called a halt.

'I'm sorry,' she said. 'I...' She shook her head.

'It's all right.' It wasn't. Her cunt had been wet, warm. We'd been so close and then the brutal halt. Time was leaking away. She'd be leaving for Cape Town tomorrow and weeks of frustration stretched ahead.

'I've had a lovely time, Simon, thanks to you.' She put her arms around me and kissed me open mouthed. Her breath was marrowy and she didn't recoil when I drew her in tight against my erection.

My good intentions died. She could be unlocked. The bunk was behind her. My pelvis to hers, my tongue exploring her mouth, I nudged her tentatively towards it, then took her by the shoulders and pushed gently until she was sitting down with me kneeling between her legs.

'What is this?' she smiled. 'A proposal?'

I felt my desire drop. But only for a moment. An old, arousing image flickered in my mind: a dark man with his face in a spreadeagled woman's lap. 'Sort of,' I mumbled. I pushed up her skirt and dipped my mouth to the fork of her body.

She gave a cry, and for a heartbeat I was afraid I'd misjudged. Her hands went to my ears as if to jerk my head back but then fell away as I nuzzled determinedly. When I eased her panties down her thighs, she made no attempt to stop me. The lips of her cunt were parting to my tongue and I could scent her excitement. 'Oh, Simon,' she murmured. 'What are you doing?'

I continued to truffle. A small shiver ran through her cunt. She was muttering something which sounded like *lost*, but her thighs were gripping my head and I couldn't be sure. Had she come? I didn't know, or care. Her legs were parted wide now and my cock felt full of sap. She was mine to take.

I groped with one hand in the drawer of my bedside table until my trembling fingers found the tin of French letters there and began to fumble it open, anxious not to tear the flimsy latex. Yanking down my trousers and underpants I managed to roll on the condom. A last lick and I lay down on top of her and began to edge my cock into the lushness of her sex.

Entry was easy at first. But as I thrust deeper, she became tighter, winced and uttered a small mew, her eyes snapping open.

'Am I hurting?' I forced myself to slow. I didn't know what I'd do if she asked me to stop.

184

'A bit. It's all right.' Her smile was brave. 'Do you love me a little?'

'No. A whole lot.' At that moment it was true.

She seemed less tight now and the smile stayed.

I pushed deeper, then deeper still and she didn't flinch, though her eyes closed again. Sensation, exquisite and almost unbearable, was spreading through my cock and belly. My increased excitement seemed to communicate and her crutch began to grind against mine. Her T-shirt had worked up to her midriff and I pushed it and her bra up above her breasts. Immediately she cupped them and began to run her thumbs around the aureoles.

The gesture, so unexpected and intimate, tipped me into a sharp stuttering orgasm.

She lay under me, her hand stroking my neck. But when I kissed her lips, she turned her head away. 'Ugh,' she said. 'I don't like the way I taste.'

'I do. I like it very much.' All the same my cock was dwindling fast and after a while I rolled off her, removed the sheath, knotted it, pushed it under the bunk, then lit a cigarette. I tried not to feel deflated.

Jessica sat up, took the cigarette from me and puffed at it rather inexpertly. 'I meant to wait,' she said. 'But when you...' She gave a small cough and handed back the cigarette. 'I'm not sorry. I'm glad it was with you and I'm quite happy to be ruined, like the maid in the Hardy poem.'

'That's good.' I made a mental note to look up the poem.

'It didn't really hurt.' Her hand went to my thigh. 'May I touch? It's so teeny and soft now, compared...' Her fingers curled around my cock. 'Like a big shrimp or sleeping baby snake. Sweet.'

I touched her throat. 'Shouldn't you...?'

'Get home?' Her expression intent, she was drawing my foreskin slowly down over the head of my cock, then back, sending small tingles through the stem. 'Yes, I should. But I'm not that keen on Mummy at the moment. She's being horrible. Really sarky about my term marks. And not only that. She snipes at the way I dress and make up, about the money I'm spending... And, of course, boys.'

'Boys?'

'People have been telling her that I've been going to the bio and dances a lot, which isn't exactly true. Then she bumped into your Aunt Betty in town, who let drop – accidentally on purpose, I'll bet – that I'd gone out with your cousin Rex.'

At the mention of Rex's name acid dripped into my gut and my cock which had been stiffening went soft again.

Jessica didn't appear to have noticed and continued to finger the flaccid flesh. 'I've hardly seen anything of Rex, but Mum called me flirty and flighty.' Her eyes lifted to mine. 'I'm not. I love you and want you and me to be together.' She laughed. 'Especially now that I'm your ruined maid.'

In her hand my cock was hardening again. The clock read midnight, but that no longer seemed to matter. This time she didn't avert her head when I kissed her and her hand moved faster on me. 'Shall we?' I whispered in her ear.

She shook her head. 'I'm a weeny bit sore.'

'This then?' Rampant now I drew her head down into my lap. For an exquisite moment her lips touched my cock, then she pulled away and sat up.

'I'm sorry,' she said in distress. 'I can't. I know it doesn't seem fair. But I just can't.'

186

I choked back my frustration. 'Don't worry about it.'

'What about this?' Her hand was busy.

'Nice.' It flitted across my mind that Jessica's handwork was competent for a novice. But I mislaid the thought as others obtruded. She was panting as she jerked away at my cock and my exploring hand encountered taut nipples. Might she let come between her breasts?

But even as I shifted on the bunk there was a hammering on the *rondavel* door. 'Simon,' my mother called, 'Simon!'

Jessica's hand flew off my cock as though it had turned into a red-hot poker and went to her T-shirt, yanking it down.

'Wait, Ma,' I yelled. 'I'm coming.'

Which was both true and untrue. My cock was detumescing fast as I dragged on my trousers, ignoring my underpants. Jessica was hanging over the edge of the bunk scrabbling for her slacks and panties.

'It's the damn phone,' my mother yelled back. 'Mrs Leighton. For you. What the hell are you up to in there?'

'Nothing.'

Barefoot, conscious of my semi-erection bulging in my trousers, I squeezed out of the door and shut it behind me. In the moonlight my mother's face was grey. Her old dressing gown hung open and I could make out her low breasts through the thin nightdress.

'You're in big trouble, son,' she said grimly, turning towards the house. 'Your girlfriend's mom is the hell-in and no mistake.'

The telephone receiver was lying like a question mark on the small hall table. I picked it up and said hello. Mrs Leighton's voice rasped down the line. 'I want my daughter home at once, do you hear? You're to keep right away from her in future. If you don't, I'll cut her off without a penny and have you run out of town.'

The line went dead.

My mother was in the kitchen boiling a kettle. Her gown was sashed and she'd rough-combed her hair. 'She's mental, that woman,' she said. 'And you're a damn fool messing around with that toptown lot. Better pack it in, son, before you land right in it.'

I was tempted to say that I already had, but grunted instead and went out the door. For once I was glad that Kathy was with Norman on the Robertses' farm.

'She's being completely unreasonable,' Jessica said as we walked through the back garden to her car. Just because I'm dependent on her at present to support me through varsity she thinks she can control every bit of my life. She simply can't see me as an adult. I think she's jealous of me, as well. She's always been odd around my boyfriends.'

She took my face in her hands and kissed me hard, her tongue seeking mine, then stepped away and got into the car. 'I do love you, Simon.'

'Snap. Ring me.'

I watched her drive away, then went back into the garden. The night had become cool and a slight breeze fanned my hot face. Above, the moon was new, a sliver of silver in the velvety sky. Standing there, breathing hard, I could still feel Jessica's embrace, provoking a renewal of desire and a frantic need for release.

Unbidden fragmentary images clicked through

my mind. Jessica under me, her fingers circling her nipples. Kathy in the shower, her arms lifting as if to greet the spray. Thandi at the tap, her soap-flecked hand going under her skirt to that dark, forbidden cunt. I tried to control them, to focus only on Jessica, but couldn't. Dizzy, I ripped open my fly and, groaning with the misery of my balked lust, rubbed and jerked until I shot into the hedge.

As I turned to walk back towards the house a shadow flitted from the peach tree to Florence's *khaya*. I called, 'Thandi!' But she didn't stop.

Twenty-seven

'You seem out of sorts, Simon,' Elizabeth said. 'What's the matter?'

'Boredom is the matter.' That wasn't quite accurate. I was in purgatory. Jessica had written only one letter to my three since her return to Cape Town, and that mainly about an unsympathetic and harrying tutor. Work wasn't producing much joy either. I made my routine calls, attended meetings of local organisations in the evenings, regularly telephoned useful contacts and kept eyes and ears open for the unexpected news item. But nothing excited me.

Elizabeth held up the sheaf of cablegrams she'd been given to sub-edit. 'This might interest you. It's a Sapa report saying that groups of Africans have been turning up at police stations in Johannesburg and elsewhere, demanding to be arrested. Some already have been. Others have been turned away. Perhaps we should be contacting Thabo Modisi? He promised to speak to me again but he hasn't.'

'Typical Xhosa unreliability.'

She frowned. 'I think he was offended because Ian cut my report of our interview to a paragraph. Anyway, there might be something doing.'

'Maybe.' Memory was jabbing me uncomfortably. Though I'd entered twenty-first of March in my diary as the starting date for the proposed Go-to-jail Campaign, other assignments and my own problems had swept it out of my mind. I was losing my grip.

I lit a cigarette and tried to concentrate. 'Have you got a phone number for Modisi?'

'He didn't leave one. Only an address.'

'No good. Our best chance is to check with the police. I'll do it.'

Our shared phone trilled. I picked up. 'Mr Brown, this is a friend,' whispered a voice I recognised. 'Many African people are at the Rhodes Street Police Station without their dompasses and there is going to be trouble very soon.' He hung up.

Affable old Silas Mkize, the criminal court interpreter, a secret PAC man? I'd sometimes wondered what his private opinions were. Now I knew and it was food for thought.

'We needn't bother looking for Modisi,' I said to Elizabeth. 'It looks as though he's led his gang to the Police Station.'

Puffing at his pipe, Grantley-Pearson nodded at my news. 'We should have taken Mr Modisi a bit more seriously,' he said when I'd finished. 'A wire has just come through that the police baton charged a gathering in Sharpeville location in the Transvaal last night and there was a march of five thousand on the municipal offices this morning, leading to another baton charge which dispersed them. Apparently an even bigger crowd is grouping at the Sharpeville Police Station. Sounds as if we have a similar situation here. Get to Rhodes Street straightaway and I'll chase up a photographer.'

The early morning autumn chill had dissipated and a warmish breeze fluttered my tie as I hurried along Victoria High Street towards the Octagon. I was a few yards from the Post Office when Carol Lategan rounded the corner at an awkward jog-trot and stopped in front of me. She was wearing a tight blue skirt and jacket and high heels and was hefting a large red handbag. Her face was flushed and her mascara was streaked.

Before I could greet her she grasped my arm. 'Kathy's in among a whole lot of kaffirs outside the

Police Station,' she panted. 'You better get there.'

'Kathy?' I spun Carol round and increased my pace. 'She should be at work.'

'Day off. We were going shopping then a matinée. We called on Violet at her florist's and there was this big crowd shouting outside the Police Station.'

My chest tight, I began to run. Still clinging to my arm, Carol ran beside me gasping out her story:

'I said we should scram. But Kathy had to take a look. There's kaffirs all over the place, but she doesn't care. Next thing she sees that young kaffir whose mother works for you...'

'Sipho!'

'Him. Plus that Coloured *ou*, not the one with the scar, the thin one. She tells me to get you – and offs into the crowd. *Mal*! And I'm clapped out – *uitgeput*.'

She released my arm. Freed, I ran past the Athena Café and on into Rhodes Street.

Normally the top end was fairly quiet on a weekday, the main activity confined to customers of the café and Violet Lategan's flower shop. The lower end, which became Jameson Street and led towards Vilakazi, was usually busier because of comings and goings at the Police Station, a small bakery and Illingworth's garage.

About a dozen whites, including some Athena staff, were clustered on the pavement outside the café looking down the street. There was a smaller group, all women, similarly occupied under the florist's awning. They looked my way as I sprinted past and I thought Violet called out.

Ahead of me the street was choked by a chanting crowd of blacks. Massed in front of the wide raised verandah of the Police Station, they filled the width of the street and spread down its length in the direction of the township. Impossible to say exactly how many, but I guessed several hundred.

And building, judging from the shuffling at the fringes.

Four uniformed policemen – two of them white, two black – stood on the verandah, their backs to the shuttered windows and green charge office door.

As I got closer I could see that the crowd was composed mainly of men, with only a sprinkling of *doeks* and berets. I was reminded of the demonstration in Victoria High Street years ago, but these participants looked younger and more informally dressed.

The chanting had become clearer: '*Phantsi namapasi*. Arrest us now.'

There was no sign of Kathy.

Ten paces from the edge of the crowd I stopped, scanning it anxiously. My heart was thumping my chest wall like a fist. Some of the demonstrators stared at me curiously. One, a youth in a baggy jersey, spat on the tarmac.

Three more white policemen appeared on the verandah: a muscular blond captain, an old sergeant I recognised from police calls as Koekemoer, and Kepler, carrying two megaphones.

A body cannoned into me from the side. Carol, heaving with the effort of her run, steadied herself against me with one hand and pointed towards the verandah with the other. 'Jesus,' she half-wheezed, half-laughed. 'It's bladdy Kepler going to broadcast to the kaffirs.'

Sergeant Koekemoer walked slowly to the edge of the verandah and beckoned. The lean figure of Modisi climbed the steps and began talking to him.

'Simon!' Sipho, flared-nostrilled, his face beaded with sweat yet incongruously wearing an overcoat, stood in front of me, hand outstretched.

'Where's Kathy?' I rapped, surprised into submitting to the elaborate Congress handshake.

He inclined his head towards the crowd. 'Over there with Ben and Seth March.'

'What are you doing here?' I demanded. 'This isn't your show.'

'Just keeping an eye on things,' he said calmly. 'Our people are confused by this campaign. Modisi was a big man in the ANC and not everyone knows he switched.' The wide-set eyes focussed on Carol, travelling from the flushed face down to the shiny shoes. He didn't hold out his hand. ' *Molo*,' he said. 'Are you press now, too?'

'No.' Carol giggled. 'You know me, boy. Kathy's friend.'

'What gives, Blackie?' Gerry Fielding, the town photographer, had joined us, puffing a little, his freckled face puce, a large camera in one hand and a smaller one dangling against his chest.

'What you see.' I indicated Sipho. 'He'll tell you.'

The crowd had grown again, swelled by a group of sixty or so people, led by two young men wearing armbands. Now I could see Kathy waving and the red beret she sometimes wore bobbing as she threaded her way towards us with Seth March beside her.

Sergeant Koekemoer and Modisi were in earnest debate, with the blond captain looking on. Modisi reached out for a megaphone, but Kepler bridled and Koekemoer shook his head violently. A hiss came from a group in the crowd. Modisi held up a hand and turned back to Koekemoer. More earnest talk, then the old policeman shrugged, nodded and made an exit through the charge office door.

Beside me Gerry Fielding was clicking away.

Modisi stepped forward to the edge of the verandah and began speaking loudly in Xhosa.

Sipho translated: 'He's telling the people that the police want them to return to the township. But he has told the sergeant that the people are here to be arrested and will not go home. Also, he is demanding to see the Station commandant about three young PAC cadres arrested for incitement in Vilakazi last night. The sergeant has agreed to take those messages to the commandant.'

Kathy and Seth March had reached us. 'Good, you got him,' Kathy said to Carol. To Sipho she said, 'Ben thinks the crowd is getting very angry.'

'The police like to frustrate the people,' Sipho said. 'It gives them an excuse to shoot.'

'You'd better get out of this, Kathy,' I said. 'You shouldn't be here.'

'I am here,' she retorted, her colour high, 'and I'm staying. The people were friendly to us, weren't they, Seth?'

'Here's Prinsloo,' Sipho said quietly.

The commandant, large and stiff backed, the sunlight glinting on the badge of his cap, had appeared on the verandah accompanied by Koekemoer and the limping figure of old Silas Mkize. Shouted remarks from someone in the crowd were followed by a collective ripple of laughter.

Sipho chuckled. 'They asked Mkize if he is also offering himself for arrest.'

Modisi had begun speaking, ostensibly to Prinsloo, but with frequent glances at the crowd, which had fallen silent so that his booming voice was just audible. Mkize, positioning himself beside Prinsloo, translated quietly, miming the gestures of the PAC man. When Modisi stopped, the crowd shouted '*Ewe*! – Yes!' and three men danced up the steps, emptying their pockets to show that they weren't carrying passes, before dancing down again.

Sipho frowned, concentrating. 'Modisi is saying the people have come in peace, but are determined never to carry passes again.'

Prinsloo listened until Mkize had finished murmuring in his ear, then said something to Koekemoer and one of the black constables. They snapped to attention, saluted and marched through into the charge office. The door slammed behind them.

Sipho nudged me and pointed down the street. A khaki personnel carrier had rolled into position behind us: two policemen in combat gear sat on its roof cradling sten guns. Gerry Fielding's camera clicked urgently.

I grasped Kathy's arm. 'Now will you go?' Shaking her head, she pulled her arm free.

Prinsloo was talking to Modisi, wagging his swagger stick as if to sweep the black man away. Modisi was answering back: from his agitated movements it was clear that he was angry.

Some of the crowd had noticed the personnel carrier. There was a rumbling of voices and shuffling of feet. I felt a prickling at the back of my neck.

On the verandah, Modisi retreated to the steps and stood there with his arms folded while Prinsloo took one megaphone and Silas Mkize the other. '*Aandag! Aandag!*' Prinsloo blared. 'Attention! Attention! I am informed that you have been persuaded by your so-called leaders to offer yourselves for arrest. I advise you in your own interests to forget this foolishness and return to your homes. Your presence here constitutes an illegal gathering and a contravention of the Riotous Assemblies Act and if you won't disperse of your own free will I will be obliged to take the steps necessary to disperse you, including the use of force.'

Limping forward to the edge of the verandah Mkize translated.

The crowd didn't like it. There were cries in English and Xhosa and a knot of women began to chant a Xhosa song which referred – unflatteringly, I guessed – to Prime Minister Verwoerd. Modisi, still on the steps, had begun a shouted dialogue with the front rows of the crowd.

'Thabo is being stupid,' Sipho said. 'He is encouraging them not to move.'

'He has to,' Seth murmured. 'Otherwise he'd lose authority with his followers. It's an *impasse*.' He grinned tightly. 'Impasse over the *dompas*.'

'Jesus Christ,' Carol exclaimed hoarsely. 'You can joke?' She took Kathy's arm. 'Time we trekked, Kath.'

'Not yet.' Kathy's attention was on the crowd.

'Arrest us,' a young man was shouting. 'We want to fill your jails. The whole country is a jail.' Others joined in. Modisi, his face gleaming in the sun, turned triumphantly back to Prinsloo.

Seth laughed. 'Any African any day can get picked up just for not having the *dompas*, but now that people are trying to get arrested the *Amabulu* don't want to know about it.'

Out of the corner of my eye I caught a glimpse of green: a Volkswagen had parked behind the armoured car. A tall, stooped man, grey faced and hollow cheeked in a navy-blue suit, was the first to get out: Grobelaar. He was followed unhurriedly by two

197

men in brown suits, both burly, one white, one black.

'Simon!' Elizabeth had arrived at my elbow. 'Ian sent me to find out how you were getting on. Is there anything I can do?'

'Run like hell,' Carol said.

'You can tell him things are tense,' I said.

'So I see.' The grey eyes traversed the crowd, then took in my companions. She might have been a spectator of a ring event at the Victoria Agricultural Show.

'Look, Blackie!' Gerry Fielding was pointing at the flat roof of the warehouse to the side of the Police Station. Two uniformed figures knelt there, rifles to their shoulders.

Loud clattering yanked my gaze to the verandah once more. The shutters were banging back to reveal gun muzzles poking out through the window bars, shadowy shapes behind them. The charge office door opened and a dozen policemen armed with FN rifles burst out onto the verandah and took up positions on either side of the commandant. The blond captain's revolver was in his hand. Simultaneously Grobelaar and his two assistants raced up the steps, seized Modisi and, before he could move, half-pushed, half-dragged him across the verandah into the charge office.

'Jesus,' Gerry Fielding breathed. 'Tough stuff.'

'Provocation,' Seth said.

The crowd, as if stupefied by the abruptness of it, fell silent and still for a moment. Then, shouting and gesturing, it surged forward, only halting as the policemen on the verandah took a step forward, raising their weapons.

The commandant had the megaphone to his mouth again. 'In terms of the Riotous Assemblies Act I order you to disperse. If you disperse there will be no trouble.'

'Release our leaders,' a youth shouted, 'or arrest us all.'

'*Ewe*,' others shouted. 'Arrest us all.'

'I repeat,' the commandant intoned, 'that you are breaking the law. If you do not disperse of your own accord I will be obliged to order my men to take action.'

His voice, distorted by the megaphone, twanged eerily into silence. Then Mkize was translating.

'They will shoot,' Seth said. 'They want to shoot.'

'*Ek dink ek gaan my onderbroekie kak*,' Carol said.

I knew how she felt. My bowels were water.

Ben March had appeared from nowhere, a blue baseball cap tilted over his eyes and an unlit roll-up in his mouth.

'Let's go.' His face was set, the scar pale in the dark skin.

For a moment I thought he meant we should leave. But he was jerking a thumb towards the verandah where the policemen stood immobile, weapons at the ready. The scene was fixed like a movie still, except for occasional flashes as the sun caught the fractional shift of a rifle.

Kathy caught on first. 'Ben means the front. If it's not just Africans, they might not shoot.'

'That's right, goosie.' Ben looked straight at me. 'Coming?'

My mouth was dry. Trust a March to frame a challenge I hadn't expected. 'Why should I?' I croaked. 'My job is to report this, not to get mixed up in it.'

'Report it from there. From the front line.' His thin smile seemed like a sneer.

'I can report it better from here,' I said.

'We're wasting time.' Seth was moving towards the flank of the crowd, followed by Kathy and Sipho.

'Well?' Ben hadn't moved.

'I answered you. Anyway, why should I risk my neck for them?'

'Because those people are our people, brother.'

'They may be your people,' I snapped. 'They're not mine. I don't go for all that shit about brotherhood.'

'That's your choice,' he said turning away. 'Your name should be Yellow, not Brown.'

Years ago this insolent *skollie* had taunted me. Now he was calling me yellow. My rage was even greater than my fear: it seemed to be my fate that my most shaming moments should be staged in front of those I least wanted to witness them.

Though my stomach was mush, my legs propelled me forward.

Elizabeth was keeping pace beside me, her face a question. Over her shoulder I could see Fielding's freckled face, sweating concern.

'Stick with Gerry and cover the general scene,' I rasped with attempted assurance. 'We'll compare notes later.' Elizabeth nodded and fell back.

Kathy had plunged into the crowd. I could make out her red beret, a bobbing marker in the dark sea. I thought she looked back towards me, but couldn't be sure.

A hand was on my arm: Carol's. ' *Wag 'n bietjie*, Blackie,' she wheezed. 'I'm coming with.'

'*Voertsek*, Carol.' Incredulity making me brutal, I tried to fling off her hand. 'You don't have to get shot with a lot of *munts* because my sister's mad.'

'Kathy's my pal.' She kept her grip on my arm, jogging with me. 'Anyway, I like kaffirs.'

There was no time to explore the irrationality of

that. We were into the crowd. Prinsloo was braying another warning through the megaphone. It went unheeded, lost against calls for Modisi's release and demands to be arrested. I could hear snatches of the anti-Verwoerd song to my left. Dark faces, some hostile, some merely curious, swung towards us as I began to push through. Once a woman caught at my sleeve and a young man stood in my way; I sensed his hatred and a desire to attack, but held up my small camera mutely and he stepped aside. I barged on, trying, as in bad moments on the sportsfield, to focus on nothing but the immediate task.

'This way.' Sipho's face was inches from mine and a sinewy hand fastened on my arm, steering me forward to where Seth and Ben, with Kathy beside them, were attempting in ludicrous *fanagalo* to persuade two men and a stocky young woman to let them pass. Sipho intervened in rapid Xhosa and the three made way.

Kathy smiled and touched my hand, then gaped at Carol.

'*Toe maar,*' Carol said. 'I'm mad too.'

Kathy's cheeks were aflame. Whatever she was feeling, high excitement was part of it. She'd always sought the danger zone – and, dog-like, I'd always followed her into it.

Perhaps out of some instinct of solidarity the crowd was thickest here. As we squeezed forward I was conscious of the pressure of hot bodies, and the clingy smell of sweat, woodsmoke and cheap soap. Choking, I wanted to strike out and free space for myself, but was afraid it would be misunderstood.

'Kathy! Simon!' Sipho had got in front of us. Seizing both Kathy's hands he began forcing a path for us by backing through the crowd while directing a flow of Xhosa at those in our way. When we came to a halt just behind the row of chanting blacks between us and the verandah he smiled, a fleeting glimmer in the ashy grey of his face. I wondered what colour my fear was painting me. Yellow perhaps.

The police had increased their numbers: more armed white policemen and, for the first time, black policemen with *kieries*.

Koekemoer, his mouth working overtime, was leaning towards the commandant and pointing in our direction. Prinsloo was nodding. Kepler had seen us, too, his awareness betrayed by his violently twitching face.

The tension had also got to Prinsloo. His jaw was set and the hand which raised the megaphone to his mouth was trembling slightly. Above the chanting his voice blurred with static:

'You have three minutes to clear the street. Disperse immediately, or I will give the order to shoot. This is your final warning.'

The armed policemen on the verandah took a step forward. The people immediately around us ceased milling and became very still. The chanting and shouting died. There was an audible click as the blond captain loosened the safety catch of his revolver. Then silence. Tangible, thick. In the midday heat the space we occupied had the smell of being about to smoulder. Kathy's fingers squeezed mine. On the other side of me Carol drew a long breath in through her nostrils.

But no one showed any sign of moving away.

Was this it? Was this how my world ended? I wanted with every tortured nerve not to believe it. In my adolescent fantasies my death had been active and heroic. Not helplessly waiting in a hot, smelly side street with a cold hand clamping my intestines and a humiliating urge to shit. Nor so soon, so wastefully soon.

Meanwhile I was registering small details with strange clarity. The high-coloured curve of Kathy's cheek in profile, the gleam of moisture in the corner of her eye. The small brown ear on the neat dark head of the woman in front of me, a round earring of red glass in the lobe. The blue diamond pattern of her companion's dress. The rigidity of Sipho's shoulders as he stood a little ahead of us, almost in the front row. Ben's copper profile, the roll-up back between his lips. Carol's plump hip against mine, her fingers biting into my arm. Beyond, the dark heads of a front row which looked looser-knit now, less of a barrier between us and the line of police whose automatic rifles no longer looked ornamental, but deadly. Kepler, the facial nerve twitching away.

'Kepler won't shoot us, at least.' Carol's whisper was bronchitic. 'His *maats* will instead.'

Ben was clicking his fingers, trying to get us to join him and Sipho. 'Stay still,' I grunted to Kathy. For answer she squeezed my hand the tighter and stepped forward, drawing me with her. Carol muttered inaudibly but shifted with me and I sensed, rather than saw, that Seth was following. Now we were part of the front row.

I felt a mad, choking desire to laugh. With every passing second it looked more certain that I was going to die for a cause I didn't believe in and among people – Kathy and Carol apart – I didn't give a toss for. And why? My ludicrous racial pride had driven me to respond to the taunts of a *skollie* and my love for my sister had done the rest. The bad joke was on me.

'You've got one minute,' Prinsloo said.

Above our heads a jet was carving through the blue of the sky, leaving a sinuous white line behind. I was conscious of a hollowness, a fierce hunger for all that had been and might have been. I closed my eyes, wishing I believed enough to pray.

When I opened them again Elias Zondi, wearing the green overalls of Illingworth's garage, was on the verandah talking to Prinsloo, his dark hand jabbing in our direction and then towards Jameson Street. The captain, revolver in hand, stepped towards them, but Prinsloo stopped him with a curt gesture of his swagger stick.

'Look,' Kathy said quietly.

From the direction indicated by Elias four women were approaching slowly in single file.

In the lead in sober grey, her cropped hair steely, a black sash slanting across her breast, was the tall figure of Miss Robinson. She was followed by Mrs Rangisamy in a white sari, her palms pressed together, then angular, grey-haired Miss Wilson, the librarian, and lastly Mrs Illingworth, the garage owner's wife, dark haired and smart in green with a touch of black at the cuffs. Ten paces behind them, walking stiffly, and carrying what appeared to be library books, old Mr Seer made an incongruous figure in his unseasonable lightweight cream suit and panama hat. As if taking an accustomed place in church, they made their way to where we stood. Without appearing to move, the row adjusted, letting them in.

Out of the corner of my eye I could see Gerry Fielding, crouched at the corner of the verandah, plying his camera, Elizabeth beside him, scratching in her notebook.

And I began to hope.

Something had been agreed between Elias and

Prinsloo because Elias was addressing the crowd in Xhosa while Silas Mkize interpreted for the commandant. Sipho, a healthier colour now, translated softly for us: 'My father says Prinsloo claims he cannot make arrests because he has no instructions and anyway there is no room in the jail for so many people. Prinsloo insists he doesn't want bloodshed and that he will release Modisi and the others later today if the people disperse peacefully now. He also promises to convey their grievances to the government.'

Sipho paused, listening, then resumed. 'Elias is advising the people to return home. He understands their anger, because it is his too. He is not PAC but the people know him and that he hates the *dompas*. He is ready to be arrested and even to die. But today is not the day. Even the PAC leaders – like Sobukwe himself – did not ask people to die today. Only to offer themselves for arrest. He says he believes Prinsloo when he says he doesn't want to shoot, but there are many in the Government who would like an excuse to kill. He asks us to remember how our people were shot down at Bulhoek and Bondelswart in the early nineteen-twenties, on the Witwatersrand in the forties, in Port Elizabeth and East London in the fifties and in Pondoland and Natal even now. Today people have again come to make a peaceful protest and again they have been answered with the threat of armed force. Perhaps the time will come when the people must meet force with force, but that time is not yet.'

Sipho stopped, grinning, and after an instant I guessed why. Silas Mkize had clearly not been translating the more fiery part of Elias's Xhosa oratory and Prinsloo was unaware of it. Momentarily, if flimsily, blacks were in control.

Elias was pointing at us.

'He's telling the people how you people are here to show solidarity,' Sipho continued, 'and how there are many more like you in the rest of the country. He asks us to sing the national anthem of the African people and go home.'

'Yes, please God,' Carol murmured, 'and if I get out of here alive I promise to be nicer to Kepler from now on.'

Elias had come to attention, right fist raised aloft, thumb extended. Faintly at first, then more strongly he began to sing:

' *Nkosi sikileli Afrika*

malupakamis'u phondolwayo.'

Beside me Sipho began to sing, then others along the row. Ben was singing, too, his voice surprisingly deep for so lean a man. Kathy was scatting vigorously in her tuneful alto. Prinsloo and his men stood silent, stony and watchful. Just perceptibly, Silas Mkize's lips were moving.

The singing swelled, sank, took off again in a powerful descant, then died plaintively away on the prayerful words with which it had begun.

' *Afrika!*' Elias thundered, fist upheld.

' *Afrika!*' responded the crowd, punching the air.

' *Mayibuye!*'

' *Mayibuye!*'

A heavy stillness followed, then slowly the crowd began to ebb away towards Jameson Street. I stood where I was, sapped, unable to believe my luck.

Kathy's eyes were glistening as she hugged Carol. 'It worked. They didn't shoot.'

'Yes,' Ben growled, 'it worked. This time.' His eyes sought mine. He grinned, the buccaneer once more. 'Well, brother, you got guts after all.' His gaze switched to Kathy and Carol. 'But you girls got more.'

'I was *poeping* myself,' Carol said. 'I still am.'

' *Masihambe* – let's get out of here before the *Amabulu* change their minds.' Sipho, his colour restored to its usual sepia, looked pointedly towards the verandah where the police were still in position. The four sashed women and Mr Seer remained facing the verandah, their heads bowed.

Elizabeth came up to us, accompanied by Gerry Fielding.

'I'm so glad you're all right,' she said. 'Our old Prep School head and the Black Sash contingent saved the day, don't you think?'

'It took a bit more than them,' Kathy said tartly. 'Elias for one.' She waved an encompassing arm. 'A whole lot of others, in fact.'

'I put it badly...' Elizabeth had gone pink. 'I do realise...'

'We'd better do some interviewing,' I cut in. My energy was beginning to return. 'Talk to Miss Robinson and Co. and I'll see you back at the paper.'

'I'll go with her,' Gerry said as she moved off. He smiled at us, lifting his camera. 'I thought you were gonners, man.'

'No pictures of me,' Carol protested. 'I'm enough in the *strond* as it is.'

Gerry laughed and clicked.

'Cold fish.' Kathy was glaring after Elizabeth.

'She was doing her job,' I said. 'And I'd better get on and do mine.'

Kathy hooked an arm round my neck and leant against me. 'I'm not going to quarrel with you today, *boetie*. See you at home.'

I tracked the departing crowd for a few minutes as it flowed, colourful and noisy, towards the township.

Where the tarmac ceased and the dirt road began, figures merged with the dust spewed up by passing vehicles. Someone began chanting, *Shosholoza*.

A hand closed round my wrist and I was looking into the bony face of Grobelaar.

'So, Brown, you've come out in your true colours, eh.' It was a statement not a question.

'I go where the news is.'

He smiled cynically. 'You took a big chance. You're lucky commandant Prinsloo is a soft man. I'd have ordered the men to shoot the lot of you – blacks, Indians, *Hotnots*, liberalists and all.'

I felt a sickening lurch in the pit of my stomach. 'I'm glad you weren't in charge then.'

'One day I will be. Then *pas op*.' He released my arm and walked away.

I'd made an enemy. But I'd worry about that tomorrow. I had a story to file.

I looked backed at the Police Station. The verandah was empty and the shutters were closed. The armoured car had gone. But as I began to walk there was a deafening metallic chattering above me and a shadow like that of some huge hovering bird fell across the street.

The helicopter descended slowly as if about to settle in the street where I stood. Then it lifted and chattered off towards the township.

Twenty-eight

When I got back to Songololo Street I found Kathy and Carol in the *rondavel*, sitting shoulder to shoulder on my bunk and listening intently to my radio.

Kathy was in her red cotton dressing gown, a towel twisted into a turban around her head. Carol wore my old gown, her wet hair loose. Cigarettes smouldered in the overflowing ashtray on the bedside table. Both were clutching bottles of Castle and there were opened bottles on the table. I picked one up and slumped down into the armchair opposite them.

'The police have fired into a crowd in a Transvaal location: Sharpeville near Vereeniging.' Kathy's face had a stripped look. 'Dozens of demonstrators have been killed.'

'I know,' I said. 'Reports were coming into the office all afternoon. Blacks have been shot dead in a nearby township as well. And there's big trouble in the Cape Town area.'

'They were unarmed. Shot like bucks on a hunt.' Kathy shivered. 'The police would have fired in Rhodes Street this morning if we hadn't been there. They wanted to. I could feel it.'

'Kepler as well,' Carol said. 'He'll want to know why I let you two drag me among a bunch of kaffirs and I've been too *bang* to face him just yet. That's why I'm here. Kathy lent me your gown. Hope you don't mind.'

'Of course he doesn't mind – it'll give him a cheap thrill,' Kathy said, clearly impatient to continue. 'The important thing is that blacks and whites acting together stopped a massacre. If only whites had joined that crowd at Sharpeville.'

'Grobelaar said to me afterwards that he would

have given the order to shoot the lot of us.' I put the neck of the bottle to my lips and took a deep swallow.

'He says that,' Kathy retorted, 'but would he have dared with whites there? *Satyagraha* is the way. Violence would only divide whites from blacks.'

I was too weary to argue with her, though Grobelaar's cold fury had left me convinced that he wouldn't have hesitated to give the order to fire. Adrenaline had carried me through the afternoon at the *News*. For two rushed intensive hours I'd worked with Elizabeth to blend our accounts of the Rhodes Street confrontation. We'd managed it in time in spite of frequent interruptions from a prowling, fidgety Grantley-Pearson, put on edge by the approaching deadline, the thick flow of news from all over the country, and, to add to his agitation, a police complaint about my 'unprofessional' behaviour. But now I felt drained, wanting only to relax.

The radio news had ended and military music was playing. I was conscious of the pair opposite me and, under their gowns, the inviting flesh, fresh-smelling from the shower. Kathy, familiar with my sly voyeurism, was well-buttoned up, but the thin cotton moulded her body provocatively. Carol, my gown loosely belted, lounged against a pillow showing a lot of thigh. When I stuck a cigarette in my mouth she leant forward clicking her lighter and the gown bulged open treating me to a generous view of her breasts. Energy began to flow back. Whatever had happened elsewhere, we'd achieved a triumph of sorts and I felt an urge to mark it somehow. More drink. Music. Dancing. Perhaps a little groping... perhaps more.

Then I remembered that Norman was coming in from the farm to take Kathy for a meal and to the bio afterwards.

'I wish you weren't going out with Norman tonight,' I said. 'We could have a *jol*.'

'It can't be helped, *boetie*.'

Carol's lips dragged down at the edges. 'My date is coming in all the way from Cradock to take me out.' She got up. 'I'd better be getting ready or it won't only be Kepler who wants to tan my arse.'

'Fuck all these farmers,' I moaned, assailed by a bitter passing thought of Rex and Jessica. 'Why can't they stay out on the range with their cattle and sheep instead of coming into town rounding up our women.'

'I'm really sorry, Simon.' Kathy was on her feet too. 'I was proud of you today.'

'I was shit-scared.'

'That makes you even braver,' she said.

'I wasn't going to let Ben March call me yellow.'

'I don't think that was your real reason,' Kathy said. 'I think you did it for me. Just like you came to Shantih's rescue at the library long ago. I love you, *boetie*.'

Stooping, she kissed me, then turned to Carol who was hovering and gripped her shoulders. 'You, too.'

'*Ag*, Kath,' Carol said, her hands going to Kathy's cheeks. 'I didn't really think. Just followed you. We did good, though, didn't we?'

Their lips met. On an impulse I couldn't define I stumbled upright and wrapped my arms around them. Wordless, we stood there.

'Kathy! Blackie! Are you there?' The bellowing from outside was accompanied by a thumping and, when we didn't reply, a rattling of the latch of the *rondavel* door.

Then the door burst open. Norman, in grey flannels, Harris tweed jacket and Victoria Old Boys tie, was on the step. I'd seen that bewildered stare before. It was how he'd looked years ago, emerging from a rugby scrum after having been head-butted.

'You're early, love.' Kathy broke away and, going over to him, dropped a kiss on his cheek. 'We were just having a bit of a natter about what happened today.'

'Have a beer, Norm.' One arm around Carol, I scooped up a bottle and held it out.

His gaze shifted from Kathy to Carol and me and then to the ashtray full of cigarette stubs. I could tell that he wasn't liking what he was seeing. 'You should cut out the fags, all of you,' he said sourly. 'You're panting like a bunch of old sheepdogs.'

'And you should cut down on the steak and potatoes – you're becoming a potguts,' I retorted.

Behind him the *rondavel* door rattled, then burst open. My mother, breathing stertorously, stood on the *rondavel* step with Sipho beside her.

'Thank God you're all right,' she said fervently. 'The Security Police have raided the Zondis' house in Vilakazi and arrested Elias. They also went to Joshua's place but the March boys were with Sipho at Rangisamy's.'

'I came to warn you that the Specials might come here,' Sipho said.

The military music emanating from the radio had stopped and the SABC newscaster was announcing that the total of deaths outside Sharpeville Police Station was now estimated at sixty-nine with one hundred and eighty injuries.

Sipho was looking at Kathy and me, his face sombre. He'd grown up alongside me, unconsidered and underrated. Now, his father and his cousin taken by the police, and in danger himself, he'd nonetheless thought of us.

'Thanks, Sipho,' I said. It was probably the first time I'd ever thanked him.

Norman shook his head. 'Mad,' he said. 'You're all mad.'

Twenty-nine

Commandant Prinsloo's complaints had been passed on to R.B. Alexander and I found myself standing in the centre of the chief's deep-piled carpet. Hair and eyebrows seeming an even purer white than usual against the angry red of his face, he harangued me from behind a massive oak desk, bare except for a picture of Mrs Alexander with their grandchildren in the garden of *The Aloes*.

'Your job is to cover the news, laddie, not become the news yourself,' he grated, his Scots accent so thick that I had trouble making out what he was saying. 'If you want to be a wee demagogue, for God's sake resign from my paper and go off and join a political party. Prinsloo is threatening to stop all future police co-operation with us.'

'I didn't mean to get involved,' I said, 'but my sister...'

He cut me short with a flap of a purple-veined hand. 'I know about all that from Grantley-Pearson,' he said. 'Very commendable, but this paper doesn't pay you to look after your sister. She's a big brave lassie from what I hear and she can look after herself. You must decide whether you want to be a Sir Galahad or work for me.'

The small blue eyes squinted at me from under the cotton-wool brows. For some reason the threat fired me up.

'I want to work for you,' I said, 'and maybe what I did was wrong. But I'd do it again.'

I waited for the verbal boot. Instead he got up and walked over to the window and stood looking down on the street before turning back into the room. 'Do you believe in God, Brown?' he asked.

That does it, I thought. Another fail mark. 'I'm afraid not, sir,' I said.

'Well I do, laddie, and I believe that we are all sinful beings who must try to atone for our sins by hard work and doing our duty to God and our fellow men. This is a black person's country and our only justification for being here is to act towards them in a Christian way. Africa is changing. Ghana and Guinea have independence and Nigeria and the Belgian Congo are on the way to it. Other countries will follow in the next twenty years. Meanwhile there is a struggle for the mind and soul of Africa between the Christian nations and the communists, and we white people of the West must mind what we do.'

He stopped. I waited, wondering where the lecture was leading. 'Peggy Illingworth phoned me last night to put in a good word for you,' he rumbled. 'She thought it very important that some young white people showed blacks that they are sympathetic. I had a call from George Gialerakis of the Athena Café, too. He thinks you stopped a local Sharpeville.'

Startled, I said nothing. Gialerakis had always been brusque with me.

R.B. went back behind his desk and sat down. 'All that may be, but my problem is that Prinsloo has issued orders that his subordinates are not to talk to you. We can challenge the decision, but we have no legal grounds. If you were in my chair what would you do about that, eh laddie?'

I'd been half-prepared for the police reprisal. Grobelaar had a hand in it, I was sure. 'Run a campaign?'

'No one would take any notice. You've put this paper in a very weak position, laddie.'

'I could try to explain myself to the commandant.'

'He doesn't want you within a mile of his Police Station.'

It was time to play the good colleague. 'Let Elizabeth take over police calls.'

I'd surprised him. The thick eyebrows wriggled. 'Elizabeth? You think she can deal with those Dutchmen?'

'Yes, sir.'

He eyed me unsmilingly, then nodded. 'All right. I'll have a word with Grantley-Pearson about it. You can go.'

Elizabeth, looking unusually flushed, came out of R.B. Alexander's office and walked over to where I was standing reading at the table. 'Apparently I've you to thank for me being given police and courts,' she said.

'I'm right out of favour and you'll do the job well.'

'I feel really small, Simon. I haven't been very nice to you and you're being utterly generous. A lot of people wouldn't have been.'

I wanted to say, 'You know why.' But the memory of my angry declaration weeks before stopped me. Instead I said, 'I was getting bored with that beat anyway.'

She shook her head. 'You can say that, but I know otherwise.' She hesitated, uncharacteristically unsure. 'I hope I can repay you one day.' She held out a hand. 'Meanwhile, thanks.'

I took her hand. I wished that I dared to try for a kiss. 'A pleasure,' I said.

Word was getting around. Mrs Langley, from down the street, had it from someone in the Rhodes Street bakery that I'd addressed the crowd. Mr and Mrs Simpson from further down thought that I'd been arrested. Mr Lategan came to the front door demanding to talk to Kathy and me about the error of our ways – and got an angry earful from my mother. Later, Carol slipped round to say the men had tried to get her to promise to have nothing to do with us. Kepler left word that he'd be seeing me.

Streets nearby had heard reports, too. Cycling to work across Pretorius Street, I was treated to a few shouts of *kafferboetie* from a trio of ten-year-olds who looked like a younger crop of Viljoens. Sarel Viljoen, now a postman and on his walk, looked as if he would like to say something ugly, but ended by sliding past me with a smirk. Mr Oldcastle, processing with his officials up the staircase to the council chamber, stopped long enough to advise me loudly to stay away from troublemakers like Modisi and Zondi and to warn Kathy to do the same.

'It's all right for bleeding hearts like Peggy Illingworth and Georgina Robinson to play with fire,' he bugled. 'They're rich and can afford it. But you've got your way to make, boy.'

The most common sign of disapproval was avoidance. Among those who seemed not to see me in Victoria High Street were the parents of some of my erstwhile classmates and a number of townspeople who in the past had been willing enough to greet me and even chat. There was nothing blatant, which made it harder to cope with because I couldn't be certain I wasn't mistaken.

Clive's reaction hurt. He came forward when I entered the bookshop a few days after the events at the Police Station, but slowly, as if reluctant. He talked about the new books but didn't invite me downstairs for coffee as usual. He pasted on a smile when Aaron Landau appeared with a bound copy of Thoreau's

Walden, which he pressed into my hands, murmuring that Kathy and I might find the thoughts on civil disobedience interesting. But by the time the old proprietor had returned to his office, Clive was on a ladder busying himself with volumes on a high shelf. My old rugby coach, Hacksaw Markham, walked past me in Station Road, as if drawn on by a seeing-eye dog.

Aunt Betty led the attack from within the family. She'd seen a copy of *Die Oosterlig*, a Nationalist newspaper, at the hairdresser's. Kathy, Carol and I featured in a centre-page picture spread devoted to unrest in the region. Unable to read the Afrikaans caption, Aunt Betty had persuaded the hairdresser to translate. It was futile for my mother to protest that we'd played no part in organising the campaign. Living on the farm, Betty had learnt beyond any contradicting that Natives hadn't the intelligence to make trouble unless put up to it by someone from a cleverer race. She'd seen with her own eyes how I kept company with so-called educated blacks – everyone knew the educated ones were the worst – and had actually let a little coolie girl kiss me right in Victoria High Street. My mother hadn't taught us to be proud of our white skins and the result was shame for my father and the family in general. Only Betty's family loyalty prevented her from taking Wilf's advice and having nothing to do with us in future.

Kathy was juggling drop scones on the griddle. 'What did you say, Mom?' she asked.

'I said I was proud of you two and she could stick her family loyalty up her bum – or up Wilf's, if she liked that better.' She grinned through her cigarette smoke. 'She hung up on me. She'll ring your dad at work and they'll agree I'm ruining you both.'

Memories of my father's anger at the time of the Defiance Campaign ran through my head like an old film, and I waited anxiously for his response. But, apart from the remark, to no one in particular, that he expected the horseshoe over the front door to be replaced by a hammer and a sickle soon, he said nothing. He was looking drawn and ill again and I surmised he had little energy for domestic confrontations.

I'd expected Norman to have some sharp words to offer about Kathy's involvement but it turned out that the Robertses – Smuts supporters from way back – thought she'd shown the kind of courage a farmer would want in a wife. What shocked Norman – almost to the point of breaking off with Kathy – was finding her and Carol in my *rondavel* in nothing but dressing gowns, and apparently quite happy to be seen by any man who chanced by, including Sipho.

'He may be just a servant's boy to you,' he'd chided Kathy, 'but he's a man, too, and he's got sexual feelings just like anyone else. No white woman should ever be careless in front of a Xhosa male. If you don't respect yourself, he won't respect you.'

I expected Jacky Hughes to cut me and he did. I expected Harry Lewis to cut me and he didn't, bounding across Victoria High Street to punch my arm. 'You've got this strait-laced *dorp* sitting up and taking notice, Blackie,' he chaffed. 'According to my old man only the no politics rule saved your editor a roasting at the Victoria Club. And getting Carol involved, too! A *Boeremeisie* defying her own people!' He laughed. 'I'd steer clear of Kepler for a bit.'

I was somewhat lifted by breezy cards from Sam Glass and Sarah Bentley and a congratulatory letter from Julian Richards. Writing from Durban, Shantih enclosed a feature from the *Nataller* similar to *The Oosterlig's*; she'd scrawled over it *Songololo Street Squad Saves The Day*.

As I did my rounds I sensed a small but definite change in the attitudes of some of the blacks who worked in the centre of town. Service from the waitresses in the Athena Café was noticeably better. The petrol pump attendants who worked with Elias at Illingworth's garage hailed me now as I cycled past, and I found myself greeted in the street by messengers, deliverymen and other previously unnoticed workers. At the *News* – because, I suspected, of Joshua's gossiping – two previously surly women cleaners now looked up from their scrubbing with an effusive *Molo Nkosi*, and Shadrach, who came round with the tea trolley had taken to bringing a cup to me first.

Joshua was like someone on amphetamines. Disappointed at missing the business at the Police Station because his driver's duties had taken him out of town, he compensated by becoming hyperactive on his return. He arrived at the house with a bottle of KWV brandy for me and enormous bouquets – bought, we learnt later, from a mystified Violet Lategan – for Kathy and Carol. It was with difficulty that my mother persuaded him not to deliver Carol's flowers in person. Next, he set about getting the BBC on an old Phillips radio he'd installed in his kiosk in the *News* basement garage and spent much of his time commuting between it and the editorial floor with scraps of information about the anti-pass campaign and the world's appalled response to the Sharpeville shootings, adding comments of his own for good measure. Though clearly irritated by this behaviour, Grantley-Pearson tolerated it, perhaps because of Joshua's special status.

What Grantley-Pearson didn't know was that Joshua was running a local information-gathering system from his 'office' down in the garage. His links included the Zondis, Silas Mkize and Caleb Mdonga and also some Xhosa labourers who he claimed were relatives on the African side. Once a highly nervous black policeman appeared, accompanied by the plump Maisie Matsomela. From him we learnt that Elias and Thabo Modisi and others in the Rhodes Street police cells were not being maltreated. This was apparently thanks to strict instructions from Commandant Prinsloo who was rumoured to be unpopular with government ministers as a result. In the course of a few days I was able to assemble a picture of a heavily armed police presence patrolling a sullenly quiet township, though there was muffled talk of a top ANC man coming from Johannesburg or Port Elizabeth to reorganise Vilakazi along the lines of a new plan devised by Nelson Mandela, heir apparent to the ANC leadership.

Sipho, I learnt from Joshua, was moving about visiting his father's ANC contacts and trying to negotiate a common front with PAC militants, while Ben and Seth were attempting to convince sceptical Coloureds in Kokville that their long-term future depended on forming an alliance with blacks.

They also called on me one evening. Ben didn't say much, but was noticeably warmer. Seth was full of the need to campaign. 'I'm giving studies a rest for a while. Action is the thing.'

He wouldn't accept that I rejected involvement. 'Your head is saying one thing and your heart another,' he said. 'You may try to sit on the fence but every time there's trouble you jump off it and take sides. Because you're one of us.'

'No,' I said. 'I'm not. What's more I want to keep my job and that means staying on the fence.'

'We'll see,' he said.

Thirty

The ragged row of overflowing rubbish bins in the lane testified that the ANC's strike call – a day to mourn the dead demonstrators – was being heeded in Victoria. Usually, some time before breakfast, a lorry driven by a white man cruised down the lane without stopping, while ceaselessly jogging black men, their heads and upper bodies crudely protected from the dust and filth by hessian sacks, grabbed up the bins and tipped their contents into the back. I'd often been jolted awake by the rumbling of the lorries and the shouts of the men. Today the silence was eerie.

Later, cycling to work, I noted that there were no blacks sweeping the pavement in front of the market, no delivery men on their powerfully geared cycles, no green uniformed men on duty at the petrol pumps of Illingworth's garage, no peak-capped doorman at Barclays Bank.

Though Grobelaar insisted to a disbelieving Elizabeth that the response to the strike call was negligible, my phone calls to shopkeepers and other employers confirmed first impressions that it was widely supported.

Press Association and radio reports reflected an eighty-five to ninety per cent response to the strike call in areas like Cape Town, Johannesburg, Port Elizabeth and East London, but weaker support elsewhere. Meanwhile in the House of Assembly, the Minister of Justice was putting through a bill to ban any organisation which 'threatened the safety of the public or the maintenance of public order', and to jail anyone who tried to promote its aims. The Minister also promised to 'increase tenfold' the penalties for encouraging or intimidating workers into strike action.

The government had decided, he explained, to stop the cowardly 'terrorists', white and non-white, who were agitating behind the scenes.

I was listening to Ella Fitzgerald's version of *Mac the Knife* when Kathy walked in followed by Sipho and Thandi. Kathy went off in search of drinks and Sipho took the armchair. Thandi sat down at the foot of the bunk. She was wearing an old cotton dress with an ugly floral pattern and her hair had been trimmed almost to her skull. There was an inept dash of lipstick on her mouth. Nonetheless there was a gawky grace about her.

Sipho came quickly to the point. 'They're going to use this new bill to ban the ANC and the PAC,' he said. 'They're out to smash the struggle organisations and there will be arrests. When that happens you will get a phone call from a woman called Joyce.'

'Joyce the Voice? It's very cloak and dagger.'

'It's necessary.'

Kathy returned carrying a tray with opened bottles of lager and a couple of lemonades. She handed Sipho a lager then stopped in front of Thandi, who hesitated fractionally before taking a lager, which she began to drink eagerly.

'How is Elias?' Kathy asked Sipho.

'All right. Thabo also. And ANC and PAC people are getting on well. Prinsloo says they will be able to see lawyers soon. But it is really Grobelaar and the Special Branch who are in control.'

'What were you playing when we came in?' Thandi said to me.

'Ella Fitzgerald singing *Mac the Knife*.'

'I like her,' Thandi said. 'I like *Dancing Cheek to Cheek* with Louis Armstrong, and *A Foggy Day in*

London Town and *Too Darn Hot*. I like Eartha Kitt, too.'

'*Tula 'ntombi*,' Sipho said. 'We're talking serious things here.'

Thandi began to sing softly, 'I wanna be evil, I wanna be bad.'

'You are bad.' His tone was mild, but there was a hint of irritation. 'Look at her,' he said to Kathy. 'Lipstick. Short skirts.'

'Why not?' Kathy said. 'She's got nice legs and she wants to show them.'

'She smokes. She runs after boys – even men.' He shook his head at Thandi in mock menace. 'You'll end up like Sibongile if you're not careful.'

'Sipho, you're a prude,' Kathy laughed. 'You talk about equality and freedom, but only as long as it applies to men.'

'That's not true,' he retorted. 'I am for all rights for women, but not these silly clothes and making up. Dignity. Women should have dignity.'

'But also the right to have fun, Sipho. To be silly if we want to. Men are always telling us how we should behave. Leave women's behaviour to women and we might surprise you.'

He looked at her soberly. 'Lots of young African women are being tempted these days. I don't want Thandi to become a whore.'

'She won't. But if you want to stop prostitution, first change men.' She smiled at Thandi. 'You aren't going to become a prostitute, are you, Thandi?'

Thandi laughed. 'Yes I am. Like Bongi. Lots of money.'

'You're talking nonsense, Thandeka,' Sipho said. 'It's the beer.' He reached over and took the bottle from her, setting it down beside his half-finished drink on the bedside table. 'Come, we've got a few people to see.' He got up. ' *Salani kahle* – stay well.'

Thandi got up too. 'Will you lend me your record, *u*Simon?' She was smiling the cheeky smile of the happily tipsy. Kathy and Sipho were looking at me.

'My pleasure,' I lied. 'Take it now.' Sliding it into the sleeve I handed it to her with a flourish.

'Good for you, *boetie*.' Kathy tweaked my cheek and went out of the door with the pair. I lit a sour-tasting cigarette. I was going soft. Once I'd only wanted to please a few useful whites. Now I seemed to want to to please everybody.

The next evening Harry Lewis caught me leaving the *News* and steered me along High Street to the residents' bar of the Hotel Victoria.

'Have you heard?' he chuckled as we settled onto high stools at the bar counter. 'Kepler Lategan has been seconded to the Special Branch, presumably for heroically holding the megaphone during that business at the Police Station. It can't be for his intelligence. Anyway, I've invited him for a drink.'

'Good one,' I said heavily. Harry must have guessed that I'd be wanting to avoid Kepler, but it was in his character to enjoy stirring the pot. Grey-suited, his thick dark hair newly trimmed and his boyish face so evenly tanned as to suggest a sunlamp rather than the sun, he exuded health and mischief. I listened while he speculated on Kepler's rise from the uniformed ranks.

'Perhaps he's been lined up specially to watch you Browns,' he joked. 'Peeping through hedges would be about his mark.'

'He's not as stupid as you think,' I countered, 'and he's a loyal Nationalist.'

'Idiots,' Harry snorted. 'Apartheid is going to wreck this country. What we need is enlightened capitalism and an incorporated black middle class. We should be buying in types like Sobukwe and Mandela, not turning them into revolutionaries.'

'You can tell Kepler that now.' Kepler, hulking in sports coat, tie and flannels, had entered through the street door, followed by Jacky Hughes, red faced and square in his blue jacket and grey flannels. In ten years he would be a replica of his father.

Scowling, Kepler came directly to where I stood.

'You fooled me for a long time, Blackie,' he said gruffly. 'But you're just as much a *kaffer*-lover as that mad sister of yours.'

'It wasn't the way you think it was,' I said. 'Ask Carol.'

His face filled with blood. 'Carol's simple and you two have been twisting her mind.'

'Nobody twisted anybody's mind. Doesn't it occur to you that we may have saved lives?'

' *Kaffer* lives?' His lip curled. 'You could have got Carol killed.'

'Well, we didn't.'

'Know what I think?' Jacky was waving a finger at me. 'I think the police should shoot every Native who can't produce a pass, because that Native is either an agitator or been got at by commies.' He grinned nastily. 'All these liberals here and overseas who are saying how upset they are by the Sharpeville shootings get on my wick. I'm upset, too. The police didn't kill enough bloody Natives for me.'

I knew I should let it go. Jacky was merely voicing what most whites thought. But in some way that I had yet to analyse I wasn't finding the old attitudes so comfortable any more.

'Perhaps you should complain to Commandant Prinsloo, Jacky,' I said. 'His force got through the day without shooting anyone and as far as I know they haven't shot anyone yet. Perhaps you should get Kepler to introduce you to his new boss, Mr Grobelaar, who thinks the way you do? Or perhaps you should get yourself a gun and go on a shoot yourself. To make it more fun you could arm the blacks so they could shoot back. Starting with the blacks on your dad's favourite housing scheme.'

Jacky took a step towards me, his head dancing on his neck, his fists clenching. 'Leave my dad out of it.'

'That's bad talk, *jong*.' Kepler growled. 'Treason talk.'

'He's right, Blackie,' Harry said lightly. 'That's going a bit far.'

'Jacky passed an opinion, uninvited,' I replied. 'I was only passing one back.' I looked at the three faces. Harry's showed amusement, but Jacky's bulged with rage and Kepler's was stiff, ominous. We might have been schoolmates once but now hatred and violence were in the air.

I drained my glass and put it carefully down on the counter. I wasn't afraid of Jacky, but I didn't want to take on Kepler. Anyway, I was in more than enough trouble. 'I came in for a beer,' I said as I headed for the door, 'not a pro-government broadcast.'

'Try the Coloured's bar,' Jacky called after me.

Thirty-one

Kathy was leaning over me in the early morning murk, shaking my shoulder.

'A woman on the phone for you,' she said, 'an African woman.'

Muzzy and irritable, I disentangled myself from my bedclothes and followed Kathy's floating nightdress across the yard and into the house. The kitchen clock read five-twenty. 'This is Joyce,' said a low voice when I picked up the receiver. 'The police took many of our comrades at three o'clock this morning.'

She recited names slowly, patiently repeating the difficult ones and sometimes spelling them. Kathy, leaning over my shoulder as I wrote, drew in her breath sharply when the woman said, 'Comrade Sipho also.'

I found Grantley-Pearson already in his office, his desk covered with messages from Sapa, Reuter and other press agencies. 'This is the big one, Brown,' he said. 'The government has declared a State of Emergency. There have been pre-dawn raids and detentions all over the country.'

'Including here,' I said, producing my list.

He squinted at me. 'How come?'

'An anonymous caller.'

He grunted and scanned the list then picked up a cablegram from his desk and stabbed the stem of his pipe at a name. 'Wasn't this chap at Victoria Boys' High?'

'Sam Glass?' Shaken, I stared at the name. 'We're sort of friends.'

'Well, I hope you're not sort of political colleagues,' he said. 'We need you here at the moment. Will you go to see his family?'

Instead of going straight back to the paper, after talking to a bewildered Mr Glass and his tearful wife I slipped into the Athena Café for a coffee.

Someone was standing looking down at me: Grobelaar, cadaverous as ever. 'Well, was Mr Glass pleased that we've stopped his son from getting into more trouble?'

'What trouble is he supposed to have been getting into?'

'I think you know,' he said. 'You're his friend, aren't you? His friend and comrade.'

'Are you going to charge him?'

'That's for Johannesburg to decide. Just wait and see.'

'What about all those you've picked up here?'

'You'll have to wait to find out about them, too.'

'Whatever people have done, pulling them out of bed at three in the morning seems like Gestapo stuff to me.'

His thin face mottled with anger. 'Certain measures are necessary for the security of our country. Some people are trying to make a revolution and one of them may be your friend Glass.'

He bent over the table, lowering his voice. 'You would be inside, too, if the commandant hadn't decided that you and your sister didn't set out to get involved in that foolishness down the street. But we're watching you, Brown. We've got eyes everywhere.'

Back at the office, I found Elizabeth talking intensely on the phone. 'Yes,' she was saying, 'yes, I know – but here's Simon now.' She held out the receiver: 'It's Jessica.'

'I just had to talk to you.' Jessica's voice was just audible on a crackling line. 'I've had a letter from Mum, saying that you were in trouble for demonstrating with a lot of Natives outside the Victoria Police Station.'

'It wasn't like that at all. Your mother got a distorted version of what happened. Some of us just got drawn into a sort of stand-off with the police. An accident really.'

'Rex says you were always getting into scrapes – and out again. But I was worried.'

'Rex? Have you been seeing more of Rex?' I could hear the jealous rasp in my voice.

'That was sort of an accident, too,' she said quickly. 'There's been Native trouble here as well. Cape Town was practically taken over by them for a while. First the city was empty – nothing happening at the docks, no deliveries of bread or milk or newspapers or anything. Then the centre of the city was swarming with Natives. Black women outside the Houses of Parliament, dancing and shouting and screaming until they were threatened with a baton charge. And an enormous march from the townships right into the city centre – they estimate about thirty thousand. Led by a schoolboy called Kgosana or something. We watched part of the march from the top floor of an office block. I was glad I was with Rex and some male students.'

'So how did Rex get into the act?' The rasp ruined my attempt to sound casual.

'I don't know exactly. He belongs to some rifle club and they were notified or got wind of it somehow and he got worried about us at the university and came to check we were okay. The marchers dispersed without trouble but Rex has heard since that the police had to use tear gas bombs on a lot of women in Langa Location who surrounded the Police Station there and wouldn't go away. Some even lifted their skirts and peed when the police tried to reason with them. I don't think I want to go on living in South Africa much longer, Simon. I don't want anything to do with all this trouble between the Natives and the government. Rex says it will never come to anything. The government just has to call in every white man who can handle a gun and that'll be the end of it. But I'd rather be somewhere you can live a normal life. Perhaps we should both just up sticks, marry and clear right out to some really civilised country. England or the United States or even Australia?'

Marry! I had the sensation of hurtling downhill on my cycle without brakes. I wanted Jessica, but not marriage, not yet. *England* ? It had always seemed a place to visit some day rather than a place to live in. Plenty of history, but grey skies delivering damp and cold most of the year. And I was chilled by the idea of an ocean between Kathy and me. 'Australia maybe,' I said. 'But we don't want to rush things, do we?'

'We must talk about it all when I'm home for Vac,' she said. 'And we absolutely must also go to the mid-year ball at the Hotel Vic. Celia and Harry will be going and Melanie and Clive will be playing. Now I must fly. Love you.'

'Love *you*,' I said as she hung up.

Elizabeth waited till I'd lit a cigarette then, sensing her gaze, stubbed it out. 'Jessica said a bit to me about leaving the country. What do you think?'

'What do you?' I fenced.

'I don't know. I'm finding what I'm doing much more interesting than I thought it would be. But that's what Jim wants after he's finished at university.'

Jim! Rex! It was evil to ill-wish decent enough men. But I did.

When I got home the others had eaten supper. Mine

was in the oven and my mother was sitting at the kitchen table listening to an SABC newsreader describing in outraged tones how crowds of blacks in cities and towns, including Bloemfontein, the stronghold of *ware Afrikanerdom*, were making bonfires of their passbooks and cheering and singing as the flames consumed them. Others had tried to hold meetings in their townships, and only police intervention had prevented attempts to burn government offices and firebomb a church.

Thandi was at the table, listening too, an exercise book and the Junior Certificate mathematics setwork propped open in front of her.

'Just in time, son,' my mother said. 'This stuff is way above my head. I've given Florence a day or two off so she can see about Sipho, but she thought Thandi ought to stay here till things get back to normal in Vilakazi. So she's catching up on a bit of overdue homework.'

The geometry wasn't difficult. The difficulty was Thandi. She was twitchy, shifting about on her stool and looking vague as I tried to explain the working of a theorem, nodding when she clearly hadn't grasped a point. 'It's no good,' I said after twenty minutes. 'We're not getting anywhere.'

She looked at me miserably. 'I must do it.'

'We can try later,' I said without much conviction.

'You both need a break.' My mother was busy at the ironing board. 'You eat, Simon, and let Thandi go and listen to records in the *rondavel* meanwhile.'

'All right,' I said grudgingly. I didn't much like the idea of letting her loose on my small collection, but she'd returned the Ella Fitzgerald record undamaged.

'Poor kid,' my mother said after Thandi had left us. 'She's trying very hard to be brave, but she's terrified that Florence will be taken next. Be nice to her, eh?'

Thandi was sitting on my bunk, flipping through an old copy of *Esquire* she'd dredged up from under it. A *kwela* record was playing which she must have fetched from the *khaya*.

Not sure what to do or say next I sat down on the edge of the bunk and lit a cigarette. She got up and went over to the player and the strains of the *Tennessee Waltz* began to fill the *rondavel*. So she remembered!

Leaving the player she came and stood in front of me, holding out her hands.

'Dance with me,' she said.

I hesitated. She was no longer a kid, and she was still black. And there were memories of unsettling moments. Did she remember those too?

'Please, *u*Simon,' she said. 'You owe me.'

I didn't want tears or tantrums and who was to know? 'Just for a bit,' I said, stubbing out my cigarette and standing up.

I'd always liked dancing and the girl could dance. Right hand, lightly clasping my left, her left hand on my shoulder, her body not quite touching mine, she matched steps as if we'd danced together before. I tried a whisk, carefully in the limited space. She followed with only the slightest initial faltering, then increasing competence. She didn't speak. Her gaze stayed fixed on a spot somewhere past my shoulder.

What was she thinking, dancing with a white? It came to me as we wheeled about that she smelled of the same soap that we had in the bathroom, not the cheaper soap normally used by servants for washing themselves as well as clothing. That would be my mother's doing.

'You dance well.' Though it was true, I spoke to break the silence.

'You too.'

The record ended. Another clicked on. She kept hold of my hand and started to twirl to Armstrong's gusty rendering of *When the Saints Go Marching In*, her skirt foaming above her thighs. *Just think of her as any dancing partner*, I told myself.

Easier thought than done. Her height nearly equalled my five foot eleven inches and under the school-type shirt the unbrassiered breasts were distractingly palpable as record followed record and foxtrot replaced waltz, giving way in turn to the clinch, spin, break and clinch of the *kwela*. 'Happy, happy Afrika,' belted the singer over the wistful cadences of a penny whistle, and suddenly I *was* happy, all that had been troubling me dissolved by the music, the movement, the brush of flesh.

When the *kwela* number ended she put on the Billy Eckstein version of *Autumn Leaves* and, with a quick glance at me, marched over to the door and clicked off the overhead light, leaving only the bedside light on. 'Nightclub style now,' she said calmly as if it were pre-agreed.

Be nice to her, my mother had said, but I doubted that her definition of niceness included dancing *binneboud* with the maid's schoolgirl daughter in the half dark. Not that what my mother thought was my main preoccupation at the moment.

'No, Thandi. Definitely not nightclub style.' I said it firmly, but I was conscious of a warmth in my groin. 'Now how about switching that light back on?'

'Just one dance,' she said, not moving from beside the switch.

'One dance.' She was going through a hard time and it was surely only common kindness to indulge her a little.

But one dance became three, with *Night and Day* succeeding *Autumn Leaves* and *Tenderly* following that and by the time it whispered to an end my hands were clasping her buttocks and she was riding the hard bulge at my crutch, her arms wrapped round me, her mouth only inches from mine, dark lipped and dangerously inviting.

With an effort I lifted my hands and stepped back from her. 'That's it.'

'One more,' she said breathily, holding up a finger.

'No,' I said, turning away from her in a clumsy attempt to hide the bulge. 'It's late and you've got school tomorrow.'

'Only one,' she persisted.

'No.' I went for lightness. 'It's chuck-out time at the nightclub.'

'Then I stay.' Looking mutinous, she sat down on the bunk.

'No you don't,' I said. 'It's been nice dancing with you. But it's time to stop. I need sleep and so do you.'

'I can sleep here with you.'

'What?' She'd said it so matter-of-factly that I thought at first I'd misunderstood her. Then it registered and the *rondavel* was suddenly smaller and hotter.

'I can sleep with you,' she repeated. She was sitting very still, looking up at me, her eyes large and shining.

'No you can't.' Panic roughened my voice. 'It's

236

out of the question.'

'You want to sleep with me.'

'No.'

'You lie,' she said. 'I felt your stick hard, that time in the car, and now again.'

'That's just a man thing. You're too young, Thandi.'

Her chin lifted. 'I'm not too young. I'm sixteen. I've done it with men. Lots of men.'

Was any of it the truth? I seriously doubted it. I tried another tack. 'Listen,' I said, 'you're black and I'm white and we'd be breaking the law. What do you think your parents would do? And Sipho? They trust me to look after you when they're not here.'

She pulled a face. 'The laws are rubbish,' she said. 'My father and my brother said so. That's why they're in jail.'

'Not for that law. If we were caught we'd go to jail. I don't want that and nor do you.'

'That old white man who goes with Sibongile wanted to give me money to sleep with him. He wasn't afraid.'

Her hurt and anger had the effect of making her look younger than her professed sixteen.

'That doesn't make it right,' I said. 'I can't be your boyfriend, Thandi. One day you'll meet a nice man of your own race and want to marry him.'

I stopped, revolted by my own phoniness, then blundered on. 'It can't be, Thandi.'

Not looking at me she got up and went over to the record player and began to sift through the records. I searched for something more to say and couldn't find it. She was proud and I hadn't expected pride. I hadn't really thought about her feelings at all.

'Borrow any record you like,' I said lamely. 'And

as many as you like.'

'I'm going now,' she said. She had taken three records and was holding them to her chest. 'You think I am too young and too stupid for you and I would make trouble for you,' she said. 'But I would never make trouble for you. I think you are just a coward.'

I put out a hand to her, but she brushed past me. I let her go then lit a cigarette and slumped onto the bunk. I should have been proud of my nobility and racial fastidiousness. The old me would have been. But somewhere I'd lost the old me.

Thirty-two

Elizabeth held up a cablegram. 'The government has just banned *The African People's Voice*.'

'That's bad.' I'd developed a grudging affection for *The Voice* and the annoyance it caused Grantley-Pearson.

'That's not all. Commandant Prinsloo has been transferred and replaced by a man named Martins. Grobelaar is pleased. He and Martins joined the force together or something like that.'

'He would be pleased. He thought Prinsloo too soft.'

'They've won, haven't they?' she said. 'The government, I mean.'

'Looks like it.' It did. Rebellions in rural Pondoland and the Transvaal continued to smoulder, flaring like bush fires now and then, but the banning of the ANC and the PAC and the widespread detentions of militants had checked protest activities in the townships. A thrill of horror and joy had swept through the nation when a white man shot Verwoerd in the head at point blank range at the Rand Easter Show. But Verwoerd was recovering and was being pronounced miraculous, even Christ-like, by his followers. Every Saturday groups of women led by Mrs Illingworth and Mrs Rangisamy, and often including Kathy, Miss Robinson and sometimes my mother, stood in Victoria High Street with placards calling for an end to the Emergency and detentions while Grobelaar and his fellow Special Branch men prowled up and down taking notes. But the Emergency continued.

'All those deaths at Sharpeville seem to have been for nothing,' Elizabeth said. 'If anything Africans seem worse off.'

Joshua, typically, remained optimistic. 'The people are reorganising. The struggle will continue.'

As April yielded to May and May crept into wintry June I became aware of a nagging depression. Letters from Jessica were few and short, though affectionate. She had decided, she said, not to abandon her studies just yet and apologised for not being able to get to Victoria before the end of the year because of a student trip and pressure of studies. This meant missing the mid-year ball but, she pointed out cheerfully, there was another in December.

She didn't mention Rex. I tried to take some consolation from that.

Five months in detention had left Sipho looking gaunter and older, yet more plausibly Thandi's brother. Facing him as he sat beside her on my bunk in the *rondavel* I was able to study the likeness. His head was bigger than Thandi's, his nose more flared, his eyes less dramatically large, but the high cheekbones, the supple mouth and well-shaped chin were similar. Detention had clearly matured him. In spite of myself, I was impressed.

'It wasn't too good inside,' he said, cradling the cup of coffee my mother had made for him. 'The first night they put about thirty of us in a small yard with no roof and only two weak lights. There were no chairs so we had to stand or squat because someone had hosed down the yard and it was wet. You'll remember that night was quite cold. Man, we shivered. Early in the morning we were put into a stinking cell. No food, no water, no blankets, no lavatory or even a sanitary pot. Only a little hole.'

He sipped his coffee. 'We shouted and banged and eventually a sergeant came, Koekemoer. He made lots of threats and went away. A lieutenant came later, then Prinsloo. Thabo spoke to him, and about two in the afternoon we got dixies of samp. Yes, samp, but we were so hungry we scooped it up with our hands. Later we got blankets which smelled of shit and piss and vomit – awful, awful. But we appointed a committee to negotiate and things got better, particularly once the PAC guys started appearing in court and could speak to their lawyers. We were moved to the prison near the Songololo – from my cell window, if I stood on a comrade's shoulders, I could actually see the bit of the river where we used to swing out on ropes, remember?'

'Of course I do.' I was feeling a prickling behind my eyes. I glanced at Thandi. Her eyes were on his face, rapt.

'How is Elias?' I asked.

'He's fine, though his stomach is still bad from the food he got when they transferred him to Johannesburg. While he was here, he was quite well treated. Nobody in Victoria prison was assaulted, not like in Johannesburg and Cape Town. Prinsloo even came to see him to ask if he was all right.'

'You know that Prinsloo is being transferred?'

'Yes. Grobelaar's work. I tell you, Simon, that man is bad. He wants to hurt, even kill. He tried to get Elias charged, but he was overruled. He told me that he was sorry the State of Emergency was being lifted and the next time the people try to take on the government they'll be ready for us and we'll drink our own blood and eat our own shit.'

He put his cup down on the bedside table. 'The leadership is still talking of negotiation and passive resistance – a national strike if talking fails. But the younger comrades are losing patience. *They* are talking of going the Cuban way.'

In spite of my scepticism I felt a twitch of my nerves: like the sensation before a rugby game or at the prospect of sex.

'The government would win.'

'A conventional war – yes. But not a guerilla war – a people's war.' He got up. 'Let us talk of this another time. Elias sends greetings and we all want to thank you for being nice to Thandi while Elias and I were inside.'

'I'm not sure I was so nice.' Thandi hadn't looked at me once since they'd arrived.

'She says you were.'

She looked at me now. '*Ewe*. You were.'

But didn't smile.

Thirty-three

Thandi was the last person I'd have expected to see outside the Hotel Vic.

But there she was with a stocky, older black woman, smoking a cigarette and leaning against the wall near the side entrance where Melanie had just dropped Jessica and me.

For a bizarre, unnerving moment, I almost believed that they, like us, were attending the end-of-year reunion dance. Colour aside, they looked the part or, more accurately, like a pair got up to *jol*: Thandi in a yellow dress which barely reached her thighs, and high heels which threatened to pitch her onto her face, and her companion in an audaciously low-cut scarlet number under a shiny black coat. Both were heavily made up and sported dangling earrings which danced and glittered under the alley lamp. Thandi wore a flame-coloured lipstick and a gaudy glass necklace. A child, I thought, masquerading as a grown-up: lamb dressed as mutton.

She was as surprised to see me as I was to see her and possibly as little pleased, but recovered quickly. 'Hello, Simon,' she said. '*Unjane?*'

'What are you doing here?' I snapped.

'Just visiting.' She waved a hand towards the rear of the hotel. 'And you?'

'There's a dance,' I said, adding abruptly, 'Does Florence know you're here?'

'She's all right,' the other woman said confidently. 'She's with me.' On closer inspection she wasn't as old as she'd first appeared. I estimated early twenties.

'I'm her aunt,' she added. 'I look after her.'

'I hope so,' I said. 'She's only an *ntombi*.'

'I'm sixteen,' Thandi scowled. 'I told you that

243

when I was with you in your room that time.'

I went hot. What was Jessica making of this dialogue? 'I didn't believe you then,' I said, 'and I don't believe you now. Anyway, you're still too young to be hanging around here.'

'My aunt will look after me.'

The unlikely aunt had been examining Jessica and me boldly. 'If you don't like your dance, come and dance with us,' she said. 'Can you *kwela*, Mister Simon?'

'*Tula*, Bongi,' Thandi said sharply. Her gaze rested momentarily on Jessica, taking in the blue satin ankle-length dress. 'Your girlfriend is very pretty,' she said to me.

'Who...?' Jessica began, but I'd had enough of the encounter and, hissing '*Pas op*' at Thandi, I grasped Jessica's arm and drew her up the steps.

On the way to the ballroom I explained awkwardly who Thandi was.

'Quite the little black madam,' Jessica commented, 'and her aunt was awful – inviting you to dance like that, even as a joke. Of course, there are quite a few students at UCT who mix with non-whites. Rex thinks they're lunatics who don't know the first thing about Natives and can't even speak Xhosa, so how can they understand them?'

I nodded, steering her towards the table where Harry and Celia were sitting, tall drinks in front of them. Her words bothered me. It wasn't that I distrusted her, but there'd been several references to Rex in the course of the afternoon I'd spent with her in Melanie's pink playroom, a meeting place she'd chosen rather than the *rondavel* or Asquith Street.

For her part, Jessica seemed unable to understand why I wouldn't throw up my job on the

News immediately and move to Cape Town.

'I want to make a complete break from Victoria,' she'd said when Melanie had tactfully left us alone. 'And you don't want to end up here like Clive, dripping with talent, but drying up slowly because he's too afraid to leave the nest.'

That cut. I'd never been to any of the major cities. Cape Town, Durban and Johannesburg loomed, exciting and attractive, but also intimidating.

'I'm not afraid,' I said roughly. 'I just need time to work things out here.'

'All right,' she said, 'but I'm keen to start making plans.'

She'd left it there, but I could feel her displeasure in the stiffness of her body when I tried to caress her, and she'd broken away after a minute, with the excuse that Melanie would be returning soon.

On the dance floor with her now I tried to put all this out of my mind. Clive and Melanie were at the Baby Grand teasing out a slow foxtrot. Someone had put out a few of the lights. But I was unable to submit to the music. I felt on edge, plagued by ugly premonitions. It made sense to leave Victoria and all my problems behind and make a fresh start. Yet I hesitated. Why?

A brief break in the music. Then another foxtrot. Jessica, rigid at first, was loosening up, moulding more to me. Over her shoulder I spotted Elizabeth with Jim Farraday. She was wearing a simple black dress which clung softly to her body, and my stomach went hollow. Unattainable as ever, yet events had forged a kind of bond, holding out a frail hope of greater future intimacy.

And that touched the core of my conflict: my fear – which I hardly dared recognse – of binding myself to Jessica. She was as good a choice as I could make: pretty, educated, clever, upper class and good company. I was hot to continue further what had begun in the *rondavel*. Yet something hard and cold in me insisted that if this were real love it should be my only love.

And it wasn't. I couldn't bear the idea of losing her. But at the same time there were other yearnings, other pictures in my mind, other whisperings of adventures to come.

A Coloured waiter was moving around the tables which encircled the dance floor. Dennis Olifant. He saw me and nodded.

Celia and Harry slid by, he in a pale blue suit, she in a strapless green top and spreading blue skirt. I felt a pinch of sympathy for the displaced Carol: toptown had won again.

More lights went out and I held Jessica tighter. Would she let me sleep with her later or would she beg off? Perhaps Melanie would lend me her car and we could slip off to the *rondavel* ?

'I want to be with you, Jessica,' I said. 'I really do.'

'Prove it by giving in your notice straightaway.'

'I'll do it soon.'

'When?'

'Soon.'

'Monday?'

'Early next year. It's only fair to them.'

'All right,' she said. But the renewed stiffness of her body signalled otherwise.

'Could I speak to you for a moment, sir?' Dennis had materialised quietly at our table, his lined face grave.

'Sure, Dennis. Go ahead.'

'I mean privately.' He indicated the passage.

'Excuse me, please,' I said to my companions.

'Oh, oh, Blackie-oh,' Harry said. 'What have you been up to? Midnight jaunts into Kokville township?'

'Shut up, Harry,' I said, rising. My mind was raking through possibilities. Dennis had no connection with anyone I knew except the Marches.

'What is it?' I asked once we were in the passage

He waited until we had stepped through a door into the back yard, a large square, edged by long buildings. Unlit but for the light coming out of the windows and doors of the rooms – some obviously staff quarters – it was oppressive with the smell of dustbins.

A loose knot of people was gathered at the closed door of one room. A big black man in a grubby vest and ragged flannels tied at the waist with rope was pounding on the door and shouting, while a woman in the blue uniform and *doek* of the hotel service staff was trying to pull him away.

'It's the young girl, Thandi,' Dennis said, heading towards the group. 'She's been calling for you.'

'Me?' I felt the muscles in my stomach tighten. 'What for?'

'She stabbed him.' Dennis pointed to a young black man with a narrow, sullen face who was necklocked by two older men, each, like him, wearing a white shirt and dark trousers. His shirt was splodged with blood and he pressed a bloodstained cloth to the biceps of his dangling left arm. 'Now she's locked herself in that room and won't come out.'

'Why?' My stomach was so tight that cramp seemed imminent.

He shook his head.

'Because she is mad,' the wounded man yelled.

'Mad and bad.'

'No, master.' The woman in the *doek* bustled up importantly. 'He was trying to force her, that man. She is drinking and smoking *dagga* in his room with him and his friends but when the men want to *kwela* her she breaks a bottle and stabs him, then runs across to that room there.' Her finger jabbed in the direction of the room where grubby vest was pounding on the door. 'The other boys run away.'

She laughed and gestured towards the man in |the vest. 'Amos is with a woman, that Sibongile, in this room but he was going outside just then to make water. The girl is in, quick-quick. Now he is locked out and she is in there with his girlfriend.'

'They are whores,' the wounded man cried, trying to wriggle free of the two men who held him. 'They wanted drink and too much money. She tried to kill me. I want the police.'

'Quiet,' Dennis said sharply. 'You're in enough trouble already, having women here.' To me he said, 'The girl claims you are her friend.'

'Her mother works for us.'

'She says she's afraid to come out unless you are here. Will you speak to her? I could call the manager but he will call the police – or that stupid fool there will. We don't want that.'

'She came with her aunt. What happened to her?'

'Aunt? I haven't seen any aunt. Just the woman they call Sibongile – who is in that room. She wants to come out but she can't get the key off the girl.'

'I don't want to get mixed up in this,' I said.

'I understand,' he said soberly. 'But if the girl doesn't leave soon somebody will call the police and then there will be hell for everyone.'

'Especially her,' said the woman in the *doek*,

'because it's past curfew.'

'What about this man?' I said pointing to the vest. 'Will he give me trouble if I talk to the girl?'

'No. He only wants to finish what he started with the other woman.'

They were all looking at me expectantly. Feeling very white and very absurd, I stepped forward and tapped on the door. 'Thandi,' I said, 'it's me – Simon Brown.'

There was rustling and scraping the other side of the door. I spoke her name again. The voice which replied was small and snively. 'The men wanted to make me lie with them.'

'Yes but you can come out now.'

'I'm afraid,' she said.

I could hear another voice, low but angry sounding, talking rapidly in Xhosa.

'It'll be all right,' I said.

'Will you take me away?'

Jesus, I thought. What a fucking nuisance. 'Yes,' I said.

The key creaked in the lock and the door opened. A scratch on her cheek and her face tear smeared, Thandi tottered forward on the preposterous high heels. Her hands lifted and for a frightening blink of time I thought she was going to fling her arms around me, but she dropped them and stood there, snivelling yet defiant. Behind her, smiling uncertainly, stood Sibongile, her scarlet dress rumpled and her nipples showing big through the fabric. Taped to the mottled, off-white wall behind her were yellowing newspaper pictures of a boxing match featuring two black fighters.

'Can you get Thandi to her parents' home?' I asked Sibongile sternly.

'No.' Sibongile was still smiling weakly. 'I am

staying with Amos.'

'Has anyone here got a car?' I asked, conscious of the futility of the question.

Heads shook and hopelessness soaked through me.

'Can you take her away, sir?' Dennis said. 'It would be best.'

'If I can borrow a car.' My mind was flicking through the possibilities: Harry, Elizabeth, Melanie. 'Can you look after her for a bit?'

'We'll look after her,' said the woman in the *doek*. She waved a dismissive hand at the wounded man, who, released by his captors, was edging forward. '*Suka wena, nja.*' He fell back, swearing.

Melanie was sitting near the band, sipping an orange juice. She dug keys from the bag beside her chair as soon as I'd rattled off my tale. 'Of course, Simon,' she said. 'Poor girl.'

My dance companions looked as if they hadn't moved from our table since I'd left. Harry grew a wide smile as I repeated my story and Celia's eyebrows arched. Jessica listened wordlessly, frowning.

'I won't be long,' I said. 'I'll just dump her and shoot back.' I touched Jessica's hand. 'Come keep me company.'

She hesitated, clearly not liking the idea much.

'It would look better,' Harry said. 'If the cops are about they might get the wrong idea and Blackie will end up reporting his own case.'

'That won't happen,' I said brusquely. I liked Harry's humour less and less lately.

'I'd rather stay where I am if you don't mind.' Jessica removed her hand.

'Remember the old miscegenation joke,' Harry

said, catching my sleeve as I passed him. 'Sowing your wild oats is all right, but *kaffircorn*...?' I shook off his hand and walked on.

'Simon!' Jessica had followed me into the passage. 'I'm not very happy about this.' She wasn't looking directly at me, but at some spot to my left.

'I'm not very happy myself,' I said. 'But I feel responsible.'

'I don't see that. The girl is old enough to be responsible for herself. If she chooses to be a prostitute that's surely her affair?'

'She isn't a prostitute.'

'She was dressed like one, and her aunt certainly is one.'

'She's been through a bad time and she's a bit wild, but that's all.' I was aware of a growing irritation. 'I know the kid well. Her mother has been with us since I was a baby. They're practically family.'

I stopped. I was beginning to sound ridiculously like my mother.

'She's more than a kid.' Jessica's face had gone white and pinched, the mouth a thin line. 'I feel demeaned by all this, Simon. It's not how I expect an escort to behave, rushing off to the rescue of some black girl.'

'Listen, Jessica.' I reached for her arm, but she stepped back. 'It's nothing to do with you. It's just that my life won't be worth living at home if I don't deal with this. I won't be gone long.'

'Be gone as long as you like. I won't be here when you get back.' She turned on her heel and walked away down the passage.

I chased after her. 'Jessica,' I pleaded, 'we can't let this happen.'

'It's very simple,' she said. 'If you stay, I'll stay.

If you go with that girl, I get a taxi home. Your choice.' Her mouth snapped shut like a letterbox flap. Her eyes glittered hostility.

It was my turn to walk away.

Dennis and the woman in the *doek* were waiting with Thandi when I arrived at the back entrance in Melanie's car. She was swaying noticeably in spite of their steadying hands on her elbows. Sibongile was nowhere to be seen.

'She is with Amos,' the woman said. 'It's better. She's no good, that one.'

'She told me there would be a party,' Thandi said. 'Dancing. Drinks. No trouble.'

'Stupid *wena*,' the woman said. 'Stay away from her or you will be in big trouble one day.'

We bundled Thandi into the back seat with some difficulty. She sat slumped, breathing hard. I hoped she wasn't going to be sick.

'Thank you,' I said to Dennis and the woman, then felt ridiculous. They hadn't done me any favours.

'You're doing a good thing, Mister Brown,' Dennis said.

'*Hamba kahle*,' said the woman as I pulled away.

I drove carefully, unfamiliar with the controls and not wanting to draw the attention of any patrolling police. In the back Thandi was babbling about the men turning nasty after Sibongile had gone off with Amos, leaving her alone with them.

'Can't you crouch down?' I said. 'I don't want you seen by the police.'

She giggled. 'Bongi used to hide in the boot of Oldcastle's car. I wouldn't do that.'

'That woman at the hotel was right,' I said repressively. 'You must stay away from Sibongile. You could have been raped, and if you'd cut that man really badly you could have been charged, perhaps with attempted murder.'

'He was forcing me – he and that other *tsotsi*. Not nice with me. Not like you.'

'Your mother isn't going to be pleased with you, *ntombi*,' I said heavily, not welcoming the reminder of my behaviour.

Thandi giggled. 'She won't find out. She's in the township.'

'What?' Startled, I took the turn into the lane behind Songololo Street too fast and wide, barely avoiding an overflowing rubbish bin.

'Night off.'

Our back gate was alongside. I slammed the brakes on. 'So where do you think you're going to sleep.'

'*Andiyazi*.' She giggled again. 'With you.'

I was beginning to wonder how drunk she really was. 'More talk like that and I'll drop you on the edge of the township and let you walk home.'

'Is all right. The *khaya* is not locked.'

'Okay, let's get you there then.' I got out of the car and yanked open the back door. She reached out a hand and I took it. She came off the seat unexpectedly quickly and stood upright for a moment, then stumbled against me.

'Dizzy,' she murmured. 'Help me.'

Again I wondered how much help she needed. 'Come on,' I said roughly, slipping an arm around her. 'Let's get a move on.'

Our house was in darkness, but there was a half moon in a clear sky and although Thandi sagged against me from time to time, I managed to keep us to the path until we reached Florence's room. A push and the door was open.

In the faint light I could make out an iron bedstead with a patchwork quilt, a small table and the old sewing machine which my mother had passed on to Florence.

Though I hadn't stepped inside it for nearly two decades, I was conscious of the familiarity of the room. The smell of lampsmoke, Sunlight Soap, a mixture of scents and Primus stove oil pulled me back to childhood and the remembered warmth of Florence's lap as she spooned some of her mealie meal into my mouth.

'Here we are.' My voice sounded as falsely cheerful as a Sunday school teacher's on a wet picnic.

Thandi didn't answer. Instead she grabbed my arm, pulling me inside. I caught the smell of a perfume reminiscent of Kathy's, blending with the slightly acrid smell of *dagga*. Then one arm hooked my neck pulling my face to hers, while the other encircled my waist locking me to her.

No, I thought. *She's black. This is taboo, a sin, a crime.*

But another voice was whispering in my head. *Kiss her*, it said. *Take her. You've wanted to. So do it.*

Then her mouth met mine: hot, open, the tongue searching, the lips gobbling. Her body was trembling, sending responsive eddies of desire through me. *It's only kissing,* I thought. *I can stop it soon and no harm done.*

But minutes later we were still kissing and straining against each other. Through the thin dress I could feel the hardness of the pelvic bone and the warm softness below. Somehow, too, we'd got closer to the bed.

'We've got to stop this, Thandi,' I panted, more

254

as a plea than a command.

'No.' Her grip tightened, thwarting my weak attempt to pull away. 'You want to be inside me.'

I could hardly deny it. Incontestable evidence of my wanting was rubbing against her and I was breathing like a runner at the end of a sprint.

'This is not a good idea,' I got out.

'It's good. I want it, also.' She was panting, too, and her fingers were digging into my buttocks.

'I must get back to the hotel.' But my mouth was hungry for hers again and an errant hand was exploring the small breasts. *No further*, I told myself. *Only this and no more.*

P*erhaps just a little more, a little further*, the demon whispered. *She asked for one more dance that time in the rondavel. This is it: a dance without music.*

I reached for the hem of her skirt, easing it up. My fingers brushed the fork of her body and felt the wetness there. One of Kepler's warnings leapt into my mind: 'If you *naai a kaffermeid*, you'll never want to do it with a white woman again.'

She wanted me: no doubt about that. She was gasping and squirming and her tongue was stabbing into my mouth. And I wanted her, wanted to push her down on the bed and bury my cock in that wet and willing cunt. Wanted her. And in some long-locked chamber of my being always had. All the things that had held me back – her colour, her youth, the risk – suddenly seemed transformed by some alchemy into reasons for submitting to the beat of my blood.

But even as I lifted her dress above her waist I knew that I mustn't take her. Not here in her mother's room. Not now while she might be high on *dagga* and probably a little drunk as well. Not after I'd been called in as some sort of guardian.

Who cares? the small subversive voice whispered. *She doesn't.*

I let go of her skirt and lifted my hands to her shoulders, holding her away from me. She was shaking violently and so was I.

'I've got to go back, Thandi.' It was meant to be gentle, but it came out gruff, brutal.

'Later,' she rapped.

'No. Now. I've got to take the car back.' The evasion sounded pathetic.

'Afterwards.'

I forced myself to lie. 'Jessica – my partner – is waiting.'

Even in the poor light, I could read her contempt. 'You don't want her. You want me. I know it.' Her hand went to my aching groin.

'You know why it can't be. I'm sorry, but it can't.' The voice was in my head again, whispering, but I closed it out. 'I've got to go to get back to the hotel, Thandi.'

'Stay.' Her fingers tugged at my belt.

'I can't, Thandi.' I caught her wrist. 'This can't work. I should never have let us go this far.' *A minute*, the voice was urging. *A minute is all you'll need.*

'It can work,' she gasped fiercely, the fingers inexorable. 'We can make it work. Never mind the *Boere* and their laws.'

'I must go.' I ripped her fingers loose and turned muzzily towards the door.

'Go, then,' she hissed. 'Go and fuck that sheepface. *Hamba! Voertsek!*'

My hand on the door handle, I stopped. My head was a jostle of images. Jessica's mouth snapping shut like a letterbox flap as she turned away from me in the corridor. Thandi's pansy eyes as I'd turned away

256

from her. The proud, angry tilt of the head.

I turned back. There was no need to speak. As I moved slowly towards her she took hold of the hem of her dress and jerked it up over her head.

'*Ngoku*,' she said, allowing the dress to flutter to the floor. 'I'm ready.'

Thirty-four

Two weeks passed before the expected letter came from Jessica. I read it in the *rondavel* while a *Piet My Vrou* was emitting its plaintive cry from a bluegum tree.

I won't attempt an exhaustive analysis of why our relationship is best ended. What happened at the hotel isn't the main reason, though I found your behaviour strange and insensitive. I'll simply say that I think our attitudes to life and our ambitions are too dissimilar for us to find real happiness together. I've come to the conclusion, too, that you are not really ready for the wholehearted commitment that I see as being essential. This brings me to something I find very hard to write because you may draw the wrong conclusions. During the difficulties of the past year I've found strength in the friendship and support of Rex. Over time our feelings for each other have grown deeper without our quite realising it. Yesterday Rex proposed to me and I feel it is only fair that you should be the first to know that we are becoming engaged. I was very fond of you (or I wouldn't have let things go as far as they did) and I still am. I hope that we can be friends as well as relations. Rex would like that, I know. I hope, too, you will find someone right for you.

My mother sniffed when I announced that Jessica had dumped me. 'I'm sorry, son,' she said. 'I liked the girl. But you weren't her style.'

'And Rex is?'

She shrugged. 'The Leightons have money and the Roys are doing well at the moment. Money goes to money. You're young, there'll be someone else.

Someone from round here, perhaps.'

Kathy didn't try to disguise her pleasure. 'You're well out of it, *boetie*. I must admit I didn't fancy that snobby little cow as part of the family.'

'Well, she will be,' I said breezily, surprised by my own cheerfulness, 'and you'll have to get used to it because once you're married you'll be living on the neighbouring farm.'

'I'm not sure I am getting married,' she said. 'If you hadn't had your own troubles you might have noticed that Norman hasn't been around all week.'

I suppressed a grin. 'What's he done?'

'Nothing – and that's half the trouble. There's been a row about the wedding arrangements. I want Shantih and Carol and Thandi to be bridesmaids and I want the Rangisamys and the Zondis and the Marches at the reception. Norman's okay about that himself, but the parents are digging their heels in. They don't mind Shantih and Co. being at the church service so much. But they're dead against them playing a leading part and what they call intermixing at the reception. They're not so worried about breaking the law – it's what all their farmer friends will do when they find out that they're rubbing shoulders with non-whites. And they call themselves liberal!'

My corked grin was beginning to leak out. She looked at me sharply. 'I don't see what's so funny, *boetie*.'

'I can imagine the reception. Ben March, smoking a *zol* and cutting the wedding cake with his flick knife. Elias Zondi asking Aunt Betty to dance the first waltz while the Indian Mynah tries to smooch you at the top table and Kepler and Grobelaar burst in to rescue Carol from the *swart gevaar*.'

She glared at me for a moment, then her frown

faded and she laughed. 'Perhaps I'll marry Norman after all and you can arrange a few surprises. And think up a few for your ex-girlfriend's wedding to our cousin while you're about it.'

Harry oozed dubious sympathy while beady with curiosity. 'Jessica was really frothing after you'd pushed off with the Native girl, almost as if she thought there might be a bit going on between you. Something the girl said about being in your room one night.' He eyed me quizzically. 'There isn't anything, is there?'

'For fuck's sake, Harry,' I expostulated, angry at his prurience and rattled by his perceptiveness. 'What do you take me for?'

'Okay, okay!' He held up his hands in mock surrender. 'I didn't believe it and said so. Celia will bear that out. Not that I'd blame you if you had.' He leant forward. 'Just between us I had a bit of a dip myself not long ago. Research, you could say.' He rolled his eyes. 'You've heard what they say about poking Native women?'

'Yes, and I wouldn't know.' I could hear the snap of anger in my voice and feel the blood heating my face.

'Well, take it from me she was magic – Black Magic. Like a marvellous animal just bred to please a man and no arguments. Plucked it. Sucked it. Fucked it. Anything I wanted and more. They can repeal the bloody Immorality Act any time they like as far as I'm concerned. You could do worse than give that *ntombi* a try – from Jessica's description she sounded quite tasty. And if you don't fancy her I could put you in touch with Black Magic. Name of Bongi. Specialises in white men, she says. Including local celebrities.'

'I've got to get back to the office.' I stood up,

fighting an urge to clamp my hand over his face and shove. Without knowing it he'd jabbed deep into a steaming core of uncertainty. After Thandi had slipped away into the blood-warm dawn, I'd lain for sleepless hours, sweating over the enormity of what I'd done. Immorality. Miscegenation. *Kaffernaai*. The words spelled disgrace, ridicule, imprisonment. If I was found out, I was finished. Finished at work. Finished among my contemporaries. Finished with the family – even with Kathy, perhaps.

But, while I called myself a disgrace, my flesh was reminding me of the uncomplicated pleasure of our sex. I could recall the warm satin smoothness of Thandi's thighs, the fervour of her kissing, the caresses of the sinuous hands on my back, and her murmured *Ewe* when at last she convulsed in climax. Perhaps because of its forbiddenness and the sharp sense of what we risked, our coming together seemed more intense than anything I'd experienced before. And as I'd spurted deep inside her I'd known I'd crave that dark body again.

For a few days afterwards I'd seen nothing of her, which got me worrying. Then early one morning she was beside my bunk smiling down at me and holding out a cup of coffee.

'For Christ's sake,' I mumbled. Acutely aware of the skimpiness of her dress and my obvious nakedness under the thin sheet, I struggled up into a sitting position.

'Is all right,' she said calmly, putting the cup on the bedside table. 'I told my mother the young master would need a hot drink to wake him up.' She sat down on the bed. I could feel the warmth of her buttock against my thigh.

'It is not all right,' I said with emphasis. 'It's

completely insane.' My heart was trip-hammering atune of fear and desire. Under the sheet my cock lifted.

'It *is* all right,' she laughed, mimicking my tone. 'My mother is cleaning the stove.' Her hand slid under the sheet.

In the weeks which followed I told myself it couldn't go on and it would be a good thing when Thandi went off to her new school in Lovedale. But when January came and she went, it wasn't the relief I'd thought it would be. I found myself missing her and not simply for her satiny skin and bold lovemaking.

I also missed her, I realised with surprise, because I'd come to like her enormously.

Thirty-five

Gerry Fielding's photograph showed the pylon sprawled ludicrously on its side among the thorn bushes.

'Good work,' Grantley-Pearson said. 'Bombs have been going off in all the main centres. A neat bit of symbolism to choose the anniversary of the battle of Blood River. An anonymous phone call, you say?'

'Yes.' I could hear Joyce calmly giving the location of the toppled pylon on the commonage and of the bomb which had failed to detonate at the rear of Mr Hughes's office in Vilakazi.

The editor lit his pipe, his eyes on me. 'Do you have any inkling who might be in the know locally?'

'None,' I lied, certain that Sipho was involved.

'Better that way, perhaps.' Grantley-Pearson looked at me assessingly. 'If this kind of activity continues the authorities will begin to play very rough indeed. If you know more than you're telling me, I hope you're strong, because you'll need to be.'

Elizabeth was on the phone when I walked into the reporters' room the next morning.

'He's not in yet,' she was saying. 'I'll tell him you want to see him.'

'Grobelaar,' she said after she'd replaced the receiver. 'He didn't like last night's story or the photograph one little bit. He wants to talk to you. Urgently.'

'Thanks for stalling him.' I lit a quivering cigarette. 'I'd better go and see Gerry first.'

'You can't,' she said sombrely. 'He's at the Police Station. Grobelaar said they would keep him there until they'd spoken to you. I'm sorry, Simon.'

'Me too.' Somehow I constructed a smile.

'Be careful,' she said quietly. 'Grobelaar is no fool.'

'I know.'

I'd a good idea who the fool was.

Grobelaar's office was a small room off the long *stoep* which ran along the back of the Police Station. Kepler was leaning against the door. He didn't return my husky greeting.

Grobelaar sat at a desk clear except for a telephone and a closed file. Mine? A bald man in a brown suit stood next to the barred window. My legs felt boneless. There was a wooden chair on my side of the desk and I made for it.

'I didn't say you could sit down,' Grobelaar snapped. 'You'll sit when I say you can. First you answer questions and no bullshit about the right to protect sources, hey? We're investigating serious crime here, even treason. I want to know who told you about this sabotage.'

'An anonymous telephone call at home.' I looked at Kepler who was scowling into space.

'Your home? Why?'

'I don't know,' I said. 'Perhaps to get me before I left for work.'

'How would he know your home number?' brown suit asked.

He'd said *he*. Did that mean that my home phone wasn't tapped – or was he trying to trap me?

'It's in the book. I encourage people to phone me at home.'

'Including blacks?'

'Anyone with a story.'

Grobelaar's reptilian eyes hooded. 'I might ask

you to make a list of all the people who know your phone number.' He bounced his pencil on the desk, frowning, then he said abruptly. 'You got a call at home when the Emergency was declared last year, didn't you?'

'I think I did, now you mention it.'

'Don't think, *jongie*. You know. Was it the same person?'

'I can't say.'

'Can't or won't?'

'I can't remember.' *Careful*, I told myself. *Don't try to be too smart.*

'Black or white?'

I pretended to consider. 'I'm not sure.'

'You can't tell the difference between a white man and a black?' Brown suit looked incredulous and I wondered if I'd seriously misjudged.

'Usually yes, but sometimes on the phone, no.'

'That's liberalists for you,' Grobelaar barked. 'White, black or in between, it's all the same to them.'

'I'm not a liberal,' I said.

'*Ag*,' Grobelaar said, 'don't talk *kak*, man. We know all about you.' His eyes flicked towards Kepler at the door.

I looked longingly at the empty chair. Had I been under surveillance or was Grobelaar bluffing? And if he wasn't bluffing did he know about the visits from Sipho and the Marches? Worse, did he know about Thandi?

'Why won't you just cooperate with us?' Grobelaar said. 'Whether you're a liberalist or not, we should be on the same side. This isn't a fight between European and Bantu. It's a fight for western civilisation and against communism. You could play your part.'

'How?' My mouth tasted of toilet paper.

'By sharing information with us. You wouldn't be sorry. Cooperation works both ways.'

The room had gone very quiet. So quiet that I could hear the town hall clock striking the hour in the distance. I cleared my throat. The sound rasped through the room. It was becoming hot. The fan wasn't switched on and I could feel the sweat gathering under my armpits.

'Well? Are you going to help your country?'

It sounded grand. An appeal to my patriotism. A call to national duty in a time of crisis and crime. And Grobelaar was in a position to respond with the kind of information which made news items. Easiest to agree, even if I meant to do nothing. Refusal would only make Grobelaar more hostile.

But as these thoughts chased each other through my head I knew I was going to refuse. Not out of any high principle. It was a long time since I'd believed that I'd enlisted in a crusade for truth. I was going to refuse because I was pretty sure that the line from Joyce led on to the man whose sister had me in a delirium of illegal desire.

'I'm sorry, Mr Grobelaar,' I said with all the synthetic sincerity I could muster, 'but I couldn't do my job properly if people thought I was trying to do yours.'

'Nobody would know.' A nerve was pulsing in his jaw.

'They would know.'

'Are you for our white race or against it?' he demanded.

'For it.'

'I'm not so bladdy sure,' he rasped. He leant across the table, wagging his finger. 'I'm not saying you are actually involved in this *donkerwerk*. But I'm warning you that if I find you have been withholding information from us about these saboteurs I will regard you as an accomplice. Understand?'

'I understand.'

'So I'm putting it to you again. Do you know anything you haven't told us about this man who spoke to you on the phone?'

Man. Again there was the possibility of a trick. If they'd been tapping our phone, Grobelaar would pounce now.

'Nothing.'

'All right.' Grobelaar leant back in his chair. 'You can go. But *pas op, of jy sal jou gat sien sonder 'n spieel.*'

'What about Gerry Fielding?' I asked. 'He knows even less than I do.'

'We'll be releasing him any minute now,' Grobelaar said. 'But I don't think he'll be too keen to help you in future.'

Thirty-six

Joshua was in the reporters' room, sitting in my chair. His face was stiff: a mask cast in grey mud. The tawny eyes burned feverishly. Elizabeth had pulled a chair close to him and was taking notes.

'Joshua's son has been picked up by the Special Branch,' she said.

'Ben!' The news didn't entirely surprise me, but I felt my throat close.

'Not Ben, Seth,' Joshua said heavily. 'He had been in Johannesburg and came back on the train early this morning, just after I left for work. They were watching the house. When he reached the gate, they grabbed him, four of them, pushed him into their car and were gone. Our neighbour saw it. She phoned me here.'

'Have you been to the police?'

He nodded. 'They won't let me see him. They will tell me nothing, except they are questioning him about a crime.'

'What crime?'

'They would not say.'

'The chief has got a lawyer taking it up with the new commandant,' Elizabeth said.

'It will do no good,' Joshua said. 'They can hold Seth for twelve days without charging him or letting anyone see him.'

'Surely he'll be all right if he isn't mixed up in anything serious,' Elizabeth said. 'He isn't, is he?'

'Seth will never talk to the police,' Joshua said. 'They will try to make him talk and when he won't talk they will kill him.'

'Oh, Joshua,' Elizabeth protested. 'It can't be that bad, can it?'

'He will not talk and they will kill him.' He got up and stood looking down at us as if we weren't there. Then, like a man refusing to concede a bodily injury, he walked slowly out of the office.

'Do you think Seth March is involved in anything?' Elizabeth's face was tight with distress.

'I don't know.' I tried to imagine the slender, diffident poet placing bombs, and couldn't. But he had the conviction and the passion. 'They'll probably give him a bad time whether he's involved or not.'

'But not kill him!'

'No. But, as we both know, they're pretty furious about the wave of bombings – and there's all that talk about extending detention.'

She gave a small shudder. 'Grobelaar frightens me. Cold and vindictive.'

The telephone rang. Elizabeth picked up the receiver, listened, then dragged a pad towards her. 'Certainly Miss van der Horst,' she said. 'Of course, I'm interested... No, it's no trouble at all.' She wrote for some time, nodding and murmuring, then hung up. 'That was about the horticulture exhibit at the Victoria Agricultural Show. It seems so ridiculous to be scribbling about flowers when...'

'The show must go on,' I said.

She winced. 'You really must stop acting so hard-boiled, Simon. Don't pretend you don't care.'

I did. A bit. But I cared far more about how my mother and Kathy were going to take the news.

They wept. I'd seldom seen either of them cry.

'He's such a gentle person to be mixed up in this awful violence,' my mother said, reaching blindly for her cigarettes.

'We can't be sure he's mixed up in it,' Kathy said.

'And we can't be sure he isn't,' I said.

'It doesn't seem like him.' Her arm went round my mother's shoulders. 'It's so cold-blooded and sneaky leaving bombs ticking away.'

'Sabotage is sneaky and the Government can't really complain because their crowd invented it,' I said.

'That's right,' my mother said. 'The *Ossewabrandwag* blew up post offices in protest against Smuts taking us into the second world war. Killed civilians.'

'That doesn't justify the bombings now,' Kathy said. 'Non-violent action can work. The government couldn't shoot every passive resister or striker if millions turned out.'

'They won't turn out to get shot,' I said. 'Not after Sharpeville. I wouldn't either. In their boots hit and run would be my style.'

Kathy had stopped crying. 'You worry me, *boetie*. I think you're getting a kick out of this violent stuff.'

'I'm not. I think it's lunatic.' It wasn't the whole truth. I felt a grudging admiration for the saboteurs' daring. They'd be caught and probably hanged. But meanwhile they were living with an intensity I envied – and for a cause they believed in.

Thirty-seven

The reporters' room clock read five-forty. The paper had long gone out on the streets and the works were silent. I'd stayed on to clear my desk of non-urgent jobs like filleting the press releases for the Victoria Agricultural Society's annual show. I wasn't keen to get home and I didn't want to begin drinking so early in the evening.

I hauled the evening paper across from Elizabeth's side of the desk and scanned the front page. Finding nothing earth-shaking, I flipped into the centre for the local news. This was even less exciting, the lead item being a court case about cattle theft in the Venterstad area, followed by the interview with Miss van der Horst.

Only three paragraphs had been given to Elizabeth's report on Seth's detention 'in connection with unspecified matters relating to national security'. His lawyer was quoted as demanding that Seth be charged or released immediately, and criticised the law which permitted the authorities to hold him incommunicado. There was a brief statement from Joshua, full of grief, rage and belief in Seth's innocence. Elizabeth had told me that Joshua and old R.B. had wanted more fuss, but the lawyer had advised that it would only make matters worse. The chief had reluctantly agreed to give private and informal negotiations a chance, and to hold back the angry editorial he'd planned.

A shadow fell across the paper. Joshua was standing there, yellow and haggard, as though my thoughts had summoned him.

'They are torturing Seth now,' he said.

'How do you know?' I demanded, not wanting

to believe it.

'My neighbour has been going to the Police Station to collect Seth's dirty clothes. They wouldn't let her have his vest. It was lost, they said. And when we looked carefully at his shirt we found some marks like blood.'

' *Like* blood?'

'It is blood. I was a stretcher-bearer in the war. I know how bloodstains look.'

'There could be any kind of reason. A nosebleed. Something like that.'

He looked at me with some of his old fire. 'No. Not on the back of the shirt.'

I felt a spasm in the region of my heart. 'Have you spoken to the chief? The lawyer?'

'They are useless because they are white and the *Boere* are white, too, so they do things in a white way. They think I am exaggerating, but I know what whites do to us black people. They talk about respecting the law even if they disagree with it. But the *Boere* only pretend to respect the law. So the lawyer will try to get a doctor in to see Seth and the chief will raise questions in the paper while Grobelaar and Martins are stalling and denying everything. They say the district surgeon will examine Seth, but the district surgeon is a government stooge. The torture will go on.'

His eyes were smouldering, accusatory. I looked away. Useless was the word for me too.

Joshua came closer and spoke again, more quietly. 'There is a policeman I know. He is very afraid, *poep*-scared, but for money will get more news of Seth.'

A shiver ran through my shoulders. 'If you're caught at that you'll go inside, too.'

Joshua removed his peaked cap and ran a hand over his forehead. 'It doesn't matter what happens to me. Seth is my son. If he stays in the cells he will die.'

'They won't kill him just like that.'

'He will not talk. He will die first. I know him.'

We were getting nowhere. 'I haven't got any money, Joshua,' I said. 'And I don't know where to get it.'

'I've got some.' He pointed at Elizabeth's chair. 'And she's got some.'

It was a long moment before I realised that he expected me to ask her.

'Fancy a beer and a game of draughts?'

It was hot in the kitchen in spite of the open door and my father had, rare for him, taken off his shirt. His skinny breasts sagged like badly ironed pockets and his skin was pasty. Obscurely repelled, I wanted to say no, but it was a long time since we'd had any kind of communication and I could tell he was worried. I'd got back from seeing Elizabeth at her home to learn that my mother had gone into Victoria Hospital for tests on what the doctors described as a 'tired and irregular heart', and that they were keeping her overnight.

'Okay.' I went over to the dresser and picked up the board and box of wooden pieces fashioned by an itinerant Xhosa gardener.

When I sat down my father pushed a bottle of beer across the table and removed the *News* he'd been reading.

'Nothing much in this rag of yours today except stuff that was in the East London paper, and a lot of drivel about the show. Oh, yes, and the piece about the March boy. What's he been up to, eh?'

'Nobody will say. But it's political.'

'Stupid. But then that's Coloureds. Hopeless cases. Always in trouble of some kind. Dillied up with drink and *dagga*.'

'Not Seth March, Dad. His brother Ben maybe, but I don't think Seth drinks or smokes *dagga*. He may be Coloured but he's bright.'

He shook his head at me. 'Degenerates –

Coloureds are degenerate, son. And Joshua March is to blame for whatever trouble that boy is in. He just won't accept he's from a lower race and he's filled his sons' heads with a lot of dangerous nonsense.'

'Let's get on with the draughts, Dad.' It struck me that he'd only been saying what I once would have said. Yet I resented his air of authority.

We played a game in silence and began the second. 'By the way,' he said casually, 'that girl of Florence's was here earlier looking for you – advice about schoolwork, she said. She's grown up fast. Legs like an ostrich. Very full of herself. Mister Brown, she said, not master or *baas*.' He huffed two of my pieces. 'Your move.'

I let him win.

Thirty-eight

Joshua was in the garage, listlessly polishing R.B. Alexander's silver Packard.

'Elizabeth said you wanted to see me.' She'd also said he was in bad shape, and she hadn't exaggerated. His face was leeched of colour and his gauntness seemed to have become skeletal overnight.

'Seth is very sick,' he said. 'That policeman I spoke about...' He stopped, his face twitching, as if he'd lost the thread of what he was trying to say.

'The one we bribed with Elizabeth's money?' I prompted.

'That one.' Joshua gathered himself with an effort. 'He says Grobelaar and two other Special Branch men were with Seth last night. They were beating him. That man, Lategan, came out of the cells with bleeding knuckles. Also he is sure they were using a shock machine on Seth's private parts.'

I felt a cold tightening of my scrotum.

'He saw the machine. In Grobelaar's office – a battery and leads – and then it wasn't there. He heard' – Joshua's eyes were screwed shut – 'screams.'

'I can't believe this!' But I flinched, imagining the high voltage pervading and twisting that thin body.

'An African cleaner, a *bandiet*, told him he looked through Seth's judas and saw him lying on the floor of his cell. Just lying there on his face with his hands between his legs.'

'Have you told the editor this? Or Elizabeth?'

'I will tell them.' He came closer. 'But it is not enough. We must get Seth out of there.'

'What?' My first thought was that grief had deranged him, but he was looking at me steadily.

'They can write about it. Nothing will happen.

They can go to Commandant Martins and the magistrate, who will say that they will inquire into it. Inquiries.' Joshua laughed harshly. 'Inquiries! There is no time for inquiries. Seth will die before anything is done.' His fingers hooked my sleeve. ' *We* have got to do something. You, me and Ben.'

His intensity was rattling me. 'But what?'

'We can break him out of that cell.' His tongue flickered over dry grey lips. 'You can get me a revolver.'

Above us, the Linotype machines had stopped, and the silence lay so heavy it seemed palpable. Joshua continued to stare at me.

'That is the only way,' he said.

I felt as if we were standing in an enormous space. The walls of the garage were miles away. A humming started up in my head.

'You're mad,' I said. 'You're talking madness, Joshua.'

'At some times of night there are only two men guarding him. Africans. With a gun we can get him out, Ben and me.'

'If anyone is shot, you'll hang. Maybe me, too.'

'If he doesn't get out, he'll die.'

I felt a rush of hatred for him and his terrifying need. I jerked my arm free. 'I haven't got a gun, and I don't know where to get one.'

'You can get a gun.' He had hold of my arm again. 'I can't get one because I'm black. But you can.'

'No one would lend me a gun. It would be traced straight back.'

'It will not be used. Just shown.'

'You can't guarantee that.' I knew I should feel sympathy. What I felt was rage at the unreason of it all. 'Let Ben show that knife of his.'

'A knife won't work. A gun will work. Point and

276

bluff. I tell you it will work.'

Again I jerked my arm free. The monstrousness of what he was proposing was crushing the breath out of me, causing my head to swim with hideous pictures. 'No,' I rasped. 'It's no, no, no.'

'We must do it,' he said.

I fought an urge to shake him. 'You're asking me, a white man, to get you, a Coloured man, a gun to free another Coloured man. I can't do it.'

His eyes closed as if he were praying, then snapped open again, blazing. 'You must do it, Simon. Seth is your brother.'

Even in his distress he was claiming equality with whites for himself and his kind. 'Look, Joshua,' I said tightly, 'I'm sorry Seth's in trouble. But he got himself there and it's nothing to do with me. So don't give me all this brotherhood shit.'

'You don't understand,' he said quietly. 'Seth is your blood brother.'

'What did you say?' The question was a reflex, like the flash burn in my chest and the roar of blood in my ears.

'Seth is your brother – your blood brother. Your mother and me became friends – more than friends – when she worked here before the war. Then I went up North and – and one leave we were a bit too happy to be careful and so... she got with a baby. You're my son.'

At first I barely took in what he was saying, understanding only that the gaunt yellow-grey face in front of me was mouthing claims which sullied my mother and insulted my father. Then the face was snapping back on the thin neck from the most unpremeditated punch I'd ever thrown. A voice was screaming that he lied. My voice.

277

He offered no resistance to my second blow, which opened up his lip. The third caught him in the throat and spun him choking against the wall.

'Wait!' he croaked and raised a hand. 'Ask...'

My knee drove into his belly and he went down into a crouch, then sprawled on the concrete floor. I shifted my weight to stamp, then stopped, held back by an onset of nausea. Stomach heaving, I ran, hand over my mouth, to the non-white lavatory at the far end of the garage and, flinging myself through the doorway, vomited into the trough of the urinal.

My head was pulsing and for a minute I stood with my cheek pressed to the chipped tiling above the urinal. Then I sluiced my face in the dirty basin and felt steadier. With juddering hands I lit a cigarette and tried to convince myself that Joshua was lying. He had to be. The alternative was unthinkable, vile – the wide mouth licking my mother's mouth and breasts, the dun thighs throbbing between her fair ones while his tainted spunk pumped into her cunt.

After pitching my cigarette into the gully of the urinal I turned to the blotchy mirror above the washbasin. My face had never pleased me much, but now it mocked me. In the poor light of the lavatory it looked dark – a dingy brown. The old nickname came back: Blackie. And the old insult: dirty. The thick black hair was rumpled and in need of a cut. Curly at the ends, though not quite peppercorn. The eyes were dark brown under heavy eyebrows. Cheekbones high. Nose straight and not thick. A wide mouth. The jawline sharp. Surely a white man's face.

But inescapably dark. Darker than my parents'. Darker than Kathy's. Lighter than Joshua's or Ben's, but nearly as dark as the fairer-skinned Seth's. So what? A lot of whites were dark. Olive skinned.

Spanish or Portuguese or Southern French ancestry showing through. Suntan contributing. A grandfather had reportedly been dark. Didn't I take after him? No one had ever said he was Coloured. But then no one had ever called him Blackie – or dirty either.

Blackie was only a play on Brown. Blackie Brown was like Dusty Rhodes or Nobby Clark. A nickname which meant nothing.

My father's face was round. He was thicker set and shorter than I was. That didn't mean anything either. No one looked exactly like anyone else in a family, not even twins, often. My mother had fair hair and blue eyes. Kathy had brown eyes, lighter than mine, but brown. Cheekbones like mine, too – almost. Joshua had high cheekbones and a wide mouth. But thickish lips. Kaffirlips, as they said. Seth and Ben had high cheekbones, too. And thin lips. Thinner than mine, more like Kathy's. That didn't mean anything either. Joshua hadn't claimed Kathy as his spawn. If he did he was a lying bastard.

Bastard. What some Coloureds were called. *Basters*. Half-castes, half-breeds, and neither-nors, too, as if they weren't complete people. It fitted Joshua.

Only, bastard or not, I'd never known him lie.

He had to be lying now. My mother would never have gone with him. No decent white woman ever looked at a Coloured, let alone slept with one. White men fucked black women, never the other way round, not even whores. Unless they were mental cases mad for a big black prick. Not your mother. Never your mother.

'*Ask!*' I could hear Joshua's words, see the damaged face. He'd been going to say, 'Ask your mother.' I wanted to obliterate both words and face, but I couldn't.

Twice I'd heard him call my mother Phyllis in a tone full of intimacy. My mother's face was thrusting into my mind now: not the face I loved, but the face which filled me with shame and unease, the loose flushed face of a woman who got drunk with inferiors and let them become over-familiar.

Did Kathy know? She'd never hinted at it. Afraid of nothing, she would have surely have said if either of us had Coloured blood. If she knew. You'd know if you had it, just as you knew you were white. Instinct told you. It came out in the way you felt, the way you were. And anyone could spot a Coloured straightaway, so everyone said. Crinkly hair. Blueish fingernails at the moons. A tint in the skin, even if it was fair. A touch of the sun – no, a touch of the tarbrush. It couldn't be hidden. People noticed.

And called you Blackie?

There was blood on my knuckles. I washed it off, rubbing the carbolic soap by the basin into the cut. You could easily get infections from Coloureds. Easier than from blacks, because of the degeneracy. Blacks were a purer race. Everyone knew that. Even Hitler had admitted it. And Thandi was pure African. And clean. As clean as I was.

Seth is your brother. You're my son. How the fuck could Joshua lie like that? The kindest explanation was that his frantic worry over Seth had sent him crazy.

A noise. I swung round. Joshua was in the doorway, leaning against the frame and dabbing his torn face with a blood-smeared handkerchief. The machines in the works had begun to hum faintly, a sign that the operators had drifted back from their dinners.

'Is it so bad to be my son?' he asked quietly.

You had to grant him guts. He could have been up the stairs to Maitland or the chief, claiming I'd assaulted him. Instead he was confronting a near-murderous younger man.

'I'm not your fucking bastard son.' I tried to tamp down my resurgent rage. 'Why are you making out my mother's a whore?'

The tawny eyes flared. 'Your mother is not a whore. We love each other. You were a child of love.'

Two strides and I had my hands around his throat. 'You're fucking lying.'

His tongue touched the smashed lips. 'Ask her,' he said. 'Just ask.'

My fingers tightened. His eyes bulged. 'Ask her,' he wheezed.

Defeated, I dropped my hands. From the start he'd offered no resistance to my violence. Nor shown any fear.

He coughed painfully into his handkerchief, his chest rising and falling.

'Speak to your mother. I'll come to your house tonight. Now I must wash.'

'If you come anywhere near the house you're dead,' I said, 'because it won't only be me who'll be after you, but my dad too.'

A smile lifted the damaged lip. 'Speak to your mother first,' he said. 'And try to get a gun.' He began to cough again.

My rage had gone. I felt weak in every muscle. 'I'll speak to my mother,' I said. 'And stay away from our place tonight, do you hear?'

He nodded and, moving past me to the basin, turned on the tap and began to splash water onto his face. 'I'll be at Rangisamy's,' he said after a moment.

I continued to stand there irresolutely. He

turned, the handkerchief dabbing at his face. He seemed to have grown taller. 'Go, boy,' he said gently. 'I know it's hard for you. But we must save Seth. Now go.'

There was a lavatory for the Lino operators on the first landing. It had a bolt inside the door and I shot it. My stomach was still churning but when I tried to puke nothing came up. Joshua's words were printing in my head. *Seth is your brother. You're my son... Ask her.*

Someone was banging on the door and shouting to be let in.

'Sorry,' I called. 'Just give me a minute.'

The face in the mirror wasn't mine. Yellow and puffy, it was the face of a *rof*. A Coloured's face?

I went to the door and pulled back the bolt. Don, a young Linotype operator, was standing in the passage. He grinned. 'What were you doing in there? Tossing off?'

'That's right.' I brushed past him. Habit carried me through the swing doors into the reporters' room. Elizabeth looked up from her pad.

'Did you see Joshua?'

'Yes.'

'Was there anything...?' She didn't finish the question, but added with quick concern, 'Are you all right? You look as if you've seen a ghost.'

'I have. My father's.'

Thirty-nine

The brandies I chucked down my throat in the Hotel Vic didn't help: by the time I got home my head was throbbing from their effect and the effort of shaping what I'd say to my mother. She'd not looked well since her return from hospital and had been told to avoid stress. Well, if there was stress, the fault wasn't mine.

She was in the kitchen rolling out pastry while vegetables simmered in pots on top of the stove and a mutton joint hissed and crackled in the oven. In the background I could hear the muttering of the old Philco radio she kept switched on in the pantry.

The scene's ordinariness choked me: could it really be that the weary-looking woman with the hank of hair gummed to her forehead was a Hottentot's whore?

I found a beer in the fridge and sat down at the table while she launched into an account of her day: of old Mrs Legrange's queer turn and the arrival of the ambulance at the wrong address, ours; of six-year old Hansie Vermaak's fall from a tree; of Violet Lategan's moans about the state of the rubbish bins. I listened edgily while waiting for the right moment to roll out my question.

The moment came when she asked for news of Seth.

'Joshua wants to try to get him out of jail,' I said.

'He would. He dotes on his boys.'

'You know a lot about the Marches, Mom.' I tried for casualness.

'I should – working at the *News* for years. Joshua often gave us a hand in the bookbinding department when he wasn't driving.'

'Why did you leave the *News*, Ma?' Although I'd thrown off my jacket and loosened my tie I was sweating.

'I left to have you. I'd managed to go on working after Kathy, but I didn't think I could do it with two of you. Your dad had work at the depot, so we could afford it.'

'And where was Joshua then?'

She looked at me sharply. 'When?'

'When you got pregnant?'

She knew I knew something. Her face had gone whiter than the flour. She pushed a limp strand of hair off her forehead. 'What's all this about, son?'

I wanted to stop. I wanted to walk out of the kitchen with the terrible questions unasked. But it was ask now or leave them forever. There was a flavour of bile in my mouth.

'I had a fight today,' I said.

'A fight? What for?'

'With Joshua. He said things. Do you want to know what things, Ma?'

She didn't reply. One trembling hand went to the back of a chair and the other to her left breast.

I swallowed. My spit was like dry crust. 'He said I'm his bastard son.'

The hand at her breast tightened, rucking the old floral dress she often wore when she couldn't be bothered with an apron. *She's got a dicky heart*, I thought. Then, *So bloody what* ?

Still she didn't speak. Neither did I. Yet everything in the room was different, had a harder, sharper definition. The air had thickened, muffling sounds from the outside. I felt as if I couldn't continue to breathe unless one of us broke the silence.

'Was he lying, Ma?' I said.

It seemed to me that she would never answer or move again. This wasn't my mother, chatty and never still, but another woman, separate and alien. She wasn't wearing a brassiere and the outlines of her low, heavy breasts were clearly visible. Images which tormented me ever since the confrontation with Joshua jerked through my mind again, vivid, obscene and – foulest of all – arousing.

Her lips were trembling now, but she got the words out almost proudly. 'Joshua March never lied in his life.'

She stood, breathing as if winded. I looked away, unable to speak. This *was* my mother. A Capie's whore. Those trembling lips had trembled against a Coloured's mouth. Those trembling hands had touched a Coloured man's cock; that body had bared itself for his use. Had she moaned with pleasure as she gave herself to him? Had the breasts which suckled me been offered to him to suck? Had the lap on which I'd sat as a child quivered for his thrust?

They'd made me a bastard. A Coloured bastard's bastard. No wonder I was called Blackie.

Tears were scorching my eyes. The room blurred. I wanted to shout abuse, to hit out at her, to hurt as I'd been hurt. 'He did lie,' I cried. 'You lied, too. By not telling me. He's only told me now because he's trying to blackmail me into finding him a gun.'

She recoiled. 'A gun?'

'He wants it to get Seth out. He believes he's being tortured.'

'Oh God!' Her hand went to her cheek. 'The poor man. And Seth! What a mess!'

Her distress fed my rage. 'It's their mess. What about our mess? Me and my – your husband, that poor sod? Did he ever get told what you were up to with Joshua? Does he know he's got a *vissie* bastard for a son?' My eyes brimming, I levered myself upright. 'Are you going to tell him now – or must I?'

She moved round the table towards me, hands outstretched. Through my tears her head appeared to be surrounded by a nimbus. 'Try to understand, son. I loved Joshua. I still do. It was never a light thing. But your dad – Eric – is a good man. Me and Joshua didn't want to hurt no one. It seemed best not to tell.'

I didn't want her touch. I desperately wanted air. Twisting away from her I stumbled out through the kitchen door. Sobs came, racking my chest.

'Simon!' She'd followed me onto the *stoep*. 'Nothing has changed. No one need know. Joshua won't talk.'

'You haven't seen him. He's out of his Hottentot head. All he cares about is getting Seth out of jail. And unless I help he'll talk.'

She came up to me and put her hand on my shoulder. 'Where is he?'

'Rangisamy's.' I shook her hand off. 'He'll talk – to force me.'

'Not Joshua,' she panted. 'He won't do nothing to harm you. But we've got to help Seth.'

'Let him rot.'

She stood for a moment. Then she turned and went back into the kitchen. I could hear her moving about, the clank of pans and the slam of the oven door, followed by silence.

The night had come down and above me the stars glittered, cool and impersonal. Where had Joshua and my mother done it, the gross coupling that had resulted in me? In the house, in the double bed while my father – no, the man who thought he was my father – was on night shift? In the bookbinding room at the *News* after everyone else had gone home? Down in the garage against the wall? In the *rondavel*? Or on the back lawn in the dark like animals?

From beyond the lane there was the wail of a locomotive and then the puffing and rattling of a train. My father – ex-father – would be off duty soon. Without will or plan I walked into the house and down the passage to my parents' room.

My mother was at the dressing table brushing her hair. She had washed her face and changed her dress. A powder compact was open in front of her.

'I'm going to Rangisamy's,' she said to my reflection. 'When Eric comes, tell him his supper is in the oven.'

Her calmness was a goad. 'Shall I tell him who you're meeting?' I snarled. 'Is that where you used to fuck, in the back of that coolie's shop? Where you still fuck?'

She'd rouged her cheeks. The colour stood out like fever-flushes against the pallor of her skin. 'No,' she said, 'and it's over. Since you were born. For your sake.'

'For my sake? That's great. You did it for my sake. What about Dad's sake? What about him, Ma? Didn't he have a sake, too? You've said yourself he's a good man. Why did you have to go and do the dirty on him? Wasn't his cock big enough and black enough for you?' I hated the filth that was jerking out of my mouth, but I couldn't halt it. 'Did you do it with the coolie, too? Or did you just suck his cock to pay for the room?'

She didn't answer, but dropped her head into her hands. Her shoulders shuddered. Her face was hidden. Her hair had fallen forward and I could only see the line of her neck, stretched as if waiting for an axe blow. Hadn't it once been common for adulterous women to be beheaded? Two steps forward and my hand could chop down. No, that would be too easy. Too kind. Women like her should be strangled slowly. Stoned. Beaten. Stabbed. Raped.

She sat there bowed. My hands were out in front of me, the fingers hooked like claws. Shaking, sick with self-disgust, I lowered them. 'You make me feel dirty,' I whimpered.

She lifted her head and turned towards me. Tears were furrowing the powder on cheeks gone shapeless, giving her face the look of a deflating circus balloon. But her tone was fierce.

'*You* make *me* feel dirty,' she said. 'You and the filthy things in your mind. If you think I'm sorry for what I did, I'm not. I often wish I'd gone away with Joshua when he asked me to. There wasn't laws like we got today and I could've gone. But there was Kathy and you and the better chances you get if you're white – and I was afraid, too, of what everyone would say. If you think that was doing dirt on Eric, you don't know nothing.'

She swept away the tears with one fingertip and groped for a box of tissues. 'I'll tell you something, son,' she said quietly, dabbing at her eyes with a tissue. 'I love you. But I went wrong with you somewhere. Maybe it's God's punishment. I was going to tell you about Joshua one day. But you never seemed grown up enough. Perhaps I should have told you long ago before you got like you are now – too good for the rest of us. A hypocrite, too. Do you think I'm too *dom* to notice what you're up to? I've seen how you look at girls, even your own sister, and how you get when Thandi's around. A girl just sixteen. Take a look at your own behaviour before you judge anyone else's. And stop feeling sorry for yourself. Think of others for a change.'

She began working on her cheeks with the tissue. 'Now get out of here and let me alone. I can't go out, looking like this.'

'No.' I moved to block the doorway. 'You're not going.' My eyes were brimming again. 'I don't want you seeing him.'

'I'm going. I've got to talk sense to Joshua. Now out!'

Back in the kitchen I sat down and picked up the beer. I didn't know what to do next. She'd said that nothing had changed. She was wrong: everything had changed. I'd taken it for granted that I was white in a world controlled by whites, where everything that was desirable flowed from being white; everything that was good, everything that mattered. In spite of what I'd done with Thandi, whiteness had remained the uniform of my selfhood and my essential superiority. Now, stripped of my uniform, I felt naked and lost. I'd begun the day white and now I was – what? All the derogatory terms I'd ever used came rolling back at me: *Hotnot. Capie. Tottie. Gamat. Skollieboy. Vissie. Neither-nor. Baster. Half-naartjie. Two coffee one milk....*

No one need know, my mother had said. I could go to work as usual, mix with my white friends, yearn for Elizabeth, go where I'd always gone without a second glance at the *Europeans Only* and *Slegs vir Blankes* signs which separated the streams of human traffic. I could drink in the Whites Only bar of the Hotel Vic, ride first class on the trains, join the Victoria Club, act the white *baas* and climb to the white top of the slippery pyramid, just as before. I was still Simon

Brown, of sixty-nine Songololo Street, officially registered son of Phyllis Brown and Eric Brown, race European, and brother of Katherine Brown, race European.

But *I* knew. The line which separated the saved from the damned, the fit from the unfit, the chosen from the unchosen, had shifted, and I was on the wrong side of it. A creature of the penumbra. Tainted and tarred. I could go on living as if nothing had changed and get away with it if I had the nerve and my secret was kept. But I'd know what I was – a play white and a bastard – and my world would never be the same.

My mother was banging about in the bedroom in what sounded like agitation, opening and closing cupboard doors and drawers and dragging a chair or some heavy object across the room. I got another beer out of the fridge and lit a cigarette. Some instinct made me examine my hands. Long. Brown. Not unlike Seth March's. A Coloured's hands? Yet they'd touched the skin of white women and the women hadn't flinched. Because they hadn't known? My mother had known Joshua's colour and hadn't shrunk from his touch. I'd felt myself superior because I was white and white because I felt superior. Did I now admit inferiority because I'd found I wasn't white? Wasn't I at least equal to any other man? And if that was true, what of Joshua and my half-brothers? What of Sipho? And Thandi? Weren't they equals, too?

I'd believed, irrationally it seemed now, that you shaped your own destiny by talent, cunning and determination, and could get anywhere no matter what and where you came from. Nothing was determined; very little was by chance. Now it looked quite different. The circumstances of your conception decided all. You had no more choice than a chocolate shot out of a machine.

I was mulling this over when my mother came into the kitchen. She had redone her face with fair success, though there was a betraying puffiness under her eyes. Oddly, she was carrying the large black handbag which went with her Sunday outfit rather than the old purse she invariably took to Rangisamy's.

She stopped, looking down at me. 'Think about this, son,' she said gently. 'You've had a shock. A hell of a shock. But it isn't the end of the world. You'll be all right. You're angry now, but one day you'll be proud of who you are. And you've always got us. Me, Kathy, Joshua and... and Eric.'

Eric now. She'd been about to say, Your dad. How had she coped through the years, living with *her* secret? I'd always thought of her as a simple woman. Strong but uncomplicated and ordinary, like any other woman in Songololo Street. How wrong could you be? She'd had a whole life I knew nothing about. She'd been a Coloured man's woman. And still was.

'Think about this, too,' she said. 'You're Joshua's son and he loves you. It hasn't been easy for him, watching you strut about like a little tin god in a Victoria High blazer while his other two sons struggled to glean an education in a scruffy prefab school in Kokville. Seeing you acting like one of the Master Race, despising him and his people and him not being able to come down on you like a father should when he sees his child going wrong. He lost that right by doing what he thought was best for you. Remember that and remember that he's in hell now with Seth in the hands of our own lot of Nazis.'

She nodded towards the cooker. 'And don't forget to tell Eric about his supper.'

She had begun to walk past me when the reason for her carrying her Sunday handbag hit me and jerked me to my feet to block her path to the door. She was taking Joshua a gun: the Luger nine millimetre automatic that the man I'd thought of as my dad had brought back as a trophy from the desert war. He'd shown it to Kathy and me once long ago, before locking it and other military memorabilia away in the bottom drawer of the bedroom cupboard. Years later I'd discovered the key on top of the cupboard. That would explain the sound of the dragged chair.

'No, Ma,' I said, grabbing for the handbag. 'Give me that.'

She stepped back, swinging the bag out of my reach. 'Leave it alone, Simon.' Edging away from me towards the passage door, she gripped the strap of the bag more tightly so that her knuckles showed white. I knew with a chilly certainty that she would swat at me rather than surrender it.

'You aren't going to talk sense to Joshua at all,' I said, taking a small step towards her. 'You've got that German gun and you're going to give it to him.'

'This is our business, not yours.' Her cheeks were pink. Her eyes glittered. Suddenly she looked younger, full of purpose.

'You're not leaving here with that gun,' I said.

'Don't try to stop me.' She resumed her edging, then paused and held up a hand. 'Ssh! Listen!'

Boots were clumping along the passage. Her face tightened and her eyes blazed at me; whether in appeal, or warning, or defiance I couldn't tell. Fingers grasped the edge of the table then released it as she managed to fix on a smile for the man who'd come into the kitchen. 'Hello, Eric,' she said. 'How was it today?'

'Boring as usual.' He glanced across at me. 'You look a bit rough. You in trouble or something?'

Out of the corner of my eye I could see my mother stiffen.

'Not that I know of,' I said. 'Unless pinching a couple of your beers is trouble.'

'Could be, if there's none left.'

'I left a couple.'

'A couple will do me.' His gaze switched to my mother travelling from her face down to her bag then back to her face. 'You going out, Phyl?'

'Just to Rangisamy's,' she said. 'Cigs and a few other things.'

'What's to eat?' he said.

'Look in the oven and see.'

'I think I'll take a shower first.' He lingered, obviously sensing something withheld. 'Sure there's nothing wrong?'

It was my chance. Four words from me could blow to pieces the rotten structure on which our family life was based. His face reflected bafflement. Hers had the rigidity of a prisoner about to hear judgment. The sense of my power was exhilarating. And terrifying.

I heard my mother's intake of breath. Then she was silent as though she'd ceased breathing.

'Just chatting, Dad,' I said.

He stared at us for a moment then nodded and left us.

My mother sat down abruptly. 'Give me a cig, son,' she said.

I held out the packet. 'You can't do it, Ma.'

Her chin lifted, though the fingers which took the cigarette were trembling. 'I've got to do it,' she said. 'And you know it.'

'No.'

A train was passing, rattling the windows. I caught the faint smell of coal smoke. My mother waited until the noise had died down.

'I'm going to do it, son,' she said.

I walked past her and looked down the passage. I could hear the faint thump as my father dropped his boots in the bedroom, then I turned back into the kitchen. My mother was drawing on her cigarette as though it were a source of oxygen.

I held out a hand for the bag. 'I'll do it.'

'No. Best that I do it.' She stood up, stubbed out her cigarette and smiled. 'A man carrying a handbag? Not in Songololo Street.'

Forty

Joshua wasn't in his cubicle in the garage and nobody knew where he was so I left a note asking him to ring me and went back upstairs.

An hour later the internal phone buzzed. 'It's Ben,' said a voice. 'Best come down.'

I raced down the stairs. No news had come to Songololo Street from Kokville over the weekend and I was anxious. As I hit the bottom step I could see Joshua behind the desk of the cubicle with Ben beside him. Even from a distance the tableau appeared stiff, unwelcoming. It struck me that Ben might be less forgiving of my attack on his father than Joshua himself.

Neither spoke as I entered the cubicle. In the harsh light of the fluorescents Joshua looked bowed and shrunken. At the sight of his face, bruised and swollen like a windfall pear, I couldn't help flinching. My work, I thought remorsefully. But there was more to it than that. All life and arrogance had gone. Despair hung about him like a smell.

Ben's face was expressionless, the peak of the baseball cap shadowing his eyes.

'Well?' I said.

Silence. Neither man moved. But as I waited for the response a single tear slid down Joshua's battered cheek.

'We were too late,' Ben said flatly. 'Seth's dead.'

'Dead?' The word came out hollow.

'They say he hanged himself in his cell just before dawn.'

'Seth hanged!' I'd seen only one corpse: a drowned black man on the bank of the Songololo: his body had been swollen, a grotesque sculpture in clay.

But hanged? The images were shadowy, from grainy films, a body turning slowly, its tongue hanging from its mouth like a tie.

Joshua straightened. 'They murdered him. They will die for that.'

'I'm sorry, Joshua,' I said weakly, 'and sorry for what I did to you.'

'That's behind now,' he said. His hand reached out and gripped my arm. The eyes shone incongruously bright in the haggard face. 'You done what you could.'

He got up stiffly. 'I must go see the lawyer again. Ben will tell you all we know so that you can put it in the paper.'

'I should go with you,' Ben said. 'You're not well.'

'No. Stay here and talk to your brother.' He squeezed my shoulder. 'You will tell your mother, eh?'

'Yes.' His calmness was awful. I wanted to say something comforting, but no words came.

He nodded and walked away, slow but very erect.

Ben was watching him. 'He's a strong man,' he said. 'The strongest. He loved Seth best, though he never showed no favouritism. You next, I think. He was always talking about you – how well you were doing at school, how good you were at sport, how we must look after you, even if you acted *bedonnered* sometimes, because your ma was a very special friend and you and Kathy were like family.' He laughed harshly. 'You *were* family – you anyway.' The narrow eyes, so like Joshua's, swung to my face. I noticed that the rims were red: the hard man had wept, too. 'What do you say about it all, hey?'

'I liked Seth a lot. And I feel bloody useless.'

'I meant about being one of us? A *bruinmens*? A *Hotnot*?'

'I don't know. Mixed up.'

296

'And angry, hey! Hating us!' He smiled bleakly. 'We've all been through it, man, us Coloureds. The people nobody wants. I used to ask, Why do I have to be Coloured? Why am I painted brown – the colour of shit? I felt I should be white. I didn't like blacks, Africans... didn't like them near me, didn't want to know them. Until one day Joshua said to me, Ben, your grandfather was white, but your grandmother was a pure African woman. He showed me an old copy of the *News* – on its fiftieth anniversary – with a picture of the non-white staff in it, and there was this very black woman with frizzy hair. A kaffir – my gran'ma. I was angry and full of hate. But that kind of anger and hate only come back to you – like puking into the wind. Because what you hate is yourself, when you should be hating the system that makes you hate yourself. Do you know what I mean?'

'I think so. When Joshua told me I *was* angry. Homicidally angry. You know all that. But now I am trying to work through what it means. What it makes me. What I should do about it. I didn't choose it and I don't like it. But I'm going to have to live with it. Like you do.'

'I didn't choose it neither. But you can choose what to do about it. Joshua taught me that. You can choose to be proud of what you are and fight for your rights.' He held out a roll-up. 'You pass as white. It gives you an edge.'

I took the roll-up. 'If you say so.'

He lit my roll-up but didn't say any more. In the works above us the Linotype machines hummed and clattered. At last I said. 'What about the gun?'

'It may still be useful.'

The noise of the machines had entered my head. Ben's eyes, smoky now, challenged mine. The scar on the lean cheek stood out. I sensed that his body had gone taut, wound up for any demands on it.

'For what?' I sucked hard on the roll-up. 'Revenge?'

He shook his head. 'I'd like to kill the vermin who tortured Seth. But if I do, it'll be with this.' His hand dipped to the pocket of his corduroys. A click and a blade jutted from his fist. At my recoil a spectral smile touched his lips. ' *Skollies* call it tongue because it tastes what it kills.'

I shivered. 'I get the joke. So why the gun?'

'Insurance.' He snapped the flick knife shut and returned it to his pocket. The eyes found mine again. 'What do you say to carrying on Seth's work?'

'So he *was* involved?' Deep down I'd known it. The abandoned studies. The coming and goings. Nonetheless, I choked as if on a tot of raw spirit.

He nodded. 'Seth was always very political. He got me in.'

There was movement at the far end of the garage. Wellington, a messenger, had entered and was kneeling down next to a bicycle to clip the turn-ups of his trousers. Other messengers would be coming in soon.

'Why me?' I took another suck at the *zol* and tried to shepherd my stampeding thoughts into some kind of order. Few people knew as much about my shoddy past as Ben March. He more than anyone had shown contempt for my callow racism and less than two years ago taunted me for cowardice. It was true that I was no longer the arrogant youth who had regarded a white skin as a guarantee of superiority. Possibly, he knew something of the changes in attitude which events and the unforeseen passion for Thandi had worked. Non-white Victoria had its own methods and sources of information-gathering. All the same I could hardly be said to match up to the specifications for a member of the underground resistance.

He didn't answer immediately. Then, 'We know you,' he said gruffly. 'You got guts and you shown loyalty.'

'Who are *we*? Who are involved?' I was playing for time.

'No names. Don't even think names.'

But my mind was already scrolling them. Joshua, probably. Surely a woman called Joyce? Sipho. And Thandi? The idea was humbling. A girl doing a man's job. Sixteen. Old enough to fuck, old enough to fight, the saying went. Even so.

'I want to think about it.'

'Sure,' he said calmly as if we'd merely been discussing my joining a sports club. A pause and then he added, 'Just remember you're a March and you owe Seth.'

There was no perceptible change of tone or the expression in the narrow eyes, but I was aware of an uncomfortable surge of adrenaline. A thought, cold as the idea of death, sliced into my mind. 'If they tortured Seth they'll be on to others.'

His look was scornful. 'Seth never talked.'

'How can you be certain?'

He smiled tightly. 'If he'd talked I wouldn't be here.'

Forty-one

The verdict at the inquest was that Seth had hanged himself while the balance of his mind was disturbed.

Solly Nathan, representing Joshua and Ben, suggested that either Seth had been strangled during interrogation or had killed himself to end his torture. Through dogged cross-examination of Grobelaar, Kepler Lategan and a duty sergeant, Nathan established that Seth had been questioned continuously in a barred office in the Police Station by a team of plain-clothes detectives, then driven away on the fifth night to Special Branch headquarters in Port Elizabeth. He'd been brought back to Victoria on the eighth day and in the early hours of the tenth had been found in his cell hanging in a noose improvised from torn bedding and his shirt looped through the bars of his cell window.

The district surgeon, Dr Sellers, testifying with constant glances towards the bench where Grobelaar sat, insisted that Seth's death was consistent with hanging, but not with strangulation. He agreed that it was just possible – though improbable – that Seth could have been forced into a position where someone else had kicked away the stool found overturned near his dangling body. He couldn't explain the causes of the cuts and bruises on Seth's face and body, including marks on his genitals, but argued they were consistent with the police account that Seth had flung himself against the cell walls and furniture in a frenzy of protest. Dr Sellers deeply resented imputations that his evidence favoured the state because his services were paid for by the state. When Nathan called for a full and independent inquiry into the circumstances of Seth's death he was rebuked by the magistrate and warned that his manner of asking questions brought him close to contempt of court.

The *News* and other papers gave the inquest full coverage and there were Opposition questions in parliament. The government cited the coroner's verdict and the need for interrogation where national security was threatened. The deceased had been 'involved with violent and subversive elements'.

'There's nothing more we can do,' Nathan said wearily in his small cluttered office. 'Unless we can produce evidence, which means persuading someone in the police to go into the witness box, we can't move forward.' He looked at Joshua. 'What about your informant?'

'Transferred,' Joshua said. 'I don't know where.' He took a handkerchief from his pocket and wiped a face which seemed to have aged ten years. 'No one is saying anything.'

'That figures,' Nathan said. 'Give me his name and I'll make inquires.'

'I cannot give you his name,' Joshua said. 'He was very afraid.'

'Joshua, Joshua,' Nathan moaned. 'Surely finding him is the most important thing?'

Joshua's face shone with anguish. 'I promised.'

Hundreds attended the funeral service in Kokville, spilling out of the red-brick church and down the path. Many went to the burial in the Coloured section of Victoria cemetery and later to Joshua's neat, surprisingly well-furnished house. A helicopter chattered overhead during the interment and Special Branch Volkswagens and the yellow Studebaker sometimes driven by Grobelaar were sinister presences both at the funeral and in the street outside the house; but there was no direct interference.

Ben and five young Coloured men I didn't know carried the coffin while Joshua walked behind. The predominantly Coloured church congregation was threaded with a fair number of whites and Africans. R.B. Alexander, his wife, Ian Grantley-Pearson and Elizabeth were in the front pews with – at Joshua's insistence – the Zondis, the Rangisamys, Shantih, my mother, Kathy and me. In the pews behind sat old Mr Tewson, and his wife, the Landaus, Mr Seer and Miss Robinson. Though Norman refused to go to Joshua's house, he sat in a back pew at the church and drove Kathy and my mother to the cemetery.

The service was long. The minister, a young man with a boxer's nose and broad shoulders, had gone to the same school as Seth. He praised his sensitivity, his writing talent and his concern 'not only for the brown people, but all people'. His death was not suicide, but must be laid at the door of apartheid.

In the buzz which followed this statement, a pretty young woman with a halo of curly hair and a skin the colour of copper, read a poem which called for rage and not sorrow, action and not mourning. Joshua, instead of reading a lesson from the Bible, chose Seth's favourite poem, Brecht's *To Posterity*:

The old books tell us what wisdom is
Avoid the strife of the world, live out your
*   little time*
Fearing no one,
Using no violence
Returning good for evil –
Not fulfilment of desire but forgetfulness
Passes for wisdom.
I can do none of this:

Indeed I live in the dark ages... Alas we
Who wished to lay the foundations of
   kindness
Could not ourselves be kind.

'I cannot forget or forgive the murder of my son,' Joshua said into the silence. 'I will not return evil for evil, but I will not rest until his murderers are brought to justice.'

Ben and others spoke at the graveside, some weeping, all with anecdotes about Seth. The pretty woman threw a bracelet into the grave and let the manuscript of the poem she'd read flutter after it.

Later in the hot jostle at Joshua's house there were more tears – and more stories. The pretty woman, a little drunk, told me she was Seth's 'unofficial fiancée', and that he'd told her he wouldn't marry or father children until South Africa was free.

'I wish I was carrying his child.' She wiped her eyes.

'If you want a March child you'll have to make it with me now, Leonie,' said Ben who was plying the mourners with a sharp red wine.

I expected indignation. Instead she laughed. 'Seth would have said that was all right. He believed in free love, though there was never anyone but me, that I knew of.'

'You knew right.' Ben kissed her cheek, splashed wine in our glasses and moved away, piratical even in his funeral suit.

'Don't mind Ben,' Leonie said. 'He talks rough, but he's got a big heart and I might do worse.' She inspected me mistily. 'I've never met you before, have I? Are you a cousin?'

'No. I'm Simon Brown.'

'Brown by name, but not by nature,' she giggled. 'Wait, I've heard that name. Let me think.' She closed her eyes and opened them again. 'I've got it – the star reporter.'

'Hardly a star.'

'Modest, too.' The big eyes seemed to have become more liquid. 'Seth said you were on the side of us *bruinmense*, you and your mother and sister.'

'Not always, in my case. But I am now.'

She touched my wrist. 'That's the main thing.'

I felt a catch in my throat and the itch of forming tears behind my eyes. Here in the Marches' home among those who'd been close to Seth and whose goodwill suffused the room, identification was easy and the temptation to confide my secret to this warm and attractive woman was strong. But caution was stronger. Play white for now, it's safest, Ben had said, and so far I'd taken his advice. I was a long way from feeling comfortable with my new self. I'd been white and now I wasn't, yet I continued to live as before, accepted as one of them by people who despised my kind, going to the places I'd always gone – cinemas, cafés, pubs, everywhere the signs read *Slegs vir Blankes*/ Europeans Only – but warily. Daily routines which I'd performed automatically had become acutely conscious, fraught with the need to dissemble. I no longer walked the streets of Victoria as an ordinary citizen, but as an actor, an impostor, a reluctant undercover agent whose premonitions of exposure alternated with a peculiar feeling of power.

Over Leonie's shoulder I could see Kathy talking to Ben. Once she'd have been the first to know my secret. I'd have rushed to tell her, needing her to share my burden. But I'd held back, not sure why beyond a dreary consciousness that we were not as we had been.

Events were raising barriers between us; differences and resentments and a growing sense that our paths were dividing. Her abhorrence for violence was total. If I gave Ben the answer he wanted and she got to know of it, I risked the loss of her love. That knowledge, mingled with pure fear of what I was being asked to undertake, tortured my days and nights, disrupting my sleep and destroying my appetite. But, to complicate my agonising, Ben's challenge, while it scared me, carried a seductive thrill. I'd always felt myself to be a spectator, an observer from the sidelines: here was not only danger but the glamour of being involved in significant action. What was more, it was flattering to be trusted. And so I see-sawed between acceptance and rejection.

Ben moved away, dispensing more wine, and Thandi appeared at Kathy's side. As always lately, the sight of them together and the thought of what they might say to each other touched off a thrill of uncertainty. More secrets. Beyond them, my mother was standing close to Joshua. Too close. Secrets again. Too many secrets. And too dangerous to tell.

Leonie was talking about Seth and her plans to bring out a collection of his poems with tributes from those who had known him. I let her run on, preoccupied with my internal conflict. 'Perhaps you'd write something for it?' she wound up. 'About your friendship across the colour line?'

I nodded, but felt an internal flinch at the falsity of my position.

'Introduce us, Simon Legree.' Shantih had joined us, her arm around Thandi. She smiled at Leonie. 'He is much too fond of good-looking women, this boy. We were getting jealous, hey Thand?'

'*Ewe.*' Thandi gave my arm a small sharp pinch:

it reminded me of Florence's sly disciplinary tactic when I was small.

'Leonie Muller,' Leonie said. 'Seth's fiancée. I mean I *was* his fiancée.'

There was a brief, sad silence. Then Shantih said, 'We must see that Seth will not have died for nothing.' She drew Thandi forward. 'I'm Shantih Patel and this is Thandi Zondi, a sister in the struggle.'

'I also knew Seth,' Thandi said quietly. 'He often talked about how well you sing and write.'

'He mentioned you, too,' Leonie replied. 'Don't you have a brother, Sipho?'

After a few minutes Shantih steered me away from the pair. I went reluctantly: I wanted a chance to suggest to Thandi that we slip off to the *rondavel*.

'This is a sad time, Simon,' Shantih said. 'But it's good to see so many people showing support for the Marches. You, too.'

'That surprises you?'

'No. Right from that meeting on Table Rock, when you were so angry with Seth and Ben and me for being there, I felt – and it was strange – that something interesting was going to happen between you and us. A connection. And I was right, wasn't I?'

'Yes. Until then I thought being white made me lord of all. You three challenged that. I didn't come out of it very well. Or what followed.'

She chuckled and squeezed my arm. 'Shocks change us, Legree. For better or for worse. You don't come out of it too badly.'

Thandi was looking at us. I flapped a hand to acknowledge her. She grimaced, whether in simulated anger or the real thing I couldn't tell, then looked away.

Meanwhile Shantih was going on, her tone mock-wheedling. 'I want to ask you a favour, Simon.'

'Ask it.' Perhaps it was the drink, perhaps the spirit flowing through the gathering, but I felt benign.

She hesitated, then said: 'Could Kathy and I have the *rondavel* for a few hours? Please don't say no. I have to go back to Durban tomorrow.'

That meant no sex with Thandi. 'I thought that phase was over.'

'Is anything strong ever really over? It'll be a very long time before I see Kathy again. She wants me at her wedding, but I can't face it. So please, Legree.'

I was well caught. The temptation to say no was powerful, but I could hardly explain a refusal. 'All right,' I growled. 'But look out for Norman prowling around or Kepler Lategan peeping through the quince hedge.'

She pulled my head down and kissed my cheek. 'You'll always be my white knight,' she said lightly and was off across the room to where Kathy was talking to Mr Seer.

Elizabeth in a sober grey dress was standing with Joshua and my mother. I was about to make my way over to them when Thandi's fingers pincered my arm.

'You are flirting too much, *u*Simon,' she breathed in my ear. 'You must talk to me now.'

I couldn't tell from her face whether she was serious or joking, but her breast was brushing my arm and her thigh was pressing against mine. Desire swept through me.

Clearly it was at work in her, too. 'Can we go to your *rondavel* by-an'-by?'

'No,' I replied mournfully. 'It's already booked.'

Her eyes glinted. 'You and who?'

In spite of my frustration I couldn't help grinning. 'Not me. Shantih and my sister. But you wouldn't know about that kind of thing, *ntombi*.'

Her chin went up. 'I know about it. More than you. We can go to my mother's *khaya*. She is going to Vilakazi with my father after this.'

'Others might see us.'

Again the chin lifted. 'Let them.'

It was time to talk to Ben. I found him having a smoke on the front *stoep*. 'I'm on my way,' I said. 'And I've made my decision. I'm in.'

'Good.' His face showed neither surprise nor pleasure. 'It fits in nicely. Comrade Stephen will be at Rangisamy's next Thursday night.'

'Who is Comrade Stephen?' Now that action was imminent, I felt a panicky urge to stall.

'You'll see. Stephen is his code name.' I thought I detected the embryo of a smile. 'Mine is Albert. You must choose a name for yourself.'

I quelled a nervous urge to laugh. 'Call me Ishmael.'

'Be there.' He pushed me towards the steps.

I was halfway down the street and pondering whether I could even now back out of the assignation with Ben and 'Comrade Stephen' when the Carters' white Chrysler pulled up alongside me. Elizabeth leant across and opened the passenger door. 'Can I drop you somewhere?'

'Thanks. I'm for Songololo Street.'

Elizabeth drove carefully, slowing to a crawl whenever children or dogs appeared. 'What wonderfully resilient people the Marches are,' she said earnestly. 'Especially Joshua – so dignified and controlled.' She braked to let a mangy dog of unidentifiable ancestry cross ahead of us. 'He did make a strange remark to me, though. I was saying how sorry I was about Seth and he replied that he was going to have to find consolation in his remaining sons. I thought there was only Seth and Ben. Isn't that odd?'

The temptation to tell her – to surprise or even repel her – was as powerful as the urge to touch, but I sucked back the risky words. 'Yes,' I said instead. 'It's probably the strain.'

'Probably. And there was that strange accident, wasn't there. Don, the Lino operator, thought that there was some kind of fracas involving you and Joshua down in the garage.'

'Don got it wrong. Joshua was on his way to work early. It was still quite dark. A cat ran out into the road. Joshua swerved to avoid it and fell off his bicycle, that's all.'

'That's what Joshua said.' The grey eyes flickered to my face. 'You've changed, haven't you, Simon? No one would call you a racialist now.'

I couldn't resist: 'Put it down to the complexion. Dark. Or dirty, depending on the point of view.'

'No!' The car veered as Elizabeth swung the wheel to bring it to a halt under one of the ragged bluegum trees that lined the side of the rutted road. She cut the engine and turned a flushed face to me. 'I want to have this out. You've changed, but so have I. You keep reminding me of how horrible I was to you long ago. I was a snobbish and ignorant little cow. I didn't know much about boys and I'd never encountered anyone quite like you. So wild and rough.' She gave a small laugh. 'I was afraid of you touching me. I remember that I had dreams.'

'What sort of dreams?' The car had become hot and in spite of the open windows I could smell her perfume, wine and, subtly, something else.

'Unsettling dreams. Not the dreams a nice girl should have. They frightened me.'

309

'And now?' I was breathing faster. Was I sensing, as one animal might recognise the readiness of another, an undertow of shared desire? Or was I deluding myself, addled by drink and the emotion of the wake?

'As I said, I've changed. Only...'

'Only?'

'There's Jim. I love him.'

Jim. And Thandi, too, loyal and loving, picking her way through Kokville and then along the back lanes to Songololo Street to be with me.

'That's it then.'

'That's it. Otherwise perhaps...' She leant towards me. Her mouth met mine, stayed for a second. Then she drew away and restarted the car.

On the road ahead three curly-haired skinny girls were playing hopscotch in the dust, oblivious of us.

My people.

Forty-two

From the outcrop of boulders we could see Table Rock against the cloudless sky and beyond it Long Mountain with just a trace of Victoria's haze lurking in the foothills. In the valley below us stood the pylon which was to be our target. We'd spent some time calculating how long it took to get to it from the road above us where 'Comrade Stephen' – previously known to me as Sam Glass – had parked his car.

The sun was lighting a small fire on the back of my neck. I slapped at the spot. All I was short of was sunstroke.

'Are you all right?' Sam's lean face showed concern.

'Just a bit off colour – probably funk.'

'Wait till the actual job. I had the shits all day before my first mission.'

'You won't come on this one?' I could hear the plea in my voice. With Ben and Sipho in the *rondavel* the night before I'd watched him patiently rehearsing us in how we'd place the dynamite against the pylon's legs, affix the detonators and then set the timing device which would give us an hour to make our getaway. What had struck me then, as now, was the calm authority he'd developed since his detention during the State of Emergency. Sipho had the same air and Ben packed passion like muscle. Beside them I felt callow and fraudulent, a kid play-acting among the grown-ups.

Sam shook his head. 'I'm back to Jo'burg. Anyway, it'll be better if we aren't seen together too close to boom-boom time. Someone might just draw conclusions. You'll be all right: the others know the routine.'

He accepted a cigarette. 'After the job, stay away from each other for a while. In fact you three should consider breaking up and reforming after a couple of jobs. An all-white group might be an idea.'

'All whites? I thought we were supposed to be fighting apartheid?'

'Sure, but we have to be practical about security. A white group would be less likely to draw attention.'

I'd an impulse to tell him my news, but remembered Ben's advice to stay mum and said instead, 'I've hardly joined this mad organisation and I'm expected to recruit other lunatics.'

'We're not mad,' Sam said. 'We're blowing away a reactionary system so that we can build a country that includes everyone – Africans, Whites, Coloureds, Indians – a rainbow nation.'

He dropped his *stompie* and trod on it carefully. 'It wouldn't do to start a veld fire, would it?'

'I don't think my sister would thank us. Her future husband's farm is just over the mountain – next to my uncle's.

'Perhaps she can persuade him to turn it into a collective and we'll be able to practise guerilla tactics there.'

'Don't bet on it. Kathy hates any kind of killing.'

'No one likes it. But we have to face the possibility.'

'She thinks it's an inevitability.'

We'd reached the road. Sam grabbed my arm. 'Listen.'

The moment I heard it I saw it. The brown Chev pick-up slewed round the corner in a cloud of dust, slowed and halted beside us. I registered Norman at the wheel, then Rex against the far door and Jessica between the two.

'Jesus, Blackie,' Norman exclaimed, 'this is the last place I expected to see you. Sam, too.'

'Just visiting.' Sam paused fractionally but went on smoothly: 'Blackie's considering buying my car, so we came for a spin. How are things?'

'Fine, fine,' the trio chorused. It might have been the sun, but I thought Jessica reddened.

Norman climbed down heavily from the Chev's cab. 'They're demonstrating a new John Deere over at the show grounds,' he said. 'Rex gave me a ring and suggested we meet at the crossroads and ride in together.' He sounded defensive. Rex and Jessica hadn't moved or contributed an audible word since the initial greeting, though they'd murmured to each other.

'You're looking well, Jessica,' I said. 'Are you on vacation?'

'Yes, thank God,' she said. 'You're looking well, too.' She was silent for a moment, then added, 'We want you to come to the wedding. Your mother and Kathy, too.'

I looked at Rex. He was staring at Sam thoughtfully. Jessica elbowed him gently, 'I said we all want the Browns to come to our wedding, darling.'

'Sure, sweetheart,' he said. 'Sure. Sure.'

The cosy endearments grated. I'd no right to rancour, but I felt it.

'We'd better be getting on,' Norman said. 'Tell Kathy I'll be round soon, Blackie.'

'Give my love to Aunt Phyllis,' Rex said.

'And my best wishes – to Kathy too,' Jessica said. I waited till the Chev had pulled away before I exploded: 'Shit, shit, a thousand times shit.'

'A little more than kin and less than kind, eh?' Sam said sympathetically.

'That's just it. It seems you can't choose your in-laws any more than you can choose your parents.'

'True.' His eyes were on the moving cloud of dust. 'Do you think they swallowed my car story?'

'Yes.'

'It might be wise to find a target somewhere else.'

'I'll discuss it with the others. But I still fancy this spot.'

The black eyes glinted. 'Is that an objective judgment – or are you influenced by the attractive idea of inconveniencing your relatives?'

'Nothing could be further from my mind.'

Forty-three

'The circuit's checked,' Ben said. 'You two get away and I'll set the timer.'

He crouched over the small plastic lunch box which contained the timer, batteries and circuit which would send the current coursing along the fuse to the detonators. Sipho and I had attached these to the dynamite stacked against the legs of the pylon which loomed above our heads like some prehistoric quadruped.

My mouth was as dry as the sand of the *dongas* we'd walked along to get to the spot and my heart was like a clapper about to shatter its bell. Setting the timing device was the danger moment. A fault in the system or an error of judgment and our flesh would smear the mountainside. I tried not to think of the activist in Natal who'd been scraped off the wall of the pass office he'd intended to destroy, or the driver who had lost both legs in a premature detonation near Boksburg.

'*Lungile.*' Sipho had my arm and was pulling me away and up the mountain. He and Ben had conducted their own recce, briefed by Sam.

We straggled up the steep, stubbly slope, putting our feet down carefully and aiming for the clump of thorn trees which was the first stage on the route back to our car. Although there was a sliver of moon, the trees were just visible against the dark mass of the mountain.

Ben caught up with us as we rounded the trees. 'All set,' he said. 'Fifty-five minutes and the fucker will blow. Jesus, but a *dop* would go down well.'

'*Ja.*' I wanted a drink badly, but the urge to shit was more urgent.

We slogged on, not talking, towards the jagged line of treetops showing against the navy blue of the sky. I could hear our soft footfalls in the stillness and the howling of a distant dog. Soon our feet were crunching on the stony car track which led into the trees.

'*Strond*!' Ben's fingers nipped my arm. It was a moment before I made out the bulk of a large car which seemed to squat across the track in front of us. 'How come we didn't hear this?'

The answer didn't matter. Our borrowed Austin was parked around the bend ahead, just off the track before it petered out in front of a derelict hut.

It was well hidden.

It was also cut off now from the only way out.

We stopped, straining to see ahead. No one spoke. We knew Robert Oldcastle's Buick and why it was there. For a moment I was back on Table Rock, binoculars to my eyes, focussing on a white man with a black girl. But now the question was: what if the observed had become the observer? Not only was our car trapped by his, but he and his companion might have seen it. Unlikely, but a possibility too dangerous to ignore.

We must have stood for only a few seconds trying to work out what to do, but it felt like infinity. Then Ben's hand dipped into his pocket, re-emerging to thrust a metal object into my hand. I didn't need to look to know what it was. He pulled on the surgical gloves he'd worn to set the timer and went round the Buick trying the door handles. Locked. He swore quietly and moved on. Gripping the Luger, I followed, Sipho just behind me.

Our car was where we'd left it. In the moon's weak light the number plate was dimly visible. I half-expected to see Mr Oldcastle beside it. His absence was more nerve-racking, peopling the shadows with waiting figures.

'He won't have seen it,' Sipho murmured.

Ben shook his head. 'We can't be sure.' He opened the boot and fished out a wheel spanner.

We edged forward. As we rounded the next bend I tried to imagine what Mr Oldcastle would do. My gloomy guess was that he'd face us in spite of the embarrassment of being found with a black girl. An ugly outcome seemed inevitable. The automatic dragged my hand down and, though the night was warm, the thought of having to use it made me shiver.

'He'll be with Bongi Sibande.' Sipho had slid past me to Ben's side. 'She's his usual woman.'

'You grab her,' Ben said. 'I'll sort out Mister.'

Sibongile! Thandi's 'aunt'. Whatever she was, she wasn't an enemy. And yet – I shrank from the grim logic of it – she was as dangerous to us as Oldcastle.

We'd reached the ragged clearing round the hut. The broken door gaped, yielding to pitch blackness. Ben pointed first to himself and then towards the door before holding up a hand to me to indicate I should stay where I was.

'Aren't you taking the gun?' whispered Sipho.

Ben held up the wheel spanner. 'This will do. And if it doesn't...' His hand went to his belt and as it came away I heard the faint click of the blade, then another as he closed it. 'And you?'

'These.' Sipho raised his hands, judo-style.

'Let's go.' Clutching the spanner, Ben began picking his way towards the hut, Sipho behind him. I tried telling myself that they'd only knock Oldcastle out and frighten the woman into silence. Why then was I nudging the catch of the automatic off safety with trembling fingers?

At the hut door they stopped, listening. Then they were gone.

For stretched seconds the silence in the clearing was absolute and pure. Then it shattered. Thumping. Shouting. A thin scream which sliced the night.

Sibongile, naked breasts bouncing, burst out of the door, pursued by Sipho. Seeing me she baulked and swerved towards the trees. It was her undoing. Sipho was onto her from behind, flinging her to the ground.

I stood rigid with indecision, the automatic half-lifted. A crash from inside the hut and Ben and Mr Oldcastle staggered through the doorway, locked together. The latter was wearing nothing but a long-tailed shirt which flapped about his thick hams, and, incongruously, socks held up by suspenders. There was a large dark stain on his neck and another smaller one on his back, but he had one huge hand on Ben's windpipe and the other on the wrist of the hand which held the knife.

'*Mbulale*, Simon!' Sipho shouted. 'Shoot, man!'

Ben's knife clattered on the stone doorstep and his knees buckled. I glimpsed his face: livid, his eyes bulging, his distorted mouth shiny with phlegm. On heavy legs I lurched forward and put the quivering barrel of the revolver to Mr Oldcastle's ear. I tried to speak, to urge him to release Ben, but my throat was closed. He recognised me. The eyes, bloodshot in the sweating face, popped; whether in surprise or rage, I couldn't tell.

I wasn't aware of firing the first time, only the dull crack and then the convulsive heave of the big body. Oldcastle sagged against Ben and seemed to sigh. Now I could feel the trigger under my finger.

Shaking violently I pushed the revolver against the dark mess beside his ear and squeezed.

Again a report like a twig snapping. Gulping air, Ben stepped clear. Mr Oldcastle swayed between us, then pitched forward, hitting the ground with a thud and a rush of air like that from a punctured bicycle tyre. Absurdly, the thought flashed into my head: *What will I say to Melanie*? Then I was vomiting uncontrollably.

I was hazily aware of Ben taking the Luger from my hand and repeating hoarsely, 'Okay, brother, okay.' Still reciting the mantra, he marched me out of the clearing and propped me against a tree trunk.

He was breathing brokenly and even in the semi-darkness I could see that his face was bruised and his neck swollen. But his hands were steady as he pulled a small tin from a pocket and extracted two hand-rolled cigarettes.

'You did good,' he said, lighting both cigarettes and holding one out to me. 'I fucked up. I could hear him grunting away and I thought, he's old and boozed and on the job – easy. I didn't expect him to be such a tough old bastard. Or so quick. He heard me and spun off the girl. I got one hard hit in but he knocked the spanner out of my hands and gripped me by the throat. I pulled my knife and stuck him – once, twice. No joy. I'm telling you, man, I thought I was gone.'

I risked a queasy drag on the roll-up. It was acrid, yet comforting. *Dagga* now, I thought woozily.

'Listen,' Ben went on earnestly, 'you had to do him. He'd have shelfed us, no mistake. Anyway, he's no loss. He liked fucking black girls, but he was no friend to black people.'

'I know his daughter.' Melanie's face was in front of me. Grieving. Reproachful. I wanted to retch again, but my stomach was empty.

'She might be better off.'

'She loved him.'

'*Ag*, he was one bad bastard.' He squinched his *zol* carefully between his fingers. 'Come. We can't hang about.' He turned and walked towards the clearing. I dropped my smoke, trod on it and followed.

Neither Sipho nor Sibongile was visible, but noises were coming from inside the hut. Someone had dragged Mr Oldcastle's body away from the entrance and flung a blanket over the head and torso, though the legs jutted out, ridiculous in their suspenders. Death without dignity.

'Mind the blood, hey.' Ben stepped over a sticky-looking dark patch in front of the doorway.

Inside, Sipho was talking quietly to Sibongile, the scene weakly illuminated by a small candle stuck in a Castle Lager bottle on the floor. Beside it was a half-full bottle of brandy, some empty Coca-Cola bottles and two grubby-looking glasses. A mattress, covered with a sheet, was spread on the floor with a jacket, trousers, shoes, a tie and an enormous pair of underpants piled on top. Sibongile, crouched against the wall, was whimpering as she tried to pull on a high-heeled shoe. I could smell a sickly sweet odour which was different from the scent of sex. Then I had it. Blood. Oldcastle's. On Ben and me.

Sipho looked up. 'I've found his car keys. She says they didn't see our car. Too *jags*. He was very drunk and just wanting to jump her bones.'

'What a *gemors*,' said Ben. The wheel spanner was at his feet. He picked it up then gestured with the Luger towards the cowering woman. 'If she talks we're all dead.'

Sibongile began to wail.

'*Tula wena*,' Sipho said. She subsided into whimpering again.

'I'm buggered if I want to get hung because of a whore who goes with white men,' Ben said.

'It's a problem.' Turning towards Sibongile Sipho rattled off several sentences in Xhosa. She shook her head vigorously, replying in a low voice.

'She says if we let her go she will never say anything to anyone.'

'I understood her,' Ben said. 'But I don't believe her.'

Sipho reflected then shrugged. 'I don't like to kill her, but she knows us.'

'No, no,' Sibongile cried out. 'I don't know you. I won't talk. Not me, never. True's God. Please, my lords, please!'

Ben took a step towards her, the Luger dangling. 'You're a whore and whores lie.'

She cringed away from him, her hands coming up as if in prayer. 'I do not lie. Please, my lord. I will do anything you want, anything. Please.'

Ben raised the gun, the scarred face implacable. He's going to kill her, I thought. 'Ben,' I said shakily. His left hand went up. In the silence he'd commanded I believed I could hear the hammering of Sibongile's heart, but it might have been my own.

Ben knelt down so that his face was level with hers. 'Now listen, bitch,' he said. 'If ever you talk to anyone, you are dead. Even if all three of us are taken by the police and locked up and hung, our friends will get you and kill you. Not nice and quick like your white *outjie* was killed, but very slowly. They'll cut out your eyes and your tongue and your whoring *poes* and your heart, and throw them to the dogs. You understand?'

She nodded.

Ben looked across at Sipho. 'Agree?'

'Yes.' Sipho handed the bottle of brandy to me, shoved the glasses and the Coca-Cola bottles among the clothing in the middle of the sheet, drew up the corners and knotted them.

'Tell her in Xhosa,' Ben said.

'I understand.' Sibongile's voice was barely a whisper. 'Thank you, sir.'

'All right.' Ben pocketed the gun. 'You don't know us. You never saw us. You were never on the mountain tonight.'

'*Ewe, nkosi.*' She grabbed his hand, kissing it. 'Thank you, thank you.'

He pulled his hand away as though she'd bitten it. 'Come, then. Hurry!' After a quick survey of the hut he stepped over to the candle and snuffed it out. I looked at my watch. Time was bleeding away. Twenty minutes before the pylon went.

Sipho thrust the candle and lager bottle inside the bundle. He spoke to Sibongile again and she came over and picked it up.

Outside Ben motioned me towards the feet of the body while he took the shoulders. 'I'm already marked,' he said, indicating a clotted patch on the shoulder of his jersey and stains on the front. '*Who would have thought the old man to have had so much blood in him.* Seth used to recite that. Shakespeare, isn't it?'

I fought down the urge to vomit again and gripped the feet determinedly. But when Ben lifted the head and shoulders, the body proved too limp to lift, the bottom sagging to the ground. I forced myself to step between the legs and hook my arms under the knees, shuddering at the contact with gelid flesh.

We followed Sibongile and Sipho down the

track. The blanket had slipped and Oldcastle's heavy genitals flapped obscenely. I began to develop a superstitious fear that he was coming alive.

Perhaps sensing my growing panic, Ben launched into a quiet monologue. We had to get Oldcastle and his car as far away from the area as possible so that no one would connect his death with the blowing up of the pylon. With luck no one would visit the hut and rain would wash away the blood outside.

'I know a place,' he said. 'I'll drive whitey's car and you follow in the Austin.'

We reached the Buick. Helped by the still snivelling Sibongile we managed to manoeuvre our grotesque burden into the boot. The bundle of items from the hut followed. Then Ben and I stripped off our jerseys, his soaked with blood and mine lightly spattered, and squeezed them into the remaining space.

'Okay.' Ben handed me the Austin's keys. 'We're heading down the mountain then turning off to an old quarry I know. If I'm stopped just keep going, eh?'

Sipho was studying his watch. 'We've got fifteen minutes to get away.'

'It's enough.' Ben dragged the brandy bottle out of his pocket and held it out to me. 'Best all have some of this. The girl, too.'

I concentrated on following the Buick's tail lights. Sipho's Xhosa murmurings to Sibongile in the back were oddly soothing. My earlier nausea had gone and helped by the brandy and the *dagga* I felt detached and oddly lucid. I'd killed a man, the father of a girl I liked. I could claim the gun had just gone off, but I'd deliberately pulled the trigger the second time. Of course, I could try to shift the blame. Onto Ben for bringing the automatic along. Onto both Ben and Sipho for entangling me in their cause. Onto Joshua. Sam...

But that would be false – all of it. I'd joined in freely and for my own confused reasons. Anger came into it. Resentment. Vanity, too. Perhaps even a wish to prove myself a man. A new man to match a new identity. There was also a need I couldn't quite define. To matter perhaps. The catch was that mattering had become a hanging matter.

Ben was turning left. Our lights picked out tracks leading off the road and twisting out of sight. I followed, the old car jolting uncomfortably. After a quarter of a mile the Buick halted. Ben got out and came to my window. 'Who'll stay with the girl?'

'I will,' Sipho said. 'In case someone comes.' He laughed, a brittle sound. 'We don't want our comrade on an Immorality charge.'

'We don't,' Ben grunted. 'Sabotage and murder are enough for one night.'

As Ben nosed the Buick between the complex of sheds, cranes and chutes, I realised I'd been to this quarry years before with Kathy. It had been abandoned even then, its charm the very dereliction which allowed us to explore the empty buildings and idle machinery and, best of all, to swim in the small lake formed by the water trapped in its deepest pit.

'That's right,' Ben said when I told him. 'I came here, too, with Seth and once with a goosie I was mad keen on. We got caught swimming *kaalgat*.'

Water glinted ahead and Ben brought the car to a halt facing down the slope. He'd already opened all windows. 'Just hope the bloody quarry is as deep as it used to be,' he said. 'With luck the car will fill up and sink. I'm going to jam the throttle and leave it in gear.' He held out the bottle of brandy. 'Grab this and out you get.'

I climbed out. The Buick began to creep forward. It picked up speed, then the driver's door swung open and Ben tumbled out, rolling clear as the car's front wheels struck the water. Dazed, I watched him scramble up and run towards me.

'Pray it goes right down, my brother.' He took the bottle, hoisted it to his lips, then handed it back.

I drank, almost choking. The car continued to roll into the water. It appeared to float, rocking slightly. Then the long bonnet dipped and there was a loud sucking sound.

'Better *waai*.' Arm around my shoulders, Ben turned me about and began walking me up the slope. 'There's no point in waiting. If it goes, it goes. If not...' He took the bottle again and drank.

As he lowered the bottle there was a dull rumble and a small flash lit the distant sky. A storm coming, I thought. But Ben was pounding my back.

'At least we got one thing right tonight,' he exulted.

At the corner of the lane behind Songololo Street Ben stopped the Austin to let me out.

'*Moenie* worry *nie*,' he said. 'It's going to be okay.'

'Best we don't meet for a while,' Sipho put in. 'Carry on normally and stay calm.'

I did feel calm as I walked through our back gate. What was done was done. Sooner or later I'd have to face the events of the night and the hideous wrong done to Melanie. But now I was on automatic: a zombie. I'd smoke a fag and finish the brandy in the bottle which Ben had let me have. Perhaps I'd toss off and then go to sleep. Or try to.

Halfway up the garden path I stopped. Light was shining through a gap in the *rondavel* curtains. Immediately I imagined Grobelaar waiting for me, but rejected the thought as guilty jumpiness. Thandi I knew to be in Vilakazi, looking after young cousins. The most likely visitor was Kathy.

Nonetheless I approached slowly, my heart beating to a heightened rhythm. In spite of discarding my jersey and having made another check for bloodstains I could still smell the sticky-sweet stench I'd sniffed in the watchman's hut. *All the perfumes of Arabia will not sweeten this little hand.*

The door was slightly ajar. Gripping the neck of the brandy bottle I edged the door open wider and peered in.

Norman was sitting on my bunk, his back against the wall, his eyes closed and a copy of the *News* open on his lap. He jerked awake, blinking furiously.

'Where've you been, Blackie?' he growled. 'We've been trying all over town for you.'

I'd hoped I wouldn't have to use the flimsy alibi I'd concocted. 'With some of the guys from work, boozing and playing cards.' I held up the bottle. 'I won, too.'

He frowned, rubbing his face with his big paw. 'It's bad news, Blackie. That's why I'm in from the farm. Your mom's not well. Heart again. She's gone into intensive care and Kathy and your dad are with her now.'

Forty-four

White dominated Victoria General Hospital. The walls, the shuttling nurses, the bed linen: all white. It was as though the authorities believed that whiteness would repel all disease. Though I'd scrubbed myself under the shower and put on clothing freshly washed and ironed by Florence, I felt unclean as I made my way towards the one-bed ward to which the white-clad receptionist had directed me. Unclean and smelling faintly of blood.

My mother smiled feebly as I walked in. Against the chalk-white pillows her face was grey and I detected grey streaks in her hair, which I hadn't noticed before. Kathy sat on one side of her and the man I now thought of as my stepfather on the other. He looked nearly as ill as my mother, sallow cheeked under the stubble, his eyes red rimmed, his shoulders slumped. What was he going through, I wondered, this sad person who seemed to matter so little to anyone and didn't even know I wasn't his son?

Kathy's face showed strain, too, though she was carefully made up and was wearing a freshly ironed blouse. She looked at me unsmilingly. 'So you finally turned up? We did everything but send the police out looking for you.'

'I was with some of the boys from work,' I said.

'Bad lad,' my mother said weakly. 'You always were a night owl.'

'Bad girl,' I said with a jollity I didn't feel as I took her hand, 'scaring us like this.'

'I'll be up and about soon,' she said. 'I can't be laying in bed all day. Too much to do.'

I nodded, humouring her.

Kathy, my stepfather and Norman went back to

Songololo Street. My mother dozed and didn't talk much, but was emphatic that I shouldn't tell Joshua she was ill. 'He'll try to barge in here. It'll only cause trouble and he's had enough of that just lately.'

Kathy returned alone and pulled me out into the corridor. 'She's sicker than she knows,' she said, puffing hard at one of my cigarettes. 'The specialist thinks they may have to operate on her aorta. She won't listen – bangs on all the time about getting home.'

She flicked some ash into one of the ashtrays placed at intervals along the corridor. 'She's been ordered not to smoke and she keeps trying to cadge a fag. Don't you go giving her one, do you hear?'

'I won't, sis.' I looked at my watch. 'I've got to get to the *News*.'

She came closer. 'Where the hell were you last night? Norman said you looked terrible. Stank, too.'

'I told him – playing cards with some of the boys.'

'Till five a.m.? You hate cards.'

'Not when I'm winning. And there was a bit of a barney.'

She studied me. 'I believe you. Thousands wouldn't.'

By the time Elizabeth got back from her morning round I was fidgety with anxiety. Don't worry, Ben had said. But I was troubled by forebodings featuring the hut, the old quarry and Sibongile.

'Much happening out there in the world of crime?' I said as casually as I could.

'I'm not sure. None of the senior policemen is around. They're out in the district, apparently.'

In spite of my resolution not to smoke in her

presence, I lit up. 'No idea why?'

'None. But Melanie told me this morning that she's reported to the police that her father didn't return home last night. They aren't taking it particularly seriously, but Melanie is. He keeps odd hours, she says, but he's always in by early morning.'

Grantley-Pearson came into the reporters' room behind his fuming pipe. 'I've had a call from the town clerk of Venterstad,' he said. 'They've been without electricity since after midnight and so have some farms on the same grid. It may be connected to damage to a pylon.'

'Sabotage?' Elizabeth uncapped her pen.

'Quite possibly. Explosions have been reported in Johannesburg, Durban and Cape Town. Check with your friend Grobelaar, will you, Liz?'

'He was out earlier. I'll try again.'

'I could check with farmers in the area,' I said eagerly. 'We could get pics.'

'Let's see what Elizabeth comes up with first. Pictures are out, by the way. The government feels we're aiding and abetting saboteurs by publishing pictures of their successes.'

Elizabeth's repeated phoning got Grobelaar and an admission that a pylon had been blown up.

'He's pretty cagey about local investigations, but he did say that we could expect countrywide arrests soon.' She clicked paper into her typewriter carriage. 'He also let on that the Uniformed Branch are beginning to take Mr Oldcastle's disappearance more seriously.'

I was glad she wasn't looking at me.

After work I spent an hour with my mother. She was perkier, but more fretful. 'There's so many orders outstanding,' she fussed. 'I'm doing the bridesmaids' dresses for the Probart wedding and I may be doing the cake as well.'

There was also a plea for a cigarette, which I evaded by pretending I'd run out. I was relieved, if rather ashamed, when a nurse ejected me because it was supper-time.

Halfway down the hospital drive a plump black nurse caught up with me. 'You are Mr Brown?' she said pleasantly.

'That's right.'

'I've got a message for you from Comrade Sandy.'

For a moment I didn't register. Then I'd got it: Sipho's code name. My heart began to thump. 'Okay.'

'He says not to worry about Bongi. She has gone to Johannesburg. Everything will be fine.'

'And?'

'That's all.' Her smile was a flash of perfect teeth. 'I hope your mother gets well soon. *Hamba kahle.*' She turned back towards the hospital.

Belatedly I recognised her voice: Joyce. 'Thanks,' I called. She lifted a thumb.

Everything will be fine. I wished I shared the optimism.

Kathy stood at the kitchen table jabbing her finger at the item in the stop press of the *News*.

'This was you, wasn't it?' she demanded. 'This is why nobody could bloody find you!' She ignored my head-shake. 'I never believed that tall story of yours about being with the boys. I just hope Norman does.' The finger levelled at me. 'That's why you were on the mountain with Sam Glass, wasn't it?'

'Utter coincidence,' I countered.

Her glare was pure contempt. 'You were

involved, Simon. You're in this with Sam and God knows who else.'

'No,' I said. But I knew my face was betraying me.

'You're going to kill someone, or get killed yourself, if you don't get caught first. And it scares me, *boetie*, it scares me so much that I've half a mind to turn you in.'

I was back with the horror. *Oldcastle's body. The stains on the shirt. The mess beside the ear.* Confession to Kathy would feel like a deliverance, but confession was unthinkable. 'Look,' I said, 'I can't admit it. You must understand that. We're on the same side now. You always wanted that. But it's obvious that *satyagraha*, strikes, demonstrations and all the rest aren't working. People need some victories and the sabotage campaign is giving them a few.'

'My God, you've changed,' she said harshly. 'A violent revolutionary all of a sudden. Spouting communist slogans like Sam Glass and Sarah Bentley and a few others who should know better.'

'Including Seth. He died for what you call communist slogans.'

I'd meant to sting her and I had. 'That's unfair,' she cried. 'I loved Seth. He was one of the real oppressed with a real excuse for what he did, not a campus communist.'

'Nor am I, and maybe I've an excuse, too.' I was tempted again to pour out all: Joshua's revelation, the nightmare on the mountain, even the involvement with Thandi. But no, I'd crossed into a territory I couldn't ask her to enter.

'What excuse?' she said when I didn't go on.

'Nothing,' I said. 'I see things differently from the way I did, that's all.'

'I can tell that,' she said sadly. 'I've longed for you to change and I never thought I'd wish you'd stayed as you were, but I do.'

Forty-five

The Sapa report on my table at the *News* announced that scores of people had been detained in pre-dawn raids across the country.

Unsettlingly, no names were given, but I was pretty sure that Sipho hadn't been taken or Florence would have said something that morning.

I shot downstairs to the garage. Joshua had already heard the news on the radio. 'It's bad,' he said. 'But we're all right. No Specials came to our house.'

My heartbeat steadied.

'Look after yourself, hey!' Joshua's hand went to my shoulder.

Since Seth's death and the scandalous inquest verdict of suicide, white had crept into the thick hair and beard and more lines scored the gaunt face.What lay ahead might be worse.

There was so much to say and no time to say it.

I caught his hand, squeezed. 'I will. You, too.'

Elizabeth was at her typewriter when I got upstairs. 'They've found a body,' she said bleakly. 'Mr Oldcastle's. It's murder.'

My legs turned to sponge. Somehow I got my backside onto my chair. 'How come?'

'Itinerant sheep shearers saw the tip of an aerial sticking above the water in a disused quarry off the Venterstad Road. Otherwise it would have gone unnoticed for ages. The details are horrible. He'd been stabbed, shot and bundled into the boot of his car. The police say they're ruling out nothing, including revenge. He had no money on him so it might have been robbery.'

'Is that all?'

'All so far.'

No mention of Sibongile. No mention of the bloodstained clothes in the boot. No mention of blood at the abandoned hut on the neighbouring mountain or the sabotaged pylon nearby. Were the police missing connections or were they holding back information as part of their strategy? I forced out the question. 'Has Melanie been told?'

'Yes. I've just come from her house and she's devastated. On the verge of collapse.'

I felt close to collapse myself. I'd been finding it nearly impossible to concentrate on the ordinary details of my life. I was sleeping badly, long periods of insomnia alternating with blood-splashed dreams which had me waking in a sweat. I was restless and listless by turns at work, really only interested in the political and police news, yet afraid of betraying myself by showing concern. Now I had to add hypocrisy to my crimes by ringing Melanie.

I forced myself to dial the Oldcastle number, my mouth dry and sour with the falsity of what I was doing – and felt a shameful relief when Dorcas answered, saying that Melanie wasn't well enough to see visitors or even to talk on the phone.

Meanwhile, Florence brought a message from Sipho suggesting a meeting at Rangisamy's.

Rangisamy was welcoming, but Mrs Rangisamy was aloof as she led the way to the back room. I smelled a difference of views between the Indian couple and thought of the rift between Kathy and me.

The word from Johannesburg, Sipho said, was that neither 'Stephen' nor a close comrade 'Rose' had been scooped up in the recent raids, but the Special Branch were hunting them.

'So we're all right for now,' Sipho said crisply.

'But if they take Comrade Stephen it'll be time to *voertsek* – very fast.'

He went on to outline the R-plan. Rangisamy would drive us across the border into Lesotho. From there we'd be taken north and then perhaps to Europe.

'What's happened about the girl – the whore?' Ben lolled on the sofa, toying with an unlit hand-rolled.

'Sibongile is safe across the border.'

'But will she stay there?'

'The organisation will see that she does,' Sipho said confidently. 'Let's meet in a few days. If it gets hot, it's the R-plan.'

Ben left first, going out through the shop. Sipho sat down next to me. 'Simon,' he said, 'Thandi has told me about you and her. She's serious. What about you?'

My head jerked involuntarily. How our positions had shifted! I'd been the young white *baas* with all the advantages of my colour. Now he was a warrior, like his ancestors, and I was under interrogation, with even my white identity resting uneasily on deception and lies.

'Well?' he prompted.

What could I say? What would a Xhosa man do in my position? Shamingly, I'd no idea beyond vague recollections of talk about *lobola* and compensation for acts of seduction.

'I'm serious about *her*,' I got out. 'It isn't a light thing, not a white man-black girl thing, like...' – I hesitated at the name – 'like Oldcastle. She is why I'm with *you* – one reason anyway.'

He frowned, then nodded. 'You *are* with us. I knew that when you killed Oldcastle.' He gripped my arm. 'Just remember the risks you are taking and watch out, eh? You are part of the movement now.'

Tipsy with relief I grinned at him. 'I'm not likely

to forget.'

Elizabeth trailed into the reporters' room. Her face was drawn and she sat down heavily. A late night with Jim perhaps? The thought pinched a nerve.

'Melanie is in hospital,' she said. 'A psychiatric ward. She tried to kill herself. Sleeping pills and then...' – her voice faltered – 'she slashed her wrists. Dorcas found her in the bath or it might have worked.'

In spite of the January sun flooding the office, I felt cold.

'I'll go and see her tonight,' Elizabeth went on. 'The doctor thinks she might try again. Apparently she blames herself for her father's death.'

A carousel of images flickered through my mind. Oldcastle slumping to the ground. The body with its grotesquely flapping genitals. And I was the author of it all, anonymous and malign – and denied even the release of confession.

The phone rang. I jumped, believing for a terrified, superstitious moment that my secret was out.

It was Kathy. 'Mom's had a stroke,' she said tersely. 'I'll stay with her till tonight. Come soon as you can.'

The phone shrilled again as I recradled it. 'Simon, it's Julian Richards,' the voice announced unnecessarily. 'I'm in Johannesburg, stringing for a couple of overseas papers and I've just learnt from a source here that Sam Glass and Sarah Bentley have been picked up by the Special Branch. In a public library in Yeoville. Disguised in business suits, Glass with a little Hitler moustache – Jewish humour, that. Quite by chance a right-wing student happened to see Glass going in and recognised his walk. So the pair was brought to book, so to speak. Sorry, that's not very funny. I thought you'd like to know and maybe do a bit of background digging for us.'

'It's not funny at all,' I said. 'But I am glad to know.'

Forty-six

Florence was in her *khaya* working her sewing machine. She listened with eyes tightly closed while I repeated what Julian had told me, then switched off the machine and got up to put on a *doek* and light coat.

'I will tell Sipho,' she said.

After she'd locked the *khaya* door she turned to me. 'You must be careful.'

'Don't worry,' I replied. 'I will be.'

'There is stew for you and Miss Kathy in the oven.'

'Thanks, Florence.' I wanted to say a lot more, but was choked. The unspoken history between us couldn't be voiced now.

She touched the *doek* then the lapel of her coat. 'I will look after your mother when she comes out of hospital.'

'I know that.' I'd an impulse to hug her, but she was already moving down the path.

'You're great, Florence,' I called after her. '*Hamba kahle.*'

She held up a clenched fist and went on and out of the back gate.

Rangisamy briefed me in the small room where he stored Basuto blankets. 'Tomorrow morning early, say six o'clock, you must be here. Come by the back. Dressed ordinary. No suitcase. Only briefcase or carrier bag.'

'As late as that?' I queried. 'Isn't it risky?'

'It cannot be done before. My van goes from here into the district every day just after six. Anyway, the SB won't be dreaming of looking for you in a *koeliewa.*'

He laughed. I laughed, too, less comfortably.

'Tonight,' he went on, 'it would be best if you are staying with a friend. If your Johannesburg comrade has been talking, the SB will be looking for you at home, at work, in the streets, every place.'

'I don't think he'll have talked.'

The usually cheerful face looked mournful. 'Even very brave people are talking if they are tortured. Seth March was one in thousands.'

I was scared again. It wasn't the gut-emptying fear I'd felt after killing Oldcastle; it was more like the expectant fear I'd felt earlier under the pylon. On my way back to Songololo Street I was conscious of a disturbing tingling under the surface of my skin. I'd been walling out thoughts of what was ahead. Rangisamy's matter-of-factness had knocked the wall down. Normal existence was cancelled.

Criminality. Flight. Exile. These had been just words. Now they meant more than I felt I could bear: abandoning everything familiar, loved, trusted, safe, and stepping into the threatening unknown. Kathy, Thandi, Elizabeth, erased from my life. My mother. Joshua. Against the sky I could just make out the shape of the mountains which ringed the town: they were fading into the dark. I flung my head back and let out a howl.

A voice called my name. Startled, I shied. A whirr of wheels and Tilly Peters shot by, waving. Days ago I'd laughed and joked with her in Temple's Milk Bar: now she was frightening me. I had to take hold.

I lit a cigarette and thought about Rangisamy's advice. It was straightforward and sensible.

Stay with a friend, he'd said. But who could I trust and by what right? The answers were: hardly anyone, and none. Who would readily hide a fugitive? As a black township dweller I might have found someone willing to hide me. In white Victoria, even to liberals, a saboteur would be a pariah who should be reported to the police immediately. Harry was just anarchic enough to enjoy putting up a person on the run. But Harry was a blabbermouth. My best bet would be to book in at an hotel. Not the Hotel Vic but one of the lesser places off the Octagon.

There were several carrier bags in the *rondavel* but I rejected them for a briefcase and began to pack, spreading trousers, shirt, underwear and socks on the bunk.

Behind me the door squeaked and for the second time that evening I shied.

Thandi stepped inside wearing the navy skirt and white shirt of her former school. I felt a wrench of anxiety.

'Is something up?' I asked.

'I've come to pack for the young master,' she said. 'Also I have a message from Sipho. He will meet you at the shop tomorrow.' She took a jersey from my hands and carried it over to the bunk. 'Where are you going tonight?'

'To the hospital first, then I'm not sure. Hotel perhaps.'

'No. Come back – to the *khaya*. The *Boere* will not look for a white person there.'

'I'm not so sure.' But her nearness was kindling the familiar need.

'I will watch for them. If they come, I'll warn you.'

'And how will you do that?' I felt myself losing the struggle against desire. Had she chosen the childish clothing to disguise or provoke?

She thought for a moment, frowning, then darted over to the chest of drawers and pulled out a hideous check pattern handkerchief, one of a set given to me by Aunt Betty. 'If the Specials are here I will tie this to a gate three houses up.'

I could smile at her naivety: a reminder of the gap in our ages, but her fierce optimism was lifting my spirits.

'Not a bad idea,' I said. I took her by the shoulders and pulled her to me, knowing that my assent had nothing to do with sense or safety and everything to do with my need to fuck and fuck again and through fucking forget – if only for an hour or two – the terrifying uncertainty of what was to come.

'She's really bad,' Kathy whispered as I reached the bedside. 'The doctor thinks she might rally, but I'm afraid she's slipping away.'

My mother's face lent grim support to Kathy's words. The eyelids were down. The shrunken mouth drooped at the corners. I could hear a low arrhythmic buzz: her breathing.

'Keep talking to her, *boetie*, though I don't know if she's registering,' Kathy went on. 'Can you stay with her till midnight? I need a nap.'

'Sure.' Kathy clearly needed rest. Her face was like putty and her eyes were tired. Even her hair looked lustreless. 'I've left you some stew.'

She kissed my cheek and left.

I was in for a long vigil. Thandi would wait. Nothing, I'd learnt, stopped her going after what she wanted.

'Simon!' I jerked round. Elizabeth was at the door. I went out into the corridor.

'How is your mum?'

'Not too good. How is Melanie?'

'They wouldn't let me see her, but I had a word with the nurse – we were at Girls' High together. She says Melanie believes she killed her father.'

'*She* killed him?'

'Yes. It's all very complex but it has to do with ambivalence or something – loving him and hating him at the same time for what he did to her.' She registered my puzzlement. 'You don't know?'

'Know what?'

She hesitated, then said, 'He abused her love for him after his wife died. It went on for years, then he turned to young African girls. Melanie blames herself, not him. They say that's common.'

Elizabeth came closer. I could smell her perfume. 'I have to go. Jim's waiting. I hope your mum gets better soon.'

I watched the slender figure walk away. I'd have liked to say goodbye. Instead I was left with regret and guilt. So I'd killed an evil daughter-fucker and should be feeling good about it. But I'd caused her breakdown, not Oldcastle. And I wasn't going to get a chance to try and make amends.

Hours passed while I sat holding my mother's hand. A nurse brought me a coffee and a biscuit and a houseman looked in. But most of the time we were alone. I talked to her quietly, relating humdrum stories of happenings at work and then slipping in as neutrally as I could that I'd probably be going away for a while and she wasn't to worry. She gave no sign that she'd heard.

Kathy arrived shortly after midnight. She looked fresh in a new red sweater and green corduroys and, from its springiness, I surmised she'd washed her hair.

'Dad's home,' she said. 'He'll come and sit with Mom after breakfast. Can you do a bit more tomorrow?'

The moment had arrived. Heart pumping erratically, I got up and walked into the corridor. Kathy followed.

Facing her, I couldn't get the words out.

She wasn't going to help. She'd gone pale and a nerve pulsed in her throat.

Speech of a sort came. 'I'm sorry, Kathy,' I wheezed. 'I've got to get away.'

'Away?' she echoed. 'With Mom so ill?'

'There's been more arrests. They've got Sam Glass and Sarah Bentley.'

She swallowed audibly. 'And they're after you?'

'I think they soon will be.'

'I knew it! I knew it would come to this. All that cloak and dagger madness and now you're running away like a chicken.' She stopped abruptly. I watched her, feeling like someone waiting for the tumblers of an intricate combination lock to click into place.

Her eyes blazed in a face suddenly as white as the walls around us. 'That's not all, is it? There's something worse than blowing up pylons!' She stepped forward and grabbed my jacket. 'You bloody idiot. You had to be a hero, didn't you? And now you've really messed up.'

I caught her wrists. 'It's done, Kathy. I've got to get out or it'll get worse.'

'This is going to kill Mom. You know that, don't you?' Tears glinted on her lashes.

'She'll understand.' I managed to rip her hands free of my jacket. 'Can't you try, too? We had no choice.'

'There's always choice,' she said contemptuously. 'And now you're choosing to run away.'

'Not just for my own sake. Others are involved.'

'That's one thing you're right about,' she flamed. 'Others who didn't ask to be involved.'

We were getting nowhere. 'I've got to go, Kath, whatever you think. I'll just say goodbye to Mom.'

'Go then,' she snapped, stepping aside to let me pass.

I went up to the bedside and kissed the icy cheek. 'I'll be back, Ma,' I said. I hoped it was true.

Kathy had remained in the corridor. She twisted her head away when I tried to kiss her. Blindly, I dabbed my lips to her cheek, mumbled my goodbye and moved slowly off, fighting an urge to cry.

'Simon, wait!' I was ten yards down the corridor when she caught up with me. Her arms went round me. 'Listen,' she said. 'I can't condone what you've been doing, but you're my little brother, after all.'

Half-brother. I wanted to say it. But it, too, was a confession for another time. 'Tell Joshua that Mom's sick,' I said. 'He should know.'

'I'll tell him.' Her face changed, breaking up. 'How will I know you're all right, *boetie*?'

'I'll get word to you somehow.'

'You better.' She pulled me into a tight embrace. We stood for a long time pressed to each other.

There was no warning handkerchief attached to the neighbour's back gate. Feeling foolish as well as scared, I walked on and through into our garden.

The *khaya* was in darkness. That had been agreed. But as I twisted the door handle I was shivering.

The door opened. The curtains were closed tight and I could see nothing. Inside, I stopped, listening. I could hear breathing. My own. Ticking. Reminding me of the ticking timer on the mountain. Then a creak and a rustle and Thandi whispered 'Simon!'

Two strides and I was beside the bed, dropping my jacket and kicking off my shoes. The bedclothes soughed, then Thandi's arms were around me, pulling me down.

For a while we lay just holding each other, Thandi naked yet warm, me fully dressed but shaking violently. On the bedside table Florence's clock read a mocking three-forty-five.

She began unbuttoning my shirt and trousers. 'It's all right,' she murmured. 'It's all right, my man.'

We coupled hurriedly and fiercely as if the clock was marking off our final seconds; then more slowly, touching and kissing, nuzzling and sucking, until, locked into a rocking sixty-nine, we climaxed.

We must have dozed because suddenly the early morning sun was filtering into the room through the flimsy curtains and the clock read five. At my touch Thandi woke and, before I could speak, rolled out of bed and began pulling on her clothes.

'I'll go and see if it's clear for you,' she said.

I wished I could imprint on my mind forever the proud head with its large eyes and wide mouth, the impertinent breasts, the skinny legs. I wanted her again, her texture, her taste, the soft clench of her cunt.

'Wait,' I said. 'I've something to tell you first.'

Forty-seven

The man I'd thought of as my father was in his pyjamas at the kitchen table drinking coffee. Compunction had overcome caution and driven me up the steps and to the kitchen door.

The early morning sun fell on his rumpled, unshaven face with cruel clarity. 'Kathy just phoned from the hospital,' he said. 'There's no change. I'll be going up in a while. Coming?'

The clock on the dresser showed five-thirty. 'I can't, Dad,' I said. 'I've got an assignment out of town.'

He sighed. 'It's a hell of a business, isn't it?'

'Yes.' I felt hollow, apologetic. How would he cope with what stretched ahead?

I wished I could think of suitable – or at least memorable – parting words, but none offered themselves.

'Aren't you going to have some breakfast, son?' It sounded like a plea.

'No time, Dad.' Treacherous tears threatened.

At the back gate I stopped and looked towards the house, registering with a new sharpness the vegetable patch, the vine, the fowl-run, the fruit trees and the tap where Thandi had washed, aware of my concupiscent gaze. Beyond were Florence's *khaya* and the *rondavel*, then the back *stoep*: I half-expected to see my mother and Florence sitting there on chairs dragged out of the kitchen, shelling peas while Joshua made his way up the garden path.

My vision blurred. Time to move on.

The sky was cloudless and the day was heating up. A day for swimming, for drinks in the shade, for slithery sex in curtained rooms. Unwise to think about those things or what I'd come to feel for Thandi: there were too many if-only's for comfortable retrospection. Unwise, too, to think too much about what lay ahead. I, who knew so little of my own country, was about to quit it for another. No point in trying to pretend I wasn't afraid. I'd laughed with Rangisamy about the escape plan. But that had been yesterday evening when the dark was closing comfortably around us. Now with the sun up, I felt exposed, mortal.

A goods train was rattling and smoking down the track. Out of habit I waved. The driver waved back.

On the bridge across the Songololo I stopped. The level was low, exposing its stony base; the banks were dry and cracked, the grass wispy like a scarecrow's hair. Not much of a river, but I'd spent a lot of my life beside it. When would I see it again?

Kitchener Street next. Ugly and treeless with its low windowless sheds and oil-smeared parking bays. Empty except for two black men in dungarees sweeping the gutters. After Kitchener came Livingstone Street and the entrance to Rangisamy's backyard.

Ten to six. Thandi would already be there, having gone ahead – to say goodbye to Sipho, she said. I suspected she planned to join the Lesotho run. Stubborn. Brave. Unshakeable. When I'd told her I was Joshua's son all she'd said was 'Is better' and climbed onto my lap.

Brisk walking brought me to the corner of Livingstone Street. I rounded it. A Volkswagen was racing towards me. It slowed as it came nearer, then picked up speed again. I glimpsed Grobelaar's narrow face above the steering wheel.

I kept walking, not looking back. A squeal of tyres told me Grobelaar had braked and was probably making a U-turn. My legs gone almost dead, I walked on.

Silence. I'd expected the asthmatic engine noises of the Volkswagen. The absence of sound was disconcerting. Had Grobelaar merely braked to avoid something in the road? Was it possible that he wasn't interested in me at all? Halting, I pulled out my cigarettes and, while ostentatiously lighting one, sneaked a look down the street.

What I saw killed any hopes. The Volkswagen was parked alongside the kerb about two hundred yards down, its blunt snout pointed in my direction. They were after me all right.

The back entry to Rangisamy's wasn't far. Fifty yards. I could get there before the Branch men. But it was a near certainty that was what Grobelaar was waiting for – to see my destination and net more fish.

I considered running. I might get round the next corner, another fifty yards beyond Rangisamy's gate. It was futile. They'd get me. I was finished.

Yet I knew I had to keep going. The job now was to warn the others if I could.

Passing Rangisamy's back gate I could just see his van in the yard, a shrieking yellow with purple lettering on the side: *Rangisamy for curries, spices, herbs and all Indian delights.* There was no one in the driver's seat, but the engine was running. I could imagine Sipho, Ben and Thandi tensely waiting and felt an impotent envy.

I walked on, trying to formulate a plan. By the time I'd rounded the corner into the short street which linked Livingstone and Albert I'd thought of one.

It was flimsy. But the best I could do.

I made for Albert Street swinging my briefcase and striving for a purposeful but relaxed air. Once in Albert Street I crossed to the side of the street opposite Rangisamy's store. As I hit the far pavement I let the briefcase fall and, hamming irritation, stooped to retrieve it, taking my time in the hope that someone in the store would notice me and guess the meaning of my actions.

The shutters of the shop were up and the door was open. Inside, dim shapes were moving. I thought I saw a flash of purple sari, then a shape in Rangisamy's impeccable white drill. Resisting an impulse to gesture, I fussed with the catches of my briefcase, pretending to check them, then walked on. Though I couldn't hear or see it I sensed the Volkswagen was following and would surely be seen from the shop and recognised. If not? I didn't dare think about that.

By continuing to walk I'd get to Jameson Street and then Rhodes Street. Rhodes had the Athena Café, but it wouldn't be open yet. It also had the Police Station! Best to go into Jameson then cut up a side street which fortuitously passed the garage entrance to the *News*. Joshua or the night watchman would be there by now and would let me in. With luck I could run through the garage and out of the fire door into an alley which led into Victoria High Street. It rated almost a zero hope of success, but it was the only chance I had.

But first I had to get there.

Even as these thoughts ran through my mind I heard the revving of the Volkswagen and then it was roaring up beside me to stop with a throaty rattle. Clearly Grobelaar had tired of the waiting game.

'*Wag 'n bietjie*, Brown.' I stopped. Grobelaar leant across his passenger to peer up at me. The passenger, I noted, was Kepler. Suddenly I felt the cold calm of resignation.

'*Goeiemore*,' I said. 'Nice day.'

Kepler didn't reply, but Grobelaar smiled. 'We'll

see about that,' he said. 'You're up very early.'

'I've a lot of work to do.'

'Perhaps you've been overdoing it, hey? Too much night work, *né*? Never mind. You're due for a nice long rest.'

Kepler had climbed out of the car onto the pavement and was holding out his hand for the briefcase. I tightened my grip on the handle, knowing it useless, but childishly reluctant to surrender it. 'Why is that?' I asked Grobelaar.

'You know,' he smiled, 'and we're the ones asking the questions. I'm detaining you, Simon.'

It was the first time he'd used my forename and his smile was infinitely more sinister than Kepler's scowl.

A second Volkswagen roared round the corner and pulled up. Two big white men got out. By now Grobelaar was on the pavement as well. He motioned towards the Volkswagen's open door.

Over Kepler's shoulder I could see a stork-like figure in a white shirt and black skirt standing outside Rangisamy's, looking our way.

Grobelaar touched my arm. 'You'd better get in,' he said, no longer smiling. 'You can try resisting if you like, but I wouldn't if I were you. Besides if you come with us and co-operate you might just find out which of your good friends dropped you in the *kak*. Now move!'

I moved. But not towards the car. Instead I raised my right arm and clenched my fist in the *Afrika* salute of the African National Congress.

It was an absurd gesture which I knew would bring me no favours in the years which followed. But I felt a surge of euphoria.

And, as I twisted away from Grobelaar, Thandi

saw it.

Then I was running. I heard Grobelaar's shout, then Kepler's merging with it. What I was doing was hopeless. Madness. I'd never get away. But I ran on. Running as fast as I'd ever run. I realised I was holding the briefcase as if it were a rugby ball and flung it away. Ahead of me on the pavement a street-sweeper turned, his face a rictus of surprise. I swerved round him, hurdling his broom. Dimly, I could hear the splutter and roar of the Volkswagen's engine starting up and with it the twig-crack of what might have been a backfire or a revolver shot. I didn't care. Nothing mattered but the feel of my feet hitting the pavement, the fast throb of my heart and the energy pumping through my body. For the moment I was free.

Glossary

The rough glossary below is neither comprehensive nor for the purist but is intended to explain some words and phrases which may be obscure to many readers. **Xhosa** is the language of the amaXhosa, black South Africans who inhabited the Cape Province before the arrival of the first European settlers. It is very close to the languages spoken by other members of the massive Southern African Nguni group – e.g. the Zulu, Ndebele and Matabele peoples – and can usually be understood by them. **Afrikaans** is the language of the Afrikaners, 'white' South Africans usually descended from early Dutch settlers. It is close to Dutch and Flemish and there is much debate nowadays how much its origins owe to non-white South Africans. Literally, Afrikaner means African.

Ag, nee wat: Afrikaans for Oh, no!

Amabulu: Xhosa for Afrikaners, derived from boere (see below).

Andiyazi: Xhosa for I don't know.

Bandiete: plural of bandiet, Afrikaans-derived slang term for convict.

Bang: Afrikaans for scared.

Bedonnered: Afrikaans slang for bloody-minded, mixed-up, otherwise.

Binneboud: Afrikaans for inner thigh; dancing binneboud is sexy dancing.

Bioscope: term used in South Africa in the forties and fifties for cinema; sometimes shortened to bio.

Boer, **Boere**: literally Afrikaans for farmer, but common and somewhat pejorative slang term for prison warder.

Boetie: Afrikaans for little brother. Also sometimes

slang for close friend.

Boopcraft: the art of surviving in prison, deriving from the slang term boop or boob for prison.

Bruinmens: Afrikaans for brown person – i.e. of mixed heritage, 'Coloured'.

Dagga: Xhosa for cannabis.

Dompas: literally stupid pass (Afrikaans), the slang term for the hated pass which was a means of control of movement, residence and work and dominated Africans' existence in the apartheid years.

Dop: Afrikaans slang for drink.

Dorp: Afrikaans for small town, village.

Ek dink ek gaan my onderbroek kak: Afrikaans – I think I'm going to shit in my panties.

Ewe: Xhosa for yes.

Fanagalo: Zulu or Xhosa-based pidgin, used by many whites in ordering Africans about.

Gatvol: crude Afrikaans word for fed up (gat means hole – i.e. anus in this context – and vol means full).

Gemors: Afrikaans for mess.

Goeiemore: Afrikaans for Good Morning.

Hadedah: a greeny-grey South African ibis.

Hamba kahle: Xhosa for Go carefully.

Hayi: Xhosa for no.

Hot'not, Hotnot: slang for Hottentot; similarly Tottie.

Jags: Afrikaans slang for randy.

Kaalgat: Afrikaans for naked (literally, bare-arsed).

Kaffer/Kaffir: pejorative term for Africans used by racist and ignorant whites.

Kaffermeidnaaier: pejorative Afrikaans for someone who has sexual relations with an African woman.

Kak: Afrikaans for shit.

Kieries: heavy sticks.

Kiewetjie bene: Afrikaans slang for very thin legs.

Knobkieries: Afrikaans for knobbed sticks.

Koelie, **Koelievoëls**: Afrikaans renderings of coolie and 'cooliebird.

Kwedeni: Xhosa for boys.

Kwela: Xhosa for climb, mount and sometimes slang for sex.

Kwela-kwela is slang for a police pick-up vehicle.

Lobola: bride price.

Lungile: Xhosa for all right.

Masihambe: Xhosa for Let's go.

Mayibuye: Zulu for Let it return – i.e. Let the country return to the African people, an ANC slogan.

Molo: Xhosa greeting – Morning or Hello.

Mossie: Afrikaans slang for sparrow.

Nkosi sikileli Afrika/ Malupakamis'u phondolwayo: the opening of the anthem/hymn of he African National Congress, which is now the South African national anthem –'God Bless Africa/ Let its horn be raised'.

Ntombi: girl, young woman.

Ouboet: literally old brother in Afrikaans, but basically a familiar, friendly term, like old pal.

Pas op: Afrikaans for Look out, Watch your step.

Pas op, of jy sal jou gat sien sonder 'n spieel: Look out, or you'll see your arsehole without [needing] a mirror.

Plaasjapie: Afrikaans slang combining plaas (farm) and Japie (common name, like English Jake) to mean yokel, country bumpkin.

Poep, poeping: Afrikaans slang for fart, farting, shit, shitting.

Poes: vulgar Afrikaans term for vulva or vagina.

Rondavel: a circular building, probably thatched. Based on African hut structures.

Rooinekke: rednecks – a common term among Afrikaners for supposedly fairer-skinned English people.

Siyahamba ku Vilakazi: Xhosa – Let us go to Vilakazi.

Skollyboy, Skollieboy: slang for a thug of mixed heritage.

Stoep: Afrikaans for verandah.

Stompie: Afrikaans for cigarette butt, stub.

Strond: Afrikaans slang for shit.

Suka...nja: Xhosa for Get away...dog.

Swartgatte: Afrikaans for black arses; a pejorative reference to black people.

Sy's mooi: Afrikaans for She's pretty.

Tsotsi: Xhosa for criminal, ruffian.

Tula: Xhosa for Be quiet, Shut up.

Uitgeput: Afrikaans for exhausted.

Unjani na?: question which is part of a routine Xhosa greeting – How are you? The usual response is Sipho's in Ch. 4, Ndiphilile. Wena? I am well. You?

Voertsek: abusive Afrikaans term when addressed to humans; means 'Get away' (literally Away say I).

Yintoni?: Xhosa for What – what's going on?

Zol: township slang for a roll-up, more specifically one containing dagga.

Acknowledgements

This novel would never have got as far as the Crocus Competition, let alone won it, but for the consistent encouragement, utterly honest and invariably intelligent criticism provided by my beloved partner, Jenny Newman. My thanks, too, to my friends Hugh Lewin (for some years a cell-mate) and Nahem Yousaf for close reading and valuable comments on earlier versions. Sadly, the late John Laredo, fellow-*bandiet* and most punctilious of critics, won't see the results of his advice. I owe warm thanks, too, to Athalie Crawford and Shirley Mashiane-Talbot for advising me on aspects of the Xhosa language. None of the above bears any responsibility for any of the novel's errors and failings.

My thanks also go to all surviving opponents of apartheid, and those who struggled so bravely against a brutal system, but have not lived to celebrate its collapse.